HEROES

HEROES

Festus Iyayi

Longman Group UK Limited,
Longman House, Burnt Mill, Harlow,
Essex CM20 2JE, England
and Associated Companies throughout the World

First published in 1986
Second impression 1989

Produced by Longman Group (FE) Ltd
Printed in Hong Kong

ISBN 0-582-78603-7

This book is for
Michael Imondu and Hassan Sunmonu, Jackson Omene, Lawrence Ndika and Itse Sagay

Chapter one

It was the third year of the civil war and it was the evening of the last Friday in the month of June. There was no light in the city for fear of the air raids and everywhere it was dark and uneasy and the soldiers were nervous as they paraded the dark streets, waiting, watching, anticipating. Osime Iyere, a political correspondent with the city's *Daily News*, stood inside his bedroom by the window and parted the dark blue curtains very slightly and looked out at the military jeeps as they passed and repassed the front of his house. *It should be over very soon*, he said to himself as he let the curtains fall back into place and then he went and sat on the other side of the bed and thought about the news he had been given in the city.

'The Federal troops are three miles outside the city,' his informants had said.

'Well, that seems reasonable,' he had replied. 'Last week they were reported to be on the outskirts of the city, ready to cross the river.'

'Ah, those were rumours.'

'Yes,' he had agreed then. 'Rumours but enough to start a stampede.'

'What we are telling you now is inside information.'

'Oh, come on,' he had said impatiently. 'Don't let this information spread as the other one did. Ten people died then and several children are still missing.'

'You are a cynic,' his informants had said, angrily. 'We hate bringing you any information. You are a doubting Thomas. Do you want to hear the sound of firing and shooting before you can believe what you are being told? Do you want to see the Federal troops before you believe us?'

No, he said to himself now, leaning forward and pulling out a drawer from one of the bedside cabinets, *I am not a cynic. But I dislike the rumours. Yes, I hate rumours*. There were always rumours. Why were there so many rumours in this war?

He took out a candle from the packet that he always kept in the drawer and struck a match and lit the candle. Then he mounted the candle on top of an empty tin of milk that stood on the floor and, in the pale, yellow light of the candle, he looked round again at the room.

His writing desk was in front of him with the chair behind it. The built-in wardrobe was on his left, at the foot of the bed. Behind him where the broad side of the bed ended was the dressing table with the large mirror. Between the dressing table and the bulging exterior of the wardrobe was the door that led to the short passage on the right of which stood the bathroom and the toilet. Three other doors opened into the passage; the one facing the bathroom door led to the sitting room, the other two opposite his own bedroom door led into two other bedrooms. These were the rooms which his two younger brothers and sister had occupied before the Biafran soldiers had invaded the city. After the invasion, he had had to send them home, to Ugbegun where, he was told, they would be safe. At least, so his father had said when he sent for them.

He saw the two books that he had brought with him that afternoon on the table. He looked at them and shook his head because he knew it would be impossible to read in the yellow light of the candle. Everything was impossible now. He could not write his feature page in the newspaper because everything had to be on the war and everything printed on the war had to favour the Biafrans. If the Biafrans lost a city and it was clear that was the truth, the newspaper had to report the opposite. It was disgusting, utterly disgusting. He kicked off his shoes and removed his clothes and then he lay back on the sheets, naked, and stared at the white ceiling. *Soon we shall be rid of these inconveniences,* he thought. *The Federal troops will come and drive these Biafrans away and then everything will be different. There will be no more cruelty. The beating and the maltreatment of the people will stop.* He smiled in the yellow light of the candle, a smile that was sarcastic and cynical. *The Biafrans call themselves liberators! Ha! Liberators my foot! How can they be liberators when they treat the people like prisoners? The young man that they took away this afternoon and then shot afterwards? Was that liberation or murder?*

Yes, he wanted the true liberators, the Federal troops, to come into this city. The Federal troops would set an example. His landlord would see that he was right, his landlord who had so little faith in the decency of the Federal troops. *Oh well*, he said to himself. *It's only natural that his sympathies are with the Biafrans. After all, he is from Oganza. He is one of them. So he sympathises. But Ohiali will find out that I have been right all along.* His daughter, too, would see that he had been correct about the Federal troops. Ndudi would see that he had not been boasting when he claimed that the Federal troops were humane. 'They are humane,' he said aloud, blew out the candle and smiled in the darkness.

He turned on his side and now he could hear the wind outside, blowing very gently. *I hope it doesn't rain*, he said to himself. Then he changed his mind. *I hope it does rain but that the wind remains gentle. Please God, do not let the winds destroy my corn.* He raised his feet when he pulled the sheets down and then up again, over himself. *Perhaps the war planes will not come tonight. If they come, perhaps by the time it is dawn, I will not be alive but dead like so many others. And Ohiali will be dead too. And Ndudi and her two younger sisters and brother, and her mother. But perhaps they will not all be dead. It is possible for many to live in the same house and yet for some to be safe and unhurt after an air raid on the house. It has happened several times before. Perhaps Ndudi will be alive and I will be dead and she may not even weep. Well, why should she?* he asked himself. *Your affair was over the day the Biafrans came here. You hated the Biafrans and you hated her and you hated her father. But you stayed on in their house,* he pointed out. He shrugged his shoulders. *What else could I have done? Packed out? Packed out where? And what would have been Ohiali's reactions? Perhaps he would have informed the Biafrans and they would have come after me.*

He thought again about the bombs and shuddered. *The bombs are dreadful. Horrible. You lie in your bed and a bomb drops on your roof and then there is an explosion and you are no longer alive. I always feel naked when I think about bombs. Naked and afraid and sweating. You have no hiding place from bombs. Bombs are not like the rain. And yet both come from the sky. But why can't the planes drop the bombs on the military targets? Why did they always drop them on any target? Anywhere? Perhaps it is true the planes are flown by Egyptians. Perhaps. And Russians too.*

He shook his head. *No, the Russians are not flying the planes. I know that that is crap, pure rubbish, propaganda, Biafran propaganda.* But the Arabs were, all right. He had met somebody who had met somebody who had spoken to somebody who had been involved in recruiting the Egyptian pilots. He went back over the list of 'somebodies' in his mind and he felt uncomfortable. *The chain is too long*, he thought. *Perhaps it is propaganda, too.* He shook his head. He didn't know.

A lot of things were propaganda in this war. Many, many things. Accusations of genocide on the fronts. That definitely was propaganda. Claims of captured territories, several of them. That too was propaganda. But the maltreatment of the civilian population was not propaganda. That and the photographs of the hungry and diseased children. Those were not propaganda, they were true. How he would love to go to the war front, to see things for himself.

'And what if you get killed?' his mind asked him.

'I won't,' he answered himself back.

'But supposing you did get killed?'

'Impossible.'

'But it is possible!'

He thought about it and he shivered, because he knew that he was the only hope of his family, his father, mother and brothers and sisters in particular. He was their only hope. If he got killed, then they too would die . . .

It was in the morning that the rain woke him. He heard it on the roof top like horses' hooves and he shuddered involuntarily but thought nothing of it until he heard it driven against the window panes by the wind. The wind! The pellets of rain hit the window panes like bullets and then the wind howled very sharply, violently, and all of a sudden, he could not lie on the bed any more but sat up, the sweat breaking out on his face.

If the rain was falling without the wind, the corn would be all right. The corn loves the rain that falls without the wind. The wind always thrashes the corn, particularly if the corn is full grown and tawny green at the leaves. When the corn is full grown and its ears are almost out after the silky crown that is like so many fine strands of a woman's hair is out, then a strong wind can do anything it likes with the corn. The wind can take the corn then and pull it from its roots or break it in its middle, snap it up and afterwards the corn would be lying flat on its back, its backbone broken, paralysed and helpless. Full-grown corn always took a terrible beating from a wild, strong wind.

Osime Iyere sat on the bed and he could not move and the bile was in his mouth and in his heart as he thought about his corn at the back of the house. He sat on the bed and he could hear the wind chasing the rain up and then down the street and he knew that his corn must have taken a terrible beating. Even as he sat there, immobilised by his fear for his corn, the flashes of lightning came right through his window and they were in his room at the foot of his bed, bright and clear and dangerous as a beautiful woman. He jumped up from the bed and went and stood against the wall by the window and then, very very cautiously, he parted the window blinds and peered outside. The sky was wild and black as a young gipsy woman's hair. The floods ran wild and strong on the street, the wind was fierce and passionate as it chased after the rain, everything was wild and black and dangerous and passionate and desolate, and yet beautiful. Yes, beautiful. The wildness and the blackness outside, the dark floods that overran the shallow, hastily dug gutters, the wind, the sky, were beautiful, strange but beautiful.

He came back and sat at the head of the bed, his back against the bed post, his feet under the sheets and again he thought about the corn outside, the labour he had put into it, the opposition he had overcome, the opposition from his landlord who he felt had been against it simply because he had not planted it. Then there had been the goats and the erosion that the floods had caused. He had fought all these things and won. He had put a great deal of labour into raising the corn and by God, how much pleasure had he derived from watching the corn stalks fill out, the corn leaves broaden and green ever more darkly! How much expectation had he nursed in his mind! How much of his feelings, love and other emotions had been ploughed into that soil with the corn! How much of his warmth and blood was in the green of the leaves and in the roundness of the corn stalks!

Osime Iyere got up from the bed, took his underpants from the edge of the chair's support, put them on. Then he went to the wardrobe and opened it. He had to bend down to pick up his khaki shorts because they were on the floor of the wardrobe. He went back to the bed and after buttoning up the front of his shorts, he took out from under the bed his once-white-but-now-brown canvas shoes. He tied the lace of the shoes very slowly because he was afraid to go out to see how much beating the corn had taken from the wind.

He went out of his room into the passage and then into the toilet to urinate. It was cold and his urine steamed up at him so he had to turn his face sideways so that he would not breathe back the steam and he pressed himself harder so that the urine would come out more quickly and then it was over and he had spat three times into the toilet bowl before flushing it and now he was in the bedroom where his sister had always slept. There was a double bed here too but the mattress lay bare on the bedsprings. He opened the wardrobe door. On the right of the wardrobe were the sheets and blankets for the bed and on the left side were the hoe and the cutlass and the spade. He took the spade and the cutlass and then he was in the sitting room and, looking at the clock that hung on the wall, he saw that it was almost ten o'clock. He whistled to himself but he did not panic because he remembered that this was a Saturday and that therefore he did not have to go to the office. But tomorrow he would go. Tomorrow would be Sunday but he would go to work because that was his schedule.

Now he was outside at the back of his house and, looking at the corn as it lay on its back, he felt hollow and bitter and angry.

I ploughed myself into that soil, I manured, fertilised this corn with my love. I ploughed my warmth into the soil to make this corn grow. And now what happens? The wind destroys it all. The efforts of so many months destroyed in a single night! My love, my warmth, my labour, my expectations all wasted by the wind of a single night. My feelings, my everything! Waste. The green, shining leaves wasted!

And how much time did we have left? he asked himself. *How many days? Let me see. Let me see. Five weeks? Perhaps not five but six or even seven. No,* he said to himself. *Three weeks and a half at the most. Twenty four days and the corn would have been ripe for the reaping. Twenty four days and my labour and love would have been rewarded. But not now, at least not any more. All that is waste now. Gone with the wind, as the book said.*

He searched his mind for things he might have done, for other precautions that he might have taken. The wall was there and acted as a shield. Perhaps the wind changed its course this night. *I simply do not know. What I do know is that it is cruel for one part of nature to treat another part of it in this way. It is cruel and hard. Wind to corn. Rain to corn, yes hard. The wind acted as a butcher, slaughtered my corn, my everything.*

He put his right foot on the extended and broad side of the shovel's blade and the blade bit deep into the soil, the rain in his face and hair, a big cloud in his heart. *But perhaps there is something I can do. Yes, something I can still do and which is why I brought out the spade and the cutlass anyway. I am going to raise this corn once more. I am going to make it stand on its feet, I am . . .* He stopped because he thought he heard a loud explosion coming from the centre of the city. *What was that?* he asked himself, his heart beating rapidly. *What was that?* He listened intently but there was no need for him to listen intently for the explosions came again, not once, nor twice but several times and all of a sudden, he knew that they were the explosions made by the shells from the firing mortars of the Federal troops.

So they have come! he cried to himself. *They have come!* And now the pain in his heart from the wreck that the wind had made of his corn was temporarily forgotten. His mind was wild and his heart beat rapidly, unevenly and lifting his foot off the broadside of the shovel's blade, he pulled it out of the earth and as he turned to go back into the house, he saw that the back door of his landlord's house was open and that both Mr Ohiali and Ndudi's mother were outside, watching him.

'Did you hear the guns?' Mr Ohiali asked, coming towards him in spite of the rain.

Osime Iyere lifted the shovel and rested it on his shoulders and then said, 'Yes, I did. The sound of exploding shells.'

Ohiali turned away and looked at his wife, and she said, 'Do you think the Federal troops have come into the city?'

Osime shrugged his shoulders. 'I do not know,' he said.

He had to be careful. He could hear the sound of more guns, mainly small firearms firing in quick succession now, but he was not sure who was doing the firing. He had to be careful with these people.

'They must be Federal troops,' Ohiali said as if to himself, and even as he said it, they could all hear a great shout coming from the centre of the city.

What if a massacre is on foot? Osime asked himself. *What if this is a massacre?*

'Could be Biafran troops,' he said. 'The Federal troops are still far away. You heard the news yesterday. They are still held up at Ore and this firing comes from the river.'

Osime Iyere looked at the face of the big man and he didn't like what he saw there. He saw the fear plainly written in the other man's eyes, the fear and the uncertainty. The big man's eyes shone with his fear as his fair face glistened with the pearls of raindrops. *Only a minute,* he said to himself. *Only one minute between now as we stand here and a few months ago when I faced the corn. A minute ago, Mr Ohiali was secure and safe inside his house. But now, look at the sudden droop of his shoulders, a droop that shows even in the way his singlet hangs on him, a droop that shows in the way he avoids my eyes and looks instead at the wet ground. A minute has passed and yet what changes. But why should I have any sympathy for him?* he asked himself. *Why should I feel any pity for him? His feelings and sympathies have betrayed him enough. I am sure they are Federal troops anyway. And I am also sure that innocent people have nothing to fear.*

'Will you go to the town to find out?' Mr Ohiali asked him.

'Me?'

'Yes. You could drive to the city centre.' The man was completely drenched now.

'And if they are Biafran troops?'

'They will not be Biafran troops.'

'How can you be sure? We should wait here or . . .' and he hesitated. 'Perhaps you could go yourself.'

Mr Ohiali shook his head and his wife said quickly, 'No, Ichiti, you mustn't go out.'

'So we will wait,' Osime Iyere said and carrying the shovel on his shoulders, he went into his flat.

Osime Iyere leaned the shovel and cutlass against the wall and, drawing out a dining chair, he sat down rather heavily and tried to think. *What if they were the Biafrans? Perhaps there was a massacre afoot. Oh rubbish,* he said to himself and stood up. *Absolute rubbish. They must be Federal troops. Only Federal troops use the mortar tanks and the firing of the guns is great. But I am not going out,* he promised himself. *I am going to stay here until I am sure.*

He walked across the sitting room and now he was in his bedroom by the window. He stood there for almost fifteen minutes, the window blinds slightly parted, before he caught sight of the first tank and then the soldiers and then he was no longer in any doubt and excitedly, he cried out, 'Federal troops! One country! Federal troops! One Nigeria! Oshobe!' He laughed and danced wildly away from the windows, into the passage, into the sitting room.'

'One Nigeria!' he cried again and again. 'Long live one, united Nigeria!' He stopped only when the tears started to his eyes and his voice sounded strange to himself and he just couldn't think any more.

Chapter two

It was ten days since the Federal troops had first come into the city. Ten days when everybody had seemed to go mad with joy and everybody was generous with the soldiers and invited them to their homes and gave them free beer and they told you stories about the war. They were ten wild days and by then the Federal troops had pushed the Biafrans back and across the Niger and the war was no longer in the state now but outside it. And yet it all seemed unbelievable. It all seemed unreal, except for the dead. There were many of them, hundreds of them on the streets.

Why did they have to strip them to the waist before shooting them? Why didn't they just shoot them? Why did they have to disgrace them first, strip them down to their pants before shooting them? He hated the killings, they made him feel sick.

'But they are soldiers,' his other mind said.

'And shouldn't they be taken prisoner?'

'Well, perhaps they died in the process of fighting.'

'No,' he said to himself. 'They did not die in the process of fighting. They were dragged out from where they hid in the bushes, stripped to their pants before being shot.'

The bushes were being cleared now. The city administrator had given the order that all the bushes in the city must be cleared so that no Biafran soldier could hide there. He understood the reasons for the precautions but he could not understand the reasons for the killings.

Anyway, I am sure the killings are all over now, he thought, and looked at the front page of the *Daily News* as it lay across his desk. To avoid further embarrassment and possible molestation, all Ibos resident in the city were to report to the garrison headquarters at Ikpoba slope by the river and be registered. So the newspaper carried it. The exercise must be completed by the following Sunday, the paper said. 'Go and be registered to avoid cases of mistaken identity,' the paper said.

Well, Ohiali should see this, he said to himself. *Ohiali should see this and then he will know there is no more reason to be afraid.* He turned the newspaper over and in big bold headlines, he saw that there was going to be a cultural display at the stadium on the Saturday in honour of the Federal troops. He thought about this briefly and then he was glad that the Biafrans had no planes. Otherwise it could have been suicidal, having thousands of people in one stadium and many of them, no doubt, top military officers.

Yes, there would be thousands of people there and he knew that he would be one of them.

This whole war should be over very soon. He wanted the war to be over. He hated the guns and the shootings and the killings. Perhaps you had to pay so much to be liberated. So much in thousands of lives, tens of thousands of lives, tens of hundreds of them disgraced, ridiculed and spat at before being shot.

He folded up the newspaper, opened up his briefcase and placed the newspaper inside it. Then he pressed down the cover of the briefcase hard because of the many books already in it. He heard the locks click and then he turned it straight up and stood it on its back. He looked round at the office, at the desk of the Features Editor. *I should wait for him to come back before I go,* he thought.

He lifted the briefcase up and it was heavy with his books. *Like a pregnant woman heavy with her unborn child,* he thought. He liked the simile. Both were weighted with meaning. *Strange that I should think of a pregnant woman at this time of war. Strange, when everything is being liberated but only at the price of so many dead. I guess a pregnant woman dies a little too before her child is born. All new creation, all new birth, requires some measure of death. So it is with this our war.*

Now he could no longer wait and he pushed the door open and stepped out into the narrow corridor and then to his relief, he saw the Features Editor coming down the corridor, his car keys hanging from his fingers.

'Hi, Osime,' he called as he walked up to him. The man was plump, rather short and he was growing a stomach now as a man grows a beard. And although it was clear that the growth in the stomach area came from the beer drinking, Ade refused to give up the beer. Instead, he drank more. But he was considerate, generous and kind and all these showed in his eyes, in the way they were always moist and warm. It wasn't easy being the Features Editor. Ade had lasted three weeks already where his predecessors had lasted mostly half a week.

'You off already?'

'Yes. Almost six o'clock now.'

'What about the proofs?'

'I've read them,' Osime Iyere said, going back with Ade to the office.

'Any mistakes?'

'Of course, hundreds of them, but I have corrected them. That ought to be the work of the proof readers.'

Ade shrugged his shoulders and sat on the edge of his desk.

'You know they are not educated. Will you be going to the stadium on Saturday?'

'Yes. What about you?'

Osime smiled. 'Good for us the Biafrans have no air force.'

'I was just thinking about that.'

'You were?'

'Yes. That and the front page headlines. Do you think it is sincere?'

Osime looked Ade directly in the eye and then shrugged his shoulders again.

'Are your worried about your landlord?'

'Yes.'

'I think he had better go. He is old enough for them to know he couldn't have been a soldier.'

'Do you think they really mean it?'

'I don't see why they should lie now. There are no more dangers. Anyway, I understand the orders came from Lagos.'

'So you think he should go?'

'Yes, if he wants to stay alive.'

'I will tell him that,' Osime said, picking up his briefcase.

'And how is Ndudi?' Ade asked, a smile in his eyes.

'We don't talk to each other now.'

'Why? That's childish,' Ade said.

'You should tell her that.'

'Did you try to talk to her?'

'Yes.'

'And what happened?'

'She doesn't need my pity. Neither do her parents.'

'Give her my regards anyway. Try not to argue with her.'

'When do you come in tomorrow?' he asked to change the subject.

Ade eyed him and said, 'About midday.'

'So late?'

'Yes. I am on the civil defence tonight and that means I will have to catch some sleep in the morning.'

'See you then,' Osime said. 'And please check the proofs again before you leave.'

'And give my regards to Ndudi,' Ade said and this time he was serious and the smile was gone from his eyes and face.

Osime Iyere did not answer him but walked out of the office to the corridor.

He drove home slowly and he thought about many things. *Funny that I should be more aware of the war now the Biafran troops have gone and the Federal troops are here. I guess it is the civil defence that does it. When the Biafrans were here, I did not have to spend one night every week waiting and watching on the streets. Now I am involved as I never was before. And how do I tell Ohiali that he can trust his life to the Federal troops? How do I persuade him that it is better to go to them before they come for him and perhaps strip him and give him a shot of apeteshi before shooting him.'*

He did not want to remember that shooting incident. Each time he remembered, he shivered. No, he did not want to remember it ever. Remembering it did something to his illusions about the war and he wanted to keep them, these illusions about the Federal soldiers being good and virtuous and humane . . .

Now he was driving into his compound and he noticed that as usual, the curtains on Mr Ohiali's doors and windows were drawn. He parked the car at the back of the house and after carefully rolling up the windows and bolting the back doors, he got out of his car, lifting the briefcase at the same time out of the car. Then he slammed the car door shut and locked it with his key and put it in his pocket.

First he would go into his apartment and after he had eaten, he would call on his landlord and tell him the news. But why wait until he had eaten? Why not go straightaway and give him the *Daily News*? He changed his mind and walking to the backdoor of his landlord's apartment, he knocked on it twice. He waited a few minutes before he saw the window curtain in the kitchen part slightly and he saw that it was Ndudi's mother. He heard her going across the kitchen and then the back door was open and the woman stood there, nervous and worried but smiling.

'How are you, Osime?' the woman greeted him and moved away from the door so that Osime could enter.

'Thank you, madam, I am all right,' Osime said, going into the apartment. 'Is Oga in?'

'Yes. He is in the sitting room.'

'Good,' Osime said. 'I have something I want to show him.'

Now he was at the table eating the food that he had prepared and he was happy and relieved that he had gone to his landlord. *If he goes,* he told himself, *fair and good. If on the other hand, he refuses to go, then I will be free of any blame, later. I have played my part. I have done the best I can. The ball is now in his court. So, let him play it.*

But how can a man be so stubborn he asked himself. *Not how,* he corrected himself, *why? Yes, why should a man be so stubborn in the face of so much reason?*

As he ate, he thought about the country. *Three years ago, we had peace. Three years and it almost seems like twenty years since the radio broadcast the news without stopping to give more details about the number of people lost or captured. The war was stupid but even more stupid were the reasons given for it, the reasons that led up to it. Why couldn't the people, the leaders, have been more honest with each other? Why did they have to be dishonest to cause a war?*

He wanted the country as one anyway. He was against any division, any secession, but so was he against mass killings. He did not believe the Biafran claims about genocide. That could not be possible . . . He stopped because he remembered the dead bodies he had seen on the streets. Hundreds of them . . . but thank God they were soldiers. Yes, rebel soldiers. He hated their being killed but still, they were soldiers and that made a difference. *Some difference,* he said to himself.

He picked up the plates and he was just going to place them on the ledge of the hatch connecting the kitchen to the sitting room when he heard the sound of a car on the gravel drive outside. He hesitated, then put the plates back on the table and went to the front door and parted the curtains. When he saw that it was Ade, he undid the catch on the front door. He went back to the dining table and this time, he picked up the plates and took them into the kitchen and placed them in the sink. He washed his hands and was rinsing the inside of his mouth with the water when the door bell rang.

He lifted his head from the sink and, blowing out the water, called loudly to Ade to open the door. He opened the refrigerator and took out two bottles of beer that were icy cold from their long standing in the refrigerator.

'What are you doing?' Ade called from the sitting room.

'Bringing the beer,' Osime answered. 'How many bottles do you want?'

'Do you mean I am a drunkard?'

Osime laughed. 'No, but all journalists are.'

'Do you mean I am no longer a journalist?'

'No,' Osime said. 'You are an editor.'

'What's the difference?'

'You don't have to go out as often as we do. And be frustrated too.'

Ade laughed. 'Don't worry. You will soon be an editor. The Political Editor.'

'No,' Osime said. 'I prefer being a correspondent. I hate the desk.'

'You will see,' Ade promised. 'The General Manager often talks about your work. He likes it.'

Osime brought the bottles of beer and the glasses and set them, a bottle and a glass each, on different stools.

'What is happening in the city?' Osime asked.

'Have you seen Ndudi's father?'

'Yes. Why?'

'What did he say?'

Osime shrugged his shoulders. 'He's not going.'

'Not going?'

'No, he's not going. He says the Federal troops are murderers.'

Ade did not make any reply immediately but rubbed his stomach gently with one hand while he moved the glass of beer round slowly on the stool with his other hand. Finally, he sighed loudly so that Osime looked at him closely.

'I think your landlord is right,' he said. 'He shouldn't go.'

Osime was a bit taken aback. He stood up from the chair and his fair face and brown eyes and small moustache and beard were all involved in his surprise. The whole five feet eleven of him that was neither fat nor thin but trim and sprightly was involved in the surprise.

'You think Mr Ohiali is right not to go?'

'Yes. If he has any sense, he shouldn't go.'

'But, Ade, we are talking about the Federal troops, not about the rebels.'

'It doesn't matter,' said Ade slowly. 'It doesn't matter whether you are talking about the Federal troops or the Biafran soldiers. There are two elephants involved in this war and all round them is the grass. The grass is the one that is taking the beating. The elephants trample on the grass most crudely, most viciously. This is not our war and all talk about the Federal side or the Biafran side is an illusion. Just remember the elephants and the grass. Remember there are many sides to this war and that as the head of state said in last week's broadcast, when two elephants fight, it is the grass that suffers.'

'And you think I am on the side of the elephants.'

'Remember there are two elephants.'

'Well, I am on the side of one of the elephants and also of the grass.'

'That's impossible,' Ade said. 'You can't be on the side of the dogs of war and at the same time pity those who suffer from the war.'

Osime shrugged his shoulders. 'All I know is that I believe in having one country and those who seem bent at keeping it one at the moment are the Federal troops. So what's wrong with being on their side?'

'Oh, nothing,' Ade said. 'Absolutely nothing except that belief in one country ought not to be the same as belief in the Federal troops. They are two separate things, the ends you believe in and the means for achieving those ends.'

'So what do you want me to do?'

Ade looked at him. 'Stop believing that both are one and the same thing. They are two separate things. You may believe in one Nigeria but that does not mean believing in the Federal troops.'

'They are not murderers. They are decent, honest people . . .' He stopped because the word honesty suddenly jarred something in him.

'My landlord is a Bini man,' Ade said. 'A son of the soil. He knew some people, Ibo people. And when the Federal troops came, these Ibos ran to him for help. Mind you, these were traders whose shops had been looted. So they come to my landlord and ask for him. My landlord is kind and generous. You know him. So he takes them in. But this morning, he goes to the town and he hears the Federal troops are making a door-to-door check for the Biafrans. So he takes these people in and he opens the roof space and he hides them there. And this evening, the Federal troops come in and want to know if he is hiding any of the Biafrans. My landlord says no.

'But we heard that you took in some of them,' the Federal troops say.

'Well, I did,' my landlord says, 'but now they are gone.'

'Why did you take them in at all?' the Federal soldiers ask.

'They were my friends,' my landlord says. 'They were my friends and they were civilians.'

'But you heard about the plans they had for you?'

'Yes, but I do not believe it,' my landlord says.

'These people you hid planned to massacre you all. They had cutlasses and axes and guns all staked in the classrooms of Ebun College. You heard about it and yet you refuse to believe it,' the Federal soldiers say.

'My landlord keeps quiet and the Federal soldiers start going round the house.

'What is in the garages?' they ask.

'What should be in the garages?' my landlord answers. 'Cars and jerry cans for the petrol. Nothing else.'

'Three soldiers go out and shoot the locks of the garages and search there but find nothing. Then the other two start searching the rooms. Again they find nothing. Then one of them says, 'Perhaps they are up in the ceiling,' and my landlord says nothing. The soldiers cock the rifles and all of a sudden, there is firing. They shoot the ceiling to pieces and as the blood starts dripping down, the men laugh and say to my landlord, 'So you were hiding Biafran soldiers. You knew they were here and yet you lied to us.' Then they took him outside and shot him.'

Osime placed his glass of beer on the table and his hands trembled a little. 'You mean your landlord has been shot?'

Ade looked at him and stood up. 'What do you think I have been trying to tell you? They took my landlord outside and shot him five times in the body. Each soldier shot him once.'

'My God!' Osime exclaimed. 'You can't be serious! The Federal soldiers wouldn't shoot people like that!'

'Do you want to come with me? I know you're always hard to convince. Honestly, I think far more hard times await us now than ever before.'

'But you jump to conclusions too easily,' Osime said. 'Okay, one man has been killed, but you cannot generalise from that.'

'One man that I saw,' Ade said. 'One man, not counting the three in the roof space and the many others that I did not see. I came here actually to tell you to tell Ndudi's father to keep away from that registration camp. I have no faith in the promises made in the papers.'

Ade went to the door and then he seemed to have remembered something else. He put his hand in his breast pocket and brought out two passes. 'These are for you and . . . Ndudi,' he said.

Osime took them and looked at them. 'Thanks.'

'There is a big rush for the passes. The war commanders will be there and so only a selected audience has been given passes.'

Osime looked at the passes again and for the second time he said, 'Thank you, Ade, and honestly I am sorry about your landlord. I am shocked but it all sounds unbelievable.

'See you,' Ade said and went to his car and drove away.

Osime Iyere came back into the house and sat on the settee and looked at the bottles of beer. *My God*, he said to himself, *it can't be true what Ade said.* How could the Federal soldiers have shot civilians in cold blood? When was a killing a killing for the war and not murder? Was murder part of this war? Why did the soldiers behave in that way? They fired at the ceiling, Ade had said. They opened fire on the ceiling and then the blood dripped from the ceiling to the floor. They took the landlord out and shot him. He did not want to believe it but what if it was true? Would he not be leading his own landlord straight to his death? The war was no longer what he thought it was.

Again he remembered Ade's words. 'There are many sides to this war. When two elephants fight, it's the grass that suffers.' His landlord, and Ade's landlord were part of the grass. All the civilian population was part of that grass. And who were the elephants? The armies? Suddenly, his faith in the Federal troops was wavering. This wasn't what he had expected from the war.

He picked up the two glasses of beer, his own half-filled, and took them to the kitchen and emptied the beer into the sink. Then he left the two glasses there. He came back and took the bottles and this time, he went into the bedroom he now used as a store and drew out a carton of beer in which stood five empty bottles already. He dropped the two bottles into the carton, folded the carton up and pushed it with the toe of his foot against the wall. He stood there for a few seconds, then dusting his hands, he went out of the room and was about to enter his own bedroom when he heard a knock on the back door.

Chapter three

He went to the back of the house and his heart missed a beat. Ndudi stood there. He opened the door to let her in but she continued to stand outside, on the wet ground.

'My father would like to see you,' she said.

'Ndudi!'

She looked at him.

'Can you come in for a minute? I want to tell you something?'

She hesitated for a second, then stepped out of the light rain into the house.

I thought it was all gone, he thought. *I thought it was all over and that I had done with it. But it was always there. It has always been there and what I have held has been a bubble. And the bubble burst a moment ago, as soon as I saw the rain in her hair, looked into her eyes and remembered.*

He saw her now, the water glittering in her hair and he remembered. He saw her in all her fairness, in all her slimness and he remembered, for if ever there was a beautiful woman, then Ndudi certainly was one. But love is also politics and the coming of the Biafrans had driven a wedge between them. To be more exact, he had converted the invasion of the state by the Biafrans into a wedge. Somehow, and for a reason he could not understand, he had felt that Ndudi's father had shown a certain amount of joy, in fact, had celebrated the coming of the Biafrans. He had resented it and the love he had had for Ndudi, still very young and vulnerable then, had flickered and then gone out, leaving nothing but an uneasy darkness. But now he knew that he loved her.

He led her into the sitting room and caught her eyes going round the room. He guessed she was trying to see what had changed in the room since she had last been there.

'Ade was here,' he said.

'I saw him,' Ndudi said.

'Do you want us to stay here or go into the bedroom?' he asked.

'Anywhere,' she said. 'Anywhere will do.' He looked at her intently and sharply and now he saw the fear and the anxiety and the helplessness clearly in her eyes.

'You look as if you were being led to a slaughterhouse,' he said, turning to her as he led her into the bedroom.

She shrugged her shoulders. 'Isn't the whole world a slaughterhouse?' she asked.

'You mean this part of the world?'

'No,' she said. 'The whole world. Not here alone.' She sat down on the bed.

'You should not talk like that, Ndudi,' he said. 'We are but a small part of the world and the fact that we have a cloud here does not mean that the cloud covers the rest of the world.'

She did not say anything for some time and he turned the chair that served his writing desk towards the bed and sat on it.

'Well, what is it?' she asked at last. 'What is it we must discuss?'

'Us,' he said slowly, 'You and I.'

'Us?' she asked and covered her eyes with her hands, and lay back on the bed on her back.

'Ndudi,' he said to her and stopped because he saw the tears as they came down the side of her face. He stood up hastily and went to her and lifted her head up in the bowl of his hands and he could feel the warmth of the tears on his palms.

'Ndudi,' he said to her again. 'You mustn't cry. Nothing happened. You should know that.'

She did not answer.

'Ndudi,' he called to her again and his voice was soft and warm now with all the emotions that he had tried to suppress these past weeks. 'Ndudi, everything is all right. You mustn't cry.' He took her hands from her face and bent down and kissed her tears. They tasted salty in his mouth and he could not swallow it. He tried to kiss her on the lips then but she turned her face away in a subtle quick movement. He dropped her hands back on the bed, and stayed for a moment because he did not know what to do and because the saliva was gradually building up in his mouth, he got up from the bed and went out of the room, to the bathroom. He spat out the saliva and then he cleared his throat and spat that out too. Then he turned on the tap and rinsed his mouth with cold water.

When he came back into the room, Ndudi was sitting up against the broad board of the bed, her hands in her lap, her head against the wall, her eyes staring unseeingly at the wardrobe in front of her. Ndudi looked away from the wardrobe at him and they looked at each other and then away from each other.

'Can you forgive me?' he asked.

'It's my parents I am worried about,' she said.

'Your parents?'

'Yes.'

He felt hurt because he thought she had deliberately ignored him.

'They will be all right,' he assured her.

She laughed, a small bitter laugh that somehow made him feel as though it had been directed against him.

'Look, Ndudi,' he said now. 'I want to talk to you seriously now. Well, I know I made a mistake. I admit it. And I am prepared to do everything to set matters right between us. That's as far as we are concerned. As for the other thing, I don't think it is wrong to be happy that one's state has been liberated, that the children can now go back to school, that the markets can reopen, that everything can return to normal, or at least, to as near normal as possible. Of course, you will say things are now normal for us because we no longer wear the shoe. But I want to believe that you are part of us. After all, Oganza is still part of Midwest.'

Ndudi stood up from the bed now. 'My father wants to see you,' she said. 'Beyond that we do not want anybody's sympathy. As for us, there wasn't really anything between us. Yes, we made love. We had sex. But you know how these things are. We all make mistakes.'

'I see,' he said quietly now, seeing that the lines had hardened. 'But no matter what you would like to think, you must never imagine that I am on this or on that side. We all need help sometimes and that is why it isn't really a mark of strength to refuse help when you need it. And what I really want to do is help. If your father agrees to go to the registration camp on Sunday, I will go there with him and I will bring with me at least three other reporters and a number of photographers. We will make sure we are there from the beginning to the end. As for us, you have yourself said it. We all make mistakes.'

He watched her go out of the room and something in him went with her. He wanted to stop her, to hold her hand and tell her that they were both being foolish, very foolish. But he had his pride and warned his considerate self to stand firm. He watched her go out of the back door, and he closed the door after her and came back into the sitting room and drew out one of the dining chairs and sat on it.

Why did things have to happen this way? When she lay back on the bed and I kissed the tears off her cheeks, I thought then and sensed it too that things were going to be all right. And that was less than ten minutes ago. I kissed her cheeks and held her hands and she did not protest. It is true that I could not look into her eyes because they were moist with the salt water but I felt then that we were going to be all right. Relationships! Why did they have to be so complicated? Why did we have to complicate them when we could make them simple, honest and beautiful. Perhaps there is something in us, in each of us, that hates simplicity, that thirsts after climbing mountains and getting lost in mazes. Or perhaps it is simply because, as she says, we all make mistakes.

He shook his head because he didn't know and then stood up because he remembered he still had to see Ndudi's father.

Chapter four

Now it was Saturday afternoon and as he dressed for the cultural display at the Stadium, he thought about Ade who had gone to enlist in the army.

He could not understand Ade. Why had he gone to enlist in the army? Because his landlord had been shot in his presence? But that was stupid. What would he gain from it, except perhaps death? No, it was wrong to do what he had done. Just wake up in the morning and pack your bags and go to the army headquarters to enlist. He knew that Ade hated the army, he hated the Federal troops fiercely after what they had done to his landlord. Then why go and join them? Why go into the company of the people you hate? Well, he remembered. You joined them if you could not beat them, except of course, Ade hoped to beat them by joining them. Ah, nonsense. It was foolish, unreasonable. He could not understand it.

He went out of the flat through the back door and before getting into his car, he looked at the remaining stalks of corn that he had saved. His heart contracted when he remembered how many there had been and he closed his eyes momentarily to shut out the memory but he couldn't. He shook his head and, as he got into the car, he told himself that it was not possible for a man to shut out his memory simply by closing his eyes. Something else was necessary, something a man could not have as long as he remained alive. Death was the only blind that could shut out all memory. Living was remembering, the flame of life fanned memory, only the ashy coldness of death took away memory.

He drove along the narrow dirty streets and he saw the soldiers and the army jeeps and the guns and the helmets and the boots and every other trademark of war. Everywhere he looked there were soldiers carrying guns, guns loaded with certain death, and their faces were impassive and serious and, to him, respectable. *These are our soldiers,* he said to himself. *Our soldiers wear heavy black boots, they carry modern weapons and are serious and heroic-looking as they march. Unlike the Biafran soldiers who wear canvas shoes and share one gun between three soldiers. Yes, our soldiers are fine and good and very soon the whole business of this war will be over. Over and done with. Over and done with,* he said to himself again and he remembered the Irish teacher who had taught him that phrase, many, many years ago. Mr Muldoon had been very harsh, as harsh as a whip, but his teaching had been as unerring as the flight of a swallow.

He looked out again at the streets and again he saw the soldiers and the dirt on the streets. *This whole city is dirty,* he said to himself. *Just look at the snail shells and the empty cans and bottles and leaves and the sand and the dirty soldiers. The soldiers have to be dirty in this war,* he acknowledged. *Dirty and bold and courageous. But the city doesn't have to be dirty. The dirt is a reflection of the character of the times.*

The moving cars rode on the empty cans and the empty snail shells and the bottles and the noise of breaking glass and shells and exploding cans filled the air. The noise sounded dirty, as dirty as the rubbish whose crushing produced it.

He looked past the soldiers at the houses and they were small and low and dirty and ugly like the untarred streets. Some of the streets had once been tarred, hastily tarred and then the rains had come and washed the asphalt and stones away because they were tarred in haste and because there were no gutters in many places to receive the flood. Once tarred and now nothing more than loose stones and empty snail shells and cans and bottles, all crushed and the leaves also crushed and the houses also somewhat crushed and the people who lived in them also totally crushed and beaten down but by what he didn't know. Perhaps it was the same wind that destroyed his corn that also crushed the people and their houses, but he wasn't sure.

There were no dead bodies on the streets now, he observed. Yesterday they had been there, the bodies of the Biafran soldiers flushed out of their hiding places. They had been on the streets, he had seen at least a hundred of them, all of them stripped to their pants, and the blood still fresh, running out of their mouths and ears or chests. *But soon, it will be over and done with,* he thought again. *Yes, the Biafran leader must surrender and then the country will be one and the war will be over and forgotten. No, not forgotten,* he corrected himself. *Not forgotten but over and done with.*

Osime Iyere drove behind a taxi and as he looked, he saw the driver of the taxi bringing out the leaves of corn and throwing them into the road. He watched as the corn leaves hit the ground and then rolled several times before coming to a halt and then his car was on the leaves and he tried to avoid grinding them into the dust and then he leaned out of the window very briefly and spat out in disgust to the side of the road.

The next bunch of corn leaves came out of the front window on the right of the taxi and then there were more leaves coming from the back windows and they all hit the side of the road and then rolled several times before coming to a stop in the centre of the road. Osime Iyere was angry and at the next traffic lights he looked for an opening to draw level with the taxi but he was blocked by another taxi. If only he could get alongside the taxi where both the driver and his passengers were eating the cooked corn and littering the road with more garbage! If he could only get near enough to tell them they were pigs and dirty bastards and anything else he could think of. But he couldn't catch up with the taxi and he sat in his car, angry, waiting for the lights to change, but after some time the anger went away and he told himself it was none of his business how other people used the streets.

He drove carefully along the road. That was all that mattered. Driving carefully and avoiding accidents. He remembered the time at the Ring Road when another car had run into the rear of his car and the impact had been so great that the car had turned one hundred and eighty degrees so that when it stopped, he was facing the direction from which he had been coming. Salome had been with him then, Salome and Okah. It had been raining then and he had got out of the car, sweating, and when he examined the rear of the car, there was a big ugly dent there. The damage had been extensive. The whole left side of the car, his own side was smashed in. He trembled a little and Salome had got out of the car too, shaken, and Okah had got out and they had all confronted the small man who had driven his 1950 Mercedes Benz into his car and asked, 'Why did you hit us?'

He had been so infuriated that he wanted to punch the man on the face but he had prevented himself from doing that by walking back to his car until the man had called after him, 'Every man should go and repair his own car.'

He had walked back quickly and before the man could realise it, he had hit him twice in the face and the blood began to come from the man's nose. They had fought in the rain until more cars had come and stopped and people had come between them and then the police had arrived. And all along Salome had been in the rain, wet and shivering. It had been her birthday.

No, he didn't want to be involved in any accident, ever again.

He had had to repair his car by himself because his insurance policy had expired and the police had wanted to prosecute him on account of that. No, he didn't want to be involved in any accident, ever again.

He drove carefully now, his eyes on the road, watching out for the other cars. *I shall be there in another five or seven minutes,* he said to himself, *and then I shall see the new commanders of the Federal troops. Perhaps they will grant me an interview after the cultural display. Yes, perhaps they will and I will have the opportunity to ask about this registration business.*

He drove past the secondary school and he saw that the fields were flooded, the whole ground as far as he could see. He wondered how the students played their games or even went from one block to another. And why had the Ministry of Education not done something about it? Then he remembered the war. They could have done nothing about it with the war on.

'But the war is less than three years old,' his other mind told him.

'One year but enough to shoot everything to pieces,' he answered himself.

'Not three years,' his other mind corrected him.

'Our state was occupied for less than six months.'

'Well, one month in war is more than a decade in peace.'

'The Biafrans did not touch the school nor the revenues of the state.'

'Oh yes they did.'

'How?'

He kept quiet to think of examples but he couldn't remember any concrete examples and he was angry with his conscience. The traffic lights at Oliha market stopped him. He looked out of the window at the market and what he saw shocked him. It was as if the soil of the market was night soil and dung and dogs' faeces all mixed with muddy red water. The soil was black and slimy and dirty. No, not dirty. There must be another word for it, a stronger word. Filthy? No, not filthy. That was too weak. An eyesore? Yes, an eyesore but that was still too weak. The market was worse than an eyesore. He watched as the people moved in the slime and grease and rot and decay that was the market, he saw how wares — garri, rice, banana, vegetables and dried fish — were displayed even on the very top of the garbage and something in his head nearly gave way. Something in his stomach gave way and he felt it welling up and he took a deep breath and then his eyes watered from the pain of keeping it down and then, as the line of cars began to move, he spat out into the street and then he was away and clear of the vomit that was the market.

Yes, vomit. He had found it. Vomit. The whole market was like vomit and the people like vermin feeding on it. The market grounds, the stands, the wares, were nothing but vomit and night soil simultaneously thrown into a pool of muddy red water. The people were the maggots in the night soil or the vermin that fed on the vomit, the wares and the stands were the undigested lumps of food in the slimy vomit.

It was terrible, absolutely loathsome and horrible, what a war could cause, what three years of fighting and killing could drive a people to. He hated the rebels who had caused the war.

There were hundreds of armed soldiers outside the stadium. He could see some of them in the far away bushes, standing by the trees, holding their guns, at the ready, their teeth flashing momentarily in their dark faces as they laughed or talked. The soldiers at the gate were even more heavily armed. They stood, tall and black and unsmiling, and held the guns that were loaded with quick, instant death almost carelessly. He showed the men his pass and even as they examined it, he felt uncomfortable and uneasy because of their guns and their grenades.

There were many people in the small stadium, crowds of people and police and soldiers all armed to the teeth, watching and waiting. He saw five armoured cars in different parts of the stadium and again he felt uneasy but proud. He always loved looking at crowds of people, particularly in a stadium. He looked at the people now as they sat on the long wooden benches that were painted green on the seats to give the impression of padding and painted white on the legs and back supports and they were so colourful and beautiful that he wished he could paint the brilliant spectacle.

He saw that the cultural display had started. This was a group of very young girls who were stripped to the waist with rows of beads covering their breasts. Their short skirts were also beaded at the hem and on their ankles they wore beads and on their wrists they wore beads and more beads were woven into their matted hair. Osime Iyere watched one of the girls, one of her hands going up and making a beautiful curve in the air, one of her legs also raised above the ground and then came the sound of the cymbals and the girl was away from the group, moving to the edge of the field on the other side. His eyes followed her across the small patch of grass. He couldn't believe that a human body could move in so many successive waves, as the water does when hit with a stone. And yet this girl moved her body as if the sound of the cymbal came from the centre of her nerves and all else was nothing and she was the music and the sky and the rest of the world. Osime Iyere stood there and watched the girl, not more than thirteen, he guessed, and the sweat stood on his face with his admiration for her.

'Why are you standing there?' a soldier who had come up behind him demanded and he almost jumped. Osime Iyere began to move.

'Wait! Stand there!' the soldier ordered. Osime stood and waited.

'Let me see your pass.' Osime put his hand in his right hand pocket and brought out the white pass and handed it over to the soldier.

The soldier examined the pass and looked at Osime Iyere's face. 'Journalist, heh?'

'Yes,' Osime said. 'Political correspondent.'

The man raised his hand and pointed. 'Wing A is over there. Do not stop until you get there.'

Osime Iyere took the pass from the soldier and now he no longer kept it in his pocket but in his hand and with the soldier watching him, he walked away to the stand indicated by the soldier.

Wing A was the second class part of the small stadium and instead of being painted, the seats here were actually padded green. Osime Iyere walked up and looked across to the stand and he could see that almost all the seats had been taken and that the gate which led into the stand had been bolted from the inside and was being guarded by three soldiers.

Osime Iyere tapped lightly on the side of the gate to draw the attention of one of the soldiers guarding it and one of them looked at him and then looked away.

'I want to get inside there,' Osime said across the gate to the heavily armed soldiers. The soldiers stopped looking at the dancing girl and looked at him. One of them was a private, the second was a sergeant and the third was a lance corporal.

'There are no more seats,' the lance corporal among them said.

'But I have a pass.'

'That is not our fault,' the private said.

'The pass was issued to me from the Administrator's Office.'

'You had better go away,' the sergeant said now, the impatience in his voice clearly showing.

'And my pass?'

'Do you want your body to be carried away from here?' the private asked.

Osime Iyere looked at the man's face and the callous way the private had spoken made him angry. 'Let me in!' he demanded. 'I am a journalist.'

'So you are a journalist?' the sergeant asked.

'Yes. With the *Daily News*.'

'Do you want me to tell you what we have done to journalists in this war?'

Osime Iyere did not answer.

The sergeant laughed and his voice was pompous. 'I will tell you,' he said. 'Journalists like you we have first of all shaved and then whipped before shooting. Now go away.'

Osime Iyere stood there and the blood of his face clotted with his anger. Who did these uneducated soldiers think they were talking to?

'Let me in,' he demanded again. 'There are vacant seats over there. Look at them.'

'Seat or no seat, you cannot come in.'

'A friend of mine has reserved a seat for me in there,' he insisted.

'Where is your pass?', the sergeant asked.

Osime showed it, ready as it was in his hand.

'Let me see it,' the sergeant said again and Osime held the pass out, across the iron bars of the gate.

The sergeant took the pass, examined it and put it in his pocket. 'Now you can go away,' he said.

'What about my pass?'

'You have no pass,' the sergeant said. 'How did you get in here?'

'Give me back my pass!' Osime Iyere shouted, the anger almost choking him.

'You have no pass,' the sergeant said. 'Private Ikun!'

The private saluted smartly.

'Open the gate and take him out of the stadium,' the sergeant said. 'I want him detained for further questioning.'

The private unlocked the gate. The gate had to open inside, inwards towards the soldiers and Osime made a rush for the opening.

'You hand over my pass!' he cried.

'Detain him,' the sergeant shouted, 'and if he resists, shoot him when you get outside.'

'You bastard!' Osime Iyere shouted, beside himself with rage. 'You are all bastards!' and he held on to the gate while the lance corporal and the private attempted to break his hold. *I must not allow them to take me outside here,* he thought. *If they do, I am dead!* He struggled fiercely. People began to look at them, in their direction.

'What is it?' a Chief Superintendent of Police who had come up asked.

'That sergeant has taken my pass,' Osime Iyere said, letting go of the gate now.

'Why did he take it?'

Osime Iyere explained. The Chief Superintendent of Police looked round at Wing A and then said, 'But there are no more seats there.'

'There were seats when I came here.'

The superintendent looked at him and then away. 'Sergeant,' he said, and the man pretended to stand to attention, 'do you have this man's pass?'

'No sir,' the sergeant said. 'I do not have his pass.'

'You had better go away then,' the superintendent said to Osime.

'What about my pass?'

'He doesn't have it.'

'How can you say that when you haven't searched him?'

'He is an officer like I am,' the Chief Superintendent of Police said. 'Army officers do not tell lies.'

'Private Ikun,' the sergeant called again. 'Take this man out of the stadium and detain him.'

The man immediately seized Osime Iyere by the collar of his shirt and began to pull, push and kick him. The lance corporal joined in.

'Somebody had better stop them!' Osime heard a woman's voice demand and he was surprised because he thought he recognised the voice.

'I say stop it!' the woman cried again and pushed her way through the crowd of soldiers and policemen to where Osime Iyere was being kicked on the ground now.

'I say stop it,' she cried again, 'or else somebody will regret it,' and the soldiers looked at her and then at one another and one of them recognised her and whispered to the others. They stopped kicking him.

Osime Iyere picked himself up from the ground and his face was swollen and bleeding and his clothes were torn and he could not look Salome in the face.

'Who started this?' Salome asked and the soldiers looked uneasily at each other.

'We are sorry, Madam,' the sergeant said now. 'We are awfully sorry. We didn't know . . .'

'Okay, come with me,' she said and the men followed her and Osime Iyere also followed her and his mind was black with hatred for the soldiers.

They went past the gate that cordoned off the area of the cultural display from the rest of the stadium and they were all silent and the soldiers, those who had beaten him, kept looking over their shoulders and then back at Salome's face that was serious and angry and cold.

Now they were past the last of the gates and they were outside of the stadium and Salome led Osime aside and they talked briefly and then she came back to the soldiers and told them to go away.

'You should never get involved with soldiers,' Salome said to him now and put her hand on his face but he drew it away quickly.

'I guess you have saved my life,' he said, shaken and a little ashamed.

'Forget it,' she said. 'Don't think about it.'

He shook his head. 'I can't,' he said. 'Not any more.'

'Forget the gratitude anyway.'

'No,' he said. 'I can't. That goes with the experience.' He touched his face and nose and his fingers felt sticky with his own blood.

'You should go home and treat yourself,' she said. 'I will come to see you later this evening. That is, if you still live in the same place.'

'Yes,' he said. 'No. I mean you shouldn't bother. Please don't come.'

'Oh, why? Are you married?'

'No,' he said. 'It isn't that.'

'Then I'm coming.'

No, he cried to himself. He didn't want to start any of this thing all over again. He was not going to take any chances.

'No,' he said now, firmly. 'You can't come. You mustn't come.'

She looked at him, very shrewdly as only Salome could, and said,

'It is Otunshi you are afraid of then?'

'No,' he said. 'I am not afraid of your husband. Why should I be?'

'You heard he shot a man shortly after we were married.'

'No,' he said. 'I mean, yes, I heard it but it is not because of that that I ask you not to come.'

'Okay then,' she said. 'I won't come to your house. But let's meet at the Luna Club at eight o'clock. Otunshi goes to the war front in one or two days' time and I follow shortly after. So perhaps we shall never meet again. But come to the Luna Club at eight. You know as well as I do that the place is always deserted.'

'If I am able to,' he said.

'Yes, only if you are able to but I think you will be all right. Bathe your face in cold water. Take the water from the bottles that you keep in the fridge.'

'Yes,' he said. 'I will.'

'So I will see you then at eight.'

'Yes, at eight o'clock.' He hesitated and then he said, 'How is the major?'

She laughed immediately. 'The major is all right,' she said. 'I was representing him here this afternoon. You see, only some of the officers are here. They are not taking too many chances.'

'I see,' he said. 'And what will he be doing tonight? I mean while you are at the Luna Club?'

'He is never at home in the evenings. Can you believe . . .' she began and then stopped. 'No,' she said. 'I will see you later, that is, if you will be well enough.'

'I think I will be all right,' he said and went towards his car.

She stood there and watched him get into the car and shut the door. When she heard the engine of the car start up she turned away and went back into the stadium.

Chapter five

Osime Iyere drove back along the road, looking but unseeing, his sight blocked by the pillar of anger and hatred in his heart. He touched the swollen flesh of his face with his left hand and the pain was great not only there but inside his body. But he did not really feel the pain, because of the bitterness in his heart.

I am glad, he said to himself, *that my landlord refused my advice. Mighty glad because perhaps — no, not perhaps. No perhaps any more. I am sure I would have led him to his death. These people are not to be trusted with anybody's life. If you cannot trust them with a pass, then how can you trust them with a life?*

'You shouldn't be bitter,' his other self said to him. 'You had a mighty good opinion of the Federal troops.'

'Heroes!' he flung at himself.

'They still are,' his other mind said. 'Three men do not make an army.'

'Yes,' he agreed. 'Three men do not make an army but one man is enough to represent what the current regime stands for.'

'Brutality?' his other mind asked.

'Yes and much more. Brutality is not bad when it is necessary. Sometimes you have to be brutal to succeed.'

'You are trying to justify the killing of Ade's landlord?'

'No!'

'Then, your own treatment?'

'No.'

'Then what?'

'There are different types of brutality,' he answered himself. 'This was not simply brutality. It was sadism, fascism. You see what I mean?'

'Yes. I see what you mean, very clearly.'

'All right then,' he answered. 'I am glad you have seen what I mean. I want to be one person, not two people any more. I want to be sure I know what I mean. I have been naive, perhaps.'

'No perhaps, remember?'

'Yes. Thank you for reminding me. No more perhaps. I cannot afford to be idealistic any more. I must be realistic.'

'Remember what your informants called you?'

'Yes. And they were right.'

'Well now, perhaps you will have the sense to keep away from them.'

'No,' he said. 'You don't beat them by running away.'

'Nor by joining them either.'

'Yes. In both cases, you become what they want you to become.'

'And perhaps even worse.'

'No perhaps, worse. A traitor to yourself.'

'I can see you have changed.'

'Not completely yet. No, not completely.'

'Because you don't know what you are going to do.'

'Yes, that and other things. The bastards! The dirty bastards.'

He drove into his compound and drove the car into the garage at the side of the house. He made sure he locked up the car properly and then he walked very slowly to the back of the house. He looked at the corn and he shook his head and he said aloud, 'We have both taken a beating but we are not beaten yet. We will show them yet.'

He put the key into the lock and turned it, then drew the door outwards, towards himself.

'Osime!'

Osime Iyere stopped and turned and then looked away again because he did not want Ndudi to see the beating that he had taken.

'Osime!'

'Yes?' He went into the house. She followed him and then shut the door.

'What happened?' she asked quickly now, realising that he was in pain.

'I was beaten up,' he said to her and entered the kitchen. 'I was beaten up by some soldiers. Our soldiers.'

Ndudi did not say anything.

'Can you get a bowl and empty these bottles of water into it? I am going for the towel.' Ndudi watched him leave the kitchen with a frown.

As she bathed his face and saw the hurt look in his eyes, she felt extremely sorry for him. She felt she knew what he was feeling. She had had the same feeling before.

'Perhaps I'd better undress and go into the bathroom and you can boil some water and use it then. The bastards kicked me all over my body, even in the testicles.'

'But what happened?'

He laughed, a short bitter laugh and kept quiet.

'You don't want to talk about it?'

'No, I don't. So your father has changed his mind,' he said.

'Yes he has changed his mind. And he will go willingly to meet them?'

He shook his head and his neck hurt him. 'He should not go,' he said. 'Ade was right. No man should trust his life with this crowd of butchers. They will murder him.'

Ndudi held the towel in her hand and looked at him. 'So you have changed your mind?'

He did not answer her.

'But you will go to my father?'

'Yes.'

'And try to dissuade him from going?'

'Yes.'

She shook her head and said, 'I think it's too late. He has made up his mind.'

'He made up his mind once before.'

'Yes,' she said and stood up, dropping the towel back into the bowl. 'I am going to see if the water is hot enough.'

She went out of the sitting room and he could hear her feet in the kitchen and then she came back and took the bowl of cold water and the towel and went into the bathroom and she was there for some minutes because she had to wring the towel to squeeze out as much cold water as she could.

Now they were in the bathroom and she was using the towel soaked in hot water to press his shoulders, neck and chest firmly but tenderly.

'Put your feet in the bathtub so I can do your back,' she said and he stood up and got into the bath and sat down with his back to her.

'Your skin is broken in several places,' she observed.

'Yes,' he said. 'I can feel it.'

'And you won't tell me what happened?'

'I already have,' he said. 'Our soldiers beat me up.'

'But where?'

'The stadium. You ought to know. I asked you to come with me.'

'You didn't tell me you were going there when you went out anyway.'

'Didn't I?'

'No, you didn't.'

'I thought I did,' he said. 'Well, now, you know.'

'Yes, I know that but not why.'

He did not say anything.

'So you won't tell me that?' she asked.

'No,' he said. 'I won't tell you.'

They kept quiet and sometimes he would squirm his shoulders or tighten up his back muscles to show that he felt the pain. She would immediately release the pressure on the towel but then apply it again until he would flex his muscles again and then she would pout her lips and say, 'I'm sorry.'

When she had finished and he was alone in the bathroom, he removed his pants and examined his penis and testicles carefully. The flesh was not broken but the pain was there all right. *They really meant to kill you,* he thought. *Yes, they really meant to kill you by kicking you in the most vulnerable places of all.* He did not want to think about it, at least not now.

'Osime!' Ndudi called from the bedroom.

'Yes?'

'I think I'd better go.'

'What time is it?'

'Almost half past.'

'Six?'

'No, five.'

'Then why don't you wait?'

'It's not the time,' she said. 'It's my father. He must be waiting.'

'Yes,' he agreed. 'But wait and I will be out in another minute.'

So only an hour has passed. An hour and yet it feels like a month, a year. But I mustn't think about that sergeant or the boots of the soldiers or the Chief Superintendent of Police either. No, I mustn't think about them or else I'll want to cry or commit murder . . .

He came out of the bathroom and went into the bedroom and she stood beside the window and looked at him, naked as he was for he had left his pants in the bathroom, and asked, 'How do you feel now?'

'Very sore.'

He was putting on another pair of pants now and she looked at him with a curious smile on her face.

'What are you smiling at?' he asked her.

'I was thinking about you,' she said.

'Oh,' he said and now the smile was on his face too. 'Why?'

'Well, I am almost glad that you should have been beaten up because now you can see much better. They broke the blinkers you wore when they kicked you in the face.'

'Yes,' he agreed and he was no longer smiling now but he was not angry either. 'Shall we go to your parents?'

'Yes. Let's go.'

She was about to move away from the window when he said 'Stop! I want to look at you as you stand there,' he said. 'I want to drink in your loveliness.'

'You're crazy,' she said and came away from the window.

'You are a beautiful woman,' he told her. 'But you mustn't let that knowledge go to your head.'

'I'm not beautiful,' she protested.

'You can say what you like,' he told her. 'You can deny what you like but that alters nothing. Let's go.'

She came past him and he took her hand and she did not take it away but allowed him to hold it until they got to the sitting room. She withdrew her hand then but he did not mind. *If anything has come of this whole black business, then it's this: that I stand to win her back, that in a way, I have won her back.*

And I must have been crazy when I used the Biafran invasion to extricate myself from the relationship. Think of a kind, warm and generous woman and it is Ndudi. And yet in a moment of madness, I almost lost her. Instead of building bridges, I built a wall. This war does not want walls nor fences. It wants bridges and a bridge is what I must build with her. But I must be careful from now on. Because what I have with her is as close, if not equal to what I had with Salome.

He did not want to think of Salome, not now.

'Let's go to your father,' he said to her rather unnecessarily and she looked back at him and she guessed that his mind must have been miles away.

They went to her parents. Mr Ohiali looked at his face and said, 'You have been involved in a fight, Mr Iyere?'

Osime Iyere looked back at the man. 'Yes,' he admitted. 'With our soldiers. They beat me up.'

'Oh, I see,' Mr Ohiali said. 'Ndudi, bring Mr Iyere a bottle of beer and a glass.'

'Thank you, sir,' Osime said quickly, 'but I don't really want a drink. I came because Ndudi said you wanted to see me.'

'Yes,' Mr Ohiali said. 'But please do not refuse the beer. Ndudi,' he said again and waved at his daughter. 'Do fetch Mr Iyere the beer.'

They were quiet and Ndudi went into the dining room which was cut off from the sitting room unlike Iyere's apartment. Ndudi came back carrying the bottle of beer and a glass and an opener on a tray. She set them down in front of Osime. They did not look at each other.

Osime opened the bottle of beer and took the glass in one hand and poured the beer into it. The beer was icy cold.

Mr Ohiali watched him take a sip of beer and then said, 'Perhaps you are aware of why I asked to see you?'

Osime placed the cold glass of beer on the tray and wiped his mouth with the back of his hand. 'Yes,' he said. 'Ndudi has told me some of it.'

'Very well then,' Mr Ohiali said and in spite of Osime's swollen face and eyes, he could see the deepening rings around the man's eyes.

'I have decided to take your advice,' the man said. 'I have decided to go tomorrow morning to the Army post on the hill and register myself.'

Osime Iyere looked at the man and felt uncomfortable.

'I don't think you should go, sir,' he said carefully. 'I was wrong about the Federal troops. They will kill you. I believe that now. You said so yourself. You were right. I am seriously advising you, sir, not to go. You should stay here and let things sort themselves out.'

The man shook his head from side to side. 'I went to the city today,' he said. 'The Federal troops had gone to two of my friends' homes and shot the men in the presence of their wives. I wouldn't want that to happen to me.'

'Father!'

Mr Ohiali looked at his daughter and the rings around his eyes showed very sharply now. 'I have decided to go because the Federal troops gave the impression that if the men were not Biafran soldiers, then surely they would have gone to register themselves at the army post on the hill.'

'But they could shoot you all the same,' Osime pointed out.

'Yes,' the man agreed. 'They could but I doubt if they will. There will be other people there. They couldn't possibly shoot everybody.

Osime cleared his throat. 'You see, sir,' he said, 'at the time I first asked you to go, I did think I would be there. I thought I could get a group of our cameramen together and some other reporters. But you said you wouldn't go and then this evening, this thing happens.' He touched his face. 'Honestly, sir, I don't think you should go. These men are murderers. They have no conscience. But I'll tell you what I will do. You can move into my apartment and take refuge there. I will hide you there.'

'And if they find me out.'

'We do not know that they will.'

The man thought about this and then very slowly shook his head from side to side.

'No,' he said finally. 'There is no need to run away from your own fate. You go out and you meet it. If I should die by going to them, then I will know it was not through any fault of mine.'

You won't be there to know it, Osime thought, but he did not say anything. He saw that the man's mind was made up. He would try to see Ndudi's mother and talk to her. He had this uneasy feeling that if the man went, then the Federal soldiers would shoot him. He did not trust them any more.

Chapter six

There were concrete steps outside leading to the upper part of the two-storey building that was called the Luna Club. The concrete steps led to a door on the landing upstairs. You opened it and there was a passage, quite wide, and on both sides of the passage were the brown and red cushion chairs and you went past these until you came to the second door that opened into the wide and spacious bar of the Luna Club.

This room must have been the bedroom of the white colonial slave driver who had lived here many years ago, many years before the country became independent and another few years after independence. *They always knew how to live at the expense of others, the white colonial bastards*, he thought and now he imagined how the white colonial slave driver must have lived in this room with his wife. That is, if they ever slept in the same room, for he saw that where the bar now stood must have been another room and the toilets would have been the toilets then but the darts room would have been the sitting room. The kitchen would have been downstairs. Yes, downstairs where there were now at least ten private rooms.

If both of them lived in this room, they would have had two beds, one in each corner of the room, and each night, before going to sleep, they would meet in the centre of the room and kiss each other goodnight. He could never really understand how a man and a woman could live in the same house, in the same room, and yet sleep in different beds.

He looked out of the window. The blinds were drawn back and the louvres were open so that the air which was very fresh at this time of the evening could come into the bar. He looked out and he saw the guava trees and the mango trees and the flowers. He moved his chair further back, against the wall, closer to the wall, and he could see the dark green grass below, cut low and smooth, like the keyboard of a piano. When the grass had been recently cut, it looked wonderful. A few days or perhaps a week later when the grass had grown a little more and the blades of grass were not sharp but green and blunt and even, like a heavy blanket, then, when the sun rubbed its back as dogs do against the grass, the grass was lovelier still and its reflection was as of a mirror.

Osime Iyere saw the closely clipped grass and then he looked farther out and there was the golf course. *They really knew how to live, the white pigs. They knew how to live and everywhere they went they drove the local labour to provide them with the realisation of their dreams. But I shouldn't call them bastards,* he said to himself. *That bitterness comes out of jealousy. They did a fine job,* he thought now, sincerely. *Look at the playgrounds they provided, and the elegant houses they built. Wonderful white, beautiful houses. See how they made use of the landscape, the trees, the fruits, the flowers, everything.*

And look what's happened since their departure. Even part of the golf course has been converted to building land. The black spirit is everywhere, desecrating the land, violating it, putting up squalid, mean houses everywhere. Houses are being squeezed into all available pieces of land. Let the land take only four bricks and there's a one-bedroom apartment, but it's a house all right. Nobody thinks about playgrounds or parks or public places. No. Only houses. Only houses are necessary. See a patch of green and cover it up the next minute with a load of sand. That's how the black master who took over from the colonial master lives, like vermin. He drew his chair away from the window.

Things definitely are worse now, he thought. *The black master took over all the white colonial man's vices and when he added his own, society became blacker than the darkness, selfish, greedy, dirty, like that market, like vomit. People want power. Power and property. Houses. Positions at the top. And there are only two ways of achieving these things — the barrel of a gun or money or both. Have a gun and you can seize power from the elected representatives of the people.*

Yes, he told himself, *have a gun and you can seize a man's pass and put it in your pocket. Have a gun and be a private in the army and the Chief Superintendent of Police will be afraid to speak the truth. Have a gun and you can kick a man in his face and in his testicles and go scot-free. Have a gun and the sky's the limit.*

Or alternatively have money. Have money and you can hijack public cement from government ships on the high seas and nothing will happen. Have money and you will be made chairman of the boards of government companies from which you have previously stolen and been ceremoniously retired. Have money by stealing hundreds of millions, tens of billions of naira and become an institution.

Power grows out of the barrel of a gun and out of bags of money. Have a gun and you have the power to destroy, you have the power to kick a man in his stomach and below the belt, on his private parts, on his testicles and penis.

The white colonial masters had the servants, he thought, *and that was understandable, given their history of trading in slaves. But what happened after they left? Black men built boys' quarters, millions of them, to imprison other blacks as servants, as slaves, at the back of their houses. The black man is a bastard and an eternal fool,* he thought, *that is, the black man who occupies any significant place in the total arrangement of society.*

Stop being bitter, he said to himself. *Forget about everything. What is there to worry about? What can you do but take it lying down? So drink your beer, drink it down and submerge your anger and the bitterness. You have nothing to be ashamed of. You are helpless. They kicked you and you were helpless. It wasn't your fault. So drink your beer.*

He picked up his glass, half filled with the yellow beer, and he raised it to his lips and took a mouthful of it and he felt the cold icy beer going down his gullet into his stomach. Then as he set down the glass, he heard the sound of a car outside. A door banged and feet were on the concrete steps and he was standing up and walking across the vast bar room to the door and, as he jerked the door open, Salome walked up, her handbag under her arm and very lovely and beautiful in her smile.

She said, 'So you are here,' and walked past him into the room and sat down on his chair by the window.

'Barman,' he called.

There was no answer.

'Barman!'

'Why don't you leave him for a minute while I look at your face,' she suggested, leaning forward in her chair to examine the damage.

He let her look and then he said, 'I have taken a room downstairs. Tell me what you will drink and then we will go downstairs.'

'Let me look at your face first,' she said again and she looked straight into his eyes and saw the mist there and suddenly her doubts were gone for she knew that he still loved her.

'What will you drink?' he asked again.

'Anything,' she said. 'Anything.'

'Gin and lime then?'

'Anything.'

'A vodka on ice?'

'Anything.'

'All right then,' he said. 'I can see you are set to go.' Then he called out loudly, 'Barman!'

The barman came up from the lower part of the house and he

said, 'I am sorry, sir. I have been looking the room over. I wanted to make sure it was all right.'

'Good,' Osime said. 'Very good. Bring me another bottle of beer and for the lady here, you bring a glass of engine oil.'

'Engine oil, sir?'

'Yes. She will drink anything.'

'But, sir . . .' the barman began and stopped.

'Go on, tell him yourself,' Osime said and poked Salome in her side with his fingers.

'I will have a Coke,' Salome said. 'Bring me a Coke.'

'No,' Osime Iyere said. 'No coking business. Bring her a gin and lime. Make it a double.'

'Is that all right, madam?,' the barman asked.

'It's all right,' Osime Iyere said and looked at Salome and she looked at the barman and nodded.

'Not a double gin and lime anyway. Make it one and as small as you can.'

'The key is in the lock,' the barman said and left.

'That your first?' Salome asked, pointing to the half-empty bottle of beer on the table.

'No,' Osime answered. 'The third. This barman knows his business. He clears the bottle away as soon as it is empty.'

'Then he places another?'

'Yes, but on order.'

'You shouldn't drink so much. You never drank before.'

'I have started today. But come on. Let's go downstairs.'

'You didn't ask him for the number of the room.'

'Oh, I know it,' he said. 'Number seven.'

She picked up her handbag from the chair and together they went downstairs to the room which had a bed, a standing mirror, a table and two chairs, and a bath and a toilet. He set his bottle of beer, which was now almost empty, on the table and sat down beside it so that he was facing her as she sat on the bed.

'You shouldn't drink too much,' she said again.

'Oh, I can drink as much as I like.'

'No, you can't,' she said. 'Or else you will be as pregnant as the commander on the third front.'

'No, I won't,' he said. 'I can never get pregnant. A man can never be pregnant.'

'Oh yes. A man can be pregnant. The commander on the third

front is pregnant.'

'Is that where you were?'

'Yes.'

'And how was it there? Weren't you afraid?'

'No,' she said. 'We lived in a white house in the reservation area.'

'At the front?'

'There is no front really,' she said. 'What is a front is not a front but a town with people and this reservation area. The war goes on much further away. My husband goes for a week and then comes back. He spends two days and away he goes again.'

'Then why don't you simply live here?'

'I think I may now. Remember this place was in the hands of the Biafrans until two weeks ago.'

'Yes,' he said. 'I have a rather short memory.'

There was a knock on the door and the barman came in with a tray. Apart from the drinks, he had brought them two sandwiches.

'I thought you might want to eat,' he said, setting down the tray on the table. 'Or should I take them away?' he asked.

'Oh no!' Osime said. 'Thank you very much.'

The barman smiled and opened the bottle of beer and left the room. Osime handed the drink to Salome.

'We will drink to our meeting then,' she proposed, raising her glass.

'Very well,' he agreed and raised his glass as well. They touched glasses.

'How long ago was it?' she asked.

'You mean before you jilted me?'

'No,' she disagreed. 'Before I went away.'

'You went away after you jilted me,' he corrected her. 'And that was nearly eighteen months ago.'

'I didn't jilt you,' she protested. 'We were not even engaged.'

'That's true,' he agreed. 'So you went away and got married.'

'You said you were not ready to be married.'

'Yes. And I'm still not.'

'Then can you blame me?'

'Well, I'll have to think about that,' he said. 'That's something that needs thinking about seriously.'

He began to feel that he shouldn't have come, that it was wrong trying to recapture the past when the present was full of hope. It was true that he had loved her intensely once, that he had been broken when she had gone away and married Captain Otunshi. He had been hurt, so hurt that he told himself that all women were opportunists, until he met Ndudi. Even then, there remained a small vacuum in his mind which ached any time it became filled with thoughts of her. In fact, he had died a little and that was why he had felt this dark surge of excitement when she had emerged out of nowhere in the stadium, when he had heard her steps on the stairs a few minutes ago.

And again, he thought, *perhaps it's a good thing to have come. The best way to conquer a fear is to face it, not to run away from it. If I want to be free of her, here is the opportunity to test the strength of what remains.* He took his glass of beer and sipped it.

'What are you thinking about?' she asked, a frown on her face.

'How things never work out.'

'Life is like that,' she said. 'We cannot change it.'

'Really?'

'Well, what could you have done in my place?'

'I don't know,' he said.

'See what I mean? But come on, this is all becoming too serious. Perhaps we should have gone to a church instead.'

'I am sorry,' he apologised.

'Then let's forget about the past. The important thing is that we are here right now. We have the opportunity to be together. Should one ask more from life?'

He didn't say anything, but got up and joined her, leaving his beer on the table.

She took off her shoes and lay back on the bed, so that he sat close to her bosom and she had her hands on his back, inside his shirt.

'Those soldiers kicked me in the testicles,' he said. 'I feel the pain there.'

'They kicked you in the testicles?'

'Yes,' he said. 'The bastards did.'

Here it comes again. I say to myself that there is no need to be bitter, that I will forget about it and yet here it comes, like vomit. But I must suppress it. It does no good to carry a hatred with you to which you cannot give expression in the most appropriate way. You either forget this hatred or it will devour you.

'Why did you let them go?' she asked.

'What?'

'Remember I called you aside outside the stadium and asked you

if you wanted them punished?'
'Yes,' he said. 'How many of them would you have punished?'
'All of them!'
'The whole Federal army?'
'Oh,' she said. 'I understand you.'
'And how would you have explained to Otunshi? Surely, he would have been told?'
'Yes. But there would have been no need for me to explain.'
'How?'
'He would not have asked me.'
'Is he that much in love with you?'
She stopped moving her hand up and down his back. 'Yes,' she said and he thought he could detect pride in her voice. He turned and looked at her. 'And you?'
'What about me?' She resumed the caressing of his back.
'Do you love him?'
Again, the movement of her hand stopped and this time she withdrew her hand completely from under his shirt.
'Let's not talk about it,' she said.
'You don't want to talk about it?' She did not say anything.
'Okay then,' he said. 'Let's talk about the war. Tell me what you have seen during the war. Tell me what your husband thinks about the war.'
She covered her eyes with her hand, the one that had been inside his shirt. She was lying on her back so that she had her face to the ceiling and he was sitting beside her. But she didn't say anything.
'Salome, don't you want to talk to me?'
She didn't answer.
'Salome!'
'Yes?' she finally spoke in a small voice.
'Is anything wrong?'
'No,' she said.
'Then why are you crying?' He felt embarrassed, seeing her tears coming down the side of her face only to disappear into the pillow.
'I don't know.'
He kept quiet.
Then she said, 'Sometimes you cry and you don't know why. Perhaps it comes out of a deep-seated self-pity.'
'Do you pity yourself?'
'Sometimes.'

'But you have no need to,' he said. 'No need at all. Life is what we make of it, that is,' he added, 'after it has made us.'

'That's the problem,' she said. 'It first of all makes us.'

'You could have refused your parents' demands.'

'No,' she said. 'I couldn't have done so. I know that's what you hold against me. Why you think and claim that I jilted you. But I couldn't have refused my parents' demands any more than you could have persuaded them to let me wait. We all make mistakes and live our whole life in mistake thereafter.'

'Let's forget about it,' he said. 'Let's talk about this war, about the Federal troops, about what is now.'

'All right,' she agreed. And her voice was suddenly bright. 'What shall we say about the war?'

'Otunshi, for instance. What does he think of the war?'

'Oh, his whole career is there. We are hoping he will be made a Brigadier by the time he leaves for the front next week.'

'A Brigadier?'

'Yes, a Brigadier. That will make him a real commander.'

'Does he like the war?'

'No,' she said. 'His career is in the war but I don't think he likes the war.'

'I can't believe it. How can you take part in this war and not be part of it, particularly at his level.'

'Oh well, I don't know. But it is there. Not all who bear arms really hate the enemy. I have heard a lot of ugly things said about him, though. But he has always told me that the war cannot be won by being virtuous.'

'So that is where the brutality of the soldiers comes from then.'

'I don't know,' she said. 'I have never suffered from it and so I have never thought about it.'

'Yes,' he said. 'You wouldn't know. You have to feel what you know to really know it. Who feels it knows it.'

You don't wonder about something you know nothing of, he said to himself. *You wonder about the things you know, those of them that you feel. I never wondered about the brutality of the soldiers, I never believed it existed and even when I heard about it, I was always prepared to discount it as false or untypical. But now I know better, from experience, from personal intimate knowledge.*

'How long did you take this room for?' she asked.

He shrugged his shoulders. 'For as long as we are here. Do you want to go now?'

'No,' she said. 'I don't want to go at all.'

'But I will have to go.'

'When? Now?'

He thought she sounded somewhat alarmed. 'Yes,' he said.

'Why?'

He shrugged his shoulders.

'You mean you took this room only to come and shrug your shoulders?'

'I didn't know what I wanted.'

'But I know what I want! I want you!'

He shook his head. 'I couldn't go through with it.'

'I see,' she said. 'So you are a coward among other things?'

'Is that what you think?' He stood up from the bed.

'Look,' she said, and he turned and looked at her as she sat up on the bed. 'You don't have to blame me for everything. My coming here should show you how deep my feelings are.'

'I don't blame you for anything,' he replied. 'I simply don't want to start this thing all over again. It was pure madness coming here. We shouldn't have come here at all.'

'So you do still love me then?'

'I want to go,' he said.

'And you will not even kiss me?'

He went towards the door. 'I am sorry. You know they hit me on the lips too.'

'That's the big excuse now,' she said and stood up from the bed and gathered her clothes about her.

He could see that her eyes were bright with frustration and he thought he could also see anger there. *But why should I feel sorry for her, why should I have any conscience or feel any guilt? She left me and went to the major. She knew what she wanted then as she does now.*

He opened the door.

Chapter seven

It was the knocking on his window that woke him in the morning. He got up from the bed, sitting down at first, and then he heard the knocking again. Suddenly he was very wide awake and remembered that today was Sunday and he had promised to drive his landlord to the Army Post on the hill. He went to the window and parted the curtains and saw Ndudi standing outside.

'Go round to the back door,' he called out to her and he let the curtains fall back into place. Then he went and opened the door to her.

She came into the house and shut the door behind her and then followed him into the bedroom.

'You shouldn't be dressed in black,' he said to her.

'I can feel the whole thing in my bones,' she said. 'How are you feeling?'

'In some places better, in other places worse than yesterday.

'You shouldn't be wearing black,' he said again. 'A portent of doom.'

'Don't you think it will happen?'

'Your father can still prevent it.'

'There is no chance of that.'

'Osime Iyere went into the bathroom and looked at his face in the mirror. His left cheek was still swollen and the skin under his right eye was red and black where it was broken. How he hated those soldiers. How he despised them. *And if anything happens to my landlord, then I am to blame. I talked him into it. I put the idea into his head. But how was I to know? How was I to know that the Federal soldiers would not be liberators but conquerors? Like the Biafrans before them.*

'You could have found out,' his inner mind told him.

''But how?'

'Oh, don't ask how. You were simply naive. That is the gospel truth.'

Oh hell, he thought. *I was naive but that is the way you are brought up. You go to the university which is built away from the cities and in the mornings, the wardens come and sweep your room and make your bed and you go to the dining room and the food is cooked, ready to be served. You even went on strike when the university authorities told you to clear your own plates away. Yes, you went on strike because you felt that that was beneath you. You have never known any suffering, at least not after the first early years of your life. So out you come of the university and your ideas about people, about society, are as green as unripe oranges. You couldn't see anything wrong with the society except where it interfered with your privileges. Not with the privileges of others. You didn't see how anything could be wrong except when it happened to you. Oh yes, you did have humanitarian ideas, all students were liberals, even those of the most conservative stock became liberals at the university. But it was only verbal, this liberalism, and you forgot very easily what you had said five days before about justice and all the rest of the crap because they were merely words and words like steam have a way of evaporating very easily into the air.*

But it is never too late to learn, he told himself. *A man is a product of his experiences. You experience and then you gain a vital insight and then you know better. And so progressively, step by step, you build up your knowledge about yourself, about your neighbours and the rest of the world. And I am going to learn,* he promised himself. *I am going to learn and apply my knowledge. This experience with the soldiers is only a beginning. I did not seek it. It came to me. But you do not have to wait for such experiences to seek you out. You can go out, purposefully, after the truth. And that is what I am going to do about this war. I am going to find out more about this war and I am going to write about it. I am going to find out all that is ugly or beautiful about this war and I am going to write about it. But it will be the truth, the harsh and bitter truth. Nothing more, nothing less.*

'Osime!'

Osime turned away from the mirror and in the doorway Ndudi was standing. He wanted to smile at her but his mouth was full of lather from the toothpaste and instead, he smiled at her with his eyes.

'I am going back inside,' she said. 'Father says we should leave at about ten o'clock.' Osime turned back to the sink and spat the lather out and then rinsed his mouth.

'You don't mean you are coming?'

'Yes, I am.'

'But isn't that what your father wanted to avoid?'

'I am going but my mother is not coming,' she said.

'You are not going,' he said. 'I am going and your father is going.'

'No,' she said. 'If anything happens, at least one member of our family must be there to see it happen.'

'But why you?'

'Because my mother cannot go. She is weak. She has had a breakdown.'

'And your father wants you to go with him?'

'Yes. At first he did not want me to. But then he changed his mind.'

'All right then,' he said. 'I will wash my face and then I will get dressed and come out. I will be ready in about fifteen minutes.'

'I will go and tell my father.'

He listened to her steps rise and fall and there was a bang when the back door was shut.

Now he was standing outside his house and waiting for them to come out and as he looked out at the passing cars on the street and the soldiers with their guns and set faces, he felt very uneasy.

Nothing would happen. How could anything happen to a man who had gone of his own free will to register with the soldiers? And there would be many more like him there. They could not do anything bad in the presence of so many people. But he failed to convince himself. *You were beaten up by the soldiers in the presence of thousands of people,* he reminded himself. *There was a Chief Superintendent of Police there.*

But these circumstances are different, he thought. *This man goes to register with the soldiers. What harm can come of that? The soldiers have asked them to come and register themselves to save themselves from being molested in the future. What grief can come to a man who of his own free will answers such a call? There can't be any,* he answered himself but still without conviction.

The sun was out now and it was warm and bright and clear and he leaned forward on the front of the car and the engine was warm against his hands and he prayed that nothing would happen on such a lovely day as this.

'Here we are!' Mr Ohiali said, coming up behind him. Osimi straightened up and turned and he saw that his landlord was dressed in a white shirt and white trousers and that Ndudi had changed into a dark blue dress and was holding her father's hand. Ndudi's mother stood behind them and her hands were crossed under her breasts and Osime saw the fear and the pain and all the suffering of the past two weeks written on her face.

'Shall we go? Mr Ohiali asked and Osime Iyere opened the back door of the car for him.

Mr Ohiali placed one foot inside the car and said to his wife who had begun to cry, 'I will be back as soon as it is over. Don't be afraid. Nothing will happen.' Then he got inside the car and then cleared his shoe of the loose stones between the heel and the sole before placing the foot inside and shutting the door of the car.

'You can sit with your father at the back,' Osime said to Ndudi.

'No, let her sit with you in the front,' the man said and Ndudi went to the other side of the car and opened the door at the front and sat down.

'Madam, we shall be back,' Osime said to Ndudi's mother and he got into the car, started the engine, engaged the gears and moved away.

He looked at Mr Ohiali through the mirror and he could see the man looking back at the house and at his wife standing there, her hands crossed under her heart, afraid and weeping, and he turned his face away from the mirror because his own eyes became misty.

The Army Post on the Hill had been a police station before the Biafrans invaded the state. But because of its strategic position — it commanded the entrance into the city and overlooked the river and the city — the Biafran soldiers had expelled the policemen stationed there and converted it into a command post. The Federal troops came and drove them out but instead of returning the place to the police, they occupied it in their turn and now used it for detaining suspects and registering all people who came from the Biafran-held areas.

The Army Post occupied both sides of the road. You crossed the bridge over the river and then you drove some fifty yards up the road and on both sides of the road there was nothing but white sand and then the grass before you came to the road block where the soldiers stopped your car and questioned you.

'I have come to see your commander,' Osime said to the soldiers and they bent down, two of them, and looked inside the car. The other soldiers, about twenty of them, stayed ten on each side of the road, some of them standing, the others lying on their bellies, their guns in front of them, ready to fire.

'What for?' one of the two soldiers asked. He spoke very bad English.

'My friend here has come to register,' Osime said.

'I see,' the other soldier said. 'I see, Biafran.'

'No,' Osime said. 'He is my landlord.'

'Biafran,' the man repeated. 'Nyanmiri.'

Osime did not say anything.

'No need to see Commander. Commander has business, other business. He registers there. You leave your car here and you walk there.' The man pointed to the right-hand side of the road and Osime saw the low buildings, three of them, painted brown.

'Can I park the car properly?'

'Yes, over there,' one of the two soldiers said. 'Over there but the girl stays in the car.'

'My wife,' Osime said.

'Okay, your wife. What is her name?'

'Ndudi.'

'Ndudi?'

'Yes, Ndudi.'

'Nyanmiris answer Ndudi a lot. She, Nyanmiri?'

'She is my wife,' Osime said and put the car in reverse and parked the car away from the centre of the road.

'If they come back to you, don't say anything,' he said to Ndudi and came out of the car.

'You going with him?' one of the soldiers asked.

'Yes,' Osime said and smiled falsely.

The soldiers hestitated and then one of them said, 'Okay, you go and come back in five minutes.'

'Thank you,' Osime said but in his mind he said, 'Curse' instead of 'thank'.

'They called me Nyanmiri,' Mr Ohiali said.

'They are illiterates,' Osime told him. 'That was why I asked to see their commander.'

'Yes, they are illiterates,' Mr Ohiali agreed but his face was set and serious and Osime did not make any reply.

Everywhere there were soldiers and they all carried their guns carelessly.

They came to the first of the buildings and Osime saw that there were many people there.

'Mr Ohiali!'

Mr Ohiali turned as three men walked up to them. They were all dressed in shirts and shorts of khaki material and Ohiali began to talk to them in his language.

'You have come to regiser?'

'Yes.'

'We also came to register.'
'And how are they doing it?'
'Well, they call you up when it is your turn on the line and then they begin to question you.'
'About what?'
'Your address. And your business. And what you did during the occupation.'
'And then what happens?'
'Nothing, they ask you to wait.'
'What for?'
'We don't know,' the man said. 'We have been questioned already but as you can see, we are waiting.'
'And you can't go away?'
'No, you can't.'
Osime Iyere went to the front of the line and he could see a second lieutenant, a sergeant and two lance corporals sitting behind a desk and a man standing in front of them. They were questioning him and making notes on two separate sheets of paper.
'Why did you come here?' the second lieutenant asked the man.
'It was in the newspaper,' the man said. 'I am a trader and I have lived here for eight years.'
'Any houses?'
'No,' the man said, 'I have no house.'
'Eight years and you could not build a house? Are you not an Ibo man?'
The man smiled. 'What I sell are clothes and there is very little money there.'
'You mean you sent your money home to your brothers to buy arms for this war?'
'No, sir,' the man said hastily. 'I have three sisters and they are here with me in the city.'
'But we have a letter which says you gave the Biafrans money for arms.'
'No, sir,' the man said. 'That cannot be true.'
'Are you saying we are telling lies?'
'No, sir, but . . .'
'All right,' the lieutenant said. 'Go out there and wait.'
'We believe in one country,' the man said.
'Go out there and wait.'
'I never paid out any money.'

'Go out there and wait!'

The man turned aside and the soldiers wrote something on one of the two sheets of papers and laughed.

'Next!'

Now almost an hour had gone by and they were on to his landlord and he was standing in front of them and they were asking him questions.

'We have a report here that you are an officer in the Biafran army,' the second lieutenant said.

Mr Ohiali looked the man straight in the eyes and his voice was quiet. 'No,' he said. 'That is not true.'

'But you were seen commanding troops on the Ogoja front.'

'I have been in this city since the war,' Mr Ohiali said. 'There is a man here who can vouch for me.'

'Yes?'

'Yes. He is my tenant and he brought me here, even now.'

'So you do have a house?'

'Yes,' the man said. 'I own a house. I have lived here for more than twenty-five years.'

'And the money you gave to the Biafrans?'

'I have never given them money.'

'Can you swear to that?'

'Yes,' the man said. 'I have never had any contact with them. I can swear to that.'

'And the plot that you people hatched to kill all the men in this city?'

'I was not party to that plot,' the man said.

'But you knew about the meeting. You knew about the guns and the matchetes and the axes that were piled up in the classrooms at Ebun College in the city.'

'No,' Mr Ohiali said. 'I knew nothing about it.'

'And you can swear to that as well?'

'Yes.'

'Then who was involved in the plot? Every man who has since come forward has denied involvement in the plot. Each one of you has denied helping the Biafrans, giving them money! Then who was involved?'

Mr Ohiali did not say anything.

'Well?' the lieutenant asked.

Mr Ohiali shrugged his shoulders. 'I can only speak for myself,' he said. 'I do not know what others did during the time of the occupation.'

'Okay then,' the second lieutenant said. 'Go and wait,' and the sergeant picked up his blue ballpoint pen and wrote something on one of the sheets of papers and passed it to the second lieutenant who looked at it and nodded and pushed the paper back to the sergeant.

Now they had interviewed all the men, about two hundred of them. The sergeant stood up and the talking among the men died away. 'The men whose names I am going to call now,' he announced, 'are to report here every Sunday morning at seven o'clock. The next set of people are to go away and report to the K division of the Nigeria Police Force every two weeks on Sunday mornings at eight o'clock. The last set of people are to wait here for further interrogation.'

Osime Iyere watched the faces of the men as their names were read out and he saw how they looked at each other, uneasily at first, and then with relief as they heard their names. Then came the last set of names. There were nine of them and Mr Ohiali was one of them.

They separated these last nine from the rest of the group and herded them against the wall and told the rest of the men to go away.

Osime stepped out of the crowd as they jostled among themselves and hurried away. Osime stepped forward and approached the second lieutenant.

'Excuse me,' he said and all the soldiers frowned and looked at him.

'What is it?' the second lieutenant asked, standing up.

'I am the tenant that one of the men spoke about, one of the men who you now hold.'

'Yes?'

'I want to vouch that he was speaking the truth.'

'Do you want to say you attended the meetings with him?'

'No,' Osime said. 'But I know the man and I have been his tenant for three years. Even before the war.'

'And you are from which state?' the man asked.

'I am from this state.'

'Which part of it?'

Osime told him.

'And what is your job?'

'I am an editor on the *Daily News*.'

'A journalist?'

'Yes.'

'I see,' the second lieutenant said. 'We have had a lot of problems with journalists in this war.'

'I am not here to cause any trouble,' Osime said.

'But journalists always cause trouble and we have had to be very severe with some of them in this war.'

'I simply want you to know the truth.'

'Corporal!' the second lieutenant called.

'Yes, sir!'

'See this man to the road block.'

'But excuse me . . .'

'You have been dismissed,' the sergeant said, 'unless you want to be one of them.'

Osime Iyere looked at Mr Ohiali where he stood with the others against the wall, five soldiers in front of them, and said, 'I will be back. Don't be afraid. Nothing will happen.'

The lance corporal followed Osime Iyere.

'Can I see the commander?' Osime Iyere asked.

'The second lieutenant will be angry,' the man said and Osime looked at him.

'Isn't there a way I could see him?'

'I could leave you before . . .' There was a shot and then another and then three more and Osime could see two bodies lying on the ground away from the wall and the five soldiers were holding their guns and pushing one of the remaining seven away from the wall, into the open space that led to the banks of the river. Then there were four more shots and another body lay on the ground and even as he looked, Osime saw his landlord break away from the rest of the group of men and make a run for the river.

There were immediate shouts but the soldiers let him run for some time for they must have known that on that bare naked ground, the man hadn't the slightest chance in the world. Then just as he reached the bank of the river, there was a sudden outburst of gunfire. It looked for a moment as if Mr Ohiali would make the river. Then he seemed to bend over backwards and crumble as the bullets hitting him first propelled him forward and then broke his back and he fell not forward but on his back, his face twisted, his hands frantically but unconsciously trying to push his intestines back into his stomach as they came out of the large gaping hole in his belly.

Osime Iyere watched and he could not believe his eyes and all of a sudden he felt very sick and he was holding his stomach and bending down over the grass and the vomit came out of his mouth and the water came out of his eyes.

The lance corporal watched him and then turned his face away and spat on the grass, twice.

'Do you still want to see the captain?' he asked.

'Yes,' Osime nodded and gathered up two handfuls of sand and covered the vomit with it and wiped his eyes with the back of his hand and stood up.

'Now can I see him?'

Not that this will achieve anything, he thought. *What I have just seen is murder and nobody can bring these people back, but I want them to know that I know it was murder and that it will not do to attempt to justify it when it appears in the papers, for he would describe it exactly as he had seen it. He did not want to think about Ndudi.*

Chapter eight

The captain's office was in a long narrow building that had only one door opening into it. In all, there were four rooms and you entered the first room through this single door by stepping on a cement block that had been placed on the ground to serve as a step. You entered this first room and the wooden benches were arranged against the wall and there were many soldiers, all of them armed, sitting on the long benches.

You went through a door that connected this room to the next and here a soldier sat behind a big typewriter placed on a high wooden table, and there were three other chairs on which five soldiers were managing to sit by bringing the chairs up against each other and these five soldiers were all talking to the one who typed. Then you went through another door and came to another room which had a carpet of red and blue on the floor. There were easy chairs here too and a girl sat behind a padded desk on which was another typewriter. Beside the typewriter was the telephone and then a notebook and a pencil and the girl was leaning back in her chair and talking across to two army officers sitting in the easy chairs. A man in a big *agbada* who Osime guessed was a contractor sat on one of the easy chairs.

The soldier who escorted him stopped here and saluted smartly and briefly and then stood aside, and the two officers, one a sergeant and the other a second lieutenant, looked at him questioningly but it was the private and his escort who answered.

'He is here to see the Commander, sir,' he said.

'What about?'

'About the shooting,' Osime said, and told himself that he had to be patient or he would lose his temper and he didn't want to lose his temper, not now.

'What shooting?' the second lieutenant asked.

'That is what I want to see the Commander about. I am from the *Daily News*.'

'The two officers looked at each other and the second lieutenant said again, 'You can discuss this business of the shooting with me. The captain is busy.'

Osime looked him straight in the eye and shrugged his shoulders.

'Then your name will appear in the papers,' he said very quietly, and the second lieutenant frowned because he knew the full implications of having his name in the papers when there was another and senior officer in the next room.

'Can I see your identity card?' he asked, more to save his face than for any other reason.

Osime put his hand into his back pocket and drew out the card and handed it over to the sergeant who was nearer him. The man looked at it and then passed it on to the second lieutenant who again looked at it and Osime remembered his humiliation at the stadium and bit his upper lip.

'All right, journalist,' the second lieutenant said and there was venom in his voice. 'You can see the captain.'

'And my card?'

'You will get it back after we have finished with you,' the sergeant said and stood up and walked the short distance to the connecting door and knocked feebly, very feebly, on it. He waited a few seconds, then turned the handle and, opening the door, went inside.

Osime Iyere waited and he could hear the voices inside the door and then the sergeant came out and handed Iyere back his card and asked him to go inside.

These army officers certainly know how to live, Osime told himself as he entered the office and observed the rug on the floor and the heavy easy chairs and the long table and the drinks cabinet. To his surprise the captain stood up as he entered and offered him his hand. Osime took it and made an effort to smile and then he sat down on the chair that faced the captain and the man said, 'Well now, Mr Iyere, what can I do for you?'

Osime Iyere sat back in his chair and again he saw his landlord running zig-zag across the sand of the river bank, and heard the sound of the shooting and saw his landlord plunge forward, and then seem to fold at the knees and dissolve like salt that has absorbed a lot of water. He shook his head vigorously because the smell of his vomit was back in his nose and the water was almost in his eyes.

'So what can I do for you, Mr Iyere?' he heard the captain ask again and he was back and the smell was replaced by a cold bitterness and anger.

'It's my landlord,' he said, and his voice was quiet so that he himself became surprised at the deadliness of it.

'What about your landlord?' the captain asked.

'He has just been shot. He and the others.'

'Where?'

'Here, on the grounds and on your orders.'

'No,' the captain said. 'No, you must tell me what happened. I have given no orders for any shooting.'

Osime looked the captain straight in the eye and the man looked back unflinchingly and Osime decided that perhaps he was speaking the truth. He told him the story.

The captain was silent for a while as he thought it over and then he said, 'I am sorry, Mr Iyere, that this thing should have happened. But this is a war and so many things happen that we cannot account for, at least not directly.'

'You mean . . .'

'I don't mean anything,' the captain said quietly. 'You must always remember that this is a war. The war kills, it kills people.'

'You mean . . .'

'I have told you what I mean,' the captain said. 'There is nothing we can do. It is unfortunate but it is the truth.'

'You mean your soldiers have the right to kill anybody?'

'Not anybody. You are alive.'

'My landlord was not a soldier. He was a civilian. He came here to report to you on your orders. And yet you refuse to do anything about his murder?'

The captain looked at Osime's face and smiled suddenly, and then, just as suddenly, the smile was gone. You could have said he had a hidden switch in his mouth which he used to turn the smile on and off. Now he stood up and paced the room and then he came back to his desk and pressed the push of the bell and it rang out shrilly and a lance corporal came into the room and stood to attention.

'Open that filing cabinet there,' he said to the lance corporal, seeming now to be unaware of Osime's presence. 'Open it and bring out the brown envelope that contains the photographs.'

The lance corporal went to the corner of the room and brought out the large brown envelope and placed it on the table in front of the captain.

'You may go,' the captain said to the lance corporal who saluted and went out. Then the captain pushed the envelope towards Osime.

'Open the envelope and look at the photographs,' the man said.

Osime Iyere sat back in his chair and stared at the captain.

'Go ahead. Open the envelope and look at the photographs.'

Very slowly, Osime drew the envelope towards himself and bending the flap over backwards, drew out the pack of photographs. They were face down and he saw that the back of the first photograph had the stamp of his own newspaper. *What they do to journalists,* he thought. *Yes, what these barbarians do to journalists!* He turned the pack of photographs over on its face and then suddenly, his heart missed a beat and his mouth became dry and he wanted to look away but he couldn't.

'My God!' he cried. 'Oh my God!'

'Go on. Look at all of them,' the captain said and now he was sitting back in his chair and his eyes were black and full of hatred.

'Look at them,' the captain said. 'These are photographs that were taken by your own people and sent to us at the war front. The dates are stamped on the backs of the photographs. Look at those too.'

'Oh my God!' Osime murmured to himself and now he could no longer look at the photographs and dropped them back on the table on top of the envelope.

'The Biafran soldiers did that,' the captain said quietly. 'They took the women, raped them in front of their children and husbands and then, as if that was not enough, drove those long sticks through their vaginas into their wombs. Then they cut the throats of the men and the children. Cut their throats and severed their heads from their bodies. And all these are civilians. None of them had ever even spoken to a soldier. But that didn't stop the Biafran soldiers from carrying out their barbaric acts. We are human beings too. So if you want to write about this morning's shootings in the papers, think of these photographs and write about them. We even conduct inquiries to establish the guilt of the men that we shoot. We cross-examine them, but those women and children and men were cross-examined with knives and long sticks and rape . . .'

'Yes, I understand,' Osime said. 'I understand everything now.'

'Good,' the captain said and stood up and Osime also stood up.

'You must always understand that this is a war, it is a civil war but that does not make the war any better. If anything, it makes it worse.'

'One more thing, Captain . . .'

'Yes?'

'Can I have the body of my landlord so that I can have him buried?'

The captain thought for a while. Then he nodded his head and stretched out his hand. 'Yes,' he said. 'Tell the men I have given you permission to take his body away.'

Osime looked at the man's outstretched hand and turned away without taking it. The captain laughed. 'I thought you really did understand,' he said and then he pressed the bell and again the lance corporal appeared but this time only to escort him out of the building.

'Will you go for the body now or do you intend to come back later?' the lance corporal asked.

'I will come back,' Osime said. 'I have his daughter waiting in my car.'

'I am sorry,' the lance corporal said.

Osime said nothing.

'I am sure these things can be prevented,' the man said again. 'Being a Biafran soldier does not condemn a man, being a civilian even less.'

Osime looked at the man and he was surprised. 'Then why are you in the war?'

'I needed a job and again I believe in one country.'

'I believe in that too,' Osime told him. 'But I don't believe in the war any more.'

'I am sorry,' the man apologised again. 'I believe in fighting a war but I am not a murderer. There is a difference between killing armed men and shooting civilians.'

The man held out his hand and Osime hesitated and then took it and the man said, 'I will have his body waiting for you when you come back. I can at least make sure of that.'

Now he was alone and the house was empty but for him and as he lay back on the bed his mind was bitter and full of resentment.

I am surely learning from this war, he thought. *Yes, this war is a great teacher and we all are its pupils. One thing clearly stands out now. One major thing I have learnt. You do not have to be brutal to be a soldier, or rather you are brutal not because you are a soldier but because there is a sadist, a rapist, a fascist and a murderer in you who wait for war and army uniforms to give them expression.*

I have always been amazed at the human capacity to inflict pain and suffering but this war beats my imagination. This is not simply a war. This is more than a war, something dirtier than a war. I wish there was another and a stronger name for such things than simply a war, because this one involves not only the killing of soldiers by soldiers but also the killing, raping and torturing of men, women and children by soldiers.

Momentarily, he closed his eyes because he could see the long sticks that had been driven through the women's vaginas, he could see the heads as they lay on the dust severed from their bodies and the eyes of the women as they popped out even in their death and the eyes of the men and the children were closed. Then again, he could see his landlord running for the river and then he could hear the shots and see the man's hands as they worked frantically, even in those last moments, to push his intestines back as they rushed out of his body. He thought and he felt sick and his mind grew bitter.

He was amazed, too, at the human capacity to absorb pain and suffering. *We must all have shock absorbers, pain absorbers . . .* How else could Ndudi have looked at the face of her father as he lay dead and not gone out of her mind, broken down? She had stood there, dazed and speechless, and her heart that was her pain absorber had taken in the tragedy and yet not failed her. Perhaps this was the key to human survival, this capacity to absorb and not burst, this capacity even in the face of so much pain and grief to retain some hope, some dignity, some self.

But we do not have to cause the pain only to absorb it afterwards. That is the great folly. Human beings cause wars, human beings at the helm of affairs start wars. The masses go to sleep one night and next morning they wake to the sound of marching boots and shrieking jets and exploding bombs. The people are never consulted.

And any consultation that takes place is always in the form of manipulation, of propaganda. The people are manipulated into the war because those at the helm have a monopoly over the means of indoctrination and information. They can misinform. They misinform the people, they trick the people into war. The people are manipulated into a war only to have their children killed, their houses destroyed by bombs and grenades. And all the time, the generals and the politicians stand aside, away from the death and the destruction of the war and shout that it is indeed a great war. A great war for them because they lose nothing and yet gain everything. The generals and the politicians and the religious leaders and the businessmen send their children away from the country to make sure that they do not suffer from the war. But the workers and the farmers and the poor people remain and yield up their children to the war.

But how can these soldiers become so cruel? Why do they kill each other and not the generals? Or the politicians? Or the businessmen? Or the religious leaders? Why do they obey the orders to kill? Surely they must know that they are killing each other?

I have nothing against wars, he thought, *that are fought over principles. Principles that in some way deal with our questions. Where are we going? How are we getting there? But the present war is a war that arises from the greed of a few men. No principles are involved here because even if the country remains one or is divided, nothing really changes. Changes may occur at the top as new people jostle for power but lower down, where I come from, the farmer and the worker will continue to live in mud houses and starve and be ignorant and sick and yield up their children for senseless wars. If we were asking which way, east or west, if we were asking one man one loaf or one man many loaves and millions of other men no loaf at all, this war might have made sense.*

There ought to be a referendum among the people about any proposed war. The people ought to vote and by each ballot box there ought to stand written the history of all the sufferings and deaths and destructions, and finally, the ideas and principles behind all of the past wars. There ought to stand on every street bold placards declaring the aims and principles behind the proposed war so that the people could see whether the war was in their interests. They would be informed about the possible sacrifices required of each class in the society. The people would see their sacrifices in terms of death and destruction and violation and humiliation and labour and compare these with the profit and power and exaltation of the generals and politicians and religious leaders and businessmen. They would make the comparisons and see whether the war was in their interest and whether they were willing to carry the cross for the rest of society.

But the people never have a chance to make a choice! They never do because they get misinformed and manipulated. They never get told that the reason for the war is the greed of those in power for more power. And so, the people get manipulated into a war and their daughters get raped, and their sons get shot. All of them are killed one way or another. Their daughters die with their tongues and eyes popping out, their sons get shot or beheaded. The people get beaten down, blinded and beaten down.

No, he concluded. *This is not a war. This is an investment in blood and destruction by those at the helm of affairs with the expectation of profit.*

Osime stood up because he heard his name called. It was Ndudi.

'I will be with you in a minute,' he called out to her and hesitated in the room because he was embarrassed. *I took him to his death*, he thought. *I took him to the hill to have him shot.* He came out of the room into the sitting room and Ndudi stood there, against the door in black, dazed, her eyes swollen, her hair dishevelled. *She has finally had it*, he thought. *It has finally reached her*. He felt deeply sorry for her and desperately guilty for the tragedy.

'My mother wants us to take his body home,' Ndudi said.

'Home?'

'Yes. To Oganza.'

'That is near Asaba?'

'Yes. We wondered if you would drive us there. Neither of us can drive.' He looked at her and then at his hands as he thought about what she had said. The road was bound to be dangerous. The Federal troops had got to the bridge but anything was still possible.

'Will you?' she asked. 'We also need a coffin. To put him in.' She began to cry.

He did not say anything but went into the bedroom and took out his identity card and his notebook and a ballpoint pen and his wide-brimmed cotton hat. He changed his shirt for a black one and then he changed his trousers for a thick pair of blue jeans. He went into the bathroom and took his toothbrush and the half-used toothpaste. He came back into the bedroom and drew out the last of the drawers and took out the pack of chewing sticks. He went back into the bathroom where he replaced the toothbrush and toothpaste and took instead the two combs, the big one and the small one. He took the towel.

Again he came into the bedroom and took from the wardrobe the brown carrier bag that held his camera. He looked round the room, at the writing table, at the unmade bed, the wardrobe whose doors were open now. *I may never come back here again,* he thought, and he went out of the room and locked the door and placed the key in the room where his sisters used to sleep before the war.

Chapter nine

Ndudi sat with him in the front of the pick-up van. Neither of them said anything to each other. They could hear the sobs of the woman as she sat at the back of the van with her three other children and the body of their father. She sobbed loudly and then she was quiet for some time. Then she wept loudly again and the children cried as well. But he did not stop or say anything. *There are times,* he thought, *when tragedies not only bind us hand and foot but tie our tongues as well.*

I am glad, though, that I called at the office and told them where I was going. At least, they will know if I do not come back. And if Salome goes there today, or tomorrow, she will know as well. It is a pity I couldn't keep the appointment. It is a pity that she will go there and wait for me in vain. It is a pity about this girl as well, he thought as he glanced sideways at Ndudi, at her fair but serious face. *It is a pity about her father. It is a pity that I am driving this car.*

'How many check points have we crossed?' he asked her now and she shook her head and did not answer.

'It does not matter,' he said to her.

He tried to work out in his mind how many checks there had been. About fifteen, he thought. Fifteen which meant one for every three kilometres. And each time, they took the lid off the box and looked at the body there. They searched the car, they asked questions and it was obvious they were nervous as they carried the automatic AK 47 Kalashnikov rifles. Always the bayonets flashed in the sun. Always the men had their fingers on the triggers. It was the bayonets that worried him, the bayonets that were jack knives sharpened on both sides and ending sharply and flashing dangerously. Also he saw the machine guns flashing between the leaves of the bushes as they stood on the tripod mounts. He wondered why they didn't get general purpose machine-guns, but he did not ask because of the voices of the soldiers.

'Where do you say you are going then?'

'To Oganza.'

'Oganza?'

'Yes.'

'We took it only two days ago.'

'We published it.'
'Did you show our photographs?'
'Yes. Some photographs.'
'Which newspaper did you say you worked for?'
'The *Daily News*.'
'Journalist, eh?'
He did not say anything.
'So you couldn't bury him in Benin?'
'No. My wife wants him buried at her home.'
'You say he was shot by mistake?'
'Yes.'
'He wasn't a Biafran?'
'No.'
'And how is Benin?'
'Quiet.'
'See, we liberated it. We liberated it and they pushed us here.'
He did not say anything.
'What is the name of your wife?'
'Ndudi.'
'Nyanmiri.'
'Nigerian,' he said.
'Nyanmiri,' the soldier insisted and he did not say anything.
'We also took Ishan,' the soldier said. 'But I wasn't there. I was on the Ehor front. We took Benin.'
'It was a fine job,' Osime said.
'Did you see the truck load of Biafrans we blew to pieces near the General Hospital?'
'I heard about it.'
'You should have seen it! They were coming back from Ore and attempting to make for Sapele Road. But we had come up round East Circular Road and down Sapele Road and we met them close to the hospital. By the prison.'
'I heard about it.'
'We had the Russian armoured cars that have a range of over 350 miles and the lieutenant put a cannon right into the engine of the lorry and it carried it back and scattered it in front of the hospital. There must have been over fifty Biafrans there. But we couldn't count them, you see. You couldn't say which part belonged to whom.'
'Our newsmen and photographs brought back the reports,'

Osime said.

'Any cigarettes?' the soldiers asked.

Osime lifted his carrier bag to the front seat beside Ndudi and brought out a packet of cigerettes and offered it to the soldiers and they said, 'Well, journalist, you can go and be sure to bring us good news on your way back. Be sure to write something good about us when you get back to Benin.'

'Sure I will,' he promised each time and drove away.

He drove slowly because of the road blocks and the trenches and the soldiers. At the back of the van the woman and her children sobbed loudly now and again. In between, it was quiet. Ndudi did not say anything and he kept his eyes on the road, thinking.

Always there was the movement of soldiers along the road in jeeps and vans and trucks, sometimes on foot. He looked at their eyes as he passed them and the eyes were expressionless and the faces were set and determined. Somehow, he felt sorry for them. *They are the ones doing the fighting,* he thought. *The ones being killed in this war and yet probably nobody ever will learn anything about them. It is a pity.*

As you come in to Agbor the road meanders and the ground now is increasingly hilly and on both sides of the road, there are trees that are no longer very tall and the undergrowth is short. As you come to the top of one hill, the ground slopes away in front of you and beside you and you can see a long way around, and if it is sunny as today is and quiet as today is, and in the evening too, you begin to wonder if indeed there is a war on. You look around and you see the beauty of the landscape and become envious of the trees whose branches seem to mingle with the whiteness and the softness of the evening clouds in the horizon. You travel a little more distance, downhill now, and as you get to the foot of the hills, the woman sobs and you are reminded of the body in the car. And then you begin to climb again, this time slowly up the steep hill and as you get to the top of this second hill, there is a sudden burst of fire and you stop and the quiet dissolves into the heat of your fear rising inside. You stop and then from both sides of the road, a dozen soldiers suddenly appear and now you know there is indeed a war on. You can see the soldiers and this time they are really nervous because now and again there is a burst from the Kalashnikovs and you look to see what is being fired at but can see nothing except the tense faces of the soldiers.

'Where do you think you are going?' the sergeant asked and they were on the road and at the back of the van with two of their soldiers and already, they had the lid off the box.

'To Oganza,' Osime said and the man gave him back his identity card and shook his head.

'You can't go any further,' the sergeant said. 'The Biafrans control the road between here and Onicha-Ugbo.'

'I thought we had got as far as Asaba,' Osime said.

'Yes,' the sergeant said. 'But this is the war front and here one day is a very long time. The Biafrans retook part of the area yesterday morning.'

'How did it happen?'

'I don't know,' the sergeant said. 'But I know the Biafrans are pulling their troops back from the Delta because they have no chance there now. And these troops are desperate and want to get to Asaba to cross the bridge. Otherwise they are cooked and they know it.'

'That means your men at Asaba are cut off?'

'That means that the Biafrans are trapped between us and our troops at Asaba. But they are desperate and we are patient. We have over two thousand men at Asaba ready to cross the bridge.'

'And you don't think it advisable that we should continue?'

'No.'

'And the . . .?' Osime pointed to the box inside of the van.

'He is not in a hurry now, is he?' the soldier asked.

Osime did not say anything but looked at the surrounding whiteness of the trees' trunks and the greenness of the trees' leaves and then at the narrow stretch of road ahead. He did not look at the soldiers.

'You think we might give them information about your positions?'

The sergeant looked sharply at Osime and all his face was involved in the smile, the way faces are involved when the smile is sincere.

'I am worried about that,' he admitted. 'That is, if you come across them. The Biafrans stay in the bushes, well away from the roads. They are not an organised force any more.'

'We would like to go ahead,' Osime said. He did not want to think of the body. The box had been opened so many times that it could begin to suffer.

'Which part of Midwest did you say you come from?'

Osime told him.

'You are very fair-complexioned.'

'My parents.'

'They are not here for us to see. Can you speak your language?'

'Yes,' Osime said and now he felt a little sick because he knew what was going on in the officer's mind.

'Okay then, say something,' the sergeant ordered and Osime looked into the dark face of the man, the eyes that were red and bloodshot, at the green and yellow steel helmet, the whole six feet of the man.

'I feel like spitting into your face,' he said in his language and the sergeant smiled. He did not understand.

'Why did you say that?' one of the other soldiers asked and Osime turned and saw the man standing away from the rest at the edge of the road, on the other side.

'What should I have said?' Osime asked but the soldier did not leave his position. He continued to stand there, rifle at the ready, his face black even against the sun.

'Something better,' he said now.

'I want to go,' Osime said. 'You're delaying me.'

'We delay you for your own safety.'

'Aidenoje,' the sergeant called and the soldier came over now, the metal butt of his gun folded forwards, his fingers on the trigger, his left hand gripping the forehand guard of the gun firmly so that the gun was between his half folded right hand and his body. 'What did he say?'

'He is from our area, sir,' the man Aidenoje said. 'He wants to take the risk.'

There was a sudden burst of gunfire from one of the far away trees and the soldiers looked quickly at each other and then at the sergeant.

'They are all nervous,' the sergeant said now. 'They get nervous when the night approaches. The Biafrans are good soldiers.'

Osime did not say anything.

'Well then,' the sergeant continued. 'This is what you tell them when you see them. You tell them there are at least two divisions here. You tell them there are trucks and armoured cars and carriers and machine guns. You tell them we shall be in Asaba tomorrow morning.'

'And what do I tell them at Asaba?'

'You tell them the truth. That we are waiting for reinforcements from Benin, Ore and Lagos.'

'Sure I will,' Osime said.

'And remember to tell your newspaper how good and brave we are. Remember to send them our photographs.'

'Sure I will.'

'Journalist!'

He looked at the sergeant.

'Good luck and be careful.'

They shook hands briefly and looked each other in the eyes and then Osime got back into the car and drove away. He did not look in the mirror.

It is strange here on the front, he thought. *People here are nervous and suspicious but decent. In the towns they loot the houses and rape the women and shoot the young men. At the front they shake hands with you and wish you good luck. But they ask you many questions. And if you are a journalist, they want you to write in the papers that they are good and brave. They want you to put their photographs on the front page. When I get back, I am going to write more about this war and try to tell the people how decent some of them really are, deep down. That is, if I get back.*

Without taking his eyes off the road, he looked at Ndudi. 'Are you afraid?' he asked her.

She did not say anything for some time and he thought she wasn't going to say anything at all but finally she said, 'Yes. Back there.'

He looked at her and he was surprised. 'You were afraid of them back there?'

'Yes. I was afraid of them. I hate them. They are killers.'

'Not all of them,' he said.

'They are all the same,' she insisted. 'They are all murderers and rapists and killers.'

'I understand,' he said simply and she kept quiet.

Later, she said, 'Why do you keep telling them I am your wife?' He shrugged his shoulders. 'Seems the natural thing to say and having said it once, you want to keep it up.'

It was her turn now to say, 'I understand.'

They did not see any Biafran soldiers on their way to Asaba. Once, they heard the firing of guns but that was far away and they kept on the road. Twice a car came past them going in the opposite direction and in one there were several men and in the other a man and a woman wearing a bright red scarf, but they did not stop and neither did Osime. You could see a few of the places where fights had taken place, where underneath the trenches, the bodies of the soldiers had been buried. You saw the mounds of earth and the upturned bushes and the hastily cut down branches of trees and you knew that there had been a fight there.

The woman at the back of the van had been quiet for the latter part of the journey, the children too. There is something in death that angers and perhaps even frightens one at the beginning. You experience the death of your loved one and you are angry that it should have happened. You are angry in your unbelief and your fear becomes a mirror of your own temporariness, of the entire vapour of your substance. You cry in your unbelief and in your anger and in your fear. And then resignation sets in. You accept it and the tears stop coming. Cold creeps over your brain. You die a little. *You die a little with each death that occurs close to you,* he said to himself.

Chapter ten

He turned left off the main road that went down to the bridge and the river, and drove towards the town. Close to the textile factory, there was a road block and about seven soldiers stood there, their Kalashnikovs at the ready. To the right, the ground sloped away gently and although there were many trees, he could see the smooth white surface of the river Niger and beyond it, the trees and many houses where he knew the Biafran soldiers were waiting. That was Onitsha. They held Onitsha as firmly as the Federal troops now held Asaba. But for them against the Federal troops, it was only a question of time. They knew an assault was coming and were busy preparing for it.

'Oganza?' the officer at the roadblock asked.

'Yes. My wife and I . . .'

'That is close to the front. You go past Oganza and there are two villages three kilometres from each other. They are called Mkpati and Nkesio. Nkesio is next to Oganza and is held by our troops. Mkpati is next to Nkesio and is held by the Biafrans.'

'We are going to Oganza.'

'Who is he?'

'He is dead.'

'Yes, I saw that.'

'My father-in-law then.'

'Your what?'

'My wife's father.'

'Why didn't you say that in the first place? You journalists! You think those of us at the front are fools?'

He didn't say anything.

'And how was the road?' the corporal asked.

'Quiet.'

'You didn't see any Biafrans?'

'No. Once we heard the firing of guns but that was very far away.'

'So you didn't stop.'

'No. We kept to the road.'

'How did the guns sound?'

'The firing was very far away.'

'Did it sound like guitars playing?'

'No. There are no guitars being used as guns in this war.'

Suddenly, the corporal laughed and he did not stop until the tears came to his eyes and ran down his cheeks. Osime was angry seeing the man laugh at him. He did not understand why the corporal was laughing.

'Well, can we go?' he asked.

'No,' the corporal said, wiping his eyes with the back of his hand. 'You may not go. Tell us what our position is at Agbor. We have radio contact but you know how it is. There are many lies in this war. Even your own side tells you lies.'

'They are waiting for the reinforcements to come from Ore and Lagos.'

'And when are they coming?'

'I cannot say. They didn't tell me.'

'You see what I mean?' the corporal cried. 'You see what I mean? Reinforcements! Always reinforcements! We would have been at Onitsha now but for these reinforcements. Our commander takes Asaba and the Biafrans are in disarray and he telephones Lagos and tells them he wants to cross the bridge while the Biafrans are in flight and do you know what they tell him? Wait for reinforcements! Well, we are still waiting for reinforcements. And while we wait, the Biafrans have reorganised and built the trenches along the river. The Biafrans have built their own reinforcements along the river and have come from the Delta and retaken Onitsha-Ugbo. Reinforcements!'

He did not know what to say.

There was a lot of troop movement along the streets. There were the trucks, black and rugged and high. The green tarpaulins were rolled down all the way on the ones that did not carry the troops. Osime looked at the soldiers as they passed and their faces were inscrutable but serious and quiet when they did not speak. He guessed they were going to the front, to retake the land between Asaba and Agbor that had been taken over by the Biafrans only yesterday morning. He looked at the houses for signs of damage but he did not see any. The shells would have fallen on the other part of the town, not close to the river. The damaged houses would be on the other side, in the town. And there would have been many dead.

They dug mass graves along Sakpoba Road in which they buried the Biafrans. Or those accused of being Biafrans. There were hundreds of them that even the lorries could not take them and they had to dig huge graves. They dug the graves and buried them there. They had on their pants, otherwise they were naked, and they were all young except for the old civil servant they chased and caught along Upper Sakpoba Road and then shot close to the girls' college. Here, the situation would have been different. There would be only a few graves here. Most of the dead would have been loaded into the lorries and then dumped into the river, like manure.

He looked at Ndudi and she said, 'You take the road on the right that goes by the river. It is a straight road but it is a rough road.'

'Shall we have to cross the river?'

'No.'

'Is she all right?' He indicated with a movement of his head that he meant her mother.

'She is quiet.'

'Too quiet.'

'She's accepted it.'

'And you have accepted it?'

'What else can we do? He was alive this morning. That is the difficult part of it. He was alive at eleven o'clock this morning.'

He didn't like the way she was going. He had to take her mind off it.

'What time is it now?' he asked

'He was alive this morning,' she said again and bit her lips and began to cry, gently.

See? he said to himself. *I was right. I knew where she was going.*

'You must not cry,' he said and patted her on the shoulder. 'It is useless crying now. You must be brave.'

They came across the check points two more times and then they were on their own going down by the river, slowly, the road getting dark now, and very very uneven. The river was on the right and it kept them company a good part of the way. *We are each of us a little like the river,* he thought. *The river is lonely in spite of its fish and the occasional barge or canoe. Deep down it is alone and it goes alone on its endless journey. And looking at the river, we are never sure how deep it really is until we wade in. And because we are never sure, we are always afraid. Only the expert swimmer dares the current of the river and he too is afraid at the moment of contact. Yes, we are each of us a little like the river, what with our loneliness and our fear of each other. But the loneliness comes with our self-consciousness. We grow more self-conscious and more alone, more narrow.* He looked sideways, past Ndudi, at the dark water of the Niger moving away, forwards, ahead of them, like a dream.

Like the river, we all have our secrets. We kept our affair secret from her father, but he must have known about it, all the same. She sneaked into my house when he was out and sneaked away before he came back. Her mother knew about it all right. She knew about it but never once told on her daughter. He moved the van right to the edge of the road to avoid a deep hole in the middle of the road. The van creaked. The woman began to sob, loudly now.

'Are we close to Oganza?' he asked.

'One more kilometre. Perhaps less.' He glanced at her. 'You will be brave for me?'

'I don't know.'

'But you will try?'

'Yes.' She looked at him and added, 'Thank you.'

'You don't have to thank me.'

'Oh yes, I do. We have to thank you. You have risked your life for us.'

'It's nothing.'

'We are grateful,' she said.

'All right then,' he said. 'I accept the gratitude but please be brave for me.'

Why am I asking her to be brave for me? She has to be brave for herself. She doesn't have to be brave for me.

'You will go back after the burial,' she said matter of fact.

'Yes. I will go back after the burial.'

'My mother says you can have the house. I mean, use it as you please until things return to normal.'

'She has hopes,' he said.

'Yes. We all have hopes.'

'That is something to be proud of.'

'It's the only thing left,' she said. 'If you cannot even have hope, then nothing else matters any more.'

'I understand.'

'My father owned four other houses. We would like you to look after them for us.'

'Until things return to normal,' he said.

She did not say anything because the first house appeared and she began to weep loudly now.

There was a main street, not much more than a dirt road, and on both sides of it, there were mud houses and fruit trees and flower trees. Occasionally, there was a house of cement blocks and a fine roof and he saw the tiny stabs of light from the kerosene lamps, in the darkness of the houses. Then there was a crossroads. The right hand road went down to the river and the left hand road ended abruptly in front of some buildings and a large compound that had many many trees. They kept straight on.

Chapter eleven

In the morning when she came to him he was already awake and biting on the hard chewing stick, the towel round the back of his neck, on his shoulders. Her eyes were swollen from crying.

'You are awake?' she asked and he nodded but would not look at her. He had not slept at all but had thought throughout the night, until the small hours of the morning when in spite of himself, his body had gone limp and he had found himself asleep, dreaming.

'How is she?' he asked

'She is all right. She wants to see you.'

He had slept in his jeans and now he put on the shirt while he sat on the bed and then his canvas shoes. He stood up when he made the bed and he kept his back to her so that she would not see his face. *Yes, that was why I couldn't sleep. Guilt. I feel guilty. I feel guilty for his death. That was why I came, to try to reduce the guilt feeling but it only became worse in the night. It became so bad that I sat up in bed to prevent myself from hearing the voices. But it did not help.*

He heard her going towards the door.

'Ndudi!'

'Yes?'

'I am terribly sorry.'

'What for?'

'He shrugged his shoulders. 'For everything. For that outside.'

'It was nobody's fault.'

'I know that is what you all have said.'

'But it is true.'

'Then come with me.'

'You want me to come with you?

'Yes.'

'Why? Because you feel guilty?'

He did not say anything but turned away from her and sat on the bed. She went out of the door with the knowledge that she had hurt him.

In the villages that are by the river, the morning always comes early but with a mist. Later the sun always seems to rise out of the water and the mist is like clots of blood as it falls away from the communion of the sun as it breaks the surface of the river. Like tears from blood shot eyes. The dawn here is early but white with the mist and fresh and sharp on the nostrils. It is quiet as the fishermen go down the river banks to their nets, their rubber-soled slippers swishing against the whiteness of the soil. Like the sound of the wind against the green leaves. The sand is fine here, so fine that each grain is separate and white as the stars are in the sky. But all this happens only if there is no war.

War changes everything, the lives of the fishermen, of the fish and of the birds. In the place of fishermen, there are soldiers, and in the place of the white sand there are the boot marks and the long trenches along the banks of the river and now and again, you hear a loud explosion as the soldiers throw grenades into the waters of the river and the fish begin to rise to the surface of the water and float. In the place of nets, the soliders use grenades and the fish are dead before they rise to the surface of the water. The grenades are used to kill the fish to feed the soldiers, and then the soldiers are killed with grenades to feed the fish. People are killed and dumped into the river. Here there are no burial grounds and as the explosions come and go and the soldiers scream and the fish rise to the surface of the water, the birds are silent in the trees. You listen for the sound of birds and instead, you get the sound of machine guns and rifles and grenades.

This is different from lying on the white sands, your feet in the white surf of the white and black waters of the white and black ocean under the green leaves and brown fruits of the white coconut trees at the back of the Lagos Grand Hotel with the loudspeakers pouring out grand music. That life is as far away as the fish floating on the surface of the river, killed by the grenades while the fishermen sit inside their houses staring at the walls and wondering when the war will end. This is the war front, the front where death is commonplace and hope the only thread that ties the present to tomorrow. And people weep only when death is a chance visitor. Not here on the war front, where every shell, every bullet, every gun burst and every grenade brings with it a message from death.

They hadn't cried except for the widow and Ndudi and the children. They had that glassy, resigned look which said they had seen it all before, that it was nothing for one man to be alive and another dead, that crying was a luxury born out of little experience. Ndudi and her mother wept loudly but they sounded strange and so had to keep quiet afterwards. Even the old woman, the grandmother, and the old man, the grandfather, had not said a word, nor cried either. They had done their weeping a long time earlier as each exploded gun brought with it news of the dead. They no longer wept outwardly. They wept now inwardly which was much worse. *It's worse,* he thought, *when the roof leaks inside. You know then that everything is finished really. They gave me a shovel and I helped dig six feet deep, eight feet long and three feet across into the bowels of the earth. We lowered the coffin into it and the old man and woman turned away and Ndudi and her mother broke down and wept loudly then.*

He went to the windows and drew back the bolts and opened them and looked through the mist to the freshly covered grave outside. *One night already! How time waits with a carving knife! How time serves to blunt the wounds it inflicts!*

He heard the sound of cars on the road outside, and in a little while they came past and there were five jeeps, all carrying soldiers. The soldiers stood inside the open jeeps, their rifles at the ready, their eyes scanning the houses. He saw them and counted them, there were about six in all and those he could see clearly were covered in dirt and mud and looked tired and worn out. *But their fear keeps them standing,* he thought. *Their fear drives the sleep and tiredness away from them and makes them stand on their feet. Fear is the constant companion of soldiers.*

He turned away from the window because he heard the door open and Ndudi stood there by the door.

'You should keep away from the window!' she said sharply.

'Why?'

'The soldiers might shoot. They think you are an enemy. Many have died like that here.'

'How do you know?'

'Grandmother told me,' Ndudi said. 'She saw me standing by the window.'

He looked at her and smiled and because she was going to speak again, he put his fingers across his lips to indicate that he didn't want her to speak until he had told her what he wanted to tell her.

'Ndudi,' he said now and his voice was quiet and sure. 'I am serious when I say I want you to go back with me, that we should both go back to Benin.'

'What about my mother?'

'Let's not talk about your mother. Let's settle you first. Let's talk about you.'

'I can't come,' she said.

'No? But you do want to come?'

She did not say anything but turned away and he reached her just as she put her hand on the door handle.

'You don't have to cry,' he said and now he had his arms round her, and her face was buried against the side of his neck and he could feel the warm tears on his skin as they ran down his collar bone.

'I know, I know,' he stammered. 'I know I have treated you badly in the past. But I had this resentment then. I had this bad blood and this bad faith which come from blaming the wrong persons for the war. I did not understand until yesterday morning when I saw your father shot. We all may be accomplices in this war but we were not responsible for it. Those who are responsible for it are not even here. But I did not understand then as I understand now. And you may not have any reasons for trusting me. But I want you to trust me and to come with me. And there are some things I want to do first. I want to go back to Asaba to see the Commanding Officer and maybe get a story for our newspapers. Maybe I can talk to the soldiers. There is so much going on here that rarely gets to us. Of course, there are the war correspondents. We have several here but they only report what places have fallen and what places are yet to be taken. I want to write a story that goes beyond the catalogue of captured territories.'

She was standing away from him now and he saw the doubt on her face, in her eyes. He saw the decision taking shape in her mind, through her eyes and she was quiet and went away for quite some time and then she came back from where she had been and looking at her brown eyes as they looked at him and then away from him, he knew that he had won.

'You will come back for me?' she asked and the light was in her eyes.

'Yes,' he said. 'I will come back for you as soon as I have got my story and if possible, arranged our transport. That should be in the afternoon.'

'I will wait,' she said and he examined her now and saw that she still had rings under her eyes. The black blouse she had been wearing for a full day now was creased and her hair was dishevelled. But she said, 'You know now that I do love you, that I am not afraid?'

'Yes,' he said simply. 'And you must know now that spite has nothing to do with what I want for us.'

She nodded her head and he wanted to tell her what he intended to tell her mother. *But I want it to be a surprise for her,* he thought. *I want her to know that spite has nothing to do with what I want with her.*

'You are sure you will come back?'

He laughed aloud and said to her, 'You still don't trust me, do you?'

'Don't laugh at me! I'm not a child! You know I am a full grown woman!'

'Twenty,' he said.

'Yes. But I have been a woman a long time now. Even before I was born.'

'No,' he said. 'I made you a woman. You came from the Polytechnic one day after the Biafrans had come to Benin and we met in front of the house and I was greatly shaken by your beauty.'

'And your spite,' she said

'No,' he said. 'It was beauty. You are a beautiful woman.'

'You were full of hatred for the Biafrans.'

'Yes.'

'And I was an Ibo.'

'No. You were not an Ibo.'

'But I *am* an Ibo.'

'Yes. Yes. But not in that sense. Not . . .'

'Please, don't lie to me.'

'All right,' he said. 'I had hatred in my eyes and throat and nose and heart and mind. I was full of spite. And there you were, an Ibo, a Biafran.'

'A Midwestern Ibo,' she corrected him.

'A Midwestern Ibo but it did not matter.'

'And you were very good,' she reminded him. 'You were the new tenant, the journalist. And all those girls! I was angry at first, then curious. That did it.'

'You were curious?'

'Yes. Later. It was only natural.'

'Can you still remember the first time?'

'Yes. I was nervous and afraid and afterwards I cried. And then I swore . . .'

'You swore?'

'Yes. I swore to hate you always.'

He didn't say anything but laughed and looking at her, he was reminded of his tall stalks of corn, slim and tender but strong and courageous even against the rainstorms and the wild winds. It was her eyes that always gave her away, her eyes that were large and brown under the faint eyebrows. Her eyes had a way of dilating, a way of getting moist and soft and telling him what he wanted to know.

'But you never hated me long enough,' he told her.

'No. No even after you went away from me,' she added.

'But I came back.'

'No,' she said seriously now. 'I always came after you. You never came back on your own. See, you are not even back now.'

'But I will come back this afternoon.'

She didn't say anything.

'I will come back,' he said again and he was going to hold her but she took a step back, away from him, towards the door.

'Mama wants to see you,' she said.

'I will come back,' he said. 'Remember, I asked you to come with me.'

'Yes. So don't lie to me. I am not afraid.'

'I will come back. See, I leave my chewing sticks and comb and towel here. I leave my carrier bag here.'

'I believe you,' she said. 'I am a fool but I believe you. And take your bag. You will need it for the camera.'

'I will hang the camera round my neck.'

'No. Take the bag. And the towel and the chewing sticks.'

'All right then,' he said. 'I will take the bag but I will leave the other things behind.'

'Take them along too. Please.'

'Don't you want me back? Is anything wrong now?'

'Nothing is wrong,' she said. 'But I will not hold anything here for you as a ransom. I love you enough to want you free. I am not desperate. I love you. That's all.'

'And I love you,' he said. 'These words do not come easily to me because I believe in experiencing, acting my emotions. But there it is. I have said them and I mean them and I want you to come with me and I will come back.' Something moved inside him and rose to his chest and then it was in his eyes. He turned away.

I will come back, he swore to himself as he sat between the driver and the sergeant in the jeep and they rode on the road that went by the river towards Asaba. *I will come back and they will perform the rites and we will be man and wife. Let her wait until her mother tells her what I told her. I told her mother that I was in love with her daughter and that I wanted her to go back with me to Benin and she asked me as what? As my whore? And I said, no. As my wife. And she really sat up then because she had not expected it, but then she was very good. What about her husband's people? And Ndudi? And the war? She suspected, but didn't say it, that I was on the other side. I saw her struggle with it but she was very good because afterwards she cried and promised to lie on my behalf. She promised she would tell her husband's people that her husband had been aware of my intentions and had agreed. Then she mentioned the dowry and I told her I was skint and she brought out two hundred pounds and said she would give it to them and say it came from me. And then in the afternoon, when I came back, they would perform the necessary rites. But we would have to repeat them after the war. We would have to marry all over again, after the war. Yes, she was sure the war would end. It was only a matter of time. She was sure it would be best for Ndudi. The war front was no place for a girl decently brought up. I must take care for her. She would arrange everything and when I came back, we would be husband and wife. And I will come back!*

'So you are a journalist,' the driver of the jeep said and his voice shook because of the uneven road. He was growing a beard and his soldier's uniform was black from the mud and his face was dirty and his hair unkempt. He kept his eyes on the road even as he spoke.

'Yes,' Osime answered, his mind going back to Ndudi.

'Is this your first time on the war front then?'

'No.'

'Where else have you been?'

'Benin.'

'Benin? You call that a war front?'

'It was three weeks ago. Until three weeks ago . . .' *What the hell,* he asked himself. *I should be doing the questioning and he should be doing the answering! What am I doing answering the questions?*

'Journalist!'

'Yes.'

'Any cigarettes?'

'I distributed them on my way here. Where are you coming from?'

The soldier didn't answer.

'Has there been any battle?'

The driver did not say anything but continued to look straight ahead of them. *You bastard*, Osime swore in his heart. *You filthy bastard asking me questions and then refusing to answer my questions!*

'How long have you been here?' he tried again.

'Can't you keep quiet, journalist?'

Osime looked sideways at the sergeant who had spoken and the light came into his eyes. He was sitting between two soldiers in front of the jeep.

'I want to know,' he said. 'I came here to know.'

'You don't get told anything on the war front.'

'Why not?'

'You find out, that's why. You soon learn to see. You see men coming back in an open truck and they are quiet and you know that there has been an ambush and some of them have been killed. You listen to a talkative nervous driver and you know his nerves have taken a beating. You know the soldiers have been beaten.'

'I am sorry,' Osime said.

'There is nothing to be sorry about,' the sergeant said and his fair face that was black with dirt was serious and unsmiling. 'This is a war,' he said. 'You don't get sorry about anything here.'

'Still, I am sorry.'

'Well, it doesn't matter. My men fought well. There were sixteen of us. We lost ten. We were caught in an ambush. We had no chance but we fought well. Our officer escaped. He went back.' Osime didn't know what to say.

'This war is a prostitute, a harlot,' the sergeant continued. 'Today it sleeps with the Biafrans, tomorrow it comes to our side. It has no permanent friends. It has no permanent lovers. It makes love to us all but it never satisfies any of us.'

'And the dead soldiers?'

'They are in the jeep in front of us, those whose bodies we could recover. They fought and died well. You should have seen Otun. He blocked one side of the jeep with his body so we could get on the other side.'

'That was a great sacrifice.'

'A small one,' the sergeant said. 'Many of the soldiers do it in this war. It does not matter whether they are on our side or on their side. They do it and then die so that others may live.'

'Which one is Otun then?'

The sergeant smiled suddenly and a white patch appeared on

his face as he showed his teeth. 'Otun is the tall one under all the rest of them in that jeep. Otun, Emmanuel, Ikeshi and the others.'

'I am sorry,' Osime apologised again. 'Where did Otun come from?'

'We are all Nigerians at the front,' the sergeant corrected him. 'Otun was a Nigerian as we all are, as even the Biafrans who fight us are.'

'Yes, I see,' Osime said, feeling stupid but puzzled at the same time. *Where did such loyalty come from! How could people suffer so much and yet retain so much faith? How could they keep faith in the midst of so much suffering? Perhaps the suffering is to them as flame is to the metal in the blacksmith's forge. The suffering purifies them, strengthens their resolve.*

'Journalist,' the sergeant said and Osime turned and looked at the man.

'You may wonder why I tell you all this. The fact is you are a journalist. You keep records. You write in the newspapers. After this war many generals will write their accounts in which they will attempt to show that they were the heroes of this war, that it was their grand strategies that won the war. They will tell the world that they single-handedly fought and won the war. The names of soldiers like Otun, Emmanuel, Ikeshi, and Yemi will never be mentioned. The soldiers take the dirt and the ambushes and the bullets with their lives. The soldiers pay for the unity of this country with their lives and yet, what happens? Always the officers are the heroes. Always the generals, the officers take the credit. Always the generals get the praise. Always they are the heroes. Always.'

Osime listened to the voice of the sergeant and his words were like the sound of bells. They rang distinctly and clearly and went through him the way a man feels drinking a glass of extremely cold water in which there are icecubes. And yet, he didn't know what to say.

'Back there,' the sergeant was saying again, 'our officer was driven away from the ambush. The driver drove him to safety. He escaped.'

'There shouldn't have been any war,' Osime said now. 'This war was not necessary.' He felt inadequate.

The sergeant looked at him and shook his head and again, Osime was puzzled. 'To keep Nigeria one is a task that must be done,' he said with the same finality and clarity of bells. 'We must teach the Biafrans what it means to attempt to break up the country. We must teach the Biafrans a lesson.'

'Yes,' he said simply, really puzzled now. *Here is a soldier who understands the bitterness of this war, who has tasted of its bitterness and yet is not bitter. How come? I am going to learn many things in this war,* he said to himself. *Or rather, I am going to unlearn many things. At the beginning, I did not understand the cruelty of the war. I did not think that the Federal troops were capable of cruelty, until I went to the stadium, until Ndudi's father was murdered. I thought that the Biafrans were the only villains. I did not understand the war then. Now I understand it a little better although what I don't know now is much greater than what I did not understand before. I do not understand the faith of the sergeant. I am puzzled by it. You expect a man to be bitter and there is no salt in his mind when he reveals it to you. And another thing, I thought that the soldiers did not understand. That was a mistake. They understand the mechanics of this war better than you and I. They understand much more deeply than we do.*

It is a pity that I have to go back to Benin today, that we have to go back, Ndudi and I. But I could stay, he thought and quickly dismissed the thought. *We have to go back. I gave her my promise. Besides, I came here to go away today. I did not come here to stay. And what is she doing now? Will she think I am a liar like all the rest of them? Will she wait for me? Will she think that I may not come back? Will she trust me?*

The sergeant was quiet now, not saying anything, but in the quietness of his soul, Osime could still hear the man's voice saying, 'We are all Nigerians at the front. The soldiers pay for the unity of this country with their lives and yet, what happens? Always, the officers take the credit. Always the generals get the praise. Always . . .'

He turned and looked at the dirty face of the sergeant and saw that it was quiet and without bitterness. *Yes,* he thought, *I shall reproduce his words for the newspaper. I will get this story but the story will be about the unknown soldiers, soldiers unknown even when they are still alive. This war is a bitch.* He turned away from staring at the sergeant and began to look at the large low meadows that spread along the banks of the river. In there too, were trenches and guns and soldiers. Come the signal and the mutual slaughter would start.

Chapter twelve

The army camp and headquarters was scattered across a number of buildings on the grounds of old St Barnabas College. The college was closed down now and each building was occupied by a different section of the army. The open fields formed the training grounds for the soldiers.

'Which is the office of the Commanding Officer?' he asked and the sergeant pointed to a long building that stood in the centre of the other buildings.

'But we're not going there. We're going to the building on the left, to the battalion commander. The ninety-seventh battalion.'

'We will meet again?'

The sergeant looked at him as he stood on the road and nodded his head. 'Perhaps when the war is over.'

'Yes. Perhaps when the war is over. You have my address and my name and any time you are passing through Benin, do not hesitate to call me. You can stay with me.'

'Thank you very much, journalist, I mean Osime,' the sergeant said, calling him by his name for the first time and he took Osime's hand and shook it and the laughter was in his eyes now. 'And don't forget my name too. Audu. Sergeant Audu and maybe tomorrow Captain Audu!'

'You will become a general,' Osime said.

'A good general,' Sergeant Audu said. 'A general from the ranks. Goodbye, journalist.' The formality was back, although the friendliness was still there.

'Goodbye, sergeant!' Osime raised his hand in a mock salute and then the jeep drew away from him and he was alone on the road.

There were soldiers in the fields in white singlets and blue shorts performing exercises. You could hear the voices of the officers shouting commands and see the faces of the soldiers glistening with sweat. There were soldiers in the corridors of the buildings too. He could see them walking to and fro, like the pendulum of bells, their guns at their sides. They looked stern and strong and capable. But there was a certain amount of nervousness too. He could feel it. He could almost taste it. The buildings were old and low and solid, the paint was off the walls now and the roofing was yellow and brown and black with rust. My God, he thought, *what would happen if the Biafran planes came here the way they came to Benin after the fall of the city to the Federal troops? The way they had raided the airport in their three small planes that were equipped with machine guns. They should be here, several of them, fully manned with one soldier sitting on each mount, watching and waiting.* He couldn't see any anti-aircraft guns.

That was what had happened at Benin. They had anti-aircraft guns and still the Biafrans came. It was the first Sunday after the arrival of the Federal troops and it was in the morning. He was awake then and he heard the sound of the planes as they passed overhead, flying low, and then he did not hear them for three minutes. Then he heard the loud explosions and the rapid gunfire from the anti-aircraft guns and then it was quiet until suddenly, the planes came roaring over his house. It happened twice and loud explosions also came twice and then he was in his car and driving furiously to the city. He heard it all later. Three planes on the ground had been hit, the runway had been strafed and the only soldier who had attempted to mount the anti-aircraft gun had been shot. The other soldiers had scattered hastily. Later, the army officers had come from the church service but then it had been too late. The Biafran planes had returned safely to Uli Ihiala but even before they had landed at Enugu, the Biafran radio had announced the raid. Fifty enemy soldiers and ten planes destroyed, the radio announcement claimed. Airport buildings destroyed, runway completely strafed. He remembered now his surprise and admiration at the daring of the Biafrans.

It did not matter that the pilots had been white mercenaries. What mattered was the success and daring of the raid, what mattered was the possibility and the organisation of the raid. He remembered his anger then and later his sense of shame and humiliation. And he had not been alone. Along with the shame and humiliation had come a great sense of insecurity. How come all the officers had been at church? How come only ten soldiers had been left to guard the airport.

But all that was before his landlord was shot, before he had been humiliated himself at the stadium. That was when he began to educate himself about the war. He began to understand the war until he had nothing but hatred for it because he came to see how the war had arisen. He had come to see the war as the result of the struggle for power between individuals, as the result of the very contradictions in the rulership of the country. He understood then why as many as a hundred soldiers guarded the governor's house and as few as ten guarded a whole airport. Nothing had changed. The same greed, the same hunger for power, the same disregard for the rest of the country which the politicians had practised were taken over by the military after the coups. Only the individual rulers mattered. The other sixty million-odd Nigerians were for slaughter either at the war fronts or in their beds in the cities and villages.

And that is what Sergeant Audu meant, he thought. *Sergeant Audu is a patriot but he understands that those who carry the cross for society always get crucified in the end. The generals see to that. Only one section of the population continues to carry the cross while the generals and politicians and businessmen all profit from this war. To them, the war is only another market with opportunities for profit. Sergeant Audu and Ikeshi and Emmanuel carry the cross and drink the gall while the generals and politicians and businessmen compliment each other and make speeches showing them to be the men of honour, the heroes.*

What is needed, he thought, *is a third army. An army to ask questions about the purpose of this war, about the reasons behind this war. The third army will sit among the soldiers, Biafrans and Nigerians alike, and tell them that this is not their war, that they are shooting at the wrong enemies. The real enemies are the politicians who robbed the country blind, who looted the country and prompted the generals to intervene. The third army will turn their guns on the generals, line them up and shoot them one by one, the generals of both armies, and then the soldiers will lay down their arms and go home. Then the dispute about the unity of this country will stop. The third army will clean up all the filth and mess and then we will be in business to make a fresh start. Yes,* he thought, *there ought to be a third army and I am going to be its first recruit.*

Five soldiers stood at the door and each of them carried an automatic rifle and wore grenades around their waists. He looked at them and he could see their nervousness now in the way they stood and looked at him.

'I want to see the Commanding Officer,' he said to them, looking into the red eyes of the corporal.

'What?' the corporal asked and his voice was suspicious and his bushy eyebrows seemed to come down over his eyes which narrowed in suspicion.

'I want to see the Commanding Officer,' he repeated. The corporal laughed and Osime knew the man did not take him seriously.

'Don't put your hand in your pocket,' the corporal said sharply as Osime's hand went towards his back pocket to bring out the card with his name and address on it. Osime stopped.

'I am a journalist,' he said now.

'Journalist?'

'Yes. I want to see Brigadier Murtala Mohammed.'

'He is away,' the Corporal said. 'Come next year.'

'And Obasanjo?'

'Who?'

'Obasanjo,' Osime repeated. 'I understand he is here too.'

'I don't know him,' the Corporal said. 'Never heard of him. Is he a soldier?'

'I want an interview with the Commanding Officer,' Osime persisted. 'I've come from Benin to get the interview. You know, how things are on the front, the problems, the difficulties . . .'

'Oh, I can tell you that,' the Corporal offered.

'Yes?'

'Of course. One of our problems is getting rid of journalists.'

The other soldiers smiled and their eyes were bright but they did not laugh.

'I am going back to Benin today,' Osime tried again.

'Corporal Adu!'

'Yes, sir!'

'What's going on there?'

'A journalist, sir.'

'Journalist?' A soldier appeared with two pips on his shoulders so Osime knew he was a captain.

'Good morning, Captain,' Osime said, moving between the corporal and the other soldiers and past them so that he stood just outside the door but face to face with the captain as he stood inside the room. 'I am the political editor of the *Daily News*. I am here to see the Commanding Officer. I want an interview.'

'You're a journalist?'

'My name is Osime.'

'Journalist,' the captain said matter of fact. 'Follow me.'

Everybody from the press is a journalist to them, Osime thought as he followed the captain along the corridor. But he was used to being called 'Journalist' now. He didn't mind. *But they do not like us*, he thought. *They resent us.*

The captain stopped in front of the sixth door along the corridor. It was already open and he went inside. There were four other soldiers there, two of them officers, one a major, the other a lieutenant.

'Sit down,' the captain said to Osime, indicating a chair in the centre of the room. Osime sat down and put his bag on the carpet beside his chair. He looked at the captain and then he understood. He was in the centre of the room and there were five of them sitting all around him. This was going to be an inquisition.

'Have you ever been here before?'

'No,' Osime answered and the major shook his head.

'Then how come you are here now?'

'There is always a first time.'

'That's right. But this interview? Who sent you?'

'I am an editor. I make my own decisions.'

'You mean you came all the way from Benin just to have this interview?'

'Yes and no.'

'What do you mean?'

'I took a body to Oganza. We buried him and then I came here for the interview.'

'A body?'

'Yes. My father-in-law's.'

'You are married to a Nyanmiri then?'

'They are Midwesterners.'

'Your wife is a Nyanmiri?' the captain who had brought him into the room asked.

'The Biafrans are Nigerians. We are all Nigerians.'

'Biafrans?'

'Well, rebels.'

'Which newspaper did you say you came from?' the major asked.

'The *Daily News*.'

'And you can prove it?'

'I have my card.'

'The rebels print cards showing them to be generals and officers in our army.'

'I am an editor, the political editor of the *Daily News*.'

'Have you got a copy of your newspaper with you?'

'No.'

'What?'

'You asked if I brought a copy of my newspaper with me and I said no. I didn't bring any.'

The three officers in the room looked at each other and then the lieutenant who was very tall and very dark stood up and went to the major's table and they talked in whispers and then the lieutenant went out of the room.

'Your story is weak, journalist,' the major said. 'Very weak. But you will not be the first nor the last Biafran spy to have attempted to come here in the guise of a newspaper man. And captain, tell him what we have done to them.'

The captain laughed. 'Why sir, first of all we cut off their tongues, then had them shot afterwards. In front of this building, on the field.'

'Good,' the major said. 'Now, journalist, tell us who you are.'

Osime looked round at the four men in the room and the anger was in his eyes. 'I am not a spy,' he denied. 'I cannot tell you a lie to give you the satisfaction of shooting me. You want to know who I am? Check the old issues of the *Daily News*. My column is there twice a week. My photograph, my name and what I write.'

'We don't read the newspapers,' the major declared.

Osime shrugged his shoulders. 'Then you will just have to take me to the Commanding Officer, Brigadier Murtala Mohammed.'

'The C.O. is in Lagos.'

'Obasanjo, then.'

'Who?'

'Obasanjo.'

'Who's he?'

'One of your top officers here.'

'What is his first name?'

He told them.

'We don't know him,' the major said. 'Murtala Mohammed, yes, but he is away in Lagos.'

'Then there is nothing more I can say,' Osime said, suddenly feeling weak and tired. 'I came here from Benin yesterday evening. I was seen at several checkpoints on the Benin-Asaba Road. Besides, I cannot speak Ibo.'

'You are married to one of them.'

'So the people of Asaba are rebels?' He didn't care any more now. He was fighting for his life.

The soldiers didn't say anything.

'And are you saying there are no officers in the Nigerian army who are married to Ibos?'

The soldiers continued to ignore him and his voice sounded strange even to himself in the room. *Sergeant Audu said it*, he thought now. *This is where the officers fight their wars, in the rooms where they interrogate innocent people. Fight. No. They have no stomach for that. They get driven away from the ambushes. They get driven away from the war fronts to offices where they can terrorise and intimidate unarmed people.*

The tall lieutenant came back into the room and went and spoke with the major, and then he went and sat down. Osime looked past the major at the window. *Only glass louvres. But they will probably shoot me as soon as I get clear of the room. They did it to Ndudi's father. They let him run until he almost reached the river, then they shot him from behind, in the back.*

'Well, have you arranged the execution squad?' he asked and suddenly the major laughed and stood up and came round his desk to stand in front of him.

'We are sorry, journalist,' he said.

Osime did not say anything.

'My officer has checked your story out. We know you write for the *Daily News*, that you are its political editor. But you cannot blame us for being thorough. This is a war. Now tell us what you want.'

Osime looked at the man as he held out his hand. *I must be crazy*, he thought. *I must be crazy taking a man's hand who has abused and insulted me. But hadn't the man said that this was a war? I am learning. I am learning that the war changes people, that you doubt others to survive, that war destroys trust, that it brings out the animal locked up in the human heart. And heroism too.*

'Tell us what you really came for,' the major said again and he was no longer standing but sitting at his desk.

'I came here for a story,' Osime said and his face was serious. He looked at the major and although he did not know it, the dislike was clearly written on his face.

'What story?'

'The position of the war. What difficulties, what problems.'

'We have no problems. The rebels are in retreat on all fronts.'

'Can I see the Commanding Officer?'

'I am the Commanding Officer of the Brigade,' the major said

'And the Commanding Officer of the Division?'

'He is away in Lagos.'

'When is he expected back?'

'We don't know.'

'And who acts when he is away?'

'He is away too. You have to talk to me.'

'Yes,' Osime agreed. 'But you have no problems.'

'No. But you can tell them we have crossed the Bridge. Tell them we are now at Onitsha.'

'Sure.'

'So you see, we are agreed. Goodbye.'

Osime stood up, feeling humiliated and defeated. They had humiliated him but told him nothing.

He looked at the faces of the men in the room as if wanting to remember them forever. He went out of the door. He came to the verandah of the building and again, he saw three men in *agbada*, all carrying briefcases. He guessed they were contractors. The soldiers who had first stopped him were still there. He looked at them and he felt bitter. *What decency we have,* he thought, *the war makes bitter. Or perhaps we never were decent deep down. We simply pretended to be until the war came and then we acted naturally. We act the way we are, callously, indifferently, selfishly. Like scum,* he thought and spat into the side of the road, between the sand and the grass.

The war is the great excuse for our natural vices, or how else could we have shot Ohiali so cold-bloodedly? How else could we have driven long sticks through women's vaginas and watched their eyes come out of their heads? We are wicked and barbaric deep down. Yes, war provides a measuring rod of our decency, of our humanity. Why, the law provides that we must be decent, civil to one another in time of peace and to make sure that we are, we get punished when we break the law, when we misbehave. We keep within the bounds of civility out of fear of the law, out of fear of punishment. But in time of war, there are no laws any more. We are strictly on our own, we are answerable to ourselves then. And see what happens. We loot our neighbour's property, we set fire to his house because we say he is on the other side. We loot, we burn, we rape, we murder, lie and steal. We exhibit our vomit then, we show ourselves up for what we really are. And what we really are is ugly and slimy and poisonous and dark and weak.

He spat again, this time on the road, in front of him where he must pass. *That is what most of us are. Spittle.*

Chapter thirteen

Osime Iyere walked down the road quickly and his mind was overcast by his anger. *They threatened to shoot me, the second time in less than a week. They threatened to shoot me because I came in there to ask for an interview, because I dared to say I was a journalist. They are all bastards and were born wicked and cruel and miserable. They are all . . .*

He checked himself. It was a sign of immaturity to be bitter in this war. Bitterness was the great darkness in which all light goes out. *Yes,* he thought. *I cannot be bitter. I may get angry but I must guard against bitterness. There is too much prejudice around already for me to add my bitterness to it. One has to be careful in this war. One has to make sure not to get bent. The war is the great furnace in which we are all being forged. And we must come out of it not worse, but better.*

Osime Iyere walked down the road and now he was on the Asaba-Oganza Road and waiting for a taxi. The river stretched out beside him, the river along which were the trenches. He could see the bridge, high and long and gleaming in the sun. That was where the Federal troops would cross. There and then there would be the boats across the river. It would have to be at night. And the boats would have to cross silently because on the other side, the Biafrans would be waiting. He did not want to think about the day it would happen, he did not want to think about the soldiers that would be in the boats. *I shall be far away from here and in Benin. I shall be far away and Ndudi will be with me and by then, perhaps she will have learnt to trust again.*

He saw a car coming down the road and shifting the carrier bag to his left hand, began to wave down the car. There were three occupants in the white Peugeot 404 and as the car drew level, the driver looked at him and smiled but he did not stop. The car continued down the road. He waited there another hour and five cars passed. Two were military jeeps which did not stop. Only one of the other cars stopped and asked him in Ibo where he was going. But he did not speak any Ibo and when he answered in English, the occupants of the car looked at each other and drove away.

She will not be expecting me, he thought. *She thinks I am a cheat like all the rest. But I will surprise her. She will see me and her faith in people will come back, even if she does not go back to Benin with me, even if she changes her mind. But she will see me and her faith will be restored. She will learn once more to trust. She has suffered a lot, and she is a brave woman. She will see that I came back, that I did not go away.*

It was important to him that he went back, more important, he began to realise, than anything he had ever wanted in his life. He wanted her to know that he had not been lying to her. He wanted to see her again. She must be waiting for him, even though in her heart she might not believe that he would ever come.

He waited for another hour and although more cars came, no one offered to give him a lift. *How can I let her know that I have waited for two hours? How do I communicate to her that I am standing by the side of the road now, waiting to come to her? Telepathy is the privilege of a few minds. And this waiting is beginning to kill me.* He looked at his wristwatch. Exactly two hours, five minutes and thirty seven, no thirty eight seconds now. Waiting.

He was reminded of the time he had gone with the Governor on his visits last year before the invasion of the state by the Biafrans. They had gone by road and arrived at the Oba's palace unannounced.

'The Oba says you should wait, your excellency,' the secretary in the palace had apologised.

'Thank you. We will wait,' the Governor had answered. They waited for twenty minutes and then the Governor began to get restless. He spoke with his aide-de-camp who stood up and went to the palace secretary.

'Can you please remind his royal highness that we are waiting?' Osime heard the aide-de-camp say to the palace secretary.

The palace secretary looked helplessly then at the aide-de-camp.

'Well?' demanded the aide-de-camp.

'I . . . I . . . cannot, sir?' the palace secretary stammered.

'What?'

'You see, sir, his royal highness is in the lavatory.' Osime had heard the palace secretary say, and had restrained himself from laughing. *Thirty minutes!* he had said to himself then. *What could his royal highness be doing in the toilet for half an hour?* Then he had smiled to himself. *First of all, his royal highness has to get rid of all those robes and beads, unless perhaps they now make a special hole through the robes. And then considering that his royal highness reaps where he does not sow, that he has the food of hundreds of millions of others in his stomach, and the blood of hundreds of millions of slaves on his head, he should stool for hours. He should get the stench of his parasitism and treachery firmly in his nose and eyes. He should suffocate in both.*

And what about the Governor? Is it not a fact that last year he and the head of state went to Ubiaja for a week with a carload of women? And then what happened when Theresa threatened to expose them? Did they not have her silenced? They went to bed with her, the head of state first, then the Governor, and then they had her silenced because they would not accept responsibility for her baby. They had her killed in a car crash near Ehor. She was killed, her unborn baby with her. But that was after the head of state had first stripped naked and gone to bed with her and afterwards told her that she had satisfied him as no other woman had in his life. So Theresa had confessed before they silenced her. They are all the same. They hand over to each other the baton of misery, treachery and parasitism. It is a relay race in which the runners are the Obas and the generals and the police chiefs and the businessmen and the old politicians who now have no real trade, politicians without politics suffocating in frustration and envy of the force chiefs and, because they do not have the guns, trading their frustration and envy for parasitism, treachery and misery. He came back out of his reverie just in time to see his royal highness come into the room, his royal highness whose face was beaded in the sweat of his labour from more than an hour of sitting at stool.

Now Osime Iyere came out of his reverie just in time to see a car coming down the road and he began to wave with both hands, including the one that held the bag.

The pick-up van went past him and then stopped and began to reverse back.

'Where are you going?' the driver asked

'Oganza.'

'Ten naira.'

'Ten naira?'

'Yes. This is a war.'

'All right,' Osime agreed. 'Where do I sit?'

The man looked at Osime and then at the bag. Osime quickly drew out the camera and his notebooks. 'I am a journalist,' he told him. 'I carry no weapon.'

'Okay then,' the man said. 'Sit here in front with us.'

The woman who sat beside the man moved further inside and Osime opened the door of the car and got in.

'Where are you from?' the man asked.

'Benin.'

'You are a Bini then?'
'No. Esan.'
'What part of Ishan?'
Osime looked at the man thoughtfully. 'Why do you ask?'
'We had a business at Uromi before the war.'
'And you left it?'
'Yes. Five weeks before the Federal troops came.'
'You are an Ibo then?'
'Yes,' the man said without emotion. 'I am a Midwestern Ibo. But I had to leave.'

Osime understood. Perhaps that was what Ohiali should have done. *Ohiali should have taken his family and gone away before the Federal troops came and then he would not have been there for me to persuade to go and be killed. But how does one ever know these things? How can one ever know that come another day and one will be dead? You would have to be supernatural to know, and that is impossible.*

'And you are going to Oganza?'
'Yes,' Osime replied.
'Any business there?'
'My wife is there.'
'Your wife is from Oganza?'
'Yes.'

The man shook his head then and Osime wondered what the man had in his mind until he said. 'We are from Oganza. And you are our in-law. Whose family then?'

'Ohiali.'
'He has his house by the road?'
'Yes.'

'See?' the man said to his wife. 'What would have happened if we had not stopped? We would have left our in-law behind. And now, young man, you must forget that we ever asked for ten naira. That wouldn't be fair any more.'

'I don't know what to say,' Osime said

'Then don't say anything. We know the Ohialis. And anyway, anybody who marries from Oganza marries our daughter. He is our in-law.'

'What do you think of the war?' Osime asked.

'The war?' and the man laughed. 'The war is like a woman, deadly. We all suffer in this war.'

'And you think it will end?'

'Of course,' the woman said now. 'Sooner or later, the Federal troops will cross the bridge and then the war will be over.'

'So you think the Biafrans will lose.'

'We know they will lose. Even the Biafrans know they will lose. You look at the Biafran soldiers, children of sixteen and seventeen wearing black canvas shoes and carrying daneguns. And then look at the Hausa soldiers, at the Federal troops armed with rifles and automatic guns and planes and tanks . . .'

I shouldn't have asked, Osime thought. *I should just have kept quiet because feelings are strong in this war and nobody sits on the fence, not any more.*

The man continued to talk as he drove along the narrow uneven road. He drove slowly and carefully and then they came to a sharp bend that was on high ground so that the river stood clearly out to the right, gleaming and sweating under the sun, and in front of them, as the road sloped away gently forward, they could see a long convoy of army jeeps and trucks coming towards them. The man stopped his car and parked it on the edge of the bush away from the road. 'We must come down from the car,' he said now. 'There is trouble. There are too many of them this time.'

They got down from the car and stood beside it on the road, near the bush and the man went behind the van and undid his zip and began to urinate on the grass. The woman stood with Osime and she was quiet and he looked for the fear in her eyes but couldn't see any. And then the first jeep came past, holding several soldiers who looked at them as they stood on the ground, well away from the road. About ten trucks passed before the jeep came and stopped beside them, and the army officer, a captain, beckoned to the man as he stood beside his wife and he walked towards him. They spoke for less than a minute and then the man came back.

'We cannot go to Oganza,' the man said. 'The Federal troops have pulled out of Oganza and abandoned it to the Biafran troops. We must turn back and follow him to Asaba.'

'But I want to to to Oganza,' Osime said.

'The captain says you can't.'

'Oh yes, I can.'

'Are you coming or not?' The man got into the car.

Osime looked at the woman as she stood on the road beside him and shook his head. He got into the car and then the man's wife got in and shut the door after her. The man waited until the jeep of the captain had pulled ahead on the road and then he brought the van into the road and reversed in front of the next truck.

'This is what the war means,' the man said vacantly. 'You leave your children at home and travel five miles to buy food and before you get back, you are in a different country and your children are in a different country.' The woman began to cry.

'Is this the only road?'

'Yes. But there is the river.'

'We will try the river then,' Osime said hopefully.

'No,' the man said. 'The river is a death trap. You will get shot. Only this time you will have a choice as to who kills you — the Biafrans or the Federal troops. The Federal troops are preparing to cross the river and the Biafrans are waiting on the other side. Nothing crosses the river now except the fish and they swim underneath the water.'

'Then how do I get to Oganza?'

'You can't, not until the Federal troops take it back.'

'But I have to go back there. I've got to get there!'

The man did not say anything and the woman continued to weep, loudly now.

My God, Osime said to himself. *Oh my God! I should have taken her with me. Ndudi should have come with me!* He did not want to think about what the Biafran soldiers might do to her. He closed his eyes.

Now I understand why the soldier laughed when I said I had been at a war front before and claimed that Benin was the war front. This is the war front, the front where nothing holds, even for a single morning. She'll understand, he thought desperately, *she'll understand that it was the war that cut me off. It is important that she understands because up to now, she has only known me in my spite, not in my love. She only knew me in my hatred, in my ignorance.*

Last night as I tossed on that bed, it suddenly came to me that I had to make a decision. Either she came with me or I left without a trace. I must have loved her all along. I must have loved her and yet I faced her with my hatred. Love and hatred are like two sides of a coin, love on one side, hatred on the other, and both roll on the edge, the third side, which is life. All along I must have kept love down and turned the hate side uppermost. Then I changed sides last night after rolling on the edge since the coming of the Federal troops. I recognised then how much courage, how much strength there was in this woman, I recognised that my hatred was born out of ignorance, and that neither of us was to blame for this war. It is a war of words, rumours and lies. At every turn the war is accompanied by a lie, a lie used by each side to frighten its own people so that they are prepared to stand up and be counted. I bought this lie. I bought it whole-heartedly and brought it home and wrapped around it a coil of hatred which I took to Ndudi. Thank God I turned in time. Thank God she hadn't gone away from me or else when I turned it would have been too late. I would have suffocated in my love.

'Journalist!'

He opened his eyes and the man pointed ahead of them. 'We have stopped.'

'Why?'

The man looked at him and shrugged his shoulders, 'I don't know.'

'Have I been asleep for a long time?'

'Ten minutes, maybe.'

He turned to the woman as she sat beside him. She was still weeping. He felt he had to say something to her.

'They'll be all right,' he said. 'You'll see. Your children will be all right.'

'Oh my God!' the woman wept. 'Oh my God!'

'They will be all right,' Osime said again.

It was a long convoy. There were as many jeeps as there were trucks and civilian cars. The tanks and the armoured cars stayed at the very end of the convoy.

Inside the car, the woman continued to weep and Osime sat quietly, having realised that it was useless trying to reassure her. You did not tell people at the front what was all right and what was not. They knew themselves. They new there was real trouble.

'What is your real name, sir?' he asked the man.

'Umunna,' the man said voicelessly.

'And I am Osime Iyere,' Osime said.

'Why have we stopped?' the man Umunna asked now.

'I don't know. Do you think it is anything serious?'

'No,' the man said. 'It can't be. It can't happen again.'

'No,' Osime said. This could not be an ambush; the Biafran soldiers would have had to retake Asaba to launch an ambush here. But what if it was? Was that why the man was getting restless?

'Did it happen before?' he asked.

The man Umunna did not speak at once, but finally, he breathed in deeply and with the coming out of the air said, 'Yes. Twice before.'

'Twice?' he asked.

'Yes. The last one was last week. Five days ago.'

'I see,' Osime breathed.

'About two hundred soldiers died. Two hundred soldiers on the Federal side. About fifty on the Biafran side.'

'That many? We did not hear about it.'

'Events like that do not go out. But the Biafrans would have announced it. They would have announced it again and again until the whole world learnt about it.'

'Yes. But we did not hear about it.'

'But I don't think it is the Biafrans holding us up this time.'

'There's no gunfire.'

'Yes,' the man Umunna agreed. He wiped his face with the broad palm of his hands and you could see that his eyes were tired and his mouth drooping a little and his hair whitening.

'Do you have a son in the war?'

'Yes. Two. One joined up with the Biafrans and the other is with the Federal soldiers.'

'Then you are in the middle,' Osime said.

'The Biafrans are ill-equipped,' the man Umunna said as if he had not heard him. 'They are ill-equipped and inexperienced.'

'And young,' Osime said, and the man Umunna looked at him quickly and sharply.

'There is no middle in this war,' he said finally.

Many soldiers came down from behind them and went past them on each side of the car, on both sides of the road. They went slowly, their guns cocked, their faces scanning the surrounding bushes. Osime Iyere looked at them as they went past and he could not read anything on their faces. There was no shouting, simply a deadly, stealthy silence.

'I think we are beginning to move,' the woman said suddenly and both of them turned to look up the road and then at her. She had stopped crying but her eyes were serious in her fair face and her headtie was on her lap, close to her knees. She was a little too fat. You could see that in the roundness of her arms. She wasn't a tall woman. He had seen that when earlier, they had got down on the road.

The convoy began to move. It went at a slow pace and after some minutes, they passed some of the soldiers and there were many boot marks printed on the soft soil of the road. Some of the soldiers were inside the bush.

'Do you think they saw something?' Osime asked.

'Perhaps.'

'Or perhaps a car broke down,' the woman said.

'Perhaps,' Osime answered. 'I was afraid over there.'

The woman looked at him and he thought he saw a light come into her eyes but it went away and she said, 'We are afraid all the time in this war.'

'Fear dominates the second front,' Osime said

'What?' the man Umunna asked and turned to look into Osime's face.

'Nothing,' Osime said.

They drove on in silence but now they were going at a much faster pace. Osime was thinking about Ndudi, and also about Salome. *What I had for Salome was real, but she killed it with the news of her impending marriage to Otunshi. I didn't believe her at first. Believing her meant that all the time we had sworn to each other about our loyalty, about our faith, about our love, she had had something going on with Otunshi, that she had been disloyal, faithless. I didn't believe it until she showed me the invitation cards, but strangely enough I never hated her. I moved house to escape her and came face to face with Ndudi and the fact of Biafra at my door. So I took my pain, my distrust and my vengeance to Ndudi. And she did not complain. Not once. I told Ndudi I did not believe in love when she said she loved me. I told her this every time I made love to her and I watched her cry and after some time, she did not cry any more. She called me a cynic. She called me a pagan. But she did not hate me. Ndudi saw all the other women who came to me, she saw me in my intimacy with them but she did not hate me. That is strength,* he thought. *Strength is retaining your faith in the face of contradictory evidence. It does not matter in what, so long as the original faith remains. It is essential that we do not change in our fundamentals. A woman shocks you by betraying your faith in her. You absorb your shock but you retain your faith in woman, in man, in humanity. And we must retain your faith in our ability to survive this war. This war will pass but we will remain. Faith is the antidote to fear. Not spiritual faith. Just good, warm, human faith.*

Now they were on open ground where the houses began and the road was better.

'We are back at Asaba,' the man Umunna said. 'We cannot leave the convoy, though.'

'What will you do?' Osime asked him.

'I will try to get back one way or another.'

'How?'

'I don't know. But I will keep my wife here.'

'I will come with you.'

'Do you really want to?'

'I must get back to my wife.'

'It wouldn't be wise,' the man said. 'Think about it. The Biafrans will be there.'

'Yes,' Osime agreed, the helplessness coming back. 'But will you take a message there for me?'

The woman began to cry again. The man Umunna looked at her and turned away.

The convoy turned into the grounds of the Midwest Hotel and the first jeeps stopped and the man Umunna brought his van to a halt by the road, clear of the other cars and the jeeps.

'You will give her my message then?' Osime asked as he stood on the road and gripped the man's outstretched hand. 'And you will be careful?'

'Yes.'

'And thank you both.'

'There is no need to thank us,' the man said. 'Your people were good to me. And now you are our in-law.'

The woman didn't say anything. She was wiping the tears from her face with her headtie.

Osime walked away from the van towards the jeeps that held the soldiers. He stopped by the first jeep and went round it to the other side where the sergeant stood and introduced himself and gave the man his card.

'I was with the convoy,' he said finally. 'Why did we stop?'

The sergeant examined the card and gave it back to him.

'We thought we saw more rebel soldiers in the bush.'

'But there were none?'

'Did you hear any shooting?'

'No.'

The sergeant turned away from him and walked to the back of the jeeps and spoke to the soldiers who sat inside it and in a little while, they came down from the jeep and stood together, the grenades they wore around their waists touching each other. The sergeant came back.

'Why did you abandon Nkesio and Oganza?' Osime asked again.

'Can I look at your card again?' the sergeant asked and Osime suddenly had an uneasy feeling in his stomach as his mind went to the stadium and the soldiers.

He brought out his identity card and handed it over again to the sergeant.

'Your card is not signed,' the sergeant said finally.

'Not signed?'

'Are you pretending you do not know?'

'The card is signed by the General Manager and the Editor-in-Chief.'

'How long have you been here?'

'One day.'

'And you were with the convoy?'

'Yes. I was . . .'

'How come?'

Osime tried to explain again. Why were these people always on the offensive? Why were they always so hostile?

'So your wife is a Nyanmiri,' the sergeant said.

'A Nigerian,' Osime said, the anger leaping to his chest and almost choking him.

'A Nyanmiri,' the sergeant repeated, spoiling for a fight.

You are a Nyanmiri, Osimi said in his mind.

'What?' He had seen Osime's lips move.

Osime did not say anything.

'You will come with us,' the sergeant said suddenly.

'Thank you,' Osime said. 'I will be glad to do just that.'

You bastard. Your pear is ripe. Eat it. Eat it and choke on it.

Chapter fourteen

The former St Barnabas College had been converted into a camp for the soldiers. You came into the camp through the road that ran between the football fields and stopped in front of the huge building that had held the library, the principal's office, the teachers' office, the assembly hall and the gymnasium. When you entered this building, there was a long narrow passage, the doors opened into the former offices of the principal and his deputy and the principal's secretary. All three rooms were large and were used by the officers of the division. On the left hand side, two doors opened into the school's former library and the teachers' office. The library books were on the floor now. Most of them had been destroyed or removed by the soldiers, first by the Biafran soldiers who used the pages of the books for wrapping cigars or toilet purposes and then by the Federal troops who continued where the Biafrans had left off. The former office of the teachers had contained several desks and chairs, but most of them had been removed and stood around the building. It was in this room that Osime Iyere had been questioned by the major and the officers in the morning.

At the end of the passage was the door that opened into the large assembly hall. You had to climb some steps before you came to the door and it opened into the raised part of the hall which served as the stage. You stood on the stage then and looked into the vast empty hall and at the end there were the wooden structures that served as the gymnasium. Many doors opened on each side into the assembly hall.

The road went round the assembly hall on both sides and walking either way, you could see the three long buildings that had been the classrooms. Further away, if you went by the right of the assembly hall, you saw first the church and then the large building that had housed the principal. The Commanding Officer of the Division lived there now.

You continued down the road that went away from the back of the large assembly hall and there were more fields and trees on both sides of the road until you came to the small ugly building that was the camp's electricity generating room. You went past it, and came to a small roundabout and the road branched left and right while another continued straight on to the first of the four buildings that had served as dormitories for the students. Each of the buildings was shaped like the letter E. The soldiers slept here now and each building took five hundred soldiers, not counting the five sergeants who slept in a small room attached to each wing that must have served as the store. Two other dormitories stood far away from the rest, surrounded by trees. One of these was used as the hospital while the other held the prisoners of war.

The first four buildings faced each other and in the middle was the large kitchen and dining hall where the soldiers had their meals. On each side of these dormitories, there was a three-bedroom house that had served as the housemasters' quarters when the school had been a school and there was no war. The army officers occupied these houses now. Behind three of the dormitories there were more fields and trees and houses. Some of these houses served as officers' quarters, others were used as stores, depots or simply offices. These houses stood at the very edge of the fields and behind them was a wall ending in a fence of wood and wire which ran round the camp on three sides except on the side that directly faced the highway. On this side of the camp there were six houses, two of which were quite large. They had housed the school's vice principal and the senior tutor. Now, one was the officers' mess while the others housed the officers.

Osime Iyere lay on the bed and covered his face with his hands. The beds were arranged in two straight rows, double decker beds. On either side of him, the soldiers were asleep in their uniforms and boots. There were no mattresses on the beds, only mats and pillows. The pillows had no pillow-slips and were brown from the sweat of past use and torn in many places so that the pieces of foam continually came out and had to be pushed back in. The pillows stank, the soldiers stank as they slept in their uniforms and boots. There was no water. The Biafran soldiers had destroyed the pipes before they left. They had dug up the pipes and twisted and broken them. They had also thrown grenades into the soakaway pits and blown up their concrete covers. The dormitories stank but the soldiers were always tired, so they slept.

Outside, he could hear the footfalls of the soldiers as they paced to and fro in the corridor, four of them keeping watch in this section of the building. They would be there for four hours and then four others would take over. When he had come here in the evening, he had looked around to see if he would find any of them. He had gone behind each of the buildings and then into the large dining hall and come out again and gone round the officers' quarters that stood one on each side of the dormitories. He hadn't seen any. Then he had gone to the edge of the fields, where the other houses stood, and he hadn't found any either. It was then that he had gone to the sergeant.

'There aren't any anti-aircraft guns here at all.'

'Yes, there are,' the man had said, looking out of his small window.

'I didn't see any.'

'They are there, one near the main building, half-way between it and the church under that almond tree. Then there are two more, one on each side of the C.O.'s quarters.'

'But these guns are of use only to the officers. What about the soldiers?'

'The mechanised units have their machine guns and tanks.'

'I am talking about *you*. What if you are attacked, suddenly? It happened in Benin just before I came. They went to the airport.'

'We heard about it.'

'Well, the same thing could happen here.'

'Impossible.'

'That was what they said in Benin. And yet see what happened.'

'That's our problem, journalist. We will take care of it. Anyway, we will teach you how to shoot tomorrow. That is, if you want to learn.'

'Thank you. I want to learn.'

'And we will give you a uniform.'

'Good. I appreciate that.'

'You will take my photograph?'

'Yes. Whenever you're ready.'

'Now?'

'No. Tomorrow morning. This place stinks. The smell is killing me.'

'The rebels did it. They are mean. Very mean.'

'I guess you have done the same thing somewhere else?'

The sergeant had looked at him then and smiled suddenly but had admitted nothing.

'What do you think of this war then?'

'We will win it.'

'Do you like it?'

The sergeant had turned away then and when he came back he asked, 'What did Sergeant Audu say your name was?'

'Osime Iyere. And he said you were Sergeant Kesh Kesh.'

'The sergeant is an intimate friend of mine.'

'That is why I came to your unit. He told me his unit would take some time reorganising. He lost many men.'

'Yes. He is lucky to be alive. They are in the mechanised battalion. But where did you meet him?'

'On the road from Oganza. He had been involved in an ambush near Nkesio.'

'Yes. And do you know the captain of their company was made a major this morning? "In recognition of his bravery," the citation said. The captain who ran away, who was driven away from the ambush. Audu got nothing. Audu who was trapped and had to fight his way out. The man who abandoned them got promoted but those who died, who fought were never even mentioned.'

'Yes,' Osime Iyere said. 'That is how it has always been. They always get the credit. Audu told me. This is a bitter spiteful war.' He paused and then asked again, 'Do you like it?'

'Like it? I'm a professional soldier. I was in Kaduna when the war broke out. I was already in the army. I did not come to the war for a job as many of the soldiers did. I already had a job.'

'Then what happened?'

'I went first to the Nsukka sector. When the rebels couldn't kill me there, they moved me to the Port Harcourt sector. But that wasn't enough. I got transferred to the Midwest. We came in from Okene and then entered Auchi. And while some went towards Benin, we came through Agbor. The rebels are yet to kill me. But tell me, why didn't you stay with your kind, with the other journalists? Why did you ask for a special dispensation from the Major to stay here?'

'I like it better here.'

'Then don't complain about the stench, about the smell.'

'I won't, not any more.'

'Well then, journalist. You don't mind if I call you journalist?'

'No.'

'Good. Well then, do you like being a journalist?'

'Yes. But I don't touch certain kinds of stories.'

'There is only one kind of war,' Sergeant Kesh Kesh said. 'There is only one kind of war and in it, you either kill the enemy or you let him kill you. You cannot take chances in a war. You cannot afford to.'

No, Osime said to himself now. *There are different kinds of wars. A civil war is different from a war between two countries and there are even different kinds of civil wars. You need to examine the idea behind a war. This war has no idea, only greed behind it. The unity of the country was not threatened until the politicians and their partners in corruption allowed their greed to run riot. Didn't you hear what the man Umunna said? 'Your people were good to me.' We never had any quarrel with the Ibos, nor did the Ibos have any quarrel with the Hausas or Yorubas until the politicians and generals allowed their lust for power and greed for profit to run riot.*

That is why the war has no blood in its veins. It is dizzy, it sags, it does not provoke, it does not excite. It has no spirit, no romance. There is nothing in it for a man or woman to die for. Talk about the war in Zimbabwe or in Vietnam! Talk about the Russian civil war, talk about the resistance of the Binis against the whites, talk about Jaja of Opobo and you have wars with ideas behind them, wars with romance in them, wars worth fighting in, worth dying in. Not this war. Certainly not this dull monotonous war that began with and is based on the greed of a few individuals.

He felt bitter and resentful but helpless. He remembered feeling this way once before. It was before the war. He had been sent to investigate why the government wanted to take the hotels back from the Lebanese managers. First he went to the official in the Ministry. 'They pay us rent worth five thousand pounds a year,' the official had disclosed. 'They make on average from the hotels a hundred and fifty thousand pounds a month. When you deduct their expenses, they make a net profit of one hundred and twenty thousand pounds a month. Multiply that by twelve and you have close to one and a half million pounds a year.'

'And they pay you only five thousand pounds a year?'

'Yes.'

'Who negotiated the agreement?'

The official in the ministry had refused to answer any further questions. So he had gone to the state hotels board and discussed with the chairman of the board. 'This matter was before the state executive council for two years,' the chairman had confirmed. 'Every time it came up, some ministers would insist that the management of the hotels remain in foreign hands while others would support our cause. The split made it impossible for the executive to reach a decision on the matter until last month, when the new minister for industry was appointed. He produced evidence to show that the ministers revealed that those who were opposed were in the pay of the Lebanese. One of the ministers had a permanent room in one of the hotels to which he frequently took his concubines and once, he received a cash payment of twenty thousand pounds from the Lebanese.'

'I don't believe it!' said Osime.

'Oh yes, it is true. Last year, our board made an offer to the government. We wanted to take over the hotels and pay a monthly rent, I repeat a monthly rent, of twenty thousand pounds to the government. The proposal was rejected out of hand.'

'This is unbelieveable!'

'And that's not the end of the matter. The Lebanese man at the top says in his returns that every three months he sends two Nigerian members of staff for training overseas. We investigated this claim. We found out that it is true that two Nigerians are sent to London every three months. But they don't go there for any training. The Lebanese man at the top has a disabled mother whom he keeps in London. The Nigerians go there as servants to her. The Lebanese himself is building a multi-million pound hotel in London, building it out of the proceeds from our hotels.'

'So where do you go from here?'

The chairman shrugged. 'Actually nowhere. The case remains indefinitely adjourned. The minister himself has recently become reluctant. Some say he has been bought as well. And we have no direct access to the chief executive except through the minister. The chief executive is aware of the matter but we are not sure of his position. They are all being bought and sold, like yams at a bazaar. There is nothing we can do.'

Osime came back to the office, seething with rage. He was so angry that he got the story out in two hours and wanted to run it straightaway. Then the editor-in-chief saw it and called him to his office and then they both went to see the General Manager. As soon as the General Manager saw the name of the Lebanese he shook his head.

'No. We can't use this story,' he said.

'But the story is true!' Osime argued.

'I don't care whether it is true or not,' he replied. 'Kill it. And in future, I want to read everything you write before we publish it.'

Osime threatened to resign and the editor-in-chief laughed at him. 'The general manager is a political appointee,' he said. 'Today he is here, tomorrow he is gone. We will wait.'

So they waited but he did not leave until March, two months after the coup, two years later and by then, the military were in power and went straight into making their own arrangements with the businessmen. Osime's story was forgotten. But he never forgot about it nor the bitterness and helplessness either.

The trouble is that we are afraid to speak the truth lest those whom our truth offends tear out our tongues. We get so frightened that when we are told that we are at war, that we must sacrifice our lives for the war, we do not ask, whose war? Which war? Why war? We let the Lebanese go on cutting our throats in our own country, even supplying them with the scalpels. We do not ask the politicians to stop helping the Lebanese to cut our throats, we do not tell the generals that we will not take part in their wars because we are afraid. We are so terrified that we take the knives that they hand over to us and begin, in our half sleep and terror, to slaughter each other.

And that is why I am the first recruit of the third army. I am not going to sleep any more. It is time the soldiers understood that this is not their war, that they are fighting the wrong enemy. The generals and the politicians and the businessmen are their enemies in life as in death, in war as in peace. These are the people they should be fighting, not the Ibo farmers or the Ibo workers.

Sergeant Kesh Kesh wondered why I did not go with the other journalists. The fact is that in the short time that I was with them, I felt alienated from them. All they wanted was news about women and all they talked about was women. There are beautiful women at Asaba, they all said. Didn't I want to come out to meet them? The women were willing. They fully recognised that they were a conquered people and that we were their conquerors. What rubbish! What utter, stupid, indescribable rubbish! A people are never conquered. Defeated yes, but never conquered. Asaba people conquered? Rubbish. It was rubbish because it asked the wrong questions. The journalists ought to be asking questions about the war, not asking the generals' questions. No wonder that in all their dispatches there is nothing but news of conquerors conquering territories. It was then that I decided I would rather live with one of the units than with people of my own kind. I felt alone, completely alone there.

I still feel alone now. What I am involved in is not a matter for individuals. What I am involved in is a matter for a large group of people, for the people as a whole. Most probably then, I will get shot. But then, you only live once. I have only one life and only one death to claim it.

He looked at the green luminous dials on his watch. Nearly four o'clock, and he hadn't closed his eyes once. What was Ndudi doing now? Was she asleep? And the Biafran soldiers? Had they touched her? She would have been expecting him.

And that's another thing. You spend all your life groping in the darkness and as you emerge at the end of the tunnel the light is so strong it blinds you. So you go back to the darkness, perpetual darkness. We never ever have enough energy left to run the most important race. I could suffocate now in my love and she would not even be aware of it. Because my love is useless unless she takes part in it. If I love her and she knows it but does not eperience it and share it, then my love is useless to her and to me. I would be like the plant that flowered in the desert or in the darkness. Nobody saw it. Love has meaning only when it is shared, only when another takes part in it.

He turned on his side and rested his head on his hand. He really felt lonely now. He could still hear the footfalls of the sentry and inside of the dormitory, several soldiers were snoring. They snored and made a great noise and then there were his own thoughts and then there was the smell from the sweat of the sleeping soldiers and from the open soakaway pits at the back of the buildings to keep him company, and keep him from sleeping.

He fell asleep once and dreamed of Ndudi. She was holding the red suitcase and she was standing in front of their building, tall and elegant and beautiful, and he went to her and smiled at her but she turned her face away and when he wanted to help her with her suitcase she refused, and then Mr Ohiali came out of the house and he was frowning and in his hand he held a cutlass. Osime Iyere turned quickly away from the house and behind him he could hear Ndudi's voice saying 'Don't come back! Don't ever come back!' He awoke then and looked at his watch and found out that he had been asleep only half an hour. He did not attempt to sleep any more.

And so the Biafran soldiers had regained Ogwashi-Uku, he had been told by the other journalists. The Biafran soldiers operating in the Kwale area had crossed over to the three Ukus and taken them over. The fighting had been fierce and many soldiers had died. And that was why the Federal troops had decided to abandon Nkesio and Oganza. They wanted to concentrate their forces in the coming attempt to regain the lost areas. Perhaps that attempt would be made today.

Chapter fifteen

Now it was morning and although he had been expecting them, the sirens still startled him. The soldiers jumped out of their beds and dashed for their guns and gunbelts in the same movement. There was a fever of movement, of activity, and in less than five minutes, the dormitory was empty. Only the rucksacks remained, hanging from the bedposts or lying on the floor near the foot of the beds. The rucksacks and the grenades.

Sergeant Kesh Kesh met him on his way out.

'Well, journalist? Did you sleep well?'

'No. I didn't sleep at all.'

'You don't like the conditions then? You want to return to your kind?'

'No. It's not that. I kept thinking. I couldn't sleep.'

Sergeant Kesh Kesh slapped him on the back and his dark face shook with laughter. 'I understand,' he said finally and seriously. 'Many nights I lie awake thinking.'

'What about?'

'The war. My wife, children, father, mother. The soldiers . . . But come. Remember my photograph? We will take it this morning.'

'Yes. I dreamt about that too.'

'You dreamt about it? Journalist, you are a funny one and I think I like you. Come on. I will introduce you to the other soldiers in the section. You will remember your section and then your company and battalion. Forget about everything else. Just remember those and Sergeant Kesh Kesh and you will be all right.'

Sergeant Kesh Kesh was a large man, tall and broad-shouldered and his face was dark but had an open quality. The eyes were frank and the nose was large. 'You will stay with me,' Sergeant Kesh Kesh said. 'You will not perform the exercises. You will stay with me and afterwards the corporal will teach you how to shoot.'

They went outside. It was still dark. He looked at his wristwatch. It was a quarter to six. The drill went on for an hour. When it was over Sergeant Kesh Kesh came back and led him towards a group of soldiers.

'You are going to be with this section all the time and it is good that you know them and they know you. How long do you intend to stay?'

'Until you retake Oganza.'

'Your wife then?'

'Yes.'

'Sometimes I wish I could go back too.'

'That's natural.'

'No, sometimes I really want to quit. I have been at the front three years now without leave, without anything.' Osime didn't say anything. 'You think this war will end?'

'Yes. It has to. The longest war in history lasted one hundred years.'

'My God,' Sergeant Kesh Kesh laughed. 'Are you saying my children, grandchildren and great-grandchildren may take part in this war?'

'And your great-great-grandchildren, unless of course . . .' He let the words hang in the air.

'Unless what? Listen, journalist, when you speak to me you must always say everything before you stop.' He slapped Osime on the back.

'Unless the soldiers on both sides are fed up first. If the soldiers get fed up and simply go home there will be no war.'

'But that is not practicable! This war has to be fought and lost or won.'

'Who said so? Did you, sergeant, start this war?'

'No. But to keep Nigeria one is . . .'

'Yes. Sergeant Audu said the same thing.'

'So you see, journalist, there is nothing we can do. Unless of course . . .'

'Unless what?'

Sergeant Kesh Kesh looked at him and laughed, 'See, I caught you.'

Osime Iyere laughed too and said, 'Listen, sergeant, when you speak to me . . .'

'I will always say everything,' Sergeant Kesh Kesh completed if for him.

They came to the group of soldiers and Sergeant Kesh Kesh pushed him in front of one of the soldiers who had a bar on each of his shoulders.

'Corporal Kolawole here is the section commander,' Sergeant

who were walking ahead of him looked at each other
ghed. 'You didn't do anything wrong,' he spoke for

t make any mistake. You are all right by us. Isn't that

e stocky Patrick said.
e man Obilu agreed.
third man said until all the eight of them had said it.
he soldier Patani asked. 'I told you you're all right by
t worry. We're your friends, not your enemies.'
ou bring a camera?' another of the soldiers, whose name
kobi, asked.
, I brought a camera.'
l you take our photographs then?' the soldier Olu asked.
our photographs and help us send them away?'
es. After you have taught me how to shoot.'
ee,' Olu said, flinging out his arms, 'I hand over to you all
knowledge about shooting.'
I do the same,' Kokobi said.
'Well?' Patani asked. 'You now know how to shoot. May we take
e photographs?'
'Yes,' Osime said, laughing. 'Only I left my camera in the
dormitory.'

'You left your camera in the dorm?'

'Yes. Anything wrong?'

'Oh yes. You may as well say goodbye to it. There's a lot of stealing going on in the dorms. A camera! That's good money.'

'Then you'd better wait.'

'What? We have to teach you how to shoot.'

'Later.'

Osime Iyere hurried back towards the dormitory and went straight to the bed on which he had slept. The camera wasn't there. He went into Sergeant Kesh Kesh's office and he was there eating from the aluminium plates.

'You shouldn't have left your bag out there,' Kesh Kesh said. 'You are lucky I got back to the dormitory before the soldiers did. It's there, in the corner. I kept it for you.'

'Thank you very much. You've saved my life.'

'Is the camera that important?'

'Yes. You'll see what I mean when you see your photographs.'

Kesh Kesh introduced Kolawole. 'He will teach you how to dismantle and then assemble the gun. He will teach you how to shoot — by four o'clock this evening.'

'Yes,' the corporal said without looking at Osime Iyere.

Osime Iyere held out his hand to the corporal and the corporal took it and squeezed it very hard, while looking Osime in the face. *I will not give you the pleasure of seeing my pain*, Osime told himself, and smiled into the eyes of the man and although he could not understand the reason for it, he could see hostility plainly written there.

'The corporal will introduce you to the men.' Sergeant Kesh Kesh said and went away.

Osime shook hands with each man as he was introduced.

'And so,' Corporal Kolawole announced. 'We now have a spy in the section whom we have to teach how to shoot. He says he is a journalist.'

Osime Iyere didn't say anything.

'Private Patani!'

'Yes, sir.'

'Give him your guitar.'

Patani came over, slipped the cord that held the gun in place from his shoulder and passed the Kalashnikov to Osime.

'And remember, spy, that the gun is loaded,' the corporal warned him. *I ought to take a stand now*, Osime told himself. *I must take a stand before this man succeeds in making me out to be a spy.*

'I am not a spy, corporal,' he said now. 'You heard what Sergeant Kesh Kesh said. I am a journalist.'

'Journalist, eh? Journalist, spy? What's the difference?'

'A great difference, corporal,' Osime said quietly. 'When you use the word spy, you insult me. When you say journalist, you tell everybody what I am. You may call me by my name, my professional name, corporal, but don't insult me.'

'Did you hear that, boys? He's a spy but he wants to be called journalist!' The soldiers stood quietly and listened but they didn't say anything.

If I hit him, Osime thought, *then he will have an excuse for shooting me. This man wants an excuse to kill. The war is the great excuse but that is not enough for this corporal. He still wants other, personal, excuses and I will not give him any. I will not be provoked. This man had an ulcer before I came here and by the time I am gone, he will still have the ulcer. He's not going to feed me to it. I will not be provoked, not by this man.*

'And when you get back,' the corporal continued now, 'tell Sergeant Kesh Kesh that I called you a spy. Okay. Tell him that I say you are not a journalist but a spy. Tell him and then see what happens.'

I will not be provoked, Osime Iyere said to himself. 'You will teach me how to shoot then?' he said aloud, and he thought he saw the light come into the eyes of the soldiers. But he wasn't sure because Corporal Kolawole was looking at them too.

'Teach you how to shoot? Of course, of course. We won't give them an excuse to say we do not know our duty. Now watch.'

Corporal Kolawole slipped the cord that held the gun from his shoulders and in the same movement knelt down on the grass. Osime Iyere watched him as first, he dismantled the gun and then reassembled it. The speed of the man was frightening.

'See, journalist?' Corporal Kolawole said, standing up. 'We know our business here and if it comes to shooting, we can do even better.'

Osime Iyere looked at the faces of the soldiers and he could see the admiration and respect in their eyes. He could see their confidence in the way they carried the guns and stood on the grass. He looked at the corporal and in spite of himself, he felt a respect for the man.

'I could never do it as fast as that,' he admitted 'but I can try. How does it work?'

'Two ways,' the corporal boasted, forgetting his hostility. 'The single shots and the automatic shots. When you want the automatic, you do it this way,' and Osime watched him as he placed the front end of the change lever in a central position. 'When you want the single shot, you move it this way,' the corporal said and he switched the change lever from its central position downwards so that it was fully depressed. 'Of course, if you do not want any shot at all, then you play the guitar like this,' and this time the Corporal pushed the front end of the change lever to the top position. 'The trigger is locked now,' the Corporal said and pointed the gun at Osime Iyere and pressed the trigger and Osime's heart missed a beat. The gun did not fire.

'All right,' Osime said, the fear going away from his eyes but still remaining in his voice. 'I will try it,' and he repeated the movements that the corporal had just demonstrated before him. 'Can I shoot?'

'No!' the corporal said o…
until Patani has taught h…
range. Then you may sho…
is a different business from f…
that shooting a gun is differen…
with women. There is no prosti…
fried eggs here, nor of butter …
requires intelligence, intelligence an…
to fire this gun and kill a moving m…
your women. But then I do not expe…
you to try to understand this guitar and…
to your prostitutes. I expect you to lea…
had returned.

But he has stopped using the word spy, Osim…
say anything. Corporal Kolawole walked a…

'And now,' Patani said, 'if you will follow…
will go to the north side of the camp and pract…
Remember, you must know how to shoot and s…
o'clock. The Sergeant said four o'clock but with …
by two o'clock or earlier. What have you got to sa…

This man uses the word journalist without spite, Osime…
*corporal spits it out like the early morning saliva that you wa…
your mouth. It smells and you spit it out. But this man says it …
bitterness.*

'I want to know,' he said now to the man Patani, 'and the…
I know the better.'

'That's the attitude,' the man Patani said. 'That is the co…
attitude.'

And Osime Iyere began hesitantly, 'Can you tell me why th…
corporal was so bitter?'

'Bitter?' the short stocky soldier, Patrick, asked. 'He wasn't bitter.'

'He was just telling you the truth, that's all,' Patani said and Osime Iyere realised that he had made a mistake. They thought he was asking them to tell on their comrade. He tried again.

'What did I do wrong then?' he asked.

'Do wrong?' another of the soldiers asked and he turned and he saw that it was the tall, fair-complexioned Obilu.

'Yes,' Osime persisted. 'I must have said something that was wrong or offensive or something. I must have made a mistake.'

'Did you learn to shoot then?'

'No. I remembered the camera. I came back for it. I'll go back now.'

'There's no hurry. How did you make out with the corporal?'

'He is very good with the gun.'

'Did he break your fingers?'

'My fingers?'

'Yes. I saw it when he took your hand.'

'Oh. It was nothing.'

'Kolawole is a good man.'

'I just said that.'

'I mean, he was much better than he is now. You know what happens. If you don't get killed first, then the war has a way of getting to you.'

'I understand.'

'Oh come on,' Sergeant Kesh Kesh said rather shortly. 'To hell with all that understanding, with all that politeness. Kolawole, Audu and I all enlisted in the army at the same time. Last year, the man was a sergeant, he got the rank before us but he got reduced in rank.'

'Why?'

'He disagreed with the major on matters of procedure in front of the men. The Commanding Officer said it was bad for morale. So the sergeant got punished. We lost three hundred men in that battle and many more were injured on account of following the major's procedures.'

Osime Iyere didn't say anything and Sergeant Kesh Kesh stopped eating and shook his head. 'Why don't you say something?'

Osime shrugged his shoulders. 'What can I say?'

'All right' Sergeant Kesh Kesh said angrily. 'The major was made a Lieutenant Colonel this year. That's the Nigerian army for you.'

'Perhaps the major did some other things between last year and this year.'

'Perhaps,' Kesh Kesh agreed. 'But that doesn't solve Kolawole's problem. A man gets reduced in rank, a very good and capable man at that, and he becomes bitter.'

'But he is taking it out on the wrong people.'

'There is nothing he can do to the officers. He carries his grudge like an ulcer but there is nothing he can do about it. The lieutenant colonel is in charge of administration now, doesn't even go to the front any more.'

'That still doesn't solve the corporal's problem.'

'Yes. But the man has no spirit left for the war. He loves the war but he has no spirit left for it. It is a terrible position to be in.'

'Yes. I understand now, perhaps better than I did before but I always make allowances.'

'And another thing,' Sergeant Kesh Kesh said, pushing his food away, 'the meat is tough, badly cooked. Perhaps it is dog meat. It is tough and the blood still comes from it. I mean . . .' He stood up. 'I wasn't talking about the meat. Oh hell,' he fumed. The new Commanding Officer has come. That means we may start the push for the three Ukus tomorrow morning or even this evening. He has called a meeting for this morning. He can't wait until he has found his feet. Our battalion commanders are meeting him at eight this morning and then he is going to address us all after that meeting. He is going to tell us that we must be up and moving tonight.'

'Who is he?' Osime asked.

'A Brigadier. Brigadier Otunshi.'

'Brigadier Olu Otunshi?'

'Yes . . . The very man. Do you know him?'

'No. But I have heard about him.'

'A real bastard,' Sergeant Kesh Kesh said. 'We were together in Port Harcourt. He sends out his troops on the eve of pay day. A real slave-driver. A real, mean bastard. But you'll find out if you stay here long enough. You'll come to understand what I mean.'

'Yes,' Osime nodded, standing up. 'I'll certainly find out.'

Chapter sixteen

There must have been at least two thousand soldiers gathered in the field in front of the big assembly hall. When Osime Iyere saw the large number of soldiers he prayed silently that the Biafran planes would not come. Every now and then, he looked up at the sky and it was blue and clear, even behind the trees, except low down on the horizon where both earth and sky touched. Here there were the cumulus clouds and they were red and golden brown now from the sun.

They would be chicken to the hawks, he thought. *You only needed one of those small planes, like the ones that came to the airport at Benin and everything here would be finished. Even that anti-aircraft gun would be useless,* he thought as he looked at the mount of the gun and saw the four soldiers there. *The soldiers will take cover in the church. They will abandon the gun. If they get the chance.* He felt naked, naked and defenceless as he had never felt before.

Brigadier Otunshi came at twenty-three minutes to nine. He timed it to the minute because he kept looking from the sky to his wristwatch and then back to the trees and the sky.

Brigadier Otunshi stayed ten feet away from the first line of soldiers. Behind him there were the captains and the majors and the lieutenant colonels and the colonels of the army. They all stood behind him, their hands holding the short staffs behind their backs. Brigadier Otunshi was a tall, heavily built man, fair in complexion. *Perhaps that is why Salome went with him*, Osime Iyere thought. The man was tall and bulky but imposing and handsome. He saw the dark eyebrows, the short moustache, the dark brown eyes, and he was impressed. Yes, he understood now, why Salome had gone with him. He was handsome and he had the power and money, too. *But she says she does not love him, that she always loved me. That's rubbish. How can you love somebody and desert him? Ndudi is different. She had every reason to leave but she stayed. That is love. Love is staying when you have every reason to go away.*

Brigadier Otunshi used the loudspeakers and his speech was over before it had begun. To win the war, he said, was a task that must be accomplished and every soldier had a duty to fight for his country when it was threatened either by external or internal enemies. The internal enemies were the rebels, they caused the war. They were greedy and inhuman and atrocious in their treatment of people. Soldiers who did not have a stomach for the war could go home, although as everybody knew deserters were liable to be executed when caught. There must be discipline in the army, he told them. Complete discipline and dedication and loyalty. The alternative would be chaos and anarchy, the qualities of the rebel army whom they were going to drive out from the three Ukus immediately; when, the battalion commanders would tell them. The soldiers must be in a continuous state of readiness.

'I told you the man was mean,' Sergeant Kesh Kesh said as they went back to the dormitory. 'You'll see, we'll be on the move this evening.'

'Dedicated to duty then,' Osime said.

'Dedicated? You must be joking. You'll see. Are you going to the party?'

'I'm not sure.'

'You must be there. He said all journalists, that means you must be there.'

'All right then. I will be there.'

'You won't forget about us? You'll bring us some of the whisky?'

'You want some of the whisky?'

'Yes, why not? The soldiers may not drink but the officers can get drunk.'

Osime Iyere did not say anything.

'And be careful of his wife.'

'His wife?'

'The Brigadier has the most beautiful wife in the Nigerian army, and he treats her like a queen. He shot a major in Port Harcourt just for looking at her. He shot the major in the eye with his pistol.'

'My God!'

'The Brigadier is the most jealous husband in the Nigerian army. So don't look at her when you get there.'

'What happened to the major?'

'He was lucky. He only lost one eye. And Otunshi was a brigade commander then. He wasn't a Brigadier, just a colonel.'

'You think his wife will be there?'

'Yes, she'll be there. Asaba is a captured and consolidated territory. That means it is safe.'

'What happened to Murtala?'

'He went to Lagos.'

'How was he?'

'An excellent officer. A fine soldier. Very dedicated and honest. Oh yes, one of the very best. But you understand the politics of this war.'

'Politics?'

'Yes. If you stay here long enough, you will see it.'

'I will stay long enough to see Oganza recaptured.'

'Then let that be next year.'

'Otunshi didn't say that.'

'Let that be at the end of the war.'

'You do not wish me well then? We are no longer friends?'

'God forbid,' Sergeant Kesh Kesh exclaimed. 'I want the war to end today. I want Oganza to be taken today. I want you to stay journalist.'

'Perhaps I will go and see your family when I get out of here.'

'You will go to Kesh Kesh?'

'Yes. I will go there and tell them that you are an excellent soldier.'

'You will go to Kesh Kesh and do that?'

'Yes and even more.'

'Then you are my friend, journalist, and you will see how they will receive you, like a king. My family is good. My wife Samantha, we got married three years before the war. Two boys. That's what we have. Two beautiful boys. And Kesh Kesh! Oh my God! Don't say it.'

They came to the building and entered it and went through the dormitory between the two rows of beds until they came to the door that opened into the small room where the sergeant slept and Sergeant Kesh Kesh opened the door and they went in. Sergeant Kesh Kesh sat on the bed and removed his combat helmet and held his face between his hands. Osime Iyere sat on the chair that stood away from the small table.

'Look,' Sergeant Kesh Kesh began, still holding his face in the broad of his hands, 'two weeks ago I was due for leave. We had been here for a week and I finally persuaded them to give me leave. And do you know what happened?'

Osime Iyere shook his head. Sergeant Kesh Kesh did not see him shake his head but lifted his head away from the broad of his palm, his eyes staring at the white of the ceiling now warped brown by the leaking roof and the rain.

'My papers were signed by the officer,' Sergeant Kesh Kesh began again in a small voice. 'Genuine papers and I thought of my children and had big dreams. I thought I would stop over in Benin and do a little shopping. I went on the morning that my leave began. But I only got as far as Agbor.'

'What happened?'

'You must have come across them on your way here, journalist. They are everywhere, the military police. They told me to come down from the jeep and I did and I gave them my papers and they looked at them and one of them shook his head and said no, I couldn't continue. It always begins with one of them shaking his head. This one is short and dark and he shakes his head and says no, the papers do not appear genuine. I cannot continue. I look at him and I try to explain. The papers are genuine. Can't he see the signature of Colonel Odah? Can't he see the signature of the major? The papers are genuine. I haven't been on leave for three years now, since the war began.

'The short, dark, small man does not change his mind. He shakes his head and says the papers are fake, the signatures are forged. Perhaps I am a deserter. At this time, I am mad enough to shoot him but I am not armed. You leave your arms behind when you are going on leave unless of course, you are a senior officer.

'The military police held me for almost seven hours. I was hungry. I was frustrated but there was nothing I could do. There were five of them, each of them armed and ready to kill. There were about seven of us, all of us unarmed. Around four o'clock in the evening a jeep came and they ordered us into the jeep, they took us in the jeep to the Red Sector.'

'The Red Sector?'

'Yes, that is the Kwale Area. It is the most dangerous front in this war. You have the water and the tall grass and the rebel soldiers. You do not see the Biafrans but they see you. They operate in small groups of three or five. You go after them and invariably you do not come back. Either the rebels get you or the water gets you. They sent me to the Red Sector and each time we went out I was lucky to come back alive. Sometimes you are in a boat and they come from under the boat and overturn it and you are in the water and the next thing they have bayonetted you and escaped. If you are still alive by the time the crocodiles come, they complete the work.

Many times you would hear the cry of the soldiers, you would hear them screaming and you would close your ears but the cry would continue in your own soul. You would be thinking then only of escape.'

'It must have been terrible.'

'Yes. It was terrible. It was awful. Every time the soldiers went out, they always wrote letters and left them behind. They were not sure they would come back.'

'How did you get away from there then?'

'I escaped,' Sergeant Kesh Kesh said with dignity from the bed.

'I spent one week there and then I escaped. I left them and came back here. It was dangerous but I made it. When I got back, I went and made a report but up till now nothing has happened. Do you know what the man said, the first time I told him?'

Osime Iyere shook his head where he sat on the chair.

'The man said I should be happy that I made it back here. He said he thought it was a useful experience!'

'He actually said that?'

'Why should I lie to you, journalist? The man said there were so many deserters these days the Military Police could not take any chances.'

'I will go to Kesh Kesh,' Osime promised.

'You will be my brother,' Sergeant Kesh Kesh said and got up from the bed and wiped his eyes and Osime looked away.

There was a knock on the door and the man Kolawole came into the small room.

'The major wants to see you,' Corporal Kolawole informed him.

'The major?'

'Yes. The others have just gone there.'

'Then we must be getting ready to take off,' Sergeant Kesh Kesh said.

'They will not even wait until we get paid. Six days to pay day and we must be on the move.'

'The raking units are pulling out,' Corporal Kolawole said.

'Yes. That's the Brigadier's style. See you then, journalist. And remember the whisky in case you go to the party and come back to find us still here.'

'I will go with you on the road.'

'No, journalist. You will come only after we have taken the town. You must be alive to go to Kesh Kesh. Remember?'

'I will have nothing to do here,' Osime said regretfully.

'There are the prostitutes,' Corporal Kolawole suggested with spite.

'They will be waiting for you, corporal,' Osime Iyere flung back. 'That is, if you come back.'

Corporal Kolawole laughed and Osime was surprised. 'Sure I will be back, journalist,' he promised. 'But not for the prostitutes. To claim my medals.'

'Remember, Kola,' Sergeant Kesh Kesh said as he went out, 'the journalist must know how to shoot today. Before we leave,' he corrected himself.

They went out of the small room and Osime Iyere debated between going to the mess and going to see the Biafran prisoners of war in the building that stood next to the one they used as the hospital.

'You will come with me,' the man Kolawole said, making up his mind for him. 'You will come with me if you are not afraid to see how we shoot. If you have no more business with the whores.'

Osime Iyere did not say anything but followed the man. The soldiers were sitting on their beds in a corner of the dormitory.

'So you are back, journalist,' they all said and he nodded his head and smiled.

'What now?' he asked. He carried his camera with him this time.

'We have the business of the shooting to finish first.'

'No,' Osime disagreed. 'We have the business of the photographs to finish first.'

'Then what are we waiting for?' the man Patani asked and looked at Corporal Kolawole.

'I will take the corporal's photograph as well,' Osime Iyere offered.

'I don't like photographs. No . . .'

'Oh come on, corporal,' Patani urged him.

'The journalist is all right,' the soldier Olu said in Yoruba.

He took their photographs one by one and after each take, he wrote down the name of the soldier against the number of the take. Corporal Kolawole refused to come.

'What do you think of the war then?' he asked them all.

'We will win the war,' Olu boasted.

'We will teach the rebels a lesson,' Kokobi promised.

'What kind of lesson?'

'A severe lesson. We will kill them all.'

'Why?'

'Listen, journalist,' the short stocky Patrick began but Patani interrupted him.

'Journalist, in a war like this, those who caused it are the rebels. You heard what the Brigadier said. They are the internal enemies. They want to break up our country.'

'You really think so?'

'What do you mean?' asked another soldier, the very quiet one. Osime faced him directly and tried to remember his name. Ituah, he remembered.

'What I mean, Ituah, is that you have to be really sure that they caused this war.'

'Of course they did,' Patrick insisted.

'Who are they?' Ituah asked on his behalf.

'Let the man finish,' Patrick demanded.

'I mean that there are different categories of rebels. Surely you do not mean that the Ibo soldier who carries the gun is as big as Ojukwu? Surely, Ojukwu is the biggest Biafran?'

'Yes,' Patani agreed. 'But they are all rebels.'

'Just as you are all Federal soldiers. But some people give you orders. You carry out orders. You are told to move and you move. You are told to stop and you stop.'

'What does that mean?'

'I will tell you,' Osime Iyere said carefully. 'Yesterday, I met an Ibo man who had been a trader in my village. He told me that the people in my village were very good to him before the war.'

'Yes, we had many Ibos in Kafanchan,' another of the soldiers, Musa admitted. 'We were very friendly.'

'So you see what I mean then,' Osime Iyere pointed out to them. 'You were all friends and brothers and sisters until this war came. You ate together and played together. And then you wake up one morning and you are told that the Ibo man is now your enemy and a rebel. The Ibo man also wakes up and he is told that the Hausa man, the Yoruba man, the Midwesterner is his enemy. The Ibo man is told that you are his enemy. You are told to take up arms to kill each other. But who is the Ibo man? The truth is that the Ibo rebel soldier was a trader before the war. Or perhaps he was a student or a farmer or a worker. Perhaps he had no job before this war, perhaps he was unemployed before this war.'

'I had no job,' Patrick confessed. 'I joined the army because I had no job. We were trained for three weeks and then sent out.'

'And I had no job either,' Olu admitted.

'Me to,' Kokobi said.

'So you see, the Federal soldiers who the Ibo rebel soldiers see as their enemies are people like themselves. The Federal soldiers were workers before this war came, workers or farmers or students or traders or simply unemployed. And so were the Ibo soldiers. Now can't you see something wrong there?'

'Yes, I can,' Patani said.

'There is certainly something wrong there,' Olu said.

'But if the rebel soldiers are not our enemies, then who are our enemies?' Obilu asked. 'Surely we have to fight somebody? Surely we have to fight the real enemy?'

'And who is the real enemy?' Kokobi asked.

'Those who caused this war are the real enemies,' Osime continued. 'I said earlier that you were told one morning that Ibo workers and farmers and jobless had become your enemies. The question is, who told you this?'

'The head of state, of course.'

Osime smiled. 'The head of state is a general and when he makes an announcement, he sits in council with other generals and brigadiers and colonels and majors in the army. These are the real enemies and it does not matter whether they are in the Nigerian or in the Biafran army. The real enemy are the top army officers, they caused this war, they caused the war out of their greed for power and money.'

'No,' Obilu disagreed. 'The pogroms in the North started this war.'

'Rubbish!' the soldier Musa said heatedly. 'Ojukwu started the war when he announced a Biafran republic.'

'It was Aburi, the breakdown of the agreement reached at Aburi, that caused this war,' Patani told them, handing a gun to Osime Iyere.

'Listen, listen,' Ituah admonished them, 'Let the journalist finish.'

'Yes, I will finish it,' Osime promised and pressed the trigger of the gun and it shook him although he had knelt on the grass to fire it. They all looked at the faraway wall. There were no marks on it.

'You need a steady hand,' Patani told him and Osime put the gun down on the grass at his feet and stood up.

'As I was saying,' he began again, 'why don't you ask yourselves why there was no killing of the Ibos in the North five years ago? Why did it happen four years ago? After all, as Musa says, the Ibos had lived in the North for many many years and the Hausas had done the same in the East. Yet there were no pogroms then. Why?'

'The coups,' Ituah offered.

'The coups are not enough. The point is that certain people in high running positions used the ordinary people against each other for their selfish ends. The Ibo workers or farmers did not cause the coups. You did not cause the coups. This is what happens. First of all, those in positions of power abuse the positions because of their greed. They are so greedy that others of their kind who are not in a position to satisfy their own greed get jealous and angry and finally desperate. They want the positions of power for themselves. But those currently chopping don't want to leave. So each side comes down to you, the people, and says the other side does not want your progress. They are wicked and plotting to exterminate you. You must kill them before they kill you. That's how the trouble starts. Those of us who know nothing then get dragged in. They use us to fight each other. The war did not start because of the pogrom. The pogrom was directly engineered by those who ruled us. They incited us to kill each other. And where are they now? Either giving the orders or selling food and weapons to the armies to make profits. The generals, the politicians and the businessmen are your real enemies. The generals and the traditional rulers, the church leaders who prayed for each group of rulers are the enemies and when we are dead, or tired of killing each other, then they will come back. They will come back strengthened from the war. One side will win of course. But always it will be a temporary victory because new members of their kind will emerge after the war and will want to satisfy their greed. Then there will be another war.'

'Another war?'

'Yes. This is simply the first of many because the greed of the ruling class knows no limits.'

'And how do we get rid of it then, this greed?'

'You get rid of the greed by getting rid of the ruling class, the generals and politicians and businessmen and traditional rulers and church leaders and professors. You do that and then we can start afresh with new rulers. I tell you that the Ibo soldier is not the real enemy, nor are you the real enemies of the Ibo soldiers.'

'But the Biafran soldiers don't know this,' Ituah said. 'They think we are their enemies.'

'Yes, and that is the real tragedy of this war. The Federal troops do not know that the Biafran soldiers are not their real enemies and the Biafrans are ignorant of this fact as well. So you kill each other. You rape each other's women. You kill each other's children and destroy each other's homes and farms. That's the real tragedy of the war — those who get killed in it. If you ask the generals where their children and families are you will find out that they are out of the country. The rich have sent their children out of the country while the children of working people on whom the war was imposed are trapped and killed in it. They slaughter each other, butcher each other in ignorance. This is the tragedy of war.'

'I am not going to fight any more,' Obilu said. 'I drop my gun and grenades here and now.'

'They'll call you a deserter,' Patani told him.

'So what do we do?' Kokobi asked. 'We should not fight and yet we must fight.'

'I have not said that you must not fight,' Osime corrected them. 'I say you're fighting the wrong enemy. Keep your guns and your grenades. But use them against the right enemies. I have not said that you must not fight. You must if you are to free yourselves.'

'I am going to kill me a general,' Obilu offered.

'No,' Osime said quickly. 'It's no use killing one general. They will only appoint another in his place. I want you to know the truth and knowing the truth helps until there are so many who know the truth that you can do something about it. Until then . . .'

'We must go on killing our Ibo brothers,' Musa said regretfully.

'That's the tragedy,' Osime Iyere said. 'That is the tragedy of this war.'

He looked at the faces of the soldiers from one to the other and shook his head. *The generals have armed them with meaningless slogans. To keep Nigeria one . . . Biafra must stay as the sun . . . It is all rubbish, an opium constantly fed to the working people. The man who works on the factory or farms the land does not care whether he is in Benin or in Kaduna. None of them has ever left Nigerian territory and do not even care about boundaries. It is the way of the ruling class to look for territories they can plunder, loot and scavenge with impunity. They have to agree to boundaries for themselves, for their selfish reasons. Members of the working class never bothered about boundaries, about countries until the ruling class thought them up and imposed them. The ruling class need their little kingdoms. The kingdom of the working class is the earth itself. The whole earth, not just a section of it, and that is why everywhere, they work it, they work themselves because they cannot run away from it. But the generals run from one little place to another because no place is really theirs. They are the vagabonds of the earth, the bastards of the earth,* he thought and began to walk away.

'Wait, journalist,' Patani stopped him. 'You must learn how to shoot.'

'Later.'

'No time is as good as now. There may be no later.'

'Well, perhaps I'll never know how then.'

'No, journalist, we want you to know it. I insist that you stay.'

'All right then,' Osime said and stopped and came back.

'That is what we want to do. Give him the guitar,' Patani told Musa. Musa held out his Kalashnikov to him and he took it. It was still warm from the shots he had fired earlier.

'You can fold the butt back,' Patani said. 'Fold it back and you may have greater accuracy.'

He folded the metallic butt of the Kalashnikov back. 'Now, let us try again. But watch me first.'

He tried shooting with the gun for about an hour and then gave up. They all walked back to the dormitory.

Sergeant Kesh Kesh was waiting for him. 'I no longer have to leave tomorrow,' he said. 'But some of the other infantry units are going.'

'You are lucky,' Osime congratulated him.

'You call that lucky? It is no luck, my friend, to be saved from one combat for another. What it means now is that the attack on Onitsha will be soon.'

'I would rather you weren't killing each other at all.'

'But that is no longer possible. We have a war now and we must fight in it. We must live in it or die in it. I am going to eat. You need strength for this war.'

'And energy too and stupidity also,' Osime added.

'I am going to sleep.'

'You mean you will not eat?'

'I will eat after I have slept.'

'No. It should be the other way round. Come and eat, journalist. Here you eat when the food is there because you may not have it for days. Here you are sure of the meal that is ready, not the next one.'

'I will go and eat then,' he agreed, 'and maybe, sleep after.'

'Yes, sleep and go to the party. Remember?'

'Yes.'

He was lying now on the bed and his mind went back to Salome. He would have to be careful. If Sergeant Kesh Kesh was right, then he would have to watch himself. But why had Otunshi come here? Why hadn't he gone somewhere else? Yet why shouldn't he be here? Otunshi had every right to be anywhere, just as he had. He was more concerned with Salome. *What happened in Benin was good,* he thought. *It was pure madness at first but later it was good. What I have now is for Ndudi. What I had I gave to Salome but she rejected it and I would have thrown it away completely had Ndudi not saved it for me. And for her,* he thought as he bit his upper lip, *everything now remains.*

Before now, the hunt was for egoistic reasons. You met a woman and said a few words and you did not really know each other but you went to bed and afterwards, you felt proud as you looked down at the woman. That was before and it was all right then before I really understood the war, before this war made me understand our life as I had never done before. It will not do any more, this life of one woman here, another woman there. What I want is a meaningful relationship and Ndudi is good enough for me.

But what if Salome insisted? What if she insisted upon a relationship here? But would she? Why should she want a relationship when the Brigadier was here by her side? What would she get from it? What did women get from these relationships?

He understood what he got from it. He had the feeling of personal satisfaction. And the woman? He didn't know. Perhaps it was the same thing. Perhaps the woman obtained what the man obtained. *Why shouldn't she? Why should we imagine that only the man comes out with something and that the woman goes away empty-handed? Perhaps we imagine for ourselves only because hope is more on the woman's side.*

At the present time, he thought. *It could never be like that for ever or else I wouldn't be here blaming Salome for going away or waiting now to go back to Oganza. Hope has to be on both sides for it to work. And sometimes, it is only on the man's side. You hope that the woman you love will not go away. You hope that you will transcend the coming and going of the tide. You hope you will be the ocean itself. You hope that today's relationship is the beginning of the real beginning, that it will never end. You hope that the woman will become your own and that you will become her own. You hope she won't come to you to say she has found another, that she won't bring to you the ashes of a fire burnt out.*

Hope is on both sides. Sometimes it is on the woman's side and at other times it is on the man's side but it is best when it is on both sides, because then hope changes to faith and faith becomes knowledge. When you have knowledge, you become the ocean itself. The tide of hope leaves its faith on the sand, on the beach and enters the ocean, never to return. You have knowledge and you have life itself, you have faith and you have the shadow of life. You have hope and you have dreams of life. What I have with Ndudi is hope. We haven't gone beyond the tide of hope. Not yet.

But nothing remained with Salome now, except an itch which you can scratch in motel rooms or on the back-seats of cars, or in any place for that matter. And that is what makes an itch dangerous. Because you must scratch it and until you scratch it, you have no peace. He fell asleep.

Chapter seventeen

The officers' mess was in the building that had housed the vice-principal of St Barnabas College when there was no war. With the coming of the war, the house changed. The wall between the sitting room and the main bedroom had been knocked down, so that now you came into the house and there was a large hall. To the right of the hall was the high semi-circular bar on top of which were the glasses and the drinks, mainly brandy. Arranged close together round the bar on the outside were eight high stools with padded black tops. Inside the bar where the two serving soldiers stood were more drinks and a record player and amplifier and records and a small metal box into which the soldiers placed all the money from the drinks, food and other services. Behind the barmen as they stood were counters built into the wall which held more drinks, glasses and sandwiches. Where the counters ended and to the right of the barmen, there was a rusted and brown refrigerator. Past the old refrigerator was the door that opened into the big kitchen where the cooks, also soldiers, prepared the meals. There was a huge refrigerator here, also rusted and brown, but it worked perfectly. The kitchen also served as the store.

In the rest of the hall, low single chairs were usually arranged in groups of four around the round tables. The room was empty of chairs and tables now; all had been moved outside because of the party. There was a brown and yellow carpet on the floor and it was dirty. The house had two more rooms and these had beds and were called 'slaughter rooms' by the soldiers because they frequently brought their women and slept with them here. You paid two naira an hour to use a room but even then it was very popular among the officers. All the top officers of the Division came here. Once, there was a fight between two officers over a woman and one of the officers, a major, was shot and seriously wounded and died two days later from his wounds. But that did not stop the army officers. They continued to come. Sometimes, civilians who were contractors also came.

When Osime Iyere came into the mess it was still empty except for the three men and two women sitting on the high stools at the bar and drinking. The men were all journalists. Osime walked up to them and took the seat that was empty but farthest away from them and ordered his drink, a beer.

'The drinks are free tonight,' one of the men said loudly and winked at him.

'And the food,' one of the women said and laughed and added. 'But it is not ready.'

'Come on. Join us,' the first man invited him and Osime moved his drink along the top of the bar while he changed stools. Just then two women came in. One of them was wearing a long dress. She was tall and beautiful but polished as a shoe is polished because her face shone. Her arms were covered by the long sleeves of her dress. The other woman was also tall and also beautiful and she wore a red skirt and a blue blouse, both of silk, and looking at her long legs and fair face and fine eyes that looked dark at this distance, Osime forgot temporarily about the war and all his resolutions about meaningful relationships.

'My God,' the man who sat next to him moaned. 'Oh my God!

'What is it, Ekise?' the woman with him asked. She placed her hand on top of Ekise's hand as she spoke.

'It's that woman?' the man Ekise said without shame and with deep admiration. 'She is so beautiful! Look at her, see how she stands, look at her breasts, not even a brassiere!'

'Ekise,' his companion said slowly but scornfully. 'How can you? What's she got that I haven't got? And yet see how your mouth drips with saliva!'

'She is a beautiful woman,' the man Ekise said as if from very, very far away.

'You men are never satisfied,' the other woman scoffed now as Osime leaned forward on his stool against the wooden top of the bar to get a better view of the woman's face.

'Here we are — well, I will not speak about myself. There beside you sits Attracta and like her name, she's attractive. But do you notice her?'

'The grass is always greener on the other side of the garden,' one of the other journalists said. 'You are always excited by what you do not know.'

Outside they could hear the voices of two men as they talked and laughed. Their voices were loud and firm and authoritative. They were army officers, one was a major, the other was a captain.

'Why don't you go and meet her?' the woman suggested to Ekise.

'Go and tell her what you think of her.'

'Go and meet her?'

'Yes. Isn't that what you want?'

'You must hate me,' Ekise said and his face shone with his frustration. 'You must hate me enough to want me to get myself shot.'

The woman did not say anything and the third journalist who hadn't spoken so far laughed. 'That's how it is done,' he said. 'You have an itch for a woman and you take it to her.'

'I am not a fool,' Ekise said. 'But she is a beautiful woman all right.'

Outside the two soldiers laughed suddenly and then they were quiet. Three more men, contractors wearing *agbada*, now joined them.

'I won't get myself shot on account of a woman,' Ekise said. 'I'm not a fool.'

'Oh, you men are never satisfied,' the second woman said again.

'Remember that the grass on the other side is always greener,' the second journalist said again.

'We are never satisfied because it's our nature never to be satisfied,' Osime volunteered now.

'Hear hear!' Ekise applauded.

'Both men and women,' Osime said. 'And it's a good thing that we are never satisfied because if we were, we would still be living in the dark ages, in caves. Think of what love must have been like in those caves, violent, fierce, brutal, but in the end, very satisfying. But we were not satisfied. So we built modern houses and put in beds and drew up a code of conduct. But still we are not satisfied. Dissatisfaction leads to the growth of man, of mankind.'

'Hear hear!' one of the other journalists cried.

'The same goes for women,' Osime said.

'No,' the woman Attracta disagreed. 'Do you think if a man had come in here, I would have reacted the way this boy did?'

'Who are you calling a boy?' Ekise demanded angrily.

'The woman is not free to express her dissatisfaction,' Osime pointed out.

'But the man is free to do so,' the other woman said.

'But that does not mean that the woman is not dissatisfied,' Osime pointed out.

'The woman is always satisfied,' Attracta insisted. 'Chilaka,' she said, turning to the other woman. 'Tell them that the woman is always satisfied.'

'The woman is always satisfied,' Chilaka repeated.

'And that is why men continue to sit on your shoulders,' Osime said. 'Any man who wants to grow, develop or be free must be dissatisfied, always.'

'Male chauvinism,' Chilaka accused him. 'Male opportunism. Because a man wants to grow, he must always look at other women, he must always ignore the one nearest him?'

'No, I didn't say that. When I say that a man must be restless, I don't mean that he must be a flirt. If you love a woman, you will be satisfied with her and you will stay with her. But there are other things to which a man aspires. A man aspires to peace, for instance. If we were satisfied with this state of war, we would let the war drag on for ever.'

'I don't see the connection,' the woman Chilaka said.

'Well, well, well,' Ekise said. 'I thought our friend here had opinions he never wanted us to learn or hear about.'

'What do you mean?' Osime asked.

'Tell him what we mean, Idem,' Ekise suggested to the man who sat between Chilaka and Attracta.

Idem hesitated and then gathered himself together. 'We mean we don't understand you, we don't understand your holier-than-thou attitude. Am I not right, Jato?' He passed the baton on to the third journalist.

They have discussed this before, Osime said to himself. *They have discussed this thing and planned it. They were waiting for the moment to come when they could put it across.*

'He pretends he is not one of us,' Jato affirmed now from the extreme end of the bar where he sat. 'He seems to bear a grudge.'

Osime did not respond.

'Come on,' Ekise urged him, prodding him gently in the ribs with his elbow. 'Tell us. What are you sore about? You won't even talk with us, you won't eat with us, you won't sleep with us. Perhaps you do have a grudge. Let's discuss it, let's see how deep it is, how you got it.'

They are spoiling for a fight, Osime thought, and a light came into his eyes. *They are spoiling for a fight and I will give it to them.*

'The war affects each one of us differently,' he said. 'Some of us it affects profoundly, others not at all.'

'I am profoundly affected by this war,' Ekise declared at once. 'I am so profoundly affected that I left my wife and children at home and came out here to risk my life. The journalists are the heroes of this war. But who will write about them? Not even myself here.'

'So you are married?' the woman Attracta asked immediately, ignoring the rest of his speech.

'Yes, and what of it?'

'You are a liar, that's what it is. You lied to me! You told me you were single, that you were a bachelor!' Her voice rose.

'Shattered dreams,' Jato said and laughed. 'The lie has coiled up like a snake and stung its owner.

Ekise finished the beer in his glass and asked for a double brandy.

'We are profoundly affected by the war,' he began again, reluctant to let the matter rest.

'I see what you mean,' Osime said.

'No, you do not see what I mean,' Ekise disagreed.

'Oh yes,' Osime said quietly. 'You have left your wife and children. You risk your life greatly with the women and the beer and the brandy. And at the end of the week, you risk your life by sending to your paper news about another captured village. You're a hero, remember?'

'That's an insult!'

'Show me what other risks you take and I will take my words back. Talk about being profoundly affected! Talk about being heroes!'

'And what about you?'

'What about me?'

'Is spending two days at the front and thinking that you can write the history of the war from that shallow experience being profoundly affected? Is sleeping with . . .'

'Ekise!'

'Let him finish,' Osime said to Jato. 'After all, that was what you all wanted.'

'Is sleeping in the dormitory with soldiers who shoot themselves in the hands or legs so as not to be sent into battle being profoundly affected. Profoundly affected my foot!'

'You are totally ignorant,' Osime said now. 'Ignorant and blind.'

'You're the one who's ignorant!' Ekise flung back.

'And I intend to get in touch with your paper. You are wasting their money here.'

'You bastard!' Ekise said. 'You're not even a journalist!'

'No, I am an editor. You could not get a messenger's job on my newspaper!' He got down from the stool and picking up his glass with the unfinished beer in it, went outside.

There were many officers and civilian contractors outside and they were dressed in civilian clothes, mostly safari suits and *agbada*. Their women were richly dressed in lace and gorgeous materials and wore gold bracelets and ear-rings all imported from England and Italy. The woman who wore the red skirt and blue blouse and who was tall and brown and beautiful was there too and, listening to them as they all talked and joked and laughed, Osime wondered if there was a war on at all. They all sat around the tables in the night that was white from the whiteness of the moon and cool from the cold breath of the trees and the waters of the river. The wind was the breathing of the trees and the river, gentle, serene. It was a beautiful night.

Some of the men got up and went into the mess and Osime could hear the music from the record changer as the barman put on the records. *When will she come?* he asked himself. *When will she come? If she went to my office as we arranged, then perhaps they would have told her that I had gone to Oganza. But she still won't expect to see me here. So it is going to be a surprise. I must make sure it isn't a big surprise, or else Brigadier Otunshi will notice. So I must stay out here in the whiteness of the moonlight where she will see and recognise me from the distance but where her husband will find it impossible to notice the change in her expression, if there is a change in her expression.*

He thought about what Ekise had said about the soldiers. The ignorant fool! He wished he had hit him in the mouth to prevent the rubbish from spilling out. What indescribable ignorance! If only he would stay with the soldiers and find out why they shot themselves in the leg. If only he would spend some time with the real soldiers instead of chasing after women and drinking beer and whisky and brandy. Then perhaps he would find out about the soldiers sacrificing their lives so that others might live. He would find out too how the officers avoided the ambushes while the rank and file got slaughtered. Of course there were many crude and cruel soldiers in this war, rank and file soldiers. But they had their reasons, reasons which he had now come to understand.

At first, he thought, *I did not understand. So I stood on the side of the Federal troops against the Biafran troops and when the Biafran army was driven away and the Federal troops came, I changed sides. But this time, I was on the side of neither the Biafrans nor the Federal troops. I was made neutral by my hatred for both, that is, after the Federal troops took my pass at the stadium and kicked me in my testicles, after they murdered Ndudi's father in cold blood as he ran for the river, after I saw the headless bodies of men, women and children, butchered by the Biafrans. I saw these things and I was neutralised by my hatred for the soldiers and told myself that the Nigerian had an innate natural tendency to inflict pain. I told myself that we were born cruel and callous and evil and degenerate.*

But that was before I came here and met Sergeant Kesh Kesh and the rest of the men. I met them and then something broke my neutrality and gradually as dawn heralds the first coming of light, I began to understand. I began to understand that we were all born neither more nor less cruel nor kind than the other. We become bad only after we were born, not before. And this after is what matters most. This after is connected with our training, with our upbringing, with our socialisation. The rank and file become murderers only after they have been trained in murder by their officers. We all become evil and degenerate and cruel and fascist after we have been trained by those who rule us, by the circumstances under which we live. The system generates its own contradictions. An irresponsible, undisciplined ruling class produces an irresponsible undisciplined ruled class.

Corruption always begins from the top. Before the war, corruption was in the very breath of the ministers and presidents and businessmen and politicians and traditional rulers and church leaders and army generals and police commissioners. It was there and we all reeled in it. It is still there now and we are still reeling in it. But the war brought out a stench greater than that of our corruption, so it temporarily covered it up. Let the war end, and the corruption will resurface. Always it begins at the top and simmers down to the bottom, so much so that the messenger becomes corrupt, the office cleaner becomes corrupt. Always, it is a disease brought on the rest of the people by the ruling class enshrined in their constitutions. They manufacture treachery, cruelty, callousness and shamelessness and then peddle these as commodities to the people, like all the other commodities of a neocolonial capitalism.

What is worse then? The soldier who shoots himself in his own hand to prevent himself from getting killed or the general who kills hundreds of thousands of men in war to retain his power? There are two armies, two sides in this war, the army of officers and the army of rank and file soldiers. The army of officers has somehow persuaded the rank and file that they must kill each other to preserve the unity of the country. The rank and file think they are fighting for the unity of the country whereas they are fighting to keep one section of the ruling class in power and another section of it away from power.

I must give the generals credit for doing their homework properly, he thought bitterly. *They know that the most nationalist of our population are the working class from which all the rank and file come. So they used the nationalist sentiment. 'To Keep Nigeria One is a Task that Must be Done', or to defend the survival of the new Biafran nation is a task that must be done. And the soldiers on both sides swallow the bait, for they have this deep love for their country which comes from having all their hopes in it. All their life is ploughed into the earth of their country, all their possessions are in it. They are firmly rooted in their country. But the same is not true of the generals and the politicians and the presidents and the ministers and the professors and the businessmen and the traditional rulers and the bishops. They have no love for their country because at a moment's notice they can pack their bags and go to another country where they have exported their loot. And this is why they are so treacherous, why spies are recruited from their ranks, why they commit the greatest crimes and sell their country, why they were the natural collaborators for the slave traders from Europe and America and the Middle East. All that talk about unity is nothing but hypocrisy.*

Unity is only important to them if it means a larger territory and more people that they can plunder. But they know the importance of love, all right. They know that love binds as nothing else can and that the working class are bound hand and foot to their country because they love their country fiercely. And they take this love and build it into a war song for the rank and file soldiers from the working class. The rank and file sing the song and their chests swell and their eyes brim with hatred for the false enemy, the wrong enemy. They carry rifles or drive tanks and go into mutual slaughter. And behind them, the generals sit and laugh and calculate their profits, the businessmen and the traditional rulers, the president, the ministers, the politicians, the bishops and the professors all sit and laugh and calculate their profits. All built on the blood of the dead or the sweat of the living among the ranks of the working class.

Listen to the speeches of the politicians and generals and presidents. They all begin with 'this country'. 'This country, Nigeria.' 'This country must do better.' 'This country cannot afford to let things get worse.' Always, it is 'this country', something impersonal, to be used and exploited. But listen to the talk of the workers and the farmers and the rank and file soldiers. Always, it is our *country. 'Our country Nigeria.' For the working class, it is always* our *country and this brings out in them the ultimate sacrifice.*

And Ekise opens his foul mouth to talk about the soldiers who shoot themselves in the hand to avoid being killed in a war that is not their own!

He says nothing about the soldiers who sacrifice their lives, get themselves killed in a war that is not their own. Osime regretted now that he had not struck him in the mouth and knocked out a few of his teeth. That would have taught him a lesson. In the end, though, it would not have mattered. The problem was not to shut Ekise up but with shutting up the generals and the politicians and the businessmen, the traditional rulers and the bishops and the professors. And that was why, he thought, a third army was needed, a people's army to fight the people's war . . .

'Excuse me, sir!'

Osime turned. A soldier stood in front of him holding a tray and on the tray there were glasses that held different drinks. Osime looked at the drinks and shook his head. 'I need a beer,' he said and placed his glass that held the yellow stale beer on the tray. 'Bring me a bottle of beer and another glass.'

'The soldier went away. *Don't forget Sergeant Kesh Kesh,* he reminded himself. *Sergeant Kesh Kesh asked you to bring him a bottle of whisky and you promised him you would.*

Chapter eighteen

It was typical of the indiscipline and irresponsibility of the ruling class, thought Osime, to measure their own importance by the length of time they kept others waiting. They had said seven o'clock and one and a half hours had gone by and still, they had not come. Until Brigadier Otunshi had arrived, nothing could start off.

And that's how they give us bad names. Always they are late and then everybody else says that the African has no sense of time, that he is never punctual. They use the practices of the ruling class to label entire peoples, entire continents. Always when the invited guests come, the people are waiting, the people are always the first to arrive but because the guests of honour are always late, they turn round to say the people are always late. The whole society is judged on the practices of the ruling class. And because the practices of our rulers have always been dark, we become the dark continent, because these practices have always been shameless and backward, we become the shameless and backward societies. Because they are stupid and cowardly, they make us out to be stupid and cowardly. They make us look . . .

'I have brought the beer,sir.'

Osime turned and again the soldier stood there and this time he held the bottle of beer and the glass.

'Shall I open it?'

'Thank you.'

The man gave the glass to Osime and bringing out an opener from his breast pocket, he opened the bottle of beer and passed it to Osime.

'Thank you,' Osime said again and momentarily the whiteness of the moon was there in the man's face as he smiled.

'So there you are!' another voice exclaimed and Osime turned. Jato was standing there.

'What do you want?'

'They seem to be taking their time to come.'

'What do you want?' Osime said again.

'Look, Osime,' the man Jato began. 'You mustn't assume that we planned to insult you or to pick a quarrel or anything like that.'

Osime did not say anything.

'You know how it is,' Jato continued and Osime told himself that he did not know how it was but did not say anything.

'You see one of your own kind and naturally you want to keep together. It is important in this war. You know what the soldiers do to journalists. Sometimes, say you write something they disagree with, they shave your hair. Rebel-style, they call it. Or they flog you or lock you up. In these circumstances, we have always found it better to keep together. We are all brothers in this war.'

'I am not your brother,' Osime told him.

'Colleagues then.'

'Yes, colleagues. Remember that Gowon and Ojukwu are colleagues in this war. We have colleagues too on the other side.'

'I don't mean those kinds of colleagues. We are here, on the same side.'

'Really?'

'Yes. And we have to keep together, to defend each other's rights.'

'I admit you have a point there,' Osime agreed, 'but it also depends on how many sides you see to this war.'

'True,' the man Jato said. 'Right now the most important front is the front where the journalists stand on the firing line. We have to defend that front.'

'That is not as important as the other front that I see,' Osime disagreed. 'The front where the soldiers kill each other for the wrong reasons, where the soldiers are on the firing line.'

'This is a war, man,' Jato said, completely misunderstanding him. 'In a war, soldiers are bound to die. There is nothing anyone of us can do about it.'

'Yes, this is a war,' Osime said, using the man's own language. 'It is a war and journalists too are bound to get locked up or whipped or shaved against their will.'

'You won't eat with us or sleep with us then?'

'No. But I will fight with you if the issue is worth anything.'

Jato looked at him and suddenly, he smiled. 'I understand you,' he said. 'And what you have said shows real commitment. Now, tell me . . .'

He was the first to see her. She stood on the right-hand side of Brigadier Otunshi and there was another woman with her who was flanked on the far side by another army officer and a civilian in *agbada* who he guessed was a contractor. The white moonlight washed her face and in the silvery grains of the moonlight all of her glowed and even the man Jato who stood with him gasped and then gaped at her beauty. The moon was like a neon light on her blue and white long dress and even her eyes flashed as she smiled and her lips that had lip gloss on them were like rose petals under the rain, velvety and plush but fresh and clean and beautiful. She did not even see him as she walked close by, flanked by her husband and the other men into the mess.

'She is the most beautiful woman I have ever seen in my life,' the man Jato said and his voice shook because he was strangely affected.

'Yes,' Osime agreed simply. There was nothing he could say.

The old pain he thought was gone was back and it was in his chest. He knew now that the pain never went away. You superimposed something else on it but it never went away. What he had superimposed on it was Ndudi and his new young feeling for her. This old wound ached now, even under the youthfulness of the other feeling that he had now.

It never goes away. It always remains and not for nothing a man's memory. It is the meeting that brings the pains back. You meet and inside you moves the current of the river in which you bathed many years ago. But you feel the current and it is as if you had never been out of the river, out of the stream. And if what you have now is new and young, the call of the stream is greater and the pain is much more intense. You need courage then, a lot of courage to hold on to what you now have.

He went inside. All the officers and the journalists were inside the mess now and Osime stood behind Jato where she would not see him. The arrangement was that they would sit outside in the chairs round the tables and dance inside the mess where the tables and chairs had been cleared away. But before anything could start, Brigadier Otunshi had to make a speech.

'He sold our arms to the rebels,' Jato whispered to him. 'He sold our arms to the Biafrans and afterwards the Biafrans used our own arms to kill our soldiers.'

'I don't believe it!'

'Ask any of the soldiers. Ask any of the journalists.'

'I heard about it but it's pure gossip. I can't believe it.'

'You had better because you are going to see a lot of changes here. Our casualty rate is going to go up, and the soldiers will be fighting a few days before their pay day.'

The man Jato turned away, disappointed and angry at his scepticism.

But I know it is true, Osime said to himself. *I know that Brigadier Otunshi sells our arms to the Biafrans and sends our troops into battle a few days to their pay day. I know that he kills thousands of men but in the end, he always wins. He sells our arms and kills our men and collects money from both sides but in the end, he always captures territories and that is what matters to the generals in this war. Corruption is everywhere. Sell your arms to your enemy and collect the money and put it in your pocket. Send the troops out into the battle before their pay day and get as many of them as possible killed and collect their pay and put it in your pocket. Capture a town and the first places you make for are the banks. It doesn't matter that they are the branches of the Central Bank. All that matters is that you break into the banks and blow the safes open with grenades and steal the money. You can always say that the Biafrans did it. The important thing is to get the money because this war is part of the whole business enterprise. And that means it must yield profits. That's why the distribution of the relief materials donated by the international agencies to the war victims is awarded as contracts to the wives and friends of the generals and the officers commanding at the fronts. That's why blankets meant for war victims are being sold in the open markets in Lagos and Kaduna and Kano. That's why the dried milk and food meant for the starving children are sold in the supermarkets in Lagos. That's why Chief Sule Adedoyin won the contract to distribute the drugs to the war victims, the drugs supplied by the international agencies, by the Cubans and the Russians and the East European countries, and why Chief Adedoyin now owns large drug stores all over the country. It was in the expectation of profit that the business community fanned the flames of the war, why the politicians fed canned meat to the dogs of war, why the bishops offered prayers for the war, why the professors rationalised the war, why the traditional rulers convened meetings for the war, why the generals gave the signal for the killings. The greed for profit and power lies at the bottom of this war and manifests itself everywhere in the conduct of this war. They were meant to ensure that the war came to pass, that more profits were achieved through the blood of thousands of our men, tens of thousands of our men and our women, of hundreds of thousands of our men, our women and our children. This whole war is nothing but one huge cry for money and power.*

'The man we saw come with Brigadier Otunshi is the army paymaster,' Jato whispered to him again.

'The army paymaster?'

'Yes, Major Dantari. Do you see the connection?' Jato turned away.

Yes, Osime said to himself. *I see the connection all right. Brigadier*

Otunshi needs the paymaster if he is to be successful in the arrangement of the fraud. The connection is everywhere, the connection between the generals, the businessmen, the bishops, the professors, the politicians, the traditional rulers, the permanent secretaries and the police commissioners, like a spider's web.

'Well, ladies and gentlemen,' Brigadier Otunshi broke into his thoughts, 'I am proud to announce to you that to celebrate the head of state's wedding, I have promised him the town of Onitsha. Onitsha will be our wedding present to the head of state.'

'Good talk!' cried one of the officers. 'A round of applause for the head of state.'

There was applause. Even the civilian contractors clapped.

'And a round of applause for the Division.'

There was more applause, more clapping of hands.'

'But to win, to take the city, to get the wedding present, we need discipline. Our soldiers are not disciplined. Many of them are cowards. See how they shoot themselves in their hands and legs. But I intend to have this discipline and you are going to help me enforce it. Thus as a first step, any soldier with hand or leg wounds will henceforth face the firing squad. They will be summarily executed.'

There was silence, dead silence.

'And now to the good news,' he continued. 'We have twenty invitations to the wedding, the largest number of invitations sent to any division.' There was a muted clapping of hands.

'The invitations will go to those officers who distinguish themselves in the capture of the wedding cake.'

Applause and laughter.

'And now, ladies and gentlemen, I invite you to eat, drink and dance!'

'Turn on the music!' one of the officers shouted. 'Turn on the music!'

Brigadier Otunshi went first to the tables that were covered with white cloth and on which were the dishes of food. Salome went with him and Osime saw how the officers and the other women looked at her, stared at her. He saw the head of Brigadier Otunshi go up in his pride, in his knowledge of the envy and jealousy of the other officers and contractors and women and he knew that Brigadier Otunshi defied them all.

Osime took his place in the queue when his turn came and behind him was a colonel and his wife and they stood side by side so that they formed a shield behind him. He saw the pounded yam and the eba and the white rice and fried rice and the jollof rice and dodo and the beans and the chicken. He saw the fried chicken and the meat and the stew. He saw the egusi soup and the ogbollo soup and in both he saw bush meat and stock fish and dried fish and fresh fish. He saw the salad in which there were carrots and cucumber and eggs and mayonnaise and then there were the shrimps in the cocktail glasses. Then on one of the tables, there were the ice buckets in which stood the bottles of champagne and Mateus Rosé and white wine. He saw the food and he was overwhelmed by its quantity and variety and he hesitated and the colonel said from behind him, 'You can always come back. Take a little now of each and then come back later.'

'And they say there is a war on?' he asked.

'It's a party,' the colonel said as if that explained everything and the woman with him laughed.

Osime did not say anything more but picked up a plate from the pile of plates on the table. Then he took some of the pounded yam and going round to the other side of the table where the obgollo soup stood, he took some soup and meat and then picked up a knife and a fork and went outside. The men stood in little groups outside, eating as they stood so that there was silence that was only occasionally interrupted. The women sat apart from their men at the tables. Osime could see Salome at one of the tables but well away from where he stood.

They should have provided us with water so that we could wash and eat with our hands, he thought, and laying the fork across his plate of food, he went round the house to the back where he found the tap. He did not place his plate on the grass for fear of snakes, so he washed his right hand only. He came round the house again, this time to the front and he was leaning against the wall and eating the bush meat when he heard her call his name quietly. He stopped in his chewing and looked away from his plate and she stood there, her face lit up with her smile, the light of the smile intensified by the white moonlight that poured from the silvery sky.

'Osime,' she said again and still quietly. 'Osime! What are you doing here?'

'Forgetting the war,' he answered looking beyond her, over her shoulders to the dark group of trees that stood on the edge of the grounds, to the white surface of the river and beyond it to the 'wedding cake' where he knew thousands of children, hundreds of thousands of men and women and children, were in the bushes, hiding, hungry, afraid, uncertain and cold. Suddenly, he couldn't eat any more. He placed the plate of food on the table nearest him and then, finally faced her. The pain he thought he had forgotten was back and the resolutions he had made about forgetting and ignoring her, all the assurances to himself that he had conquered her hold over him dissolved within him like salt in water.

Chapter nineteen

The soldiers were sleeping when he entered the block after identifying himself to the four sentries outside. He walked between the row of double-decker beds in which the soldiers slept until he came to the door that opened into the small room where Sergeant Kesh Kesh slept. His own bed was the upper part of the double-decker bed that stood against the wall. It was the last bed in the row and nearest Sergeant Kesh Kesh's room. He opened the door into Sergent Kesh Kesh's room quietly and stepped inside. It was dark and for some time, he could not see but he could hear the man's snores. Then he could see the silhouette of Sergeant Kesh Kesh on the bed. He bent forward as he shook the man on the shoulder gently but firmly.

'Sergeant Kesh Kesh!'

The man turned and grumbled and rubbed his face with his hands.

'Who's that?'

'Osime.'

'Journalist?'

'Yes.'

'What time is it?'

Osime looked at the dials on his wristwatch and they were green and luminous in the darkness. 'Almost two,' he said.

'You mean you are just coming from the party?' He sat up now.

'Yes. Here, take.'

Osime brought out one of the two bottles of brandy that he carried in the carrier bag which also held the camera and passed the bottle to Sergeant Kesh Kesh. 'It's the whisky,' he added.

'Whisky?'

'Well, brandy. Brandy is better than whisky.'

'You mean you didn't forget?'

'No.'

Sergeant Kesh Kesh lifted up one of the pillows and brought out a torch and pointing it downwards, turned it on and held the bottle of brandy in its light. Osime could see his face and it was dark but warm and alive. Osime went towards the door and turned the handle.

'Wait,' Sergeant Kesh Kesh called from behind him. 'Wait and I will break the cork of the bottle and we will drink a little of it together.'

'The brandy is yours,' Osime said. 'I had a lot of it at the mess.'

'It doesn't matter,' Sergeant Kesh Kesh insisted. 'You must drink with me.'

He broke the cork of the bottle and put the small end of the bottle in his mouth and Osime thought he was going to rinse his mouth with some of the brandy by not drinking it. But instead he swallowed the drink and passed the bottle to Osime who took a sip of it and passed the bottle back.

'You are going to sleep?'

'No. I am going out to see another journalist and then I will come back and sleep.'

'They left us out,' Sergeant Kesh Kesh said. 'They really left us out — they've gone.' He drank again from the bottle.

'You mean the infantry units have gone?'

'Those of the twenty-first battalion.'

'Then you are lucky. You should be grateful. Did you expect them to change their mind.'

'I don't know. The important thing is that they have gone and left us behind. That's what matters.' The disappointment and bitterness in his voice were very real. Osime was surprised. How could the man be disappointed because he had not been sent to the slaughterhouse? How could he be bitter about it? He did not understand.

Sergeant Kesh Kesh took a final drink from the bottle, then screwing back the cork of the bottle, placed it under his pillow. He turned off the light of the torch.

'Journalist,' he said now in the darkness. 'I did not think you would remember the whisky. But you did. I don't forget favours. I thank you now and I will thank you later. Go and come back and then we will talk.'

Osime went out into the night. It was cool outside and the moon was gone and the stars were gone also. He walked quickly because he knew it was dangerous to be out in the night. He came to the building that housed the journalists and climbed the single step and knocked on the door rapidly, but it was some time before the door opened. He stepped into the sitting room of the house. Jato shut the door behind him, and led him to a short corridor into which two other doors opened. The first door was on the left of the corridor. Jato stopped here, opened the door and entered.

'Where are your friends?' Osime asked, looking round the room, at the two single beds, one on each side.

There was a candle on the floor, in the centre of the room between the two beds. A locker stood against the door of the wardrobe and on top of the locker there was a suitcase.

'They have gone out,' Jato said now in answer to his question.

'They didn't come here after the party. They went to town with the women. But they have the room opposite. The journalist who shared this room with me before left after he was beaten up by the soldiers.'

'Why did you say I must come?'

Jato looked at him and smiled. 'Sit down and we will talk. We are together in this war, you know. We must not become enemies. And anyway, it can be lonely. I need somebody to share my ideas with.'

Osime sat on the bed. 'Is that what I took the risk for, came out for at this time of night? To keep you company?'

'Not exactly,' Jato said. He opened the locker that stood beside the bed and brought out a full, new bottle of whisky. 'I feel like getting drunk.'

'You mean twice?'

'No. I want to really get plastered.'

'Then get plastered but remember that you asked me here.'

'Of course. Here take this,' and he leaned forward and passed the glass to Osime and then broke the cork of the bottle and poured the yellow liquid into his glass. He passed the bottle to Osime.

'Let's drink to Salome,' Jato said. 'Let's drink to the queen of them all, the most beautiful woman I have ever seen.'

So that is why he called me here, Osime thought, the anger breathing like a flame inside him.

'You don't mean you invited me here just to talk about Salome?' He stood up.

Jato emptied the whisky in his glass in one go and then looked at Osime. 'Surely, you will not refuse to drink to your sister?'

Osime sat down again on the bed and poured some of the whisky into his glass and passed the bottle back to Jato. Had the man seen anything, had he heard anything he wanted to talk about? Was this blackmail?

'So she is your sister?' Jato asked and proceeded once more to pour the whisky into his glass.

'My cousin,' Osime said, watching him. 'My first cousin.'

'Why didn't you tell us?'

'Tell you what?' and he turned because he thought he could hear the sound of raindrops on the roof outside.

'That your sister was married to Brigadier Otunshi?'

'You didn't ask.'

'She is a beautiful woman,' Jato said.

'Thank you.'

'When are you going to see her tomorrow?'

'I am not going to see her tomorrow.' Osime stood up again and this time went to the door and took its handle. He could hear the rain outside very distinctly now and it was a downpour. He was angry.

'Surely you are not going back there?'

'Yes.'

'Come on, it's late. You could be shot.'

'I won't get shot. And you're drunk.'

'I'm not drunk,' Jato denied flatly. Then he added, 'Why don't you stay here? You could spend the night here.'

'I like sleeping in my own bed.'

'Nobody owns a bed on the war front. Sleep here and in the morning, you can take me with you when you go to see Salome.'

Osime looked at the drunken face of the man, the thin cheeks and the dull eyes, the bushy eyebrows and uncombed but short beard and the thick unkempt hair, he saw the man smiling in his drunkenness and he said to himself that Jato had had enough for the night.

He came away from the door and took the bottle of whisky and screwed the cork tight.

'You are not taking the bottle away!' Jato cried with real alarm.

'We have already drunk half the whisky. I am drunk.'

'We ought to finish the damned thing,' Jato swore now. 'Never start something you can't finish.'

'I have had enough,' Osime spoke for himself. 'I am already drunk.'

'Oh no, you're not.'

'I have reached my limit. I don't want to pass it.'

'Give me the bloody bottle then. Give me the damned thing and

I'll show you!' He began to whistle.

'We've had enough.'

'*You* have had enough. Jato never retreats before the storm in the teacup, before the demon in the bottle. Give me the bottle and I'll show you.'

'All right,' Osime said and gave up and passed the bottle to the man. 'You can take it and the demon. Have it and kill yourself. Get yourself stone drunk.'

Jato laughed. 'You watch me, novice,' he boasted. 'You watch me and you'll see how the demon can be put to shame in a quarter of an hour.'

He began to whistle loudly.

Osime went through the door into the sitting room and opened the front door. The rain was like a black sheet and it fell thick on the wings of a strong wind. Hastily, he shut the door and came back into the room. Jato was still whistling.

He want back to the empty bed and felt it and he saw that the spring was broken in several places and that the mattress was weak. The mattress had no covers and the pillow was dirty brown. When he lifted it, it smelt strongly of sweat and long use. He shook his head. Hadn't Jato said nobody owned a bed on the war front? He dusted the pillow by first going over it with the broad of his palm and then by thrashing it in the air of the room. He lifted the mattress off the bed and turned it on its side to get rid of the sand on it. Then he opened the window that was on the side of his bed slightly to let in the air, then because the rain came into the room, shut it again.

Osime lay back on the bed and his eyes jumped in his head and he felt himself going round and round in circles and then he sat up against the iron support of the bed and shook his head but it wouldn't clear. He wriggled lower down the bed and attempted to close his eyes again but the circles came back and he opened his eyes and tried not to sleep. He could hear Jato singing loudly now. At first, he sang the national anthem and then he began another song and it was about Salome but it wasn't a coherent song because Jato had to think up the words as he went along and what with most of the whisky already gone to his head, the words were often unintelligible. But he got Salome's name right each time.

Salome! Osime repeated to himself. He could feel her standing next to him and then the pain in his chest. He could see Salome now and they were all standing under the moonlight and she said to her husband, 'This is Osime.'

'So this is the Osime,' Brigadier Otunshi said and Osime could see the suspicion in the man's eyes as clearly as everything showed under the full gaze of the bright moonlight. Brigadier Otunshi did not offer his hand.

'Good evening, Brigadier,' Osime said. He did not offer his hand either.

'When did you come here?'

'Two days ago.'

'And what are you doing here?'

'Come on, Olu,' Salome intervened. 'What is this? An inquisition?'

'It's all right,' Osime said. 'Actually I brought my father-in-law here.'

'Your father-in-law?'

'Yes.' *Thank God it is not daylight or he would have seen the guilt in my eyes now.*

'You are married?'

'Yes.' He watched both their faces. He thought he saw the suspicion go away from the man's eyes. Salome's expression did not change. She obviously didn't believe him.

'So you are married to one of them then?'

'One of them?'

'A Biafran.'

'No, a Nigerian from Enugu.'

'From Enugu?'

'Not exactly. What I mean is that the people at Enugu are Nigerians as we are Nigerians. If you did not believe that, then you wouldn't be involved in this war.'

'Of course, of course,' Brigadier Otunshi agreed. 'The Biafrans are Nigerians but the Nigerians are not Biafrans.' He laughed a short laugh. 'So your wife is from which place?'

'From Oganza.'

'The village we pulled out of some days ago?'

'Yes. I was going back there when I met the retreat.'

'The retreat was for tactical reasons,' Brigadier Otunshi said defensively.

'Aren't all retreats for tactical reasons?' Salome asked.

'Yes, you could say that,' the Brigadier agreed. 'But what

happened to your father-in-law?'

'He was shot by the Federal troops.'

'He was a rebel officer then?'

'No,' Osime answered quietly, anger at the man's facile assumptions slowly building up inside him. 'He wasn't a soldier at all. He was my landlord. He went to register himself at the army post on Ikpoba Hill according to instructions. I took him there myself. He was murdered there.'

'I am sure it was a mistake,' Brigadier Otunshi said gently.

'The whole war is a mistake.'

'Yes,' Brigadier Otunshi agreed, and Osime was surprised until he added, 'if only Ojukwu had listened to reason.'

He was going to say something and Salome must have sensed it because she suddenly took his hand and said to him that they should go and dance. Otunshi looked at them then and even in the softness of the night, his bushy moustache looked harsh and Osime wasn't sure that the suspicion wasn't back in his eyes.

'The only way to deal with him is to do it openly,' Salome told him conspiratorially as they danced. 'If you are secretive, he becomes suspicious. Do it openly and although he is still suspicious, he doubts. He doubts and you are safe.'

Inside the mess, there was no light except for that of the moon that came in through the open windows. The room was dark and she had one hand round his side, while the other was inside his shirt, between the third and fourth buttons. He felt hot.

'That was very smart telling him you brought your father-in-law here. Do you know I almost believed you?'

Osime tried to see her eyes but he couldn't because it was dark. 'It is the truth,' he said simply and he felt her hand, the one that was inside of his shirt, come out slowly. She moved away from him.

'You can't be serious.'

He shrugged his shoulders. 'What do you want me to say?'

'But you can't be married!'

'Why do you say that?'

'Because . . . because, well, I thought you couldn't. You know, us. You and I. I love you.'

'Yes,' he said. 'And you are married to Otunshi.'

'I could leave him.'

'Really?'

'Yes. If you want me to.'

'You know you couldn't. What about the position, the money? He could become a general. How could you leave that? And in any case, I will make it easier for you. I won't ask you to leave him.'

'Osime,' she said slowly. 'You mustn't talk like that. You know you're only trying to hurt me. I love you. I have never loved anybody but you.'

'Thank you,' he said to her then. 'Thank you for loving me. Thank you for loving me and marrying Otunshi.'

'I refuse to be hurt,' she said. 'I refuse your gratitude as well.'

'Shall we go then?'

'No.' And now she moved close to him and placed her right hand inside his shirt between the buttons. He turned his face away sharply as he saw her chin come up and her mouth open.

'You mustn't,' he said to her sharply. 'You mustn't be foolish.'

'I love you!' she said fiercely. 'I love you and your unbelief is killing me, this whole hide and seek is killing me.'

'Then leave him,' he dared her and he felt the nails of her fingers bite into the skin on the side of his ribs and he winced.

She was silent.

'See?' he said. 'What did I say? What we have now is an itch, not love. Love you cannot satisfy by scratching it.'

She didn't say anything but stopped in her dance and led him outside. They had a few words with Brigadier Otunshi who offered his hand and told them to go ahead of him. For the first time, he shook hands with Otunshi, and then the five of them, himself, Salome and the three escorts went back to Brigadier Otunshi's quarters.

It was then that I needed my courage, he said to himself now. *It was then that I needed all my resolve to keep what I have got. We got to the front of their quarters and I told her I would not go in with her and at first, she didn't believe me and then, when she saw that I meant it, she sent the escorts away and held me and pleaded with me passionately. She didn't see how much I wanted to go with her, she didn't know how much I wanted to kiss her. But I realised then that when she said she loved me she has an itch she wants me to scratch for her and although I loved her deeply, as I had never loved anyone else in my life, I refused to be used. But I guess it will always remain, this itch. I guess it will always remain an itch. Or how else could she ask me to love her and no one else when she remains married to Otunshi? How can she love me and stay married to Otunshi? But I dared her and what did she do? She became frightened. But she can't eat her cake and have it too.*

With others yes, but not with me any more. In the end it must be selfishness. When she says 'I love you', she means 'you must love me'. She must also mean 'I want you'. Because her want is on a different level from love and that level merges with selfishness. What you want, you need for your satisfaction. You have a need to satisfy and so you want. The wanting is impersonal, as impersonal as wanting to eat an orange.

Ndudi, he said to himself now, *what we have may never be as deep as what I had with Salome, it may never be as fierce either, but it will keep and that is what matters. It will keep because we are each one of us unselfish. We do not demand of each other what we would not give ourselves. Of course, you are much better than I am because you were the first to be converted. You got rid of your selfishness a long, long time before I did. You never used me, not after the beginning. And that is important.*

He was confident now that he would be all right. It would not matter what happened afterwards. He felt as though the scales had been removed from his eyes, as though he had emerged from the darkness into light. But he would not forget what he had held for her, how far he had been prepared to go. It had been a very great temptation, to abandon everything, to tell her that he would give up everything for her. But his faith with Ndudi held, and he felt relieved. It held because, suddenly he realised that what Salome had was nothing but the itch. And he wasn't going to scratch it for her.

He could still hear Jato singing. He was singing the national anthem now. Osime spat in front of him on the wall when he sat up and then bent down to undo his shoe laces. He kicked off the shoes and then he was back again, lying on the bed. His eyes swam and his head seemed to spin and in the spinning there was music and it was the national anthem. He tried to break up the chase when he opened his eyes but his eyes would not stay open; after a time they closed and then the chase began again. He did not know when he fell asleep. The rain continued to fall outside.

Chapter twenty

In the morning the first thing to reach his nostrils was the strong smell in the room. He sat up in bed and looked at Jato who was still asleep but snoring on the bed and he was about to step on the floor when he saw it. 'My God,' he said. 'Oh my God!' and he edged past the vomit on the floor and opened both the windows and then came back and opened the door, and stood in the corridor and looked back into the room. He shook his head.

Outside, the rain had stopped falling and he could see a long line of jeeps and trucks and trailers, empty of soldiers. More trailers carried the boats and other equipment. There were five armoured vehicles including two tanks. *They must have come in the night*, he thought. *They must have come when we were asleep.* He spat out now on the grass away from him. *The swine! I must have inhaled the man's vomit while I slept.*

He came back into the room. He looked for the bottle and at first he didn't see it. Then he saw it under one of the man's flung out hands and he knew it was almost empty. *Three quarters of a bottle of whisky,* he thought. And shook his head. He picked up the carrier bag that held his camera and then he picked up his shoes from the floor and they were smeared with vomit. He spat on the floor, on the vomit.

He placed the bag under his arm and he went outside and wiped the shoes on the grass to clean them. Then he walked to the flowers that lined the path and broke a twig off one of them and shook it free of raindrops and cleared it of the leaves and then broke it again and placed the stronger part of it in his mouth and began to chew it.

He walked along the path towards the section of the buildings where he knew Sergeant Kesh Kesh would be waiting and twice he turned back to look at the building where he had spent the night with Jato. It was when he turned back the second time that he saw Jato waving his hands at him. A soldier stood by him. He stopped and waited.

The soldier came along while Jato waited on the single step of the house. The soldier came up to him and held out an envelope. 'From the commander's wife,' the soldier said.

'Thank you,' Osime said and tore the envelope open and brought out the letter. The handwriting was as bold and large as it had ever been and reading it, he was impressed.

'Tell the commander's wife that I understand,' he said, and the man began to walk away, back to Otunshi's quarters.

He saw Jato waving at him but he did not wave back or stop but continued down the path that led to the building that housed the soldiers. So Otunshi had gone down to the river. That meant that the battle for Onitsha would begin in a few days. And the boats he had seen must be for the river also. It was going to be a fierce battle to take Onitsha. If Otunshi was to keep his word, he must take the city this Friday because come Saturday, the head of state would be married. And today was only Sunday.

He went into the dormitory and through the long corridor made by the beds. Some of the soldiers looked at him but did not say anything. He felt strange as he walked between the beds and when he came into the small room that Sergeant Kesh Kesh had occupied there was a new sergeant there. The man had his knapsack thrown over the bed and he was shaving in front of a small mirror that stood on top of the small cupboard. *Jato is right,* he thought, *when he says that nobody owns a bed on the war front. This bed must have belonged to some other sergeant before it did to Kesh Kesh and now it belongs to a sergeant I do not even know. The most secure bed on the war front,* he thought, *is the grave, whether hastily dug to accommodate hundreds of bodies or found into the ready-made coffin of the river's depths.*

'Who are you and what do you want?' the sergeant asked, looking away from the mirror at him and then back again to the mirror.

'My name is Osime,' Osime told him. 'I am an editor with the *Daily News*.'

'Journalist, then?'

'Yes.'

'What are you doing here?'

'I came here to look for a friend.'

'A friend?'

'Yes, Sergeant Kesh Kesh. He was here yesterday evening.'

'Is your friend dark and tall and broad shouldered?'

'Yes.'

'I think they moved to the next dormitory. The one on the other side.' He pointed.

'Thank you,' Osime said.

'Where do you come from?' The sergeant asked and he stopped.

'I am a Nigerian.'

'So am I. I said, where do you come from?'
'From Midwest State.'
'What part of the Midwest?'
Osime told him.
'Is that so?' the sergeant asked enthusiastically and the hostility and suspicion were gone from his voice now. 'Are you really from there?' he asked and held out his hand. 'My name is Atake, Sergeant Atake.'
Osime took his hand. 'I am from there,' he said.
'I was there just before the war and then imagine us going back there three months ago. I knew the place and the people. We took it from the rebels.'
'Really?'
'Yes. Won't you sit down? Sit down and I will tell you about Ugbegun.'
Osime sat down on the man's bed and he watched him feeling his shaved chin and presently, the man cleared the mirror away from the top of the small cupboard and sat on it.
'There are two roads to Ugbegun from Irrua,' he began. 'The first road goes through Usugbenu while the second goes through Opoji. We came into Ugbegun through the Opoji road. But the Biafrans had expected us on the Usugbenu road.'
'How did this happen?' Osime asked.
'There were about five hundred rebels at Ugbegun. Every night we sent in a few shells from Usugbenu. We built up all the pressure on that front. So they expected our attack from there. But all the time we had built up another offensive in the Opoji area. Then one morning, it was five o'clock in the morning, we took up our positions and began the assault. In all, it lasted about thirty minutes. The rebels were caught with their pants down. They had moved all their men up the other road and here we were on this road. They were caught completely unawares.'
'You must have taken many prisoners.'
'No. We didn't. At the first sound of firing, the Biafrans got the message and bolted. Those that were up on the other road jumped into their vehicles and made for the road to Agbor. But we chased them up Eguare-Ugbegun, past the coffee plantation and the schools right up to Umenlen, one of the villages that make up Ugbegun. We only caught some fifty of the rebel soldiers, those of them that were unable to make the vehicles. It was one of our sweetest and

swiftest operations.'

'What did you do to the Biafran soldiers?'

'The rebel soldiers? They were all mostly small boys of fifteen, sixteen or seventeen. There were some old ones among them but very few.'

'What did you do to them?'

'The Ugbegun people told us they did not want any killings in their town. They sent us a deputation of elders. They said although they had been maltreated by the rebels, they did not want them shot. There was a man whose car they had seized and almost shot. He was among the deputation.'

'So you took them prisoner?'

'They are among the luckiest rebels in this war. Imagine people sending you a deputation not to kill the enemy soldiers! We were surprised. We sent them up to Benin — I don't know what happened to them there. But the victory itself was swift and sweet. I led the Federal soldiers.'

Osime stood up.

'You are going already, journalist?'

'Yes. I must see Sergeant Kesh Kesh.'

'You can come here any time you want. I will be your friend.'

'Thank you.'

'Any cigarettes, journalist?'

'No, I've none left. I'm sorry.'

'Well, so long, journalist. And remember to come here whenever you want to.'

'Thank you again.'

'Oh, it's nothing. Probably we will never meet again.'

'Sure we will.'

'You think so, journalist?'

'I'm sure of it.'

The other man gripped his hand, firmly, briefly, and then he was walking between the row of beds and then on the narrow path back towards the building where he had slept with Jato. He told himself he would see Sergeant Kesh Kesh later.

He came to the building and he saw that the door was open. Jato was inside sweeping the floor. He had first sprinkled sand on top of the vomit and was now sweeping both away. Osime stood at the entrance to the building on the step and Jato came out of the room into the corridor, and on his forehead were beads of sweat. He avoided Osime's eyes.

'So you are back,' he said, holding the broom down and away from him.

'Yes.'

'I must have got myself badly smashed last night.'

'I wouldn't know.'

'You mean you were asleep?'

'Yes.'

'I am sorry. I sincerely am,' Jato said. 'I didn't even know when it happened. I can't remember.'

'It's all right.'

'No. I mean it doesn't happen like this . . . it has never happened before.'

'There's always a first time.'

'And a last time. It will never happen again, I swear.'

'I believe you. Come on. Sweep it away.'

Jato held out his hand and Osime looked at the outstretched hand and then away.

Jato shrugged his shoulders and then bent down again and began to sweep the floor. Osime went away from the entrance to the house and stood on the road, on the path. Jato swept the floor of the room and then he came out and went to the back of the house and Osime could hear water running into the bucket. Jato came back with the bucket of water and re-entered the room.

So he is going to wash the floor of the room as well. I should have taken the man's hand when he offered it. I should have taken it, because I think the man is decent underneath. Perhaps he may be the second recruit of the third army.

He went up the step of the house and stood at the entrance. 'Do you need any help?' he called.

Jato came out of the room to the corridor, where they could both see each other and the sweat was on his face in little streams now. 'No, thank you.' He smiled.

Osime came down the step again and walked to the side of the house, on the grass. He could see Brigadier Otunshi's house from here and again he saw the open trucks that had brought the soldiers. *This is where it all ends,* he thought. *You place a thousand men inside trucks and you bring them as reinforcements to the front and they see the River Niger, and are anxious and talkative and afraid. They know that come another hour, another day, another week and they may be food for the worms as manure is food for the plants. We are each one of us afraid in this war. Those of us here at the front, and those of us training in various camps across the country, ready to be transported as cattle to the war fronts. This war is a factory and the soldiers are the raw materials. You feed the raw materials into the furnace of the factory but at the end, you do not get the product that you expect. You do not get the peace that you want. The generals get more power but you are no nearer any peace. This has got to be one of the several wars that are coming,* he thought. *This is the generals' war, the bishops' war, the politicians' war, the professors' war. This is not yet the war of the third army; and surely that will come as the day follows night. They load the soldiers into the trucks and burn them as raw materials in their factory of greed and shamelessness.*

But come the war of the third army, he thought, *and the generals and the traditional rulers and the bishops and the politicians and the police chiefs and the businessmen and the professors will be the raw materials as the soldiers from the working people are the raw materials in this war. And at the end of that war, there will be real peace, peace as peace should be.*

'Osime!'

Osime turned as he heard his name called and walked back to the front of the house and Jato stood there, bathed all over in sweat.

'I am going to bathe now,' Jato said. 'I won't be five minutes. Will you wait?'

'Yes, I'll wait.'

'Are you going to see her?'

'No,' he answered. 'We are not going to see her.'

'No?' Jato repeated in disappointment. 'Why not?'

'I don't want to go.'

'You wait!' Jato called. 'You wait and I will persuade you to go.'

Osime went into the room. It smelled strongly of Izal, and he came out again and stood on the step in the house. Out in the fields, he could see the new recruits in their blue shorts and white singlets doing their exercises. And there were the soldiers, fully dressed and drawn up in several rows. Osime could hear the voice of the sergeant barking out orders and at each shout of the sergeant's voice, the rows turned and raised their boots and brought the boots thundering down again or raised their guns first up then forward or took two quick steps forward and then stopped and then raised their guns. They were drilling them for the war.

And now, Jato had had his bath and was dressed and stood with Osime on the single step outside.

'Half past seven,' Jato said. 'Shall we go.'

'No,' Osime insisted.

Jato did not say anything for some time, then he said, 'The reinforcements came in the night.'

'I saw them this morning.'

'Did you count the trucks?'

'No. But there must have been at least a thousand soldiers.'

'That means that the offensive is going to start. The soldiers have not come here to eat breakfast.'

'That means many more dead soldiers, many more dead children and women and old people. That means greater suffering for a people who were swindled into the war.'

'Swindled?'

'Yes. We woke up one morning to be told that we were now at war. We were never consulted.'

'The Ibos seceded, remember?'

'The Ibos? Who are the Ibos?'

Jato looked at him sharply. 'Why do you pretend?' he asked.

'I'm not pretending,' Osime answered. 'You talk of Ibos as if they were all the same. When you talk of the Ibos are you referring to the generals in their army or to the men who sweep the floor in one of the Ministries at Enugu? Are you talking of the poor Ibo or the rich Ibo?'

'Are you saying only the rich and powerful Ibos made the decision to secede?'

'I don't see how you can dispute that,' Osime replied.

'What about the ordinary Ibos? Why did they rejoice when Ojukwu announced the secession? Why have they continued to fight for and support Ojukwu?'

'I am not aware that the ordinary Ibos rejoiced when Ojukwu announced the secession. And if they did, then something was seriously wrong. You don't rejoice when you are told to give up your children for a war. You don't celebrate when you know that, come another hour, your daughter will be raped, your sons slaughtered, your houses destroyed and you will be refugees in your own country. Our people were swindled into the war by propaganda. I will tell you what happens. You tell the Ibo man that the Hausa man is after his life, then you tell the Hausa man the same thing. You tell the Yoruba man that if only the Ibos left they would have jobs, the trade would be theirs. You tell the Hausa man that the Ibos have been holding secret meetings to get them wiped out. Then one morning, you arrange to have a Hausa man killed and you spread the news that he was murdered by the Ibos. That starts the pogrom. Behind the pogrom then are the rich and the powerful. The victims of the pogrom themselves do not say to themselves, we are being killed because we are not Nigerians. They do not, even in their wildest imaginations, dream of an alternative country. But then what happens? The rich and powerful Ibo man puts out the word. The Ibo man needs his own country. The Ibo man will be better off in a Biafra. The Ibo man will not be dominated in a Biafra. There will be no Hausas, no Yorubas. Biafra then is the end of all the problems of the Ibo man. The Ibo man must fight for a Biafra.

'The impression is created that the Ibo man's enemy is the man from the other tribe. In Biafra, the Ibo man will be king. Any Ibo man who doubts the word is told to look over his shoulder, at the pogrom. No wonder the Ibo man celebrates the announcement of a Biafra. But the whole thing is a swindle. It is a swindle because the decision to create Biafra is not made by the working Ibo man, it is made by the Ibo businessmen and generals and politicians. The ordinary man celebrates the decision he did not make and in celebrating it, he celebrates a lie and ultimately, his own death.'

'A lie?' Jato asked.

'Yes. A lie because in the first place, the Ibo man's enemy is not the man from the other tribe. His enemies are there in his own tribe as they are there in the other tribes. The Ibo businessman is a greater enemy to the ordinary Ibo man than the ordinary Hausa or the ordinary Yoruba man. The Ibo politician steals from the ordinary Ibo man whereas the ordinary Hausa man does not. The Ibo businessman cheats the ordinary Ibo man whereas the ordinary Yoruba man does not. The fact is that the ordinary Ibo has a great deal more in common with the ordinary Hausa and the ordinary Yoruba than he has in common with the Ibo businessman and general and politician.

'It is also a lie to talk about the Ibo man being king in the new Biafra. The ordinary Ibo man will be as much a slave, a servant, in the new Biafra as he was in the old Nigeria. He does not lose his chains by becoming a Biafran. Only, this time, they will bear the Biafran, not the Nigerian, label. And finally, it is a lie to imagine that the ordinary Ibo man will be better off than his counterpart from Calabar or Port Harcourt.

'But that's how the Ibo rulers swindled the people into the war. They told the people lies, they hid the facts. They did not tell the people about the starvation of children, about the disease, about the deaths, about the murders and the raping and the stealing. They told the people about the sun of Biafra, they did not tell the people about the darkness of Biafra. So the people celebrated a lie, a swindle.'

'Okay then,' Jato said. 'Let's agree that the Ibo leaders swindled the Ibo people into the war. But surely the same cannot be said about the Nigerian leaders? The Federal troops are fighting to end secession.'

'Rubbish,' Osime said impatiently. 'Absolute rubbish. The swindle is even greater on their side than on the side of the Ibo rulers. Where I come from, the Ibo man was a respected and loved neighbour until the Nigerian rulers put out the word. The Ibo man wants to dominate others. The Ibo men and women are planning to kill others. Lies. Absolute falsehoods. But these lies created the pogroms. And these lies were created by the people at the top out of greed for power and money. They wanted a war so they could steal more money and get more power. But they had to sell the war to the people. And as always, the tribe provided the raw material. Politicians who stole our money, hundreds of millions of naira, businessmen who robbed our country blind drove the country to war to cover up their crimes. This war then is the great cover-up, the great swindle. I tell you we were swindled into this war!'

'Then whose side are you on?' Jato asked. 'You like neither the Federal nor the Biafran generals. Whose side are you on then? Or do you think you can sit on the fence in this war?'

'No,' Osime replied. 'But as I said in the officers' mess last night, it depends on how many sides you see in this war.'

'There are only two sides,' Jato said quickly. 'The Nigerian and the Biafran.'

'And you are wrong there,' Osime argued. 'There is a third side. The people's side. The side of the working Ibo, the side of the working Hausa, the side of the working Yoruba, in short — the side of the working Nigerian man and woman.'

'But aren't we all on that side?' Jato asked. 'Aren't we all involved in this war on their side?'

'No,' Osime disagreed. 'If we all were, then this would have been a different war. Gowon would have been on the run and Ojukwu would have been on the run because they would have been on the same side where they actually do belong. The war then would have been honourable, and it would have been a pride to die in this war.'

'What you are asking for is a revolution,' Jato declared, shaking his head. 'And you know that it is impossible.'

'At the moment yes. But what today is impossible may become a reality tomorrow. Today we are unorganised. Tomorrow, the situation could be different.

'It is dangerous.'

'Walking here on the grass is dangerous.'

'Did you hear about Colonel Banjo?'

'Yes. He was sold out. He was betrayed. We were all betrayed there by a bastard of the regime.'

Jato did not say anything and Osime placed his hand on the man's shoulder.

'There are always difficulties,' he said. 'I wasn't very clear myself at the beginning of this war. Strictly speaking, I was a journalist. But a man learns. You see women and children who have nothing to do with the war being killed and something gives inside you. You lose your neutrality. But it takes more than seeing women raped and children beheaded to lose your neutrality to see clearly. You begin to ask questions, you hear people talk, you read, you learn. You begin to see for yourself that things are not what they seem. You get more and more alienated from the war.'

'But you must still be involved somehow. There is a war.'

'I am involved,' Osime defended himself. 'But my involvement is with the third army.'

'Is that the rebels' army?'

'Yes. The rebels from the Federal and Biafran armies. I detest this war, I loathe it because I understand its reasons. I know how it works and why it works. I hate it.'

'But there is nothing you can do.'

'Perhaps not just now. But who knows? Yesterday I spoke with the soldiers and I was surprised by their reactions. Some of them wanted to lay down their guns there and then. Others wanted the heads of some of the officers. I was . . .'

'That's very dangerous,' Jato warned him. 'You are playing with fire. If Otunshi had heard but . . . but then . . .'

'But what?'

Jato did not make any reply and Osime laughed. 'No,' he said.

'This is not a matter of in-laws. I believe that there has to be a beginning. Somebody has to make a beginning with the resistance. The third army must recruit its own soldiers.'

'It is dangerous,' Jato repeated. 'You do not see a fire and put your hand into it. You said you heard about Colonel Banjo. You said you heard about how he was sold to the enemy for thirty pieces of silver. What more do you want?'

'Nothing more,' Osime answered. 'Nothing more at all.'

He tried to speak as if he was light-hearted but he felt helpless and frustrated. Perhaps the third army was only a dream. One man alone cannot make an army, as one man alone cannot hold a red flag in a ring where there are many bulls. There must be other people waving the red flags, organised people.

And then he told himself that it was wrong to be hopeless and frustrated. The third army might not be formidable now, but who was to say it would not be formidable tomorrow? What was important was the possibility of the third army, the dream of the third army. *We do not need a thousand men,* he told himself. *We only need a beginning and one man is a beginning as one cloud is the beginning of the universe, as one star is the beginning of the universe, as one grain of sand is the beginning of the earth. What is important is the beginning, not the end of it. I am the beginning of the third army.*

Chapter twenty-one

Standing at the side of the house, the two men counted the open trucks and jeeps in front of Brigadier Otunshi's quarters.

'How many do you make them?' Jato asked.

'At least thirty trucks.'

'And as many jeeps. That means the war push is on. Onitsha is in the firing line.'

'Yes.'

'Let's go then.' He pointed to Brigadier Otunshi's quarters.

'No.' Osime shook his head.

'She sent the soldier for you. She sent for you.'

'No. I will not go even because of that.'

'Then I truly cannot understand you.'

'She is not my cousin,' Osime said and the other man turned and looked at him sharply and a questioning look came into his eyes.

'Not your cousin?'

'No.'

'Then you'd better not go,' Jato advised him, showing that he completely understood everything. 'You'd better leave Asaba immediately.'

'See?' Osime said. 'I knew you'd understand.'

'You had better leave immediately.'

'Otunshi doens't know that she is not my cousin.'

'He will find out.'

'Yes. If I go there. If we go there.'

'How did it happen?'

Osime closed his eyes. 'It's a long story.'

'You must not go,' Jato repeated and Osime opened his eyes and looked in front of him. He could see a man walking towards them. They came away from the side of the house and went and sat on the single step in front.

'What do you think?' Osime asked.

'The messenger's coming back.'

'Yes,' Osime agreed. 'Salome was always a very proud and insistent woman. She never gave up easily and what she wanted she always got.'

'Proud women can be vindictive, particularly when told to go to hell.'

'Hell has no fury like a woman scorned.'

'Something like that.'

'Yes,' Osime agreed.

Yes, Osime said to himself now. *There were several people there when I arrived and so she had her will and her suspicion and her pride. But I broke her self-consciousness because I refused to pay homage to her beauty. I saw it, I was moved by it and attracted to it with the force of magnets but I would not speak to the magnet. That baffled her and killed both her will and her suspicion. And it has been like that ever since. But I know what I went through the first few times I saw her. And later when we had become intimate, I knew that beauty was more than skin deep, that it took beautiful bones and beautiful blood to come up with a beautiful body. I said to myself what Jato said last night, that beauty is life experienced at a particular level of intensity. Salome had that effect on people. But I never told her.*

And I have made up mind now, he told himself. *You do not undo the pin of a grenade and hold the grenade in your hand. You throw the grenade as far away from you as possible. She must know that I have got her out of my system, out of my blood, once and for all. She must be able to look me clearly in the eyes and not see a cloud there. Because perhaps she has the impression that there are clouds still. When we met at the stadium, there were clouds and when we went to the Luna Club there were clouds. When we met there at the officers' mess, there were clouds, although by then, the clouds were false, like clouds in the dry season. What is left between us now is nothing but an itch and I have sworn that I will not scratch it for her.*

The soldier walked round the house and came out of the side and Osime saw that it was the same man who had brought the first note. He did not get up.

'From Madam,' the soldier said and gave Osime the perfumed white envelope in which was neatly folded the light blue writing paper.

Osime read the note and put it back in the envelope and folded the envelope twice and put it in his back pocket.

'Any message, sir?'

'No,' Osime said. 'Tell Madam that I have seen it.'

The soldier hesitated, then smiled and went away.

'What does she want now?' Jato asked as soon as the soldier was out of earshot.

'She expects me.'

'She is a beautiful woman.'

'Yes. You can go instead of me.'

Jato laughed. 'I feel like doing exactly that but I value my life. I will not go.'

'That's sensible. The war is a madhouse but that doesn't mean we have lost all our senses . . . Why did they send you here?' he asked Jato.

'Just my luck.'

'You mean you have such bad luck?'

'Not exactly. It's been pretty good so far.'

'And your family? Do you have a family?'

'Yes,' Jato said. 'I do have a family. A wife who is not beautiful but good enough for me, two boys and a girl. And then I have my mother. My father is dead. And, of course, there is also the extended family.'

'How many children has your mother?'

'Six. Three men, three women. I am the second and the breadwinner really.'

'It must be hard on them then, your being here.'

Jato shrugged his shoulders. 'Isn't the war hard on everybody?'

'Yes. How long are you going to be here?'

'Until Onitsha is liberated. To tell you the truth, I volunteered for the war front.'

'Volunteered for the war front? You volunteered to come here?'

'Yes. I have always been intrigued by the war. Ileuminonsen, that's my wife, was unhappy at first but she's come to accept it. And in any case, come another week and I may be back.'

'My fiancée is at Oganza,' Osime said.

'In rebel-held territory?'

'Yes.'

'And you still want to marry her?'

'What's wrong with that?'

Jato did not say anything but Osime understood. 'I do not mind,' he said finally.

Jato shrugged his shoulders. 'Good for you. But I don't think I could.'

'Well, you're out of danger,' Osime reminded him. 'You're married already.'

'Yes. With three lovely children. Oh my God,' he said suddenly. 'How I miss those children! How I miss those boys!'

'It could soon be over.' Osime stood up and Jato looked at him.

'Where are you off to?'

'To see the Biafran prisoners of war.'

'You mean you haven't been there?'

'No.'

'They are not too badly treated. They are just children mostly.'

'I want to see for myself.'

'You should.'

'And the hospital as well.'

'Yes. That too.'

'There are a few nurses there. Mostly reserved. Only the officers have permission to go with them.'

'I am not interested.'

'You have only just come,' Jato reminded him. 'Stay here one month without a woman and then go to the hospital and stop yourself from looking at the nurses.'

'Well, you should know. You have been here that long. See you later.'

He went down to the block where he was told Sergeant Kesh Kesh now had his bed. Sergeant Kesh Kesh was not in the room. He came out and walked towards the building that housed the prisoners of war. And as he went along he thought about Salome. It was over. Over and done with.

He remembered how it had been the very first time with her. The first time is always the most memorable time, and if you are lucky and not nervous, it is also the best time. And they had been lucky. He had surrendered himself completely, as completely as she had surrendered herself until nothing had separated them at all. They went through the film of flame and back and she told him, 'You have taken my pain from me.'

'Was it that much?'

'Yes,' she had answered, then added, 'It was much more. I felt you somersaulting inside me. Did you feel it?'

'Yes. You turned me inside out. That was when the somersault came.'

'They were like earthquakes inside me. What did I do then?'

'The same thing as when an earthquake moves. You screamed.'

'Have you felt it, experienced it before?'

'No, never,' he had admitted quite truthfully. 'Not once in my life. Let's celebrate it.'

'Yes,' she agreed. 'Let's love each other, now and for always.'

'That's a very long time,' he had reminded her.

'Always,' she had repeated and held him and put her arms round him. 'Always!' and she had clapped and laughed and stood up and danced round the room.

Yes, he said to himself now, *the first time is always the most memorable time and if you are lucky and it is good, then it counts for all time. And she was always a strong woman, strong but good. The bad times were when she was angry. I remember she threw a hammer at me once, and when that missed, she threw a bottle at me. And when that missed, she had walked out of the house and not come back for several days. She came back because, she said, she missed feeling the movement of the earth inside her, like in a landslide. And then she had been very very sweet for a long time until one day, she had come in and told me that she was going to get married to a man who was going to become a general. I didn't believe her then and she laughed and threw the wedding invitation at me. Still, I didn't believe she would go through with it until she actually stopped coming to my house.*

You cannot eat your cake and have it, he thought. *Let her feel humiliated and shamed, let her be bitter, but I feel myself completely free of her, completely free of the earthquake. I should celebrate my freedom as we celebrated the earthquake. I will not scratch her itch. I will not give her the satisfaction. What happened at the Luna Club was sheer, utter madness. It's all over and done with.*

He came to the building that housed the Biafran prisoners of war. He expected to find a prison guarded by a lot of soldiers but to his surprise there were only a few soldiers on guard over the building.

Out in the open, two men were surrounded by a group of others and when he went closer, he found the men were engaged in a game of draughts. One was a Federal soldier, the other a Biafran prisoner of war.

'Your move,' the Biafran said and moved a piece himself.

'Very good,' the Nigerian soldier said. 'Very good. You have entered the same trap that we set for you at Nsukka!' He laughed and moved a piece.

'And this is how we surprised you there,' the Biafran POW responded. 'This is how we escaped and later ambushed you. See?' He moved his own piece.

'And this is what happens when you lay an improper ambush,' the Nigerian soldier boasted and clapped. He offered a piece to the Biafran POW and then proceeded to clear two pieces.

'What I expected,' the Biafran POW smiled and offered his own piece and when the Nigerian soldier took it proceeded to claim three pieces. The men laughed and laughed at the move.

Osime looked for the guns of the Nigerian soldiers and at first, he did not see them until he went by the side of the building and under a tree, there were two Nigerian soldiers there and five Kalashnikovs were leaning against the trunk of the tree. He went round the building and on each side, there was a post with at least two armed soldiers. He came back to the front of the building and entered and he could see several men sleeping on the beds or just sitting round, talking or playing cards. There must have been at least three hundred prisoners.

He came out of the building and this time, he came back to the group of men playing draughts. The men were absorbed in the game now. One POW was whistling loudly and another was standing a little away from the group and talking to a Nigerian soldier.

Osime went away without talking to any of the soldiers. *The Nigerian soldier has more in common with the Biafran soldier than with the Nigerian general,* he repeated to himself. *Doubt this, say it isn't true and come to this block that houses the POWs.* He did not bother going to the hospital.

Chapter twenty-two

Sergeant Kesh Kesh stood inside the room holding the bottle of brandy in his hand.

'I told you,' he said. 'I told you that Brigadier Otunshi is a man who wants quick results at all costs. We start the push for Onitsha tonight.'

'What do you think will happen?' Osime asked.

'We will lose many soldiers.'

'How many?'

'More than half of what we throw in.'

'But you will win?'

'Yes. Brigadier Otunshi will win.'

'Do the soldiers know this?'

'No. But they will with time.'

'I will go with you,' Osime said.

'It will be dangerous. We may not come back.' He put the small end of the bottle in his mouth and took a long drink of the brandy. 'You must think about it carefully.'

'I have thought about it carefully,' Osime insisted. 'I have thought about it and I want to come. Besides, I have already told Brigadier Otunshi that I will come.'

Sergeant Kesh Kesh looked at him closely then and shook his head. 'If you want to commit suicide, then go ahead. You will come with Corporal Kolawole. He will give you a gun.'

'I don't need a gun.'

'Then you don't accompany us,' Sergeant Kesh Kesh said.

'Okay then,' Osime agreed. 'I will carry the gun. But you must also allow another journalist to come with us.'

'That's impossible,' Sergeant Kesh Kesh said. 'We want to take responsibility only for trained soldiers.'

'He is a good man,' Osime said. 'A very good man. And he desperately wants to come.'

Sergeant Kesh Kesh thought for a while and then asked, 'What is his name?'

'Jato.'

'Jato?'

'Yes. Jato. I do not know the surname.'

'He is willing too to die?'

'He wants to come with us.'

'All right then,' Sergeant Kesh Kesh finally agreed. 'Let him come and die with us.'

'He will survive this battle and all the others. We will survive this war.'

'You are an optimist, journalist.'

'And so are you. When do you leave?'

'I imagine in a few hours. The mechanised units have gone. That means we shall move next. When the shelling of the town starts, then we shall be ready to move.'

'Across the bridge?'

'Yes. Across the bridge and across the river in boats. The mechanised regiment will cross by the bridge. Some of the infantry will use the boats and cross the river. Others will cross by the bridge.'

'Which would you prefer?'

'The boats, certainly. I can swim.'

'So can I. But the Biafrans will be waiting on the banks in their trenches.'

'No. That's what the shelling and the mortar bombardment are supposed to prevent. They won't be there. They will be driven by the bombardment to take refuge in the houses in the city or in the surrounding villages.'

'There could be a lot of casualties then?'

'There will be a lot of casualties.'

'And you don't mind?'

'Look, journalist,' Sergeant Kesh Kesh said. 'There are a lot of things in this war you would never do if you thought about them a little more deeply. I would never have left my wife. I would never have killed another man. But it is a war and those who mind what happens never survive. They are always the first casualties.'

'So you do not mind killing the Biafrans.'

'They are rebels.'

'They were Nigerians before they became rebels.'

'No. They were Nigerians, then they became rebels, after which they became Biafrans.'

'We are saying the same thing.'

'No, we're not saying the same thing. Calling them Biafrans means that they are right. Now you don't kill people who are fighting for what you know is right?'

'You are saying you cannot sympathise with a man and then kill him?'

'I am saying that when I kill them, I kill them as rebels.'

'As Nigerians,' Osime said.

'Those who survive, those we liberate become the Nigerians.'

'They always were Nigerians,' Osime insisted. 'What has happened is that we are all caught up in the fight between elephants; elephants fighting for more space, more power, more money.'

Sergeant Kesh Kesh looked steadily at Osime and then shook his head from side to side. 'Can anyone really understand you, journalist? One moment, you are on their side and I wonder whether you are not their agent. The next moment you are on our side and my doubts begin to go away. And now, you are not on any side. You simply talk as all the other journalists do.'

Osime shook his head in disagreement. 'No, Sergeant Kesh Kesh. I do not talk at all like the other journalists. What I am really saying is that we all have no business in this war.' He stopped and watched for the other man's reaction. It did not come. So he continued, 'We are fighting the wrong enemies.' He stalled again and this time, Sergeant Kesh Kesh spoke up.

'Yes,' he agreed. 'Ojukwu is the real enemy. But how can you get to Ojukwu without clearing the path that leads to him? If Ojukwu surrenders, the war ends.'

'No,' Osime told him. 'The war may end on one front. But it will go on on other fronts too. Gowon is also your enemy, as much if not much more your enemy than Ojukwu.' He watched the eyes of the man and he saw the frown as it came up.

'Why do you say such terrible things, journalist? Why do you say things for which you could easily get shot?' Sergeant Kesh Kesh looked at him steadily.

Osime shrugged his shoulders and held the eyes of the other man. 'It is because I care,' he said. 'It is because it is the truth. But I will not pursue it. I will not speak of it any more. I will tell you, instead, something that happened to me two years ago. I was walking with a friend of mine on Upper Mission Road, just past the New Benin Market, in Benin City. My friend was deeply worried about what somebody had done to him. "Tell me," he asked suddenly, "how a man can know his true friends, how he can recognise his friends." And this is what I told him. I told him that you get to know your true friends only after you have become involved with them in concrete activities, that experience teaches both men and women who their true friends are. That those with whom one goes out to drink and womanise are not a man's true friends, that is, until proven so by concrete instances. And what I said then, I still believe now. You will not know who your real enemy is until this war has been fought and won or lost. But one thing I do know, though. The Biafran soldier who carries a gun and is sent to the slaughterhouse after only two weeks of training, after only two weeks of being fattened, is no more your enemy than your wife whom you were forced to leave behind in your village. Neither you nor the Biafran soldier ever had any disagreement before this war and besides, and this is more important, many, if not all, aspects of your lives were the same and remain the same still. Just like you, the Biafran soldier did not go to school, he was never sure of the next meal, he was never sure of a roof over his head, he could not rely on his health. He joined the army because of a deep sense of patriotism, although of course hunger also played a part in it. And then look at Ojukwu and Gowon. You look at the generals on both sides, the men who wear all the pips and the eagles and the crossed swords on their shoulders. These are men who for a long time, perhaps all their lives, have never known hunger, have always had servants, have never known any want. You look at these facts and if you stand where I am and care as I do, then you will come to see that Ojukwu and Gowon have much more in common than Ojukwu and the ordinary Biafran soldiers or Gowon and the ordinary Nigerian soldiers. You will come to see as I do that the Biafran soldier has more in common with the Nigerian soldier than with any officer on either side.'

All the time he was talking, he held the eyes of the other man. First he saw the cloud of doubt in his eyes and then the cloud darkened in anger and then the man's eyes became bright with interest, so much so that the shaking of his head from side to side stopped and he brought his right hand out and supported his chin with it. He knew now that he had the man's interest, no longer his suspicion, and that, he sensed, was important.

'Think about it now,' he urged Sergeant Kesh Kesh. The Biafran soldier leaves his wife at home just like you do but the generals bring their wives to the front. Those who do not bring their wives to the front go back to the cities every so often where their wives or girlfriends are being quartered. And when the town falls and you enter the villages, it's always the soldiers who do the raping and looting and burn the houses or shoot the civilians. The soldiers are encouraged to do these things by the officers so that in the end, the opinions of the men about themselves become so low that they see no difference between right and wrong. They no longer think of themselves as being human. They start to feel guilty for the whole war. But the officers wait in the background. And in the evenings, the women are brought to their quarters and they take these women and treat them as a defeated, captured people. They do terrible things to them. Then they go to the banks and blow up the safes and take the money in the safes. Again, at the end of the month, they claim for themselves the salaries of soldiers whom they have sent to be slaughtered at the fronts. But because all these things are done quietly, they end up feeling no guilt. They end up abusing the soldiers for indiscipline, for raping the women of the captured villages, for shooting the civilian populations. And all these happen on either side, on the Biafran side and on the Nigerian side. Think about it again,' he urged Sergeant Kesh Kesh. 'Ask yourself which of the soldiers leave their wives behind or engage in raping women or looting or burning the houses. Ask yourself which of the soldiers have the lowest opinion of themselves in this war. If you ask yourself these questions and answer them truthfully, you will come to see as I see and talk as I talk. You will come to see that Gowon is as much your enemy as Ojukwu is your enemy and both are the enemies of the soldiers on either the Biafran or the Nigerian side.'

Sergeant Kesh Kesh did not say anything for a long time. Then, he closed his eyes and raised his hand over his face and then opened his eyes and looked Osime directly in the eyes.

'There is nothing we can do,' he said finally. 'There is nothing any of us can do until this war ends. Neither our soldiers nor the rebels. I mean, the Biafran soldiers will not lay down their arms just like that. This war is like a fire with a lot of dry logs in it. Until the logs get burnt out, the fire will not go out.'

'That is true, sergeant,' Osime agreed. 'But it is also true that you can start to see the soldiers on the other side differently. It helps to know they are in a position similar to yours and that the real traitors are the generals on either side.'

Sergeant Kesh Kesh did not say anything.

'Do you know that as we go into battle now, arrangements are being made for the marriage of the head of state?'

'Yes. A time comes and a man gets married.'

'Yes, and he gets married at a time when men and women in whole villages are being slaughtered, when soldiers are being slaughtered at the fronts. He sends the children of other people, the husbands of other women, the wives of other men into the war and has them killed so that he can get married. And do you know what the marriage really means?'

'No.'

'The marriage makes a mockery of the sacrifices the husbands of other women are making here at the front. It makes a mockery of the entire war.'

'A man has to get married,' Sergeant Kesh Kesh insisted but the conviction in his voice had gone.

Osime stood up from the chair and the other man followed him to the door and slapped him on the back. 'Journalist,' he said. 'The truth you speak is clear but it is dangerous. You must be careful. I'll meet you in an hour. We shall be ready to go in an hour.'

'To the slaughter,' Osime added and went out.

Chapter twenty-three

The convoy of vehicles moved slowly along the road. Only the parking lights of the vehicles were on and they were to be turned off as soon as they got to the slope that went down to the river. The Nigerian soldiers did not want the Biafrans to see the lights since that would have given the Biafrans the signal that the attack was on. The plan was to get the vehicles to the bridge in the dark and then begin the shelling of the town. The tanks would gradually move forward on the bridge, followed by the armoured vehicles and then the troop carriers. The tanks would all the time be involved in the attack in order to disorganise the Biafrans and drive them away from the banks where they had dug many trenches. At the same time many of the soldiers would cross the river in boats and land on the beaches. There were to be about two thousand soldiers involved in the whole exercise and the majority of them were to cross the river in boats and canoes. Sergeant Kesh Kesh's section, as part of the mechanised brigade, was to go across the bridge.

Osime thought about the plan as he sat inside one of the jeeps and grimaced. *The Biafrans are already aware that we are on the move,* he said to himself, *for nothing is a secret in this war, particularly on this front. They would have known to the second the beginning of the attack and made preparations. All this business about moving in the dark with the parking lights off is absolute rubbish,* he thought. *But then,* he added to himself, *isn't everything about this war rubbish?*

There was dead silence in the jeep as it went slowly along the road. The men sat close to each other, their Kalashnikovs held straight up, their helmets throwing deep shadows over their faces. They kept quiet as each man thought his own thoughts and wondered whether he would be alive in the morning. But he knew that they could not contemplate their own death. Each man hoped he would escape unhurt and return home to his family after this war. If they did not hope, they would not be sitting here quietly, they would have got down a long time ago and returned home.

And there must be some fear too, he thought. *Look at me, I am myself afraid of this war now. There is this cold region in my heart, cold as the iron I hold in my hands, cold and hard as the iron and, of course, it is my fear. So there is fear and there is hope and a lot of courage too, for without the courage the men would not be sitting here either. I cannot see their faces but I am sure whatever tension there is on their faces is minor. You need a lot of courage to sit quietly in a jeep that is taking you to the slaughterhouse. You need a lot of courage to be able to sit quietly and say nothing and not perspire in your palms.*

He held up his left hand against his nose and smelt the sweat in his palm and then wiped it on the sleeve of his uniform and waited, listening, for the other men to do so. Presently, the man Jato raised his hand and wiped it on his face and then rubbed his face against the sleeve of his uniform. He smiled as he waited for more hands to be wiped on sleeves. He waited and then his smile went away because no further hand went up and he knew then that here indeed was courage. The gun felt heavy across his lap and the camera felt like a millstone round his neck. He felt strange and uneasy carrying a gun he knew he would not use. He felt uneasy and dry-mouthed. *Probably Jato feels the same way,* he thought. *But he must have been in spots like this before. He must be used to it.*

This plan of theirs is nonsense. The Biafrans must hear the loud noise of the armoured vehicles and cars. They must hear the movements of tanks and know that the onslaught is under way. Talk about a secret invasion and then get the armoured vehicles to make enough noise to be heard twenty kilometres away.

The shelling of the Biafran positions started exactly at nine o'clock. Osime had been expecting it but when it came, it gave him a big jolt and he started so violently that he almost knocked the soldier sitting beside him over sideways. He could not see the faces of the soldiers and as he apologised, his voice sounded strange in the darkness. Nobody, not even the soldier he had almost knocked over, answered him. There was dead silence in the jeep and the breathing of the men would have been heard but for the loud ejections and thundering explosions of the cannons.

The shelling was being done from three positions. There was the gun on the bridge that fired straight across the bridge into the distance. At each explosion of the shell, the men raised a shout suggesting they had made a hit. Then there were the two guns, one on either side of the river and mounted on the sides of the slope, far away from the bridge. They could hear the shouts coming from here too as each gun lighted up the night and then exploded the quiet of the night.

Flames, he thought, *flames of destruction, explosions of homes, lives, nature. How many die with each explosion? How many lives does each shell carry with it? We must be mad. Stark raving mad to raise a shout each time the shell explodes, we must be insane to be here firing these guns attempting to kill the Biafrans, the Ibos who until yesterday afternoon were our brothers and sisters and our in-laws and wives and children. My God!* He cried within himself. *How come on this harmless July night we are holding guns and going forward to slaughter our own brethren? Where did we get this madness? Who gave us this madness?*

'What time is it?'

He turned now and looked at Jato and drew his long sleeve upward and then looked at the luminous dials on his wristwatch. 'Three forty seven,' he said. 'Three fifty. Almost four. What do you think?'

'I am afraid.'

'Afraid?'

'Yes. The ferocity of the attack frightens me. But more than that, I am frightened by the silence of the Biafrans.'

'What do you mean?'

'They must be waiting for us on the other side. The Biafrans are best when you think you already have them licked. Suddenly, they come up, they surprise you and then you are on the defensive, on the retreat.'

'So you don't think they will abandon Onitsha?'

'Abandon Onitsha? Not so easily. Onitsha is the gateway to the strongest Biafran defences; Akwa, Nnewi, Owerri, Umuahia, Ihiala. No. They must be planning something. They must be planning to surprise us.' They were halfway across the bridge now

Osime looked over the side of the bridge and in the paling darkness, he could see the boats, hundreds of them, headed for the banks of the river on the Biafran side. They were going slowly and in groups of three so that they formed small but numerous islands in the river. He saw the silhouettes of the men and shook his head. It all seemed even more senseless now, senseless that these men should be in the boats in the river going into battle for a cause that was not really their own, in a war that they knew little about. *And these are the men that Brigadier Otunshi called cowards,* he thought. *These are the men he said had no courage, who shoot themselves so they would not go into battle. He called them cowards, insulted their manhood. These are the men slowly going forward across the bridge in the jeeps and on foot, across the river in boats, holding pieces of cold steel in their hands, the men in whose hands the seizure of Onitsha lies.* The guns continued to fire their cannons into the Biafran positions.

'What do you think Gowon will be doing this night?' he said to Jato, turning away from the river.

'He must be busy preparing for his wedding tomorrow morning,' Jato said.

'You mean this morning?'

'Yes. The head of state has to marry. You need a first lady to successfully prosecute this war. Ojukwu has Victoria.'

'And Gowon also wants a Victoria.'

'Which is why we have this war. Each wants what the other has and that is why on this night, Gowon is busy preparing for his state wedding.'

'And we are on this bridge and the men are in the boats and the guns are firing.'

'We shall come out of this alive?'

'You should know,' Osime said. You have . . .' He stopped because suddenly, he heard a loud shout and almost immediately, an outburst of heavy gunfire. The jeep came to a stop with a jolt and the rest of the men still in the jeep scrambled out of it and now they were all on the road, standing beside the jeep. They waited, perhaps a few minutes but it felt like half an hour. Sergeant Kesh Kesh went away from the jeep and then he was back. They couldn't see his face but his voice was quiet and very steady too, the way a doctor's voice is when confirming the death of a patient.

'You will stay here now,' he said to Osime and Jato. 'Stay here and keep your heads down and do nothing foolish because from now on, it is going to be dangerous.'

Osime was going to protest but the man turned away quickly and got into the jeep and the other soldiers got into the jeep and it began to move away, slowly. They were left on the road. The other jeeps came and went past them where they stood. He felt awkward holding the gun as he stood on the bridge.

The sound of gunfire and voices alternated and the voices were mainly screams while the gunfire came in bursts, steady continuous bursts and all the time there was the movement of the vehicles and then of feet as the soldiers scrambled from the jeeps to the road, firing automatically as they alighted from the jeeps. And all the time screams, shouts. Everywhere, they could see the bright flames of the rifles and machine guns. The slaughter was going on on the bridge, in the river, on both sides of the bridge. There were shouts and screams and gunfire, followed by loud splashes in the water as both men and boats turned over in the water. The whole surface of the water was alive with the flames of the gunfire and the voices of the men.

Then behind them, there was a loud explosion and he could feel the bridge sway dangerously and then a huge splash in the water. *They have blown up the bridge,* he thought. *Blown up the bridge from the Asaba end to cage us in.*

There was now nothing but the screams of the men and the sound of the gunfire. 'The rebels are on the bridge!' he heard somebody shout. 'They are on the bridge!' came the voice again and then there was a steady outburst of gunfire on the bridge and then voices of men as they screamed in pain.

A jeep came towards them furiously in reverse and they had to jump out of its way as it swerved first one way and then the other. They ran forward and raised a shout but it was too late. The jeep seemed to disappear in the very centre of the bridge and a minute or two passed and then they heard the rude impact of the jeep as it hit the water of the river below.

Many more vehicles had started their engines and begun to reverse but stopped, keeping their engines running.

'What's happening?' Jato asked.

'I don't know.'

'You think the Biafrans are on the bridge?'

'Perhaps.' He was holding his gun now in a firing position.

'I told you,' the man Jato said now. 'I told you that the silence of the Biafrans was unusual and now we are trapped.'

Some of the cars began moving again but stopped almost immediately because two of them had run into each other, blocking the way for the others. There was a sudden outburst of gunfire which went on for several minutes. There were more shouts and screams and then more gunfire and more screams.

'We are surrounded!' Jato screamed. 'We are completely surrounded!'

'Rubbish!' Osime screamed back as he lay flat on the road.

There was a shout and then more gunfire.

'The Biafrans are around us!' Jato screamed. 'I am making for the river!'

'Nonsense!' Osime called back, angry and impatient with the

man. He tried to look under the jeep but he couldn't see any movement of soldiers. Nothing but the shouts and screams and the flames of the guns intensified. *You must not panic*, Osime calmed himself. *You must not panic. The Biafrans cannot be on the bridge. We cannot be surrounded.* Involuntarily, his finger tightened on the trigger of the Kalashnikov and his whole body trembled as pulling it, he heard a loud explosion.

'We are cooked,' Jato kept screaming. 'Finally cooked unless we can fight our way to the other side, unless we can make the Biafrans retreat. I cannot swim.'

'We are not cooked,' Osime called back, his voice shaking. 'We will fight our way out. We will get into Onitsha and then take a boat back across the river.' *Did I really fire that gun?* he wondered. *Did I make that explosion?* He pushed the gun away from him.

'We are finished!' Jato moaned now. 'You don't realise it because you don't know that Brigadier Otunshi left soon after the attack started.'

'Left soon after the attack started?' He was surprised at the calmness of his voice, at the coldness of his mind.

'He left and took four colonels, three lieutenant colonels and some majors with him. They left for the wedding soon after the attack started. They got into three jeeps and headed for Benin to take the first plane to Lagos. They've gone, abandoned us here and now we are cooked.'

'Do the men know this?' He felt quiet and all right now.

'Sure,' Jato cried. 'Sure, they know we are finished.'

'Come on, man, steady your nerves. I mean do they know about Otunshi and the other officers, that they have gone to the wedding?'

The man Jato looked at him and shook his head. 'No, they cannot know. The attack was already well under way. How could they know?'

It was getting brighter and brighter and soon it would be daylight. He looked at his watch and it was just past five. *We have to get out of this,* he told himself. *I can swim but the height is too much from here. I have never taken such a jump before. It must be well over a hundred metres from the bridge to the surface of the water. And then, I have to take Jato with me.*

'Let's go forward,' Osime said. 'Let's move forward and see what is happening.' He picked up the gun again; it was still warm from the shot.

'We ought to get some photographs.'

'Photographs? Can't they wait?'

'I am not afraid,' Jato said.

'Let's not debate that. Let's go forward.'

They went forward on the bridge, slowly against the railings, using whatever cover they could find. They hadn't gone far, however, when Jato gripped him by the arm.

'I think we should stop,' he said.

'And take photographs?'

He did not say anything for some time. Then, 'It's the stray bullets I am afraid of. Several journalists have died that way.'

'But we have to go forward.'

'Did you see those soldiers?'

'Yes.'

'It's terrible!'

'You must have seen worse than this before.'

'Well, each time is always different. There is no similarity, no comparison with what you may have seen before.'

'But we must go forward. Listen to the firing. That comes from the end of the bridge. I am sure the Federal soldiers would have secured the head of the bridge.'

'Did you see those dead soldiers?'

'I counted fifty-seven.'

'There would have been more in the jeeps.'

'Perhaps, but we must not stop.'

'Okay then,' he said, giving up. 'Let's stop.'

A few feet away, a man was moaning and they went over to him and bent over him and felt his chest and Osime's hands could feel the blood as it soaked through the man's shirt.

'It's no use,' he said. 'The man was shot in the chest.' He looked closely at the man's face and then with a sharp movement stood up.

He looked down now at Obilu and a vision flashed before his eyes of the smile of the man, teaching him to hold the gun. He wiped the sweat off his face and in the process smeared the man's blood on his face. He bent down again to see what he could do but it was too late. The groaning had stopped and the man was dead.

'Fifty-eight,' Jato said.

'Yes,' Osime agreed thoughtfully. *Fifty-eight, and that doesn't count fifty-eight widows, fifty-eight fathers and as many mothers who have lost their sons. That doesn't count the children of the fifty-eight soldiers. More than a hundred perhaps. And then add the brothers and the sisters and the grandparents and their friends. This was a friend of mine.*

They heard another scream not far away from them and went forward and found a man who was screaming at the top of his voice and holding his thigh. And not two paces away, an officer was shouting commands to a group of soldiers who were hesitating to go forward. Still the man who had been shot in the thigh continued to scream, first in his native language and then in pidgin and then back to his local language.

'Shoot him if he continues to scream!' they heard the officer shout to one of the hestitating men who took two paces backward from the others and came over to the screaming soldier.

'It must be bad,' he said to Osime and Jato as he bent over the man. 'He must feel terrible. There are no doctors with us now. They are cut off on the other side, including the ambulance vehicles and the rescue teams.'

'You're not going to shoot him?' Jato asked.

'He is in serious pain,' the man said. And he stood up and took two paces away from the wounded soldier.

'Surely you can't shoot him!' Osime screamed. 'The man is only wounded.'

The wounded soldier must have felt that something more tragic was going to happen to him, for he stopped screaming and rolled over, slowly on the concrete surface of the bridge. He had lost consciousness. The sweat stood out now clearly on Osime's face.

It was almost daylight now and Osime could see further up the bridge where the convoy of jeeps and armoured vehicles stood in a barricade towards the Onitsha end of the bridge. The soldiers stood or knelt or lay flat down behind the jeeps and the armoured vehicles and from there kept up a steady fire which was returned just as steadily from the other side by the Biafran soldiers. On the floor of the bridge there were many soldiers, hundreds of them, lying face down or sideways and they were either dead, unconscious or in too much pain to take any other position.

There certainly were a lot of casualties and he thought he knew how they had come about. The Nigerian soldiers had been too confident of an easy victory. After the initial and long and heavy bombardment of the Biafran positions on the banks of the river, they had attempted to rush the Biafran defences in large numbers. Perhaps the Biafran soldiers had never been in those trenches at the banks of the river. Perhaps they had remained at the head of the bridge knowing that the Federal guns would avoid hitting the bridge. Wherever they had hidden, they had not returned fire until that moment when the Nigerian soldiers had attempted to land from the river and clear the bridge. Then they had opened fire. Surprised, the Nigerian soldiers had retreated up the bridge and this time, there had been a lot of confusion because it was dark. Probably some of the Nigerian dead had been killed by their own soldiers in the ensuing confusion. The confusion must have been made worse by the loud explosion which followed later, when the Biafrans detonated the dynamite they had planted at the Asaba end of the bridge.

The Nigerian soldiers must have realised what had happened because for some minutes, there had been absolute silence. That must have been when they regrouped and set up the barricades using the jeeps and the armoured vehicles. But he knew now too, that it would be just a matter of time before the Biafrans rushed these defences because, surely, the Nigerian soldiers were bound to run short of fire power, unless, of course, the crossing of the river was successful. But that, he knew, could not have been successful because here were the Biafran soldiers holding the bridge-head instead of being encircled by the Nigerian soldiers who should have landed from the river.

'Keep your head down!' he heard somebody shout and instinctively, he ducked and landed roughly on the concrete surface of the bridge that was now wet and black with the blood of the soldiers.

'How long do you think we can stay like this?' he asked and Jato looked at him and shook his head.

'I don't know,' Jato replied. 'All I can think of now is the head of state getting ready this morning for his wedding. He will be putting on his white gloves just now, trying them on, while we are held down here by the Biafrans, while hundreds of our soldiers lie dead on this bridge and many more are afloat on the surface of the river. Just think about it,' he urged Osime. 'Think about it and perhaps you will get the kind of feeling I now have in my stomach.'

Chapter twenty-four

'We have to move forward,' Osime urged him, 'just like they taught us to crawl.'

'I'm not going forward,' Jato disagreed. 'Going forward means going to the Biafrans.'

'No,' Osime said. 'We have to find Sergeant Kesh Kesh and his men, those that are left. We must find them.'

'They will soon run out of bullets.'

'It doesn't matter.'

'They are already running out of bullets.'

'We have to locate Sergeant Kesh Kesh.'

'It won't make any difference. We are cooked.'

'But not yet ready for eating. Let's move. We must find them.'

There were several more soldiers lying on the bridge, most of them dead. In one of the jeeps a soldier was lying forward on the steering wheel, the blood still fresh and running smoothly from his forehead. Some were sprawled out on the iron support of the bridge, knees buckled under, hands flung out on the outside. The barricade was arranged in a series and behind each were stationed a dozen or more soldiers now. They went past the first barricades of jeeps and trucks and soldiers and among them were a major and a captain who looked at them but did not say anything. Up ahead, they could hear the steady outburst of gunfire but it sounded as if it was coming not from the Kalashnikovs but from the rifles and sub-machine guns of the Biafran soldiers. *Perhaps*, Osime thought, *Jato is right then when he says the Federal soldiers are already running out of bullets. They are holding their fire now instead of responding and even dictating the pace.*

Sergeant Kesh Kesh was on the front line, behind one of the very first barricades. He had been wounded in the shoulder, but it was not serious and he had tied up the wound with a shirt sleeve torn from the uniform of one of the dead soldiers. His own uniform was, however, covered in blood, the blood of soldiers who had fallen on the bridge. His eyes were bright and alight, scanning the distance for any movement of Biafran soldiers. On either side of him as he lay behind a truck were two section commanders, one of them Kolawole, the other new on the job because his section commander, a corporal, had been killed.

Osime did not see Sergeant Kesh Kesh at first and looking ahead of him he had seen nothing but overturned trucks and jeeps that were lying on their sides and around them dozens upon dozens of dead soldiers and for the first time, the full extent of the massacre dawned on him. He turned violently then in full circle, and in the same movement he saw Sergeant Kesh Kesh and the corporal, Kolawole.

'Keep your head down,' he said to Jato and scrambled quickly towards Kesh Kesh who still had not seen him but was keeping watch for any movement of the Biafrans.

'Sergeant!'

Sergeant Kesh Kesh turned very slightly and his face was hard and wooden and his eyes were bloodshot but set. He could see the determination there even when they livened up momentarily as his lips quivered imperceptibly in a makeshift smile.

'You shouldn't be here,' he said at once. 'This place is dangerous.'

'Where are the others? You are wounded!'

Kolawole looked at him and he could see that the man's eyes were tired but serious.

'You shouldn't be here,' Kolawole said. 'You heard the sergeant.'

'I saw Obilu.'

Kolawole's black eyes went blacker. He didn't say anything. *What did one say at moments like this? What do you say when on the road you have several hundred dead and in the river hundreds more, perhaps? What did you say to men who had seen their closest associates die? What do you say to men who are holding out against odds that will eventually overpower them, men for whom time is rapidly running out? You either kept effective silence or you said an ineffectual, 'I am sorry'.*

'I am sorry,' he said, involuntarily, in spite of himself.

Corporal Kolawole did not look at him. He said simply, 'There is no need for that in this war. The rebels think they have us licked but they are mistaken. Brigadier Otunshi must be busy preparing to send help across the river.'

'All we have to do is to hold out for as long as possible. One hour, maybe two,' Sergeant Kesh Kesh added. 'Brigadier Otunshi has to come.'

'Yes,' Osime agreed and suddenly his mouth became bitter and his stomach muscles twitched. He winked at Jato who had come up beside him. 'So you think we'll get out of this?' He was looking for something to say.

'This is nothing compared to what we have seen before. This is absolutely nothing. You'll see what will happen in another hour when the commander has sent our men across the river.'

'I can still hear the guns from the hills.'

'Yes. They will continue to shell the city until we get out of here. The rebels won't know what hit them. But you shouldn't have come here.'

'We were worried about you. You are wounded.'

'Worried about us?' And Sergeant Kesh Kesh laughed a sudden short laugh. 'You should worry about yourselves. We are soldiers, professional soldiers. As for my wound, it is nothing. Just grazed skin. That's all it is.'

'Well, thank God for that,' Osime said, then asked, 'But where are the others?'

'Journalist, it is hot here,' Sergeant Kesh Kesh said, not answering his question. 'You shouldn't have come here. Too dangerous here, too hot here.'

'Where are the others?' Osime insisted. 'Are they all right?'

'The others?' Sergeant Kesh Kesh asked. 'Corporal, tell him.' Sergeant Kesh Kesh turned his face away and Osime saw at a glance that the hardness was back and with it a certain amount of bitterness, a certain amount of hatred for the 'enemy'.

Corporal Kolawole looked Osime in the eyes and his voice was unemotional. 'Patrick is on the road, in front of us. You should have seen him. He was one of the first to cross the bridge to get on the rebel soil. We actually made Onitsha. Patrick made it.'

Osime did not say anything.

'Well, perhaps you cannot understand,' Corporal Kolawole continued. 'He was shot in the head in the dark. And Kokobi also. He too made Onitsha. Olu was shot a few minutes ago. You must have heard his screams. They got him behind that truck on the right. And Patani and Ituah are also there, holding out now. They are there giving it back to the Biafrans. And I am here giving it back to the Biafrans also. And we will give it to them when help comes from the river.'

Osime was silent. *There are times,* he thought, *when you suddenly realise that there is nothing more to say, that everything to be said has been said and another word would be superfluous, times when you are silenced by the sheer force of events, times when your own life, even the brightest or the blackest details of your life pale into insignificance beside the sweep of the common situation. This is one of those moments,* he thought. *I wonder if I will ever be moved again by the death of someone I know, be it my mother, my father or even Ndudi. Then he couldn't think any more because he was too appalled, too overwhelmed by the scale of the massacre that he had seen.*

On this bridge Ibo soldiers lay dead in their numbers side by side with Yoruba soldiers and Hausa soldiers and Esan soldiers and their blood ran and flowed into a common pool and mixed. There was nothing like Ibo written on the blood as these men lay in death, nor anything like Hausa, Yoruba or Edo. The blood of these men gushed out and mixed freely without the illusion of labels. In death they had achieved something they had been told was impossible in life, something they had been told not to strive for, to hold suspect even where it tried to blossom or actually blossomed.

Perhaps, he started to think again, *perhaps we ought to learn from this to value what we have, to value and respect life. Perhaps from now on every threat of death will move me, every death will deeply affect me instead of leaving me cold because what we have here is unnatural. What we have on this bridge are the flowers, of our motherland, torn rudely from their stems, petals dripping blood. What we have on this bridge are the sons of peasants, the children of farmers and labourers, the first generation of workers bleeding to death. And this morning, in Lagos, the wedding goes on with the commanders of the army, the commanders of this division, in attendance. The commanders are busy drinking the blood of the nation, the blood of soldiers, young workers of the first generation.*

'They lost more men than we lost,' Corporal Kolawole said now. 'If you count the bodies further up the bridge, if you separate the bodies further up on the bridge and count them, you will find that the rebels lost more.'

Osime said nothing.

'The rebels lost more,' the corporal repeated emphatically.

'Shut up your mouth,' Sergeant Kesh Kesh said angrily.

Osime went ahead, crawling slowly, and after a time, he stopped and brought out his camera and took several photographs. And then he came back and Jato was taking photographs too and he joined Jato and took some photographs of the upturned jeeps and trucks and dead soldiers and finally of Sergeant Kesh Kesh and Corporal Kolawole as they squatted behind the jeep waiting for the attack to come. *They must think we are mad to be taking the photographs,* he thought. *They must think we are stark raving mad but the history of this war lies in the eyes of cameras as much as it does in the memories of the soldiers who survive.*

The firing was coming now from the river, although not from an area that they could immediately see because they were lying flat on the floor of the bridge on their stomachs.

'The bastards are shooting low,' Corporal Kolawole said. 'We are lucky they haven't got any grenades or shells or they would have blown us all up a long time ago. Perhaps they want the vehicles and the guns for themselves. Perhaps they do have shells because I heard them being fired across the river. Perhaps . . .'

A renewed outburst of steady gunfire on the bridge drowned his words. Osime instinctively put his head down and rolled over for better cover from the wheels of the trucks.

He could hear the noise of the bullets on the metallic body of the trucks and he was reminded of the first showers of rain on a late August afternoon. The shooting was being done by the Biafran soldiers, although occasionally, the Nigerian soldiers responded with sporadic shots. Listening to the sound of firing, he now knew why the Nigerian soldiers called their Kalashnikovs guitars. They certainly handled the guns like guitars. The way they kept up the fire even for brief moments.

Soon, they will get us anyway, he thought. *And the worst part of it is that the soldiers do not know that neither Brigadier Otunshi nor the senior division commanders are with them but have gone to Lagos for the wedding. That is, if Jato has his facts right. If Jato is right, then the help they expect from the river will not come and sooner or later, the Biafrans will rush our positions on the bridge. Sooner or later Sergeant Kesh Kesh will know that no help is coming from the river but he must not know that the division commanders have gone to Lagos for the wedding.*

He turned his head sideways to look at Jato, but he too was looking the other way, beyond the bridge to the trees and the sky far away. And there were clouds in the sky, white and black clouds laced into each other, and they hung low. He could not see the river, only the tops of the trees and they were black, inscrutable and quiet and thick. He could see birds circling the tops of the trees only to disappear in a straight dive into the river below. *Going for the fishes,* he thought. *Going for the fishes while we stay here, waiting for the bullets. And those trees are so near and yet so far away. If only we could make those trees,* he thought. *If only we could hit the surface of the river and swim to the safety of those trees. But that most be out of the question now. The Biafran soldiers would get us before we hit the water. That's the advantage of the rifle. And they have more rifles than machine guns. We will have to stay here until it is dark, until night, that is, if they do not come for us before then.*

Throughout the morning, they stayed where they were. The Biafran soldiers made no serious attempt to advance forward from their positions on the bridge. Like the Federal soldiers, they dug in behind the trucks that had been abandoned by the Federal troops in their short retreat on the bridge.

In the afternoon, the rain began to fall. At first, it was a light drizzle, then it increased to a downpour. The Biafran soldiers then increased the pressure, firing for up to ten minutes at a time and then stopping for about three minutes before resuming their fire. The Federal soldiers just ahead of Osime responded occasionally in sharp short outbursts. But they kept their heads down. Still the Biafrans did not attempt to take their positions.

They must be waiting for the night, Osime thought. *They must be counting on nightfall.*

'They don't know that the division commanders are in Lagos,' Jato whispered to him, clearing the rain off his face. 'They don't know that we are cooked.'

'No,' Osime whispered back. 'And they shouldn't be told.'

'I got some good photographs last night and just now.'

'You probably won't use them.'

'Yes, but I don't mind. Do you think it was worth it?'

'What do you think?'

'I think it was.'

'You are all right then?'

'Yes, I'm all right now. I was afraid in the night, yesterday.'

'Yes.'

'We are all of us afraid sometimes. Don't you agree?'

'Yes.'

'And you couldn't call us cowards for being afraid sometimes?'

'No, you couldn't. I am afraid now.'

'You're not a coward.'

'Thank you.'

'I mean it. Holding cameras as we did last night and just now was as dangerous as holding guns and firing back at the Biafrans.'

'We probably won't use the photographs.'

'Don't be pessimistic.'

'I am afraid now.'

'You don't have to be.'

'Perhaps you are right, but have you noticed that those guns have stopped shelling the town?'

'Guns get hot. They have to be rested.'

'I hope you're right.'

'I'm always right. I know from experience.'

'You think they're waiting for darkness?'

'Yes. And your friend here is waiting for Brigadier Otunshi to send help across the river.'

'Help will never come. The most senior officer on the bridge is a major.'

'What do you think happened to the others?'

'They must have been killed.'

'Or perhaps they escaped in the confusion. They may have gone back by boat across the river.'

'Yes, but that's not very likely,' Osime whispered back. 'Perhaps they were never on the bridge in the first place.'

'Perhaps they were never on the bridge at all,' Jato affirmed. 'I hate this rain. Just look at all the blood.'

'Mother Nature knows what she's doing. The rain is necessary to wash the blood away, back into the river where it belongs.'

'I guess I shouldn't mention it but I'm hungry.'

'If you're hungry, you're hungry.'

'Yes, you are right. I hate this war.'

'Because you are hungry?'

'Oh shut up.'

'Well, come on. You are hungry and you hate this war.'

Jato did not say anything for some time. Then, 'So you can swim?'

'Yes.'

'Good for you.'

'And you too.' Osime put the gun down now and left it standing against the body of the upturned jeep. He didn't feel he needed it any more.

Jato had abandoned his gun a long time ago. 'Not me.'

'Yes, you. When the time comes, you jump after me. I go first, then you follow. I will take you to the other side of the river.'

'To our side?'

'To the other side of the river,' Osime repeated and wiped the rain off his face with his hand.

'Surely you don't mean to the Biafran side?'
'No.'
'Then to our side.'
'I've told you, I have no side in this war.'
'Even now?'
'Yes.'
'Even if they kill you?'
'Yes.'
'Then you will get killed one way or another. You can't stand in the middle here.'
'I am not in the middle. I just believe that the soldiers on both sides are killing the wrong enemies.'
'And with that belief, they might kill you just as wrongly here. You need a side now, at least temporarily.'
He didn't say anything.
'Did you fire that gun of yours at all?' Jato asked.
'Yes. But only once. You should remember.'
'It was in the dark. You must have killed someone.'
'I don't know. I don't think so.'
'You must have killed someone,' Jato insisted.
'No, I didn't.'
'You don't know.'
'No, I don't know.'
'So you may have killed someone.'
'I may have shot someone.'
'On whose behalf did you fire the gun then?'
'On my own behalf.'
'No,' Jato disagreed. 'You could not have shot someone, I mean probably shot someone, on your own behalf. That would be murder.'
'It doesn't matter,' Osime defended himself. 'I fired the gun and so what? I did it involuntarily. Just like you did, involuntarily.'
Jato shook his head. 'I didn't fire my gun,' he said.
'You didn't fire your gun?'
'No. Not even once. Not even involuntarily.'
'But I thought . . .'
'I was afraid, remember?' Jato asked. 'I was terrified we would all be shot. I kept saying to you that we were finished, cooked.'
'I see,' Osime said finally. 'I see but I still won't take sides in this war. I have no sides, neither the Federal nor the Biafran.'

'Then you should have thrown your gun away instead of firing it. You may say in the open that you have no side in this war. But think about it privately. You had a gun and you fired it. You fired it and probably . . ., well, shot, not killed someone. You probably shot someone in a war in which you claim to have no part, no side. You . . .'

'Shut up!'

'I will shut up. But think about it. Probably not now but later. Of course, I will shut up. But you think about it. In fact, I will shut up now so you can think about it.' He turned his face the other way.

I fired the gun involuntarily. I did not fire it because I was aiming to kill a Biafran soldier on behalf of the Nigerian soldiers. There was a lot of firing then, a lot of shooting and everybody was nervous. If Jato did not use his gun, it was because his fear killed his spontaneity. He did not hold back the trigger because he was afraid he would kill someone. He held back the trigger in spite of himself, out of fear. And I mean what I have said all along. There is a third side to this war, the side of the soldiers against that of the generals, and that is the side, the front, that is the least developed, and the most dangerous because it unites the Federal generals with the Biafran generals against the rest of the people. That's why Banjo was eliminated. That's why Nzeogwu's coup was aborted. And that's why, should any of the present generals defect to that side, the side of the people, he will be eliminated by the combined strength of both the Federal and Biafran generals, both federal and Biafran businessmen, politicians, bishops, chiefs and professors as easily as they armed one section of the people against the others. Jato looks for connections where none exist. What if I did fire the gun? What of it? In my mind, I was no more acting for the Federal soldiers than he was protecting the Biafran soldiers by refusing to fire his gun. What I do know now is that each one of us must act as he sees fit in this war. And no amount of blackmail will make me declare support for a cause in which I do not believe, at least now that I know better.

A little ahead of them, Sergeant Kesh Kesh was issuing instructions to the two section commanders with him and in a moment, Corporal Kolawole crawled past them, going back towards the first positions on the bridge. The other section commander went forward, to the positions that were being defended by Patani, Ituah and the others.

Sergeant Kesh Kesh himself moved backwards and then drew level with them beside Jato. 'We are in a difficult situation,' he said. 'No radios because they thought we could make the landing and go on to consolidate our positions in less than an hour. And the help we expected from the river has not come either. Come the first hour of darkness and the rebels will come creeping towards us. They want the vehicles. They know we have some tanks on the bridge. They are going to kill us and take the vehicles and the tanks and the guns. But we are going to beat them to it. We are going to put at least five grenades under each vehicle. We are going to gather as many of the guns as we can and throw them into the river. They will not kill us for nothing. And if we are lucky, we may yet beat them, Brigadier Otunshi may yet send help across the river. Perhaps he too is waiting for the darkness. But whatever happens, I want you to jump for the river as soon as the first grenades begin to explode. Jump for the river and try by all means to keep afloat. I am sure there will be boats in the river waiting to pick us up in case everything else fails. Brigadier Otunshi will, at least, make sure of that.'

'It's a long drop,' Osime observed. 'I saw it.'

'Better that than the rebel bullets,' Sergeant Kesh Kesh replied.

'But I can't swim,' Jato said.

'There will be boats,' Sergeant Kesh Kesh assured him.

'Supplied by Brigadier Otunshi?' Jato asked.

'Yes. He won't just abandon us. They can't abandon us. They know they have good men trapped up here.'

I hope the bastard doesn't say anything further, Osime thought furiously. *I hope he doesn't open his mouth any wider.*

'But what if the boats do not come?' Jato asked. 'What if they have already given us up? After all, they have valuable equipment here. If they do not care for the equipment, surely they won't care for us either.'

'The boats will be there,' Sergeant Kesh Kesh assured him. 'You'll see. The boats will be there.'

'Yes,' Jato said simply, and Osime breathed a sigh of relief. *Always,* he thought, *there are many sides to a man. You may dislike, even hate, some parts of him but always there is a part of him to which you can relate.*

'What time is it?' Jato asked.

'Nearly six o'clock.'

'I wish the rain would stop.'

'You probably need it. Remember that in another hour, we could be in the river.'

'In another four, maybe five hours,' Sergeant Kesh Kesh corrected him.

'Why five hours, Sergeant?'

'We have to wait for the help across the river. If we wait and it does not come, then we blow up the vehicles and tanks and armoured cars and make for the river.'

'Help won't come,' Jato said flatly.

'Of course it will come.'

'You want to bet?'

Sergeant Kesh Kesh examined the face of the other man carefully. 'No,' he replied, with anger in his voice. 'It's bad luck to bet in this war. You do not bet. You just know from feeling it.'

'Well, Sergeant, I feel it then.'

Sergeant Kesh Kesh did not answer.

'I'm going to sit up,' the man Jato declared.

Osime did not say anything and Sergeant Kesh Kesh kept quiet also.

'I am going to sit up and if my back or chest stops a bullet then so be it. But I am not going to continue lying on my stomach in this pool of water and blood in which I have had no food for over eighteen hours. There are times when death is preferable to everything that life has to offer.'

'Why don't you just shut up?' Osime glared at him.

'Why should I shut up? I am hungry and afraid and tired and I can't swim. And in another five hours, I will be dead. Why shouldn't I talk? Why shouldn't I say the things now I may never have the opportunity to say again? You don't want to talk? Then you shut up. But I am going to talk.'

'Let him talk,' Sergeant Kesh Kesh said.

'My parents are farmers,' Jato offered. 'Farmers at Ughelli. I have a wife and three little children, you know, "three little children depending upon me" like in the woman's song. My parents don't know I'm here.'

'And your wife?' Sergeant Kesh Kesh asked.

'She knows. She knows and the children know but that does not make any difference. And what a story I shall tell them, when I get back! I shall tell them how we were held down by the Biafrans for hours and had to lie on our stomachs in a pool of water mixed with the blood of dead soldiers. I will tell them about the bridge, how it was blown up, about the overturned vehicles and the tanks and jeeps. I will tell them how we were abandoned by the division commanders, how they went off for the wedding of the head of state and left us to roast, or is it to drown, in the fire of the Biafrans. I will tell them all this and more.'

Osime turned and caught the eye of Sergeant Kesh Kesh and they were inscrutable, showing that he had paid no attention to Jato's statement that the commanders of the division had gone off to the wedding of the head of state.

'Let us all agree, here,' Jato proposed further, 'that whichever one of us survives this night will get in touch with the families of the others. Let us all give the pledge.'

Again, Osime caught the eyes of Sergeant Kesh Kesh who shrugged his shoulders. 'Of course we will. Right, journalist?'

'Right,' Osime agreed. 'Of course we will.'

My God, he was thinking. *How we all disintegrate in this war! How this war breaks us! Listen to the man talk and you know he is broken, you can feel the fear, as you can taste the salt of tears in your mouth. You never really know what you can do until the time comes, until the trial comes. This is the trial and the man has given up.* He felt sorry for the 'three little children'. *They will never know,* he thought. *And perhaps it's just as well.*

Chapter twenty-five

'Have you planted the dynamite?'

'Yes. At least ten sticks each. The one behind us has ten.'

'And the grenades?'

'The grenades too. Five for each truck, eight for each armoured vehicle.'

'Good. Very good,' Sergeant Kesh Kesh commended him. 'Now we will wait until it is a little darker.'

'Some of them must be coming for us,' Corporal Kolawole said. 'The bullets are passing over our heads. The bastards must be creeping, like snakes.'

'The rebels will not get us,' Sergeant Kesh Kesh assured him.

'Does it really matter who gets us?' Jato asked. 'It's either them or the river.'

'Shut up,' Corporal Kolawole said angrily.'

I wish Jato hadn't come with us, Osime thought. *I wish I hadn't persuaded Sergeant Kesh Kesh to let him come. But then,* he asked himself, *how do you really know in these things? You never know until you have gone with a man on a journey, until then, he is just like any other man. You go with him on a journey and you find out the things he can do, the type of man he is.*

'What do we do now?' Osime asked aloud. 'You have enough dynamite in the vehicles to blow up the bridge. How do we all get out? You can't set them off while we are on the bridge. We would all go with the explosion.'

'You wait here,' Sergeant Kesh Kesh said and started moving forward.

'Do I come with you?' Corporal Kolawole asked.

'No. You wait here. I want a word with the captain and the other men up front.' He moved away.

The darkness deepened quickly and the only bright lights came from the bursts of automatic rifles and they came from the Onitsha end of the bridge. The Biafrans were keeping up the pressure. *But what if Sergeant Kesh Kesh is right and the Federal troops have only been waiting for the cover of darkness before launching the second offensive?* He shook his head. *That is too much to hope for,* he thought. *That is too much to hope for because at this moment, the generals are at the party in Lagos and the war is as far away from them as we are as close to the Biafran soldiers.*

Sergeant Kesh Kesh came back after about a quarter of an hour and he was breathing unevenly. 'The Biafrans are less than fifty yards away,' he said. 'A group of them could even be nearer.'

'And our men?' Corporal Kolawole asked.

'They are going to stay.'

'My God!' Osime exclaimed. 'Didn't you explain to them?'

'I didn't have to explain, journalist. They already knew. Somebody has to be on the bridge to set off the dynamite.'

'But that's crazy!' Osime cried. 'Surely the equipment on the bridge can't be as important as the men. You don't mean . . .' His voice faded away.

'So can we go?' Jato asked eagerly.

If the man had been near him, he surely would have struck him now but Corporal Kolawole was between them..

'I will stay with the men,' Corporal Kolawole said, ignoring Jato.

'No,' Sergeant Kesh Kesh said. 'I have my instructions to destroy the vehicles and the bridge if necessary. But I have no instructions to allow you to stay. This thing must be done with as few men as possible.'

'One more man won't make any difference.'

'I think all this is crazy,' Osime said. 'No matter how much the equipment is worth, we must all leave.'

'We cannot give the Biafrans weapons with which they can kill a thousand of our men in a few weeks' time. Now, perhaps, we lose a few men. But then we save a thousand or more lives.'

Osime saw Sergeant Kesh Kesh move forward and head again for the forward positions.

'Why doesn't he just leave them alone?' Jato asked in an irritated voice. 'They are going to die, let them die. It's us he should worry about, not people who have made up their minds to be heroes.'

'Shut up!' Corporal Kolawole said savagely.

'You see what I mean?' Jato asked. 'You see the kind of people for whom our lives are now being risked?'

'You heard the corporal,' Osime told him. 'You talk too much.'

'What I am saying is that we should take our chances with the river now that we still have the opportunity.'

'They are only doing your dirty work for you,' Osime told him.

'They're doing their own dirty work, not mine.'

'Somebody has to set off the explosives. You heard the sergeant.

You can't set them off while we are still on the bridge. See that truck behind us? It has at least ten sticks of dynamite and five grenades. When the dynamite goes off, the bridge may go with it. We may all go with it.'

'And I also heard the sergeant,' Jato replied. 'The rebels are less than fifty yards away and if what the corporal here says about their fire being deliberately kept over our heads is true, they could well be less than ten yards away from where we are right now.'

'Or right on top of you,' Osime told him.

'I think we should dive for the river right now. We should do it if we want to live and God knows that I don't want to die. God knows I don't want to leave my little children fatherless.'

Osime didn't say anything. Sergeant Kesh Kesh came back and he was breathing heavily.

'We leave in a little while,' he said. 'We leave in a little while and make for the river.' His voice was broken.

'Corporal,' he said, turning to Kolawole. 'You go to the men behind us and tell them to listen for three bursts of the guitar and then make for the river. Start with the major.'

'You think we will make it?' Osime asked.

'Yes. The river is not too wide and if we are lucky there will be boats waiting to pick us up.'

'Do you still believe in that?'

'They wouldn't abandon us just like that. We have at least two hundred men on the bridge. They couldn't just abandon us.'

'Perhaps you are right,' Osime said more to keep faith than for any other reason. He knew they had been abandoned 'just like that'.

They stayed on the bridge for a long time. Sergeant Kesh Kesh kept telling them that the second assault must come and the Federal soldiers would never leave them to die on the bridge. He kept going to the forward positions and coming back and although Corporal Kolawole had long returned to assure him that everything was ready, Sergeant Kesh Kesh kept repeating his belief that a second assault must be on the way across the river. Corporal Kolawole told them that the only major on the bridge was subdued and quiet and was satisfied that Sergeant Kesh Kesh should give the signal for the departure from the bridge. He told them that another two captains were with the major and that they seemed bitter and angry although he could not understand their language.

Since they had no detonators, they had slit open a large number of sheets and soaked these thoroughly in petrol. Each thin sheet of cloth was wrapped round the dynamite and then tied to other thin sheets until there was enough length of cloth coming out of each vehicle so that when it was set alight the men would have enough time to clear to the next group of vehicles. This meant that the explosions had to start with the most forward vehicles on the bridge. Progressively, once each group of dynamite went off, the men would move further back on the bridge. If they were lucky and did not go up with the dynamite, they too would make for the river.

Corporal Kolawole began to move forward.

'Where are you off to?' Sergeant Kesh Kesh tried to stop him.

'To see my men.'

'Stay here!'

Corporal Kolawole did not answer but continued to move forward.

'I said stop!' Sergeant Kesh Kesh cried, trying not to shout.

Corporal Kolawole ignored him.

'Stop or I'll shoot!'

Corporal Kolawole did not stop.

'Sergeant, you can't shoot him. You mustn't shoot him!' Osime pleaded. They were all now in the darkness.

'The man is being a fool,' the sergeant said quietly and then his voice sank. He did not fire his gun.

Somewhere, Osime thought he could hear a cricket singing. How could a cricket sing on such a night as this? *But those rags flying above us are certainly bats,* he thought. *Bats waiting for our blood, the vultures of the night.* The moon was beginning to come out behind the clouds but slowly, as though it were shy, as though it was coming out against its wish, with great reluctance, as though it did not want to witness what was going to happen. The man Jato began to snap his fingers. He did it one by one and as he snapped each one, there was a loud eerie noise, like the breaking of wood. Osime was fed up to the teeth with the man, but he endured the companionship because he knew now that it was only going to be for a little time longer. *It will all be over in another hour*, he thought.

And now there was a great shout, then rapid gunfire, then more shouts. A man began to scream and then the scream stopped as soon as it had begun. Another man began to scream and now there was nothing but the sound of metal spitting fire, and the cries of men as they celebrated the power of the guns or succumbed to it.

And as the massacre was unleashed, Sergeant Kesh Kesh stood up and he was quiet and very calm. But the man Jato panicked. He made a rush for the railings of the bridge and collided with them and fell down and picked himself up almost immediately and before either Sergeant Kesh Kesh or Osime could stop him, he had climbed clumsily over the railings of the bridge and jumped for the river.

'You may make your jump now,' Sergeant Kesh Kesh said quietly to Osime. He removed his belt and passed it between the two supports of the carrier bag that held his camera and then replaced the belt so that the bag was firmly held in place. 'And you?' Osime asked?'

'I am not a hero. I am not a fool. The heroes are the fools. I will go with you.'

'Good,' Osime said. 'Don't do anything foolish. Don't be as foolish as the corporal.'

'No,' Sergeant Kesh Kesh agreed. 'I will be wiser than the corporal.' He held out his hand and Osime took it and pressed it clumsily and all the time, a thick cloud of feeling was rising inside him.

'Now!' Sergeant Kesh Kesh urged him. 'Now!'

Osime had the ring of the man's voice in his ears as he ran for the railings of the bridge. He cleared it and dived for the river. He thought he saw Sergeant Kesh Kesh beside him as he made for the railings of the bridge but he wasn't sure.

It was a long drop to the river and when he finally hit the water, he had to make sure he did not go too deep so that he could come to the surface almost immediately. The water was unusually cold, black and it was as if he was in the belly of an iced fish. And now he was on the surface of the water, breathing unevenly. He looked round him to see if he could locate Jato. *The fool,* he thought. *Couldn't even wait for us to go first. Even the drop might have killed him,* he thought. *It must be well over five hundred metres, from the floor of the bridge to the surface of the water.* He swam around for a while, looking for Jato. There was a large number of soldiers in the water and he could hear cries for help all around him but he continued to look for Jato. He swam over to the other side of the bridge and passed many of the soldiers, but he did not see Jato.

He was about to cross to the other side of the bridge again when he heard the first explosion. Instinctively, he looked up and even as he did so there were more explosions and then huge tongues of flames rose into the air before coming down towards the river like burning torches. And all the time, Osime was swimming as far away from the bridge as possible. There was a big fire along the whole length of the bridge now. The flames rose above the tall metal supports of the bridge and lit up the whole night even to the surface of the water. The moon was irrelevant now, even the sun would have been irrelevant now. And still the explosions continued, explosions that threw up the jeeps and the trucks and the tanks and scattered them, dissolved them so that they came down to the surface of the water in burning torches. And still the bridge held.

There was a man not far away from him and he was screaming for help. He must have just made the river and Osime turned round and headed towards the man. There was a lot of shooting coming from the banks of the river, on the Biafran side. And he knew they were shooting at them in the water. They would be easy to see because of the huge fire on the bridge. He could hear the sound of the huge fire as it burned, like the noise of branches of trees, or the sound of dry leaves under foot in the harmattan. He saw the huge fire burning and heard the sound of the dynamite as it exploded and then there were the screams of the soldiers in the water. The screams were eerie, the screams of men who could not swim but who had abandoned the devil of the bridge for the deep belly of the water, hoping against hope that they would in one way or another survive, men who had never swum in all their lives. And the Biafrans kept up the fire from the banks of the river, using their rifles to great effect aided as they were by the light of the fire on the bridge.

Somewhere, something gave inside Osime and presently it was in his eyes. He did not bother to wipe the tears away. He let them come and mingle with the water of the river that was on his face and then finally with the river itself. *That is as it should be,* he thought. *This river has already seen so much blood that a little salt won't make any difference.*

The man had had the first bellyfull of water before Osime reached him and even as he caught hold of him he was going down for the second time and his arms were flailing wildly in the water. He had to be careful to prevent himself from being knocked over.

Once, the man made a grab for his waist and caught hold of the plastic bag that held his camera and he felt the bag snap and go away from him, under, and he told himself that he understood the saying about drowning men clutching at straws. He told himself that he had to watch the man or both of them would go under. And he did it eventually. He caught hold of the collar of the man and pulled and at first, the man made a desperate grasp for his own hands, then for his head and then for any part of him that he could reach. He made sure one of his hands was free and that his two legs were free also. Still the Biafrans continued to aim and fire at the men in the water.

It must have taken him about a quarter of an hour to get both of them ashore but it seemed to him as though he had been in the water for a lifetime. He tried at once to get the water out of the man by pumping his stomach and presently, it all came out and the man groaned and then groped in the air with his hands. Looking at the shoulders of the man, Osime saw that he was a captain. He fell back on the sand, his eyes towards the sky and then he turned, sat up and looked at the bridge. The fire was still burning on it and he knew it would be a long time before it burnt itself out. The bridge still held in spite of the explosions. The bridge held in spite of the dynamite and the grenades and the screams and the blood and the sweat. The bridge held and surely that was a good thing? The Biafrans had planted dynamite under it too and blown up a section of it. What it meant was that the bridge would be out of use for a while. But it would get repaired, it would be mended and strengthened. And it must have been a strong bridge for it to have held, what with all that dynamite, all those grenades, all those screams, all that blood.

The fire continued to burn on the bridge and the Biafran soldiers continued to fire their rifles from the banks of the river. *All that remains now,* he thought, *is for us to get back to the camp and count the costs.* He thought about Sergeant Kesh Kesh, about Kolawole. Were they alive? And the man Jato?

Jato surprised me most of all, he thought. *Jato surprised me most and yet taught me most. He surprised me because I had expected him to be strong. He taught me most because I found out how to know who a man really is, what he really is. You get to know a man in periods of crisis, not when everything is normal and your only problem is how you are going to get from one day to another. That is routine living and what a man is then may not be the real man at all. You do not know a man because you go out for a drink together, because you go out to play whatever it is together. You may do this for a lifetime and you think you know the man thoroughly but you would really come to be sure only when you have faced a crisis together. It is only in times of crisis that you discover who you can trust, who can be a traitor, who can be a coward. Crisis is the screen on which the quality of a man comes to be displayed. Crisis is the natural X-ray of a man's real worth. All other situations count for nothing.*

Chapter twenty-six

All the way back to the road, the captain complained bitterly about the offensive.

'They abandoned us,' he said again and again. 'They left us to the rebels to slaughter. They abandoned us.'

He had his arm round the captain to steady him and even when they got to the road, the captain could not stand but sat on the grass on the edge of the road.

'They abandoned us,' he said again.

'We can't stay here,' Osime told him. 'We must move on.'

'They abandoned us.'

'Yes, but we cannot stay here.'

Still the captain sat on the grass on the edge of the road, his head in his hands. Both of them were dripping with water.

'Come on. Let's go.'

The captain did not move.

Groups of soldiers came and passed them by. Some went singly while others were in groups of two or three. You could tell who had been in the river by the wet clothes and the subdued manner in which they walked.

This is how you know a defeated army, he thought. *The soldiers limp back in small subdued groups and they are quiet and even when they are not wounded, they still limp somehow. They do not carry their guns, because they have abandoned them in retreat. And you do not know the officers either. The officers mingle with the soldiers and they are all one in the disgrace and humiliation of defeat.*

Somewhere ahead of them an engine started up and then presently the truck began to move and it had its full headlights on from the way it cut a big large path in the darkness. The sound of the engine lingered on in the night for a while and then died away and again everywhere was quiet except for the songs of the crickets and the occasional gunshot from across the river.

They must be celebrating, he thought. *The Biafran soldiers must be wild with the whisky of victory and it is a victory to have killed over a thousand Nigerian soldiers. It must be a victory to count over a thousand bodies on the bridge and in the river. And among the dead, there will be their own dead. The majority of them will be the sons of farmers or workers, or workers themselves. And all of them will be wearing plain tunics without any stripes, without any pips or eagles or crossed swords. Imagine turning up the faces of the dead, not only here on the bridge, not only here on the Niger but also at the Nsukka front and the Calabar front and the Port Harcourt front. And when you count all the fronts and count all the dead, you must have the greatest victory because there will be tens of thousands, and all of them will be the sons of small traders, of farmers, of workers, or else workers themselves and students. A great victory indeed but a victory in which the victor is neither the Nigerian nor the Biafran soldier but both the Nigerian and the Biafran general. The victory that the ordinary Biafran soldiers are celebrating now is not really theirs but that of the generals. What the Biafran soldiers really have is defeat. The soldiers have the defeat while the generals have the victory. But it is a defeat which the ordinary Biafran soldier will not recognise this night. It is a defeat that he will recognise many years hence, perhaps ten years from now. At that time the generals on both sides will have come together and told themselves that the war was a temporary distraction, that it arose as a result of communication problems and that there was nothing to remember or forgive in it. They will have congratulated themselves on effectively reducing the number and strength of their real adversary, the working class, and mapped out for themselves other strategies for maintaining their hold on the country. The generals will have forgiven themselves thoroughly and just as thoroughly blamed the masses for the differences that led to the war. They will have invented scapegoats to take the blame away from themselves. Ten years from now, Biafran generals will be giving away their daughters to the sons of Nigerian generals. Ten years from now, the generals on both sides will be sitting round the same table, planning how to deal with the working class.*

But the working class on both sides will still be nursing their grievances, they will still have this hatred, these prejudices and they will still not trust one another. They will remember their dead and blame each other. They will continue to accuse each other. And this is why the generals are the real traitors in this war. All traitors share three basic characteristics. They are incapable of sustained emotion one way or another, they have no conscience and as result of both, they are without shame. Traitors are incapable of hatred for long periods because the man they hate today they may have to love tomorrow in order to get what they want. In the same way, the man they love today, they may have to betray tomorrow if they are to see the advantages they desire. Their passions then are short-lived. Look at the generals. Look at them now and then look again at them ten or more years hence and you will come to see how very treacherous they all are.

He was getting very cold now and he had to speak sharply to

the captain to get him to stand on his feet and then they were off and again he had his arm around the man's waist to steady him. *The man is completely shattered,* he thought. *This is another Jato here. But his collapse is nothing to do with fear. He is shattered because he feels betrayed.*

There were men on the road, all the way back to the camp. Some of the men sat on the grass, on the edge of the road as the captain had done. Others were sprawled out on the road and these were either very quiet or groaning loudly. Still there were others who walked in a sort of trance, like the insane in their pure moments of madness. Osime saw all these men and he told himself that all these were the marks of a betrayed and then a defeated army. So too were the abandoned trucks and jeeps. *But then,* he reminded himself, *betrayed and defeated armies learn well. Wasn't that what Lenin had said? Except that this army has been defeated as a result of its betrayal by its own generals. This army has no ideals, no principles, it is engaged in a war that was false from the beginning and whatever it is going to learn will not come from the teaching of its leaders, not from a recognition of mistakes but from personal, individual experience. Perhaps some of the more conscious soldiers will see the betrayal as this captain has already done and that ought to be one of the most important lessons of this defeat.*

But how effective the learning will be will depend upon the existence of a national mood capable of explaining these events to the people and relating them to this war, to this defeat. Such a national mood will itself depend upon the existence of an organised third army, part of which would have emerged from this war, from the ranks of these soldiers who understood this betrayal. Beyond these, the learning that may take place may be no learning at all but a further deception of the masses, a deception deliberately conceived and executed to befuddle the masses, to render them perpetually incapable of understanding this war, this defeat and who their real enemies are.

He felt bitter and frustrated and resentful. Although he could not even explain it, he felt ashamed because he felt part of the army that had just been disgraced, part of the army that is today disgraced on this side and the next day, on the other side. And he was frustrated because he felt alone in his shame, in his disgrace, in his bitterness and finally in his hatred. *You need more than one person to feel this shame, this disgrace,* he thought, *because then you would be able to fight back. You need more than one man to fight a national shame, a collective action to put it right and God knows that the kind of collective action required is beyond the collective organisation that goes with the armies of today's generals.*

Yes, Hemingway is right when he says that a man alone hasn't got a bloody chance.

They got to the camp and suddenly, he felt completely exhausted. He collapsed on the grass outside. The captain went down with him.

He did not know how long he had been there and in the morning, in the first moments of wakefulness, he could not remember where he was either. He sensed he was on a surface and felt it and knew it was the grass. He closed his eyes quickly. And then he heard voices.

'It was a terrible beating,' the first voice said.

'Yes,' the second agreed promptly.

'We lost more than a thousand men. The river is full of the bodies of our dead and many of them are afloat. It is a horrible sight.'

'Yes,' a third voice agreed.

'Is the Brigadier back?'

'No.'

'Then we must act quickly. The men must not be allowed to brood over the defeat. If they do we shall be in trouble. We could have a mutiny on our hands.'

'What are you thinking of then?' the third voice asked.

There was a moment's pause and then the first voice answered slowly, 'We must direct their anger against the rebels. We must go to Oganza and eliminate all the rebels there. If we send the men against the rebels at Oganza and Nkesio, the likelihood is that they will unleash their anger against the rebels. And we must do it straightaway, right now.'

'What about the commander?'

'I am sure he will understand. He will have to understand. There is no other way anyway.' The voices faded into the distance.

Osime passed his hands over his eyes as if to wipe away a bad dream and then opened his eyes and saw the sky and it was dark blue and black with clouds so that it was impossible to guess what time of the morning it was and therefore how long he had been there. He could see the three men as they walked down the road and he guessed they were all officers but he couldn't be sure because they had their backs to him now and it wasn't a bright clear morning. He knew then that he was in the camp. He sat up and not far away from him, he could see a dark patch on the grass and then he remembered the captain. But where was the captain?

He remained in the sitting position for some time and it was only then that he sensed how cold he was inside. *I must not cath a cold now,* he said to himself sharply. *I must not catch a cold but must look for a way to get to Oganza and to Ndudi.* He did not want to think about Ndudi. *She must have given me up by now,* he thought. *And what with the Biafrans who are there, who knows how she may have changed?*

He stood up and everywhere it was quiet, like the sea after a thunderstorm, like the war front after a defeat. Everywhere was quiet and the figures that moved along the road were solitary and bent. Bent with the defeat, solitary from the retreat. How many of them had survived? Had anybody but the officers survived? Who would be there to send against the Biafrans at Oganza and Nkesio? The officers?

He walked on the edge of the grass and headed for the building where Sergeant Kesh Kesh had last had his quarters. And again, he felt wet and cold inside. He looked at himself now, at his clothes and they were still wet and crumpled and had tiny blades of grass all over them. Then he saw the remains of the plastic bag that had held his camera still under his belt and he stopped and removed them and let them fall away from him on the grass. *I must get out of these clothes,* he told himself and changed direction to go towards the building where he had spent a night with Jato.

He got to the door and tried its handle and the door opened. But when he tried to enter the room where he had slept with Jato only two nights before, the door was locked and then he remembered that Jato had the key. There was another door which opened on to the corridor but it was shut and in all probability also locked. He came back into the sitting room and looked round to see if he could find any instrument he could use to force the lock, a cutlass, a chisel, something with a flat edge. He couldn't see anything. He went outside and walked round the house, looking for a cutlass. He found one at the back of the house. It stood against the wall, opposite the tap, and he picked it up and came around the house from the other side and saw now that the window on this side of the house was open. The grass was wet with the rain that had fallen when they were still trapped on the bridge. It was wet too where he had slept. He remembered now although it probably hadn't mattered at the time and would not have mattered at all even if he had been fully conscious since his uniform had been wet anyway.

He mounted the single step to the door that opened into the sitting room and now he was again at Jato's door and as he raised the cutlass, preparatory to inserting it between the door and the door frame, the door opposite him on the other side of the corridor opened and the two journalists came out. Behind them were two girls, not the same two who had accompanied them out of the officers' mess two evenings before.

'Oh, there you are,' the man Ekise exclaimed.

'And where is Jato?' Idem asked.

'And what are you doing with that?' Ekise asked again, pointing to the cutlass.

Osime ignored both men and inserted the blade of the cutlass between the door and the door frame and pushed.

Ekise and Idem watched him and when he did not say anything, they went back into their room and shut the door.

Osime pushed the cutlass in deeper and then bent it away from him so that the pressure was on the door. The door held. He moved the cutlass up, directly in front of the key where it entered the lock on the door frame and again applied the pressure. A splinter of wood came off the door but he almost got the door open. He was shivering. He tried again, this time with less care and more force, bending the cutlass so far away from him that the blade of the cutlass formed an arc. The door burst open. He stepped into the room.

The smell of vomit was still in the room and the man's clothes lay in a heap on the bed. On top of the locker that stood beside the bed where Jato had slept there was a small suitcase. He stepped over to the locker and opened the suitcase and in it there were more clothes and some photographs. He picked up the photographs and looked at them. They were mostly the photographs of soldiers in combat uniforms and steel helmets. He went over the photographs one by one until he came across a small photograph of a woman and three children, two boys and a girl, with Jato standing behind them. He looked at the face of the woman, at the faces of the children and shook his head from side to side and then closed the suitcase and placed the photograph on top of it. And now he went over to the bed where he had slept and lifted up the pillow and underneath it, there was his shirt and his trousers just as he had left them, crudely folded. He picked them up and then dropped them back on the bed.

He took off his uniform slowly because he was shivering now. He told himself he could not afford to be sick, to be helpless. He was going to fight the cold and the shivering. He was going to pretend that neither existed. He was going to ignore them. He wrung his underpants and squeezed out whatever water remained in them on the floor and then he put them back on and then put on his shirt and then his trousers. He looked under the bed then and his canvas shoes were still there. He took them from under the bed and as he was sitting on the bed, bending down and putting on the shoes, he saw the small end of the whisky bottle and remembered.

The bottle still had a little whisky in it and he unscrewed the cover and cleaned the mouth of the bottle thoroughly with his hands and then with his shirt tails. The first mouthful of whisky tasted awful and bitter but he swallowed it and took another mouthful. *That ought to do*, he told himself, *because I must eat first or my head will be too weak for the whisky.* He put the cover of the bottle back and left it on his bed and then went over to the suitcase that was on top of the bedside cupboard and picked up the photograph. The woman had a smile on her face. Her eyes were caught up in the smile and were very bright. Her hair must have been recently dressed, the plaits were straight and there was a dazzle on them. She wasn't particularly beautiful but she was the kind of woman that the majority of men really wanted to marry. She had that sincere look that told a man he could trust her. He put the photograph in his breast pocket and leaving the door open, came out of the room into the sitting room. *No*, he said to himself. Perhaps it wouldn't do. He went back and replaced the photograph on top of the suitcase and closing the door as much as it would allow, went out.

Chapter twenty-seven

There were a lot of butterflies in the field and many of them had sky white or bright yellow wings. Florella, he knew. Then there were the egialea and these had black wings with white patches. Further down the field, he found some thalassinas too, and they were very beautiful and clean and their wings were sky-blue and very tender. He passed the butterflies thinking that they must live less complicated lives than his own fellow men, that butterflies obviously did not deceive each other, or go to war with each other but were honest with themselves and with the honey of the small yellow flowers that sprouted from the grass too in profusion. But he did not wish he was a butterfly. He wished there were more like himself, who understood this war for what it was and were willing to turn it against the generals on both sides and in the process, against all the other mercenaries engaged in this war.

At times he felt dizzy and then his head cleared and he told himself that it must be the hunger and that he must find something to eat. And then he was in the building walking between the row of empty beds and then in Sergeant Kesh Kesh's little room. He wasn't there. He came out of the dormitory and headed for the camp hospital.

The problem in this kind of defeat, he thought, *is that there are always a few wounded. Either a man survives completely or goes to hell. There is no middle way or whatever middle way there is is inconsequential. However, for an army of well over two thousand men, even two hundred wounded can create a crowd in a hospital as small as the one here or in the town itself.*

The hospital was indeed crowded, and even as he got to the door, a truck drew up outside and the soldiers jumped down from the front seats and began unloading the wounded. Inside the hospital, the nurses were extremely busy and he knew that they must have worked through the night because their uniforms were crumpled and stained with blood and there were rings round their eyes.

They were bringing in the wounded now from the truck that had just come and he had to go between two beds to allow the stretcher bearers to pass. There were two nurses on the other side of the bed and he asked them if Sergeant Kesh Kesh or Jato had been brought in as a patient and they told him they didn't know. He left them and walked behind the stretcher bearers and looked at each soldier, those whose faces he could see on each bed. He came to the end of the ward and there was a desk and there was a matron, a sister and a doctor standing round it and they were talking about the soldiers that had just arrived.

'We will have to put the mattresses on the floors between the beds or convert one of the other dormitories to a ward,' the doctor said and the matron agreed. The matron was a stout strong woman and the doctor was fat but tall. The sister was tall but slim and fair, every inch a woman. All of them looked tired, the doctor who wore the rank of a major and the stout strong matron and the tender, fine sister.

Osime asked them about Sergeant Kesh Kesh and Jato and the doctor shook his head and said he wouldn't know but that he could look round and wait to see the new arrivals and if they were not among them, then go to the other hospital and perhaps, back to the river. The matron gave him a smile and he acknowledged it. The sister did not look at him.

He waited in the hospital for another half an hour during which time he went round the patients again and saw the new arrivals. Two soldiers died in the time that he was there. There were no tears. *You do not cry in a place like this,* he guessed. *Not even if the dead is your child or parent or lover.* Death was commonplace here.

Was it possible, he asked himself, that Sergeant Kesh Kesh had stayed behind on the bridge? Was it possible that he had decided to become a fool too? Or had he drowned in the river? What could have happened? He decided he would go down to the river.

On his way to the river, he stopped at one of the houses that housed the army officers and was given some food to eat by a soldier he found in the kitchen. The soldier wanted to talk and Osime made a few noises while he chewed the boiled yam, and the soldier saw that he was reluctant to talk and left him alone.

And now he was on the road going down to the bridge and to the river. The sky was overcast with low rain clouds and he knew from the coolness of the breeze that the rain would soon start. There were a few birds about, the majority of them vultures. The bats that he had seen the night before had disappeared now into the dense foliage that surrounded the river. *The night hides a lot of things from us,* he thought. *In the night all you see are the broad outlines, you never see the details, the small but the major ones that adorn these more vivid contours.*

Each step nearer the river showed to him how total the collapse had been, how costly the betrayal had been. Sometimes, a beaten army is able to make an orderly retreat, preserving its formations, its discipline and some of its integrity. The stronger and better organised and the less betrayed an army is, the more is it able to beat an orderly retreat, the more is it able to preserve its essential, and most fundamental features. What had happened here was an indication of the level of organisation of the soldiers, the level of its strength and the degree of the loyalty of its officers. This army disintegrated completely leaving the soldiers in a sort of trance. The soldiers tried on their own to hold the bridge long after the officers had deserted them but it was already too late. The betrayal by the officers sealed the fate of the rank and file.

He saw more clearly now the extent of the collapse. There were several logs of wood floating in the river. The men must have attempted to keep afloat on anything available, on branches, even on leaves. There were hundreds of different items afloat on the river, logs of wood, boats, shirts, leaves, guns and most of all, bodies. Bodies of soldiers. There were hundreds of them on the banks of the river too and they were all dead. How many men had the Federal troops lost? One thousand? Two thousand?

Somewhere, further up the bank of the river about ten soldiers were sweating in the early morning mist and dew, digging the largest grave he had ever seen. There were also some soldiers in three motor boats on the river, fishing out the bodies. He stood there at the edge of the water and watched them. He walked back to just where the bridge started and looked at the mass of twisted metal there, armoured cars, tanks, trucks. He bent down and picked up a small piece of metal at his feet and looked at it and on it was clearly written 'Saladin FV601'. He knew the vehicle. It was an armoured car with a range of some four hundred kilometres and a maximum cruising speed of 72kph. Usually it carried a crew of three as well as a 76 mm gun, one .3 inch machine gun co-axial, a .3 inch anti-aircraft machine gun and 12 smoke discharges. He knew the car as he had known all the other vehicles that had been on the bridge — the Ferrett scout cars, the Scorpion reconnaissance vehicles, all British, all imported, and all wrecked and twisted and black and blown apart and still burning on the bridge. He shook his head and turned away from the bridge.

The motor boats were coming in now. They dared not go too far into the water for fear of the Biafran rifles. The motor boats came in slowly, dragging behind them a collection of bodies. The boats stopped not far away from where he stood and he walked towards them as the soldiers disembarked and looked at each of them carefully. Sergeant Kesh Kesh was not there. He walked away from the boats towards the men who were digging the mass grave. They must have started early because the grave was already very large but it wasn't deep. Probably four feet deep. He felt sorry for the bodies but he told himself that it perhaps didn't matter after all. What was a dead body after all? What if the river washed the sand away and the vultures had a festival? What did it matter? The men were dead.

Many of the bodies were swollen, those of them that had died from drowning. He looked at the faces of the dead soldiers and wiped the sweat from his own face. He saw the water on the faces of the men, their eyes closed or open, their mouths shut, hundreds of them, several hundreds of them: he had never seen so many dead before. It was no use searching for either Sergeant Kesh Kesh or Jato there. It would be impossible to find them. Perhaps they were there. Perhaps they were not there but among those the motor boats were now bringing in. Perhaps they were still floating on the river or at the bottom of the river. Perhaps, and he held his breath because it was the least probable of all the perhaps, they were still alive.

He walked slowly back and, looked again at the men from the boats who were now pulling the bodies out of the water. He looked at them only very briefly and then walked away, leaving them behind him. He told himself that nothing mattered now, not even his own life. There were so many dead that it did not matter who was alive. And all the way back to the camp, he was bitter and ashamed and angry and finally, he made up his mind. *If I cannot organise them, then I will do it alone,* he said. *I will do it alone, even if it costs me my own life.* He paused for a while on the road when his mind went back over what he had decided to do. Then he went on again, thinking. *When you think of killing generals with your own bare hands or even with grenades, then you think as an anarchist. You think as an anarchist because for every general that you kill, the ruling class presents two new ones. The ruling class is like a Hydra. You cut off one of its heads and it grows two more in its place. What you require then is collective action, because the evil that you confront is a collective phenomenon, collectively sustained and maintained. Therefore, if you kill one general, another will be selected to take his place. Killing one general, a hundred generals or even a million generals will be futile unless you also kill the police chiefs and NSO chiefs and traditional rulers and bishops and professors and politicians and businessmen. If you kill from the ranks of any of these gangsters, and leave the rest, then you are an anarchist, unless your action has a collective base and is part of a planned effort to kill all the others, to dispossess them totally and completely. Otherwise, the other vampires will get together and eliminate you. But I am going to kill not one but several generals for what they have done to us in this war. The soldiers are too well indoctrinated to see and what must be done has to be done then, alone.*

Bur first, I must locate Ndudi. I must get back to her or I will have destroyed her belief in people for life. And to live in suspicion of others, is worse than death itself.

Life is cheap in this country today. Life is cheap and death is commonplace. It is easier to be dead than to be alive. But living is meaningless unless you have an objective. And perhaps that is what explains this war, perhaps this is what explains our history. We have never had objectives. We have existed, we have survived by reacting spontaneously, on an ad-hoc basis to the demands of our surroundings. But we have never had any ambition to be anything beyond what we could immediately see. And a people without ambition to be great, to fulfil themselves, inevitably end up in small but extremely bitter wars. It is not that individuals have lacked ambition. We have had good men, men with ambition for the entire people, but they were confronted by a wall of men who were without ambition, men who had come first and therefore had settled first into the positions of power available. The men without ambition used their positions of power to render irrelevant the few men with ambitions. At other times, the men with ambition had been their own worst enemies, they had fought among themselves instead of fighting the men without ambition. Then there have been times when the men with ambition have been isolated and alone and overwhelmed by their isolation and loneliness.

I do not know whether I have ambition. In my office on Apricot Road, I was often complacent. I accepted the war as a patriot, I accepted the face of Nigerian unity as something on which there could be no compromise. So, along with millions of other Nigerians I branded the Ibo man a rebel. I screamed with millions of others 'To Keep Nigeria One is a Task that Must be Done!' And it seems now as if that was ten years ago, twenty years ago.

How does each of us come to be what we are? Why do I want to kill a general when others want to protect these same generals? What leads us in a particular direction? How do we change, how do we come to realise ourselves? It must be experience. When I was beaten up in the stadium I began to see a different side of the army I had worshipped and idealised. And then I came here and saw all the treachery, all the cowardice and deceit and dishonesty and corruption. I saw them and I began to feel the need for a second front. All these came from experience. But how many other journalists have been beaten up, kicked and humiliated in this war? Scores, hundreds? How many of them have seen the corruption and the cowardice and the treachery? Hundreds? And yet how many of them have felt the way that I now feel? That means then that something besides our experience makes us what we are. Call it instinct, if you like. Whatever it is, it is within the individual, this nameless thing that makes two people with identical life situations, identical experiences, pitch their tents on different sides, in opposite camps. It is beyond upbringing, family background, education. It is innate and stays deep at the heart of each one of us. We may not realise it is there but we eventually find it, and when we do, we find ourselves.

Chapter twenty-eight

He came back to the camp and made straight for the building reserved for the journalists. There was no point going back to the dormitory. Sergeant Kesh Kesh would not be there. The soldiers he had known would not be there either. *The Biafrans must be laughing to themselves this morning,* he thought. *Their commanders must be celebrating their victory.*

There was still a great deal of movement in the camp. The soldiers walked about in small groups, bewildered. Many more sat in the dormitories, dazed. And in the officers' mess, three captains had between them two bottles of whisky and where quietly swearing under their breath. The soldiers were subdued and angry, the officers were ashamed and angry. They had all taken a great beating from the Biafran soldiers. The shame was a collective one but it was felt individually. The soldiers blamed the officers, the officers blamed each other and the men.

Osime looked towards the building that housed Brigadier Otunshi. There was a lot of activity going on there too. There were several vehicles parked in front of the building, several vehicles and in them there were the soldiers and on the ground there were more soldiers. He could not see the faces of the men but he knew that they all shared the same humiliation and the anger.

He was about to enter the building when he heard a great shout behind him and then rapid gunfire. His first instinct was to stop and look back but he ran into the building and shut the door and then went to the window and looked out cautiously. Had the Biafrans attacked the camp? He heard the movement of feet behind him and turned. The man Ekise was almost touching him on the shoulder. Idem stood away at the other window.

'What is it?' Ekise asked anxiously.

Osime shrugged his shoulders. 'I don't know. Perhaps the Biafrans have come here, have attacked us right in our home,' Idem suggested. The other men did not say anything but continued to look out into the open field and search behind the buildings for any movement. At first they saw nothing, then they saw a large group of men running towards them and then behind these men came another bigger group and this time they were soldiers.

The first group of men scattered across the field but they must have known they had no chance as the soldiers came behind them from three sides at once and began firing their 'guitars'. It was all over in less than five minutes. Osime pushed the door open and ran outside, Ekise behind him.

The bullet holes were still fresh and the blood flowed freely from the wounds on their bodies. The soldiers gathered round them in a huge circle and then began to turn them over one by one. There were one hundred and eighty-seven of them, all Biafran soldiers, Biafran POWs, many of whom he had seen only two days before. He felt a chill go through him, a blizzard. And all round him, the Nigerian soldiers chanted one word, 'Nyanmiri! Nyanmiri!!'

He shook his head and began to walk back to the building. Ekise walked ahead of him, far away. He knew now the extent of the men's humiliation at their defeat. But he now knew that the indoctrination was so total, that to the men, the Biafran was the enemy, not their own officers who had abandoned them at the bridge. One hundred and eighty-seven prisoners of war. One hundred and eighty-seven young men shot in cold blood, in cold anger, in bitterness, in revenge for defeat. One hundred and eighty-seven mistakes, all fatal ones made by the Nigerian soldiers. *Yes,* he said to himself. *The indoctrination is indeed complete.*

He came back to the building and went straight to the room occupied by Ekise and Idem. Idem was sitting on the bed and on each side of him were the women he had seen earlier in the morning. Idem's head was bowed and the woman on his left had her hand on his shoulder.

Ekise half stood and half sat at the table in the room. His head was bowed too. 'It's a scandal!' he cried.

'One hundred and eighty-seven of them, all unarmed, all innocent, all defenceless,' Osime said. 'Men with whom they were playing games only the day before!'

'One hundred and eighty-seven scandals,' Idem breathed slowly.

They didn't say anything for some time. Each man contemplated the event and each man felt shaken. Ekise shook his head from side to side, then looked at Osime and said, 'We were beginning to get worried about you anyway. What happened on the bridge? Why did you ignore us so coldly earlier?'

'What happened to Jato?' Idem asked, his hands knotted together. 'Where is he?'

'Everything is so terrible,' Ekise lamented. 'Everything now.'

Even the journalists feel humiliated now, Osime thought. *Even the journalists carry the pain of the defeat.*

'What actually happened?' Idem asked again.

'We were beaten,' Osime spoke now, and now he too felt the pain, the humiliation.

'You were there?'

'Yes.' He went to the door.

'And Jato?'

'Yes. He was there too.'

'But how did it happen? How could it have happened?'

'We were simply beaten,' Osime said again and opened the door and left the room.

Ekise came out after him to the corridor. 'We have a bottle of brandy.'

Osime shook his head.

'Oh, come on. It will do us all some good.'

'No,' Osime insisted. 'It is too early.'

Idem came now and stood in the doorway.

'What are you going to do now?'

Osime shrugged his shoulders.

'We intend going back to the river,' Ekise told him.

Osime didn't say anything.

'My God!' the man Idem exclaimed and turned his face away quickly to hide the teardrops in his eyes.

I said so, Osime thought. *The brandy doesn't help. It softens you up instead of hardening you.* He turned away from Ekise and Idem and as he did so, he saw a figure walk up the steps of the house and the beating of his heart quickened.

'Sergeant Kesh Kesh!'

'Journalist!'

'Where have you been?'

'Everywhere. Looking for you and the others. You have been to the river?'

'Yes.'

'You saw everything in daylight?'

'Yes. I feel humiliated.'

'You too?'

'Yes, why not?' Osime opened the door into Jato's room and both men entered. He looked on top of the locker. The photograph of Jato's wife was still there but now it was lying face down. *Sure,* he thought. *They too would have been here. They too would have come here first.* He sat on the bed.

'Did you see the prisoners of war? How they were murdered?'

Sergeant Kesh Kesh leaned against the closed door. 'General Otunshi is back,' he announced, instead of commenting on the massacre.

'General Otunshi?' Osime asked. Nothing seemed to matter any more.

'Yes. He got his promotion in Lagos. It was announced to him in Lagos.'

'Otunshi promoted? You mean they didn't hear about the defeat, about the collapse?'

'It would not have mattered.'

'Many have sworn to kill him.'

'Kill him?'

'Yes. They feel betrayed. We all feel sold-out.'

'And Brigadier, well, General Otunshi?'

'He has arranged for court martials.'

'Court martials?'

'For the men and officers who he says deserted, who gave the Biafrans victory.'

'And you?'

'What about me? What can I do? Sergeant Kesh Kesh feels betrayed. Sergeant Kesh Kesh feels humiliated. We lost hundreds of good men on the bridge, men who were my personal friends.'

'So what happens now?'

'We wait. Reinforcements are on the way from Benin. When they arrive, we begin the push for Oganza and Nkesio to dislodge the Biafrans.'

'Is that the plan?'

'Yes.'

'And when do we expect the reinforcements?'

'Later today, tomorrow, the next day, any time.'

Osime bit his upper lip and leaned backwards on the narrow bed against the wall and scrutinised the face of Sergeant Kesh Kesh. He could see the humiliation and anger there.

'Your friend died,' Sergeant Kesh Kesh began and stopped but Osime understood and closed his eyes and momentarily, he could see and hear Jato when they were on the bridge. 'We found him in the river,' Sergeant Kesh Kesh added.

Osime leaned over towards the pillow and brought out the bottle of whisky. He unscrewed the top and handed the bottle to Sergeant Kesh Kesh and went back to the bed and sat on it. Sergeant Kesh Kesh wiped the mouth of the bottle with his hand and then put the bottle to his mouth and took a short drink and then wiped the tears from his eyes. He handed the bottle back to Osime and Osime took it and without wiping the neck of the bottle clean, took a short drink himself and coughed and the tears started in his eyes also. He wiped his face with his open hands, and then looked at Sergeant Kesh Kesh standing against the wall, close to the door in this room whose walls had been painted bright blue a long, long time ago.

'I saw a lot of vehicles in Brigadier Otunshi's compound,' Osime said.

'They are part of the reinforcements we expect.' Sergeant Kesh Kesh informed him. Sergeant Kesh Kesh removed his cap from his head and wiped his face with it, his face that was dark and tired and unshaven and sad and humiliated.

'You should sit down now,' Osime told him and the concern was evident enough in his voice.

But Sergeant Kesh Kesh shook his head and stretched his hand forward for the bottle of whisky and Osime passed it to him.

There was a knock on the door. The door opened and Ekise stood in the doorway. 'We are going back to the river,' he announced.

'The battle there is over,' Sergeant Kesh Kesh said and raised the bottle to his lips and drank the bright yellow liquid down and this time he did not cough.

'Still,' Ekise said. 'We'll be seeing you.' He went away and Osime could sense the shame and the embarassement of the man but he said nothing. Sergeant Kesh Kesh drank down more of the whisky and then he fished in his pocket and brought out a khaki envelope and passed it to Osime.

'My home address,' he said. 'It's written on the back. If anything happens, you know what to do.'

'Yes,' Osime promised. 'Assuming I do not go first.'

'Only stupid and pigheaded journalists die in this war,' Sergeant Kesh Kesh said. 'All you have to do now is wait until we have taken back Oganza and then come for your woman.'

'I will be with you when you liberate Oganza.'

'That would be foolish.'

'I have no choice.'

Sergeant Kesh Kesh shrugged his shoulders. 'Only foolish journalists die in this war. Remember that.'

'And brave soldiers too. And prisoners of war too.'

'Brave soldiers and brave officers,' Sergeant Kesh Kesh insisted.

'Yes, deserted soldiers and deserted officers and Biafran POWs.'

'No. Brave soldiers. The others are our problems.'

'How? What do you mean? Remember I was there! In both places!'

'It doesn't matter.'

'We need a third army.'

Sergeant Kesh Kesh gave him a look he could not understand. 'We will not desert,' he said.

'It would not be desertion.'

'No. It would be suicide.'

'We need a third army,' Osime repeated.

'Then you do not understand this war,' the man Kesh Kesh told him and shook his head and shifted his weight from his right leg to his left leg. The places where the mosquitoes had bitten him in the night were swollen.

Osime could count at least five places. Osime passed his hand over his own face and counted the swellings there too. He counted seven.

'What do you mean, I do not understand this war?' Osime asked.

'I am going back to the General's quarters now,' Sergeant Kesh Kesh said. 'Remember we leave at short notice.'

'You have not answered my question.'

'I do not have to answer it. You will find the answer in this war. That is, if you stay here long enough.'

Sergeant Kesh Kesh went out of the door and closed it after him. Osime continued to sit on the bed.

Later in the evening, he heard gunshots and came out of the building and he could see several other soldiers coming out of the other buildings and turning their heads as he did his and he knew that everybody was nervous. Three soldiers came past his buildings at a distance and they carried their rifles uneasily. He called out to them to find out what was happening but they did not answer. They continued to walk away to the direction of one of the camp buildings that flanked General Otunshi's quarters. He did not go back inside but sat on the doorstep of the building and some minutes later, another group of soldiers came past him and again he called out to them and asked them whether they knew what the gunshots were about. One of the soldiers told him that the deserters were being executed.

Altogether, General Otunshi executed thirty-seven soldiers and five officers. There was also talk of more arrests by the military police, arrests of soldiers and other people who it was said were eroding the morale of the rest of the men. But it was all talk and he did not know who was being arrested or would be arrested. The forty-two men who had been shot for desertion were buried in a mass grave in the open field between two of the camp buildings. Osime went over to the grave as it was being filled and, looking at the bodies of the men, some of them still dirty in their clothes, still wet from their fight on the bridge, he shook his head and the tears started to his eyes. One of the soldiers who held the spade looked at him and brushed the tears from his own face and Osime could not see the eyes of the man because of the burning pain in his own eyes. The soldier with the spade stared at him and then turned his back on him and went back to scooping the grey earth and throwing it down, on top of the heap of bodies. Osime could not see the difference between the men being buried here and those he had seen being buried by the river, on the beach. *Executied for desertion*, he said to himself, and the taste of raw bitter leaves was in his mouth. He looked at the grave as it slowly filled up, at the men as they sweated in their labour, and then away from them at the sky. A bird hovered high above them; he guessed it was a swallow because of its white breast and black wings. The bird seemed to suspend itself for a moment and then it dropped out of sight in a straight dive for the horizon. The clouds were gathering there in the horizon and he knew that some time in the night, it would rain. The rain would be heavy and then by morning, the grave would be washed clean. It would have ceased to be a fresh grave. The rain would have washed away the memory of the new dead. He shook his head. He could not believe that this was happening, that it could happen.

He walked back to the building where he now had his room and as he came level with the steps of the house, Sergeant Kesh Kesh came out of the house and stood at the entrance. There was a strained look in his eyes that told him that something was wrong.

'They are burying them,' Osime said and turned and Sergeant

Kesh Kesh followed the direction of the other man's eyes to the side of the field, near the fence where the men were still busy filling up the grave with the dark grey earth.

'There are many of them,' Osime added and turned to Sergeant Kesh Kesh.

'Yes,' Sergeant Kesh Kesh agreed simply.

'Many of them were still wet with the water from the river. Their clothes still had on them the mud from the river.'

'Yes.'

'I saw a very young one among them. He must have been seventeen. The bullet went straight through his neck.'

Sergeant Kesh Kesh did not say anything and Osime looked at him directly in the eye. 'Is anything wrong?' he asked.

'Let's go inside,' Sergeant Kesh Kesh said, and walked across the living room of the house into the short passage that held the rooms whose doors were opposite each other. Walking behind him, Osime noticed the yellow paint of the door. The paint was dirty now.

They came inside the room and this time, Sergeant Kesh Kesh sat on the bed while Osime stood by the open door.

'So, what is it?'

Sergeant Kesh Kesh looked at the cement on the floor that was broken now in several places. He removed his broad cotton hat and wiped his face with it. 'The military police are looking for you,' he said slowly.

'Looking for me?'

'Yes,' the other man nodded.

'What for?'

'I didn't find out. But I saw a friend of mine and they talked about you.'

'They talked about me?'

'They say you taught the men to disobey orders.'

'But . . .' and again, he was silent. How could they have known? He had interacted with only the men in Corporal Kolawole's company. How could the MP have known?

'You will have to leave here,' Sergeant Kesh Kesh advised now. 'You can't stay here any longer.'

'But where can I go?'

'The first place the MP are going to look is here.'

'Yes, I recognise that. Look,' he said now moving with Sergeant Kesh Kesh towards the outer door. 'Do you know General

Otunshi's wife?'

'What about her?'

'Can you get a message to her for me?'

'A message to her? How could I? It is impossible. There is a war council going on in General Otunshi's office, right beside his quarters.'

'But I must get word to her!'

Sergeant Kesh Kesh looked at him searchingly, then shook his head and left, still shaking his head.

I must reach her. Because if I do not, then I am a dead man and the best time to reach her has to be now when they are all absorbed by the meeting. I must reach her. I want to stay alive.

What if she was still in Lagos or in Benin and hadn't returned with Otunshi to the camp?

He was lucky that the first soldier that he saw in front of the duty post outside General Otunshi's quarters was the man who had twice brought him messages from Salome. He told Osime that Salome had come back and was in the house. He took Osime to the house, where he left him in the sitting room to go and look for her. The soldier came back and told him to sit down and that Madam would soon be with him. He went out and shut the door.

Salome wore a black blouse over a gorgeous wrapper that was red and golden in colour. She came into the sitting room and Osime stood up and then sat down again. Osime tried to catch her eyes, to read what could be going on in her mind but her face was inscrutable, like a blank screen.

'So you are here,' she said, and he thought he could detect signs of anger.

'Yes, I'm here,' Osime said and tried to smile.

'What is it?' She remained standing.

Osime stood up now. 'I came here to discuss a problem with you but I can see you are in no mood to listen. I am sorry I bothered you.' He took a step towards the door.

'Didn't you get my notes?' she asked as he reached the door.

He stopped and turned. 'Yes.'

'Then why didn't you answer them?'

Osime looked at his shoes, at the floor. 'You know it would not have worked,' he said. 'You know it was not really necessary.'

'Then why did you come now?' She moved towards him.

'It doesn't matter any more.'

'Tell me,' she insisted now. 'If you have bothered to come here, if you have taken the risk of coming here, you might as well tell me.'

He hesitated.

'Come on,' she said. 'Tell me.' She went and sat down on a chair.

'I understand the Military Police are looking for me,' he told her from where he stood by the door.

'Looking for you? What for?'

'I don't know.'

'Then why don't you find out? Why don't you go and find out?'

'That is not possible.'

She did not say anything for a while. Then she asked, 'And what do you want me to do?'

He came away from the door and walked round her so he could sit on the chair opposite her. He sat on the edge of the chair, his hands on his thighs. He looked her straight in the eyes and it was she who now avoided his eyes.

'I want you to speak to your husband,' he told her.

'What should I tell him?'

'I don't know. But I am sure you would know what to tell him.'

'What exactly have you done, Osime?' she asked seriously but quietly.

Osime rubbed his hands together. 'It's a long story. But the main thing is that I have been accused of demoralising the men, of asking the soldiers to desert.'

She looked at him now and he thought he could see the mist gathering but it went away. 'Did you?' she asked. 'Did you ask the men to desert?'

'No,' Osime denied. 'No!'

'Then what did you tell them?'

'That I did not believe in the war. That the war was wrong.'

'You told them that?'

'Yes.'

'And yet you deny that you told them not to desert?'

'Yes,' he said firmly. 'I deny that.'

'And now you want me to talk to my husband.'

'I want you to speak to your husband.'

She stood up and then came to stand in front of him. He looked at her feet on the floor.

'You humiliated me,' she said now. 'You humiliated me and ruined my time in Lagos.'

He did not say anything.

'Why didn't you come when I asked you to come?' she asked.

'I thought we'd been over that before,' he replied now.

'No,' she said immediately. 'We haven't been over it before. You haven't told me why you decided to humiliate me.'

He stood up and faced her. 'Will you do what I ask of you?'

'You could stay here,' she suggested.

He went past her to the door. 'Will you speak to your husband?' he asked again.

'No,' she answered. 'But you can stay here. You can stay here and I will explain to him.'

He opened the door and went out and the man who had taken him in was again at the duty post but talking to a group of other soldiers. He smiled at the group of soldiers and went past them. He sensed that their eyes followed him but he did not look over his shoulder. He told himself that nothing mattered any more, that he was now completely on his own, except perhaps for Sergeant Kesh Kesh. Yes, he would go back and see Sergeant Kesh Kesh and see what they could work out. He did not think of Salome at all. It seemed as if a wound he had carried with him for a very long time had suddenly closed up and healed inside him. He even felt a little happy, much happier than he had been since coming to the camp.

Chapter twenty-nine

That night Osime hid in the back of a jeep that Sergeant Kesh Kesh had pointed out to him. The jeep was among several others that were parked not too far from the entrance to the camp. He wondered whether any of the soldiers in the trenches around the entrance had seen him. He couldn't be sure.

Inside the jeep, it was dark and hard and everything was metal. The leather on the seats was worn and thin. He tried to see whether he could find anything inside the jeep that he could use as a pillow or to make the seat more comfortable. He didn't find anything. He leaned his back against the metal support that held up the tarpaulin so that his eyes were on the roof of the jeep.

This is their day, he told himself. *Today, they hold the loaded rifles in their hands. They have us against the wall because we are unarmed. But it will not always be like this. Perhaps the idea of the third army is not good now, not good because the soldiers thoroughly believe in the war, not good because I am a single man, not good because I have come here by accident. But all that is for now. Because I am still convinced that unless we have a third army, it is the ordinary people who will be lined up tomorrow and shot, not by the army generals this time but by the politicians who will succeed them. A change is needed, but not the way I wanted it here. The idea was right, but in the circumstances, it would have been pure anarchy. I therefore have a responsibility to survive this war.*

How I wish I had been this conscious before. How I wish I had read a little more, understood a little more and been a little less selfish. Perhaps then I would have come here as part of a planned operation by the third army.

There were many mosquitoes in the jeep and his hand kept going to his face, to his ears. Most of all he hated those that sang in his ears.

The rain came a little later, around midnight. It came at once, heavily, in bucketfuls and his mind went back to the bridge and then to his house in Benin on the morning that the Federal troops first came to the city. He shivered as he thought about the bridge, as once again he heard the gunshots, the cries of the men who had been shot, the loud explosions of the shells. He saw the confusion and the despair and the desperate attempts of the men to hold out even when it had become clear that they had been abandoned, that there was no hope.

The rain fell steadily and a short time after, it began to leak into the jeep and it was then that he realised that there were several holes in the tarpaulin roof of the jeep. He moved to a corner of the jeep, up front to avoid the rain and sat with his back against the metal partition that separated the front seats from the back. The rains continued to come, steadily, heavily and it was cold and wet and he could not rest or close his eyes for a minute because of the rain and the mosquitoes. He could feel the lumps coming up on his face from the mosquito bites, he could feel the damp coming up in his clothes and when he turned his face to look out of the jeep at the back, he could see nothing but darkness. Even the white sheet of rain was invisible now.

Perhaps I should move on, he thought. *Perhaps I should slip past the sentries and make for the town and then in the morning, I will find a way of getting in touch with Sergeant Kesh Kesh. I know he was to meet me here early in the morning but what if something prevents him from coming? What if he forgets and I am discovered here by soldiers who do not know me? I know that the man will come if nothing prevents him but in this war how can you be sure of anything?*

He could not make up his mind whether to remain or leave. He knew it would be better to go but where could he go? He didn't know anybody in Asaba, he didn't even know any place in Asaba. Where could he go?

Later in the night, he heard a great deal of movement and he moved to the entrance of the jeep and looked out cautiously. He saw the lights, the parking lights of a long convoy of trucks and jeeps. And he knew at once that at last reinforcements had come. The vehicles moved silently, even the loud noise made by the engines were silenced by the rain. He watched the vehicles file past, one by one, and then stop in the large area in front of the Mess. The trucks stopped and nobody got out of them. The soldiers remained inside the vehicles. *And that means that I must wait here or else I will lose Sergeant Kesh Kesh.* Again, his doubts returned. Perhaps the coming of the reinforcements would alter all the plans that Sergeant Kesh Kesh had made. He had to take the risk and come out of the vehicle. If he went to the building where he had stayed with Jato, he could perhaps talk to Ekise and find out whether he could go to the town and stay with one of the women he had seen with them the morning before. He came out of the vehicle.

The rain was warm at first, warmer than it had been inside the vehicle, but soon the warmth passed and the rain drops were like icy needles on his body. He walked slowly and carefully in a circle, all the time keeping to the open field. He came past the grave that had been dug and filled the evening before and something heaved inside him but he did not stop until he came under the shadow of the building where he hoped Ekise would be sleeping. He came round the house until he got to the front door and tried it. It wasn't locked, and his heart missed a beat because he thought then that perhaps both Ekise and Ikem would be out with the women.

He went into the house carefully, because he knew it was possible for the military police to wait for him there. But it was dark everywhere and pitch black inside the house so that it was impossible to see anything really. He groped his way through the sitting room of the house to the passage. He tried the door of the room where the two journalists slept. It was locked. He stood there for a second and he could hear the water dripping from his clothes to the floor, he could feel the water running down the back of his neck and over his eyes and then across his nose and over his mouth from his hair. He knocked on the door. He stood there and waited because there was no answer except for the rain outside. There wasn't any strong wind with the rain, just the steady downpour of the rain. He knocked again, this time louder. He continued to knock, louder and louder, and then finally he stopped because he knew there would be no answer. The men were not inside the room.

He came away from the door and walked back to the front door of the building. He opened the door slightly and stood there and several ideas went through his mind. He could go and give himself up or go straight to General Otunshi and demand to see him. Or he could go back to the jeep and wait for Sergeant Kesh Kesh in the morning. None of these ideas appealed to him. The rain was heavy and black and he was cold and shivering now. He was tired and hungry and he told himself that he might as well spend the rest of the night in the room he had shared with Jato. *What does it matter if they finally catch up with me here?* he asked himself. *What does it matter if I am caught and shot? Haven't thousands of fine women and men, hundreds of thousands of young men and women already been killed in this war? What would be mine but just one more murder?*

He shut the door and just then there was a blue streak of lightning and a second later, the whole building shook from the great din of thunder. *Even the skies are weeping,* he said. *Nature, all of nature is against this uninspiring and treacherous war.* He came into the darkness of Jato's room and began to take off his clothes. He was really shivering now. Still, he wrung the water off the clothes on the floor of the room, first the shirt, then the trousers and finally his underwear and socks until he stood completely naked in the room. He got more of the water out of the clothes by thrashing them in the open space of the room and then he laid them out on the table and on Jato's bed. He was shivering more now although he tried to reassure himself that he would be all right in the morning, that he would not be arrested, that the MP were not really organised or competent, and finally, that come another day or two, he would be at Oganza and would find Ndudi. He suspended all doubt, all disbelief, all hopelessness. He told himself that all these things would happen as sure as the rain fell thick like locusts on this second night after the defeat.

Chapter thirty

Osime did not sleep at all. *One hundred and eighty-seven Biafrans, dead, shot down like dogs. And forty-two Nigerians, murdered in cold blood. And hundreds of soldiers, slaughtered on the bridge. There is enough blood for a river, enough blood to float a ship. Life doesn't matter any more. So, why did I attempt to run? Why did I go and hide myself in the jeep? What was one more death in the orgy that was going on?*

But he was frightened. He was frightened for the soldier that would emerge from the war. It would be a man who had learnt a great deal of cruelty, for whom life meant nothing, for whom betrayal and treachery were commonplace. He was frightened for himself for now and for the people that would survive the war. Would it ever be possible to write the real history of this war, to capture the pain, the animal intensity of the cruelty, the razor-sharp sense of humiliation following defeat, the self-centredness of the majority of the generals, their harlotry and open treachery? Would it be possible to recount all these and more? He shivered from his fright and from his cold and from his inability to provide answers to these questions.

Becaue, he said to himself, *the most difficult time to live in is in the time of peace, not in the time of war. In war, one learns only the art of survival. In peacetime, the art of survival is not enough. The art of humanity takes over. This means that one lives on the basis of trust. Trust and generosity, and patriotism. If in peacetime, people live as in times of war without trust, without generosity and without patriotism, then the people are really finished. And this is what this war promises us, death. Look at it,* he said to himself. *The officers betray their men and get rewarded with promotion and those that work hard are shot for desertion. Those who are helpless before us are murdered, their killing is indirectly organised in order to draw attention away from the root causes of our general and national humiliation. And the tragedy is that the people are motivated in the process to attack and kill each other.*

He found sleep in the early hours of the morning but it did not last long because around four o'clock the door was noisily opened and he woke up and in the room there was a man and the light from a torch.

'I thought you would be here,' Sergeant Kesh Kesh said and turned the torch away from his face. 'We are on the move. We have instructions to take Oganza in the morning. My jeep is outside.'

Osime sat up, first on the bed, then struggled up. 'Did you look for me in the jeep?'

'Yes.'

'I'm sorry.'

'I understand. You have no need to worry now because there is a lot of movement and it is dark. The MP have been given other assignments by now.'

'So we should be at Oganza in the morning?'

'Yes. We have a thousand men. The artillery has already gone.'

'My uniform is wet and I have a cold,' Osime told him.

'You could stay behind.'

'No.'

'Then hurry. You know I do this against orders, at my own risk.'

'Yes. Perhaps some day I'll be able to show you some gratitude.'

Sergeant Kesh Kesh waved him aside with his hand that held the torch and the light of the torch went from one side of the room to the other, as his hand moved in his waving.

'I am ready,' Osime announced and walked past Sergeant Kesh Kesh into the corridor. His uniform hung damp on him but he told himself it didn't matter. He stepped outside of the building to the wet ground outside.

There was a long convoy of cars, all of them light infantry vehicles. The armoured vehicles had gone ahead and by now, they should have taken up their positions already. The convoy kept moving and stopping. They came to the position of the armoured vehicles and stopped, and Sergeant Kesh Kesh came out and after another five minutes of waiting, the convoy began to move forward, this time more slowly, the armoured vehicles in front, the infantry men walking beside the vehicles, their guns at the ready. There was no talking.

He did not know the men in Sergeant Kesh Kesh's company. They were new men who had been formed from what remained of the old formations after the defeat on the Bridge and the murder of the forty-two men. Their vehicle was half way in the convoy.

Less than half a mile to the village, the convoy stopped and the men got out of the jeeps and trucks into the road. He came down from the front of the jeep and went first backwards and then forwards with Sergeant Kesh Kesh as he gathered the men for the final briefing before the attack. Osime could not see the faces of the men.

Sergeant Kesh Kesh cleared his throat and said, 'Our task is to take the village of Oganza, consolidate it and then move on to take Nkesio. We shall take both villages with little or no casualty because the Biafran soldiers are not our match. Remember too,' and he looked sideways at Osime, 'remember from now on that the Biafran soldiers are not our enemies really. We go to these villages not to kill them but to persuade them. We go there to persuade them to lay down their arms. What happened in the camp after the attack on the bridge must not happen here. The madness that seized some of you then I understand, but it must not happen here or hereafter. You must avoid unnecessary violence. We want prisoners of war from now on, not dead Biafrans. Am I clear? Am I understood?'

There was no answer.

'All right then. We move!

Sergeant Kesh Kesh slapped Osime on the back. 'Journalist,' he said. 'You stay in the vehicle and away from the fighting this time. We shall see you later in the village.' He moved away quickly to avoid the other man's response.

He followed Sergeant Kesh Kesh's instructions and stayed in the rear while Sergeant Kesh Kesh and his men advanced, first half-walking but bent almost double and then on their bellies as they anticipated the attack from the Biafrans. But the attack did not come. And the fighting did not start until they were on the outskirts of the village when the Nigerian soldiers opened fire.

He got out of the jeep when the Nigerian soldiers opened fire and lay flat on the road beside the jeep, his head down. He heard the firing of the guns, in long steady outbursts with brief intervals. He kept his head on the ground and all he could think of was Sergeant Kesh Kesh on the road, giving the men their final instructions. Now, with his face in the mud, he kissed the ground and it was warm on his lips, and warm as the smile on his face and he told himself that he was crazy for kissing the warm earth, for smiling when all around him there was nothing but the flames of another fire, flames that brought out the cries from the men's throats. *Yes*, he thought, *I must be crazy*. And then, again, he shook his head and told himself that he was perfectly all right, that it wasn't madness to know, hearing Sergeant Kesh Kesh, that everything was not lost, that they would survive the war as they would the subsequent peace.

And now, there was a great shout as the Federal soldiers raised their voices and cries of 'Oshobe!' filled the air. He did not know whether to remain where he was or stand up and go forward. Eventually, he made up his mind and stood up cautiously at first, then broke into a run, then stopped to walk, tired and exhausted.

It was still early in the morning, perhaps not yet seven. The day was cloudy because the rain that had fallen in the night was not yet gone and the ground was wet and in many places, there were pools of water. He walked quickly now, almost running as he looked at each of the houses, trying to remember Ndudi's house. On the streets, there were bodies of dead soldiers, but they were not many.

Finally, he found the house. He found it because he saw the grave. The door was wide open and as he entered it, two soldiers came out of the house and they were zipping up their trousers and although they had this broad smile on their faces, they avoided looking him in the face, in the eye. He almost ran then into the house. In the open parlour of the house, Ndudi's mother was weeping. Ndudi's grandmother sat on a bench, her hair much greyer now. She was talking but Osime did not understand what she was saying. He tried to greet them, but they did not answer him and he went into the room where he had slept. Ndudi was there. She was lying on the floor of the room and her clothes were torn and scattered on the dloor around her.

He knelt beside her and touched her. He didn't know whether she saw him. But she kept weeping bitterly. 'They raped me again! They raped me! They raped me again!' He gathered her clothes round her to cover her up.

He stood up and went out quickly into the parlour and then outside. The Federal troops were moving in the vehicles now. There were many soldiers about now. He could not see the two men who had walked past him as he entered the house. He was not sure he would be able to recognise them. He stood outside there, dazed and frustrated but after a time his frustration went away and his mind became very clear and he began to see more clearly how much damage the war had done to these men.

All along, he said, right up to this moment, I had assumed that the callousness and the viciousness and the wildness and the brutality were natural to the men, that the men in uniform were natural rapists even in times of peace. All that is wrong, he acknowledged now. People are decent deep down and want to remain decent all their lives. But a bitter and spiteful war comes along and turns ordinary decent men into rapists, into animals, into something hateful even to themselves, into something repulsive and spiteful even to themselves. The war takes ordinary decent men and bends and twists them. It takes them and debases them and dehumanises them. The war takes them and pours its maggots into their souls, takes their decency and humanity and dignity away from them. A small treacherous war such as this comes along and finishes them completely, levels them completely because it has no ideals, no principles, no honour. Because it is based on spite, on jealousy, on treachery, on greed and on brutality. The spite and the jealousies and the greed and the smallness and the treachery and the brutality of the vast majority of its officers and generals. He felt sorry for the men. He felt sorry for the men that would emerge from this war.

They are animals, he said. *Wild animals and this wildness they always had. They are beasts. Black beasts. Wild beats.*

He went back into the house and walked past the women and went into the room where Ndudi still lay weeping on the floor. He lifted her up and placed her on the bed. He wiped her tears and stroked her hair and tried to comfort her. 'Don't cry,' he whispered to her, gently. 'It is going to be all right now. See, I came back for you. I love you. You can trust me. I'll look after you. See, I came back for you.'

He closed his eyes momentarily and then again went out of the room and out of the house. This time he saw that the soldiers were in small groups and that they were carrying out a house-to-house search. A truck and a jeep came driving up the road. The jeep stopped and he recognised Sergeant Kesh Kesh as he jumped down. Sergeant Kesh Kesh also saw him and walked towards him, quickly.

'So you have found your woman?' he asked as he approached the house.

There was quiet excitement on the man's face.

'They raped her,' Osime said. 'They raped her. Your soldiers raped her.'

'I am sorry.'

'Sorry?'

'Well, yes. What do you expect me to say?'

Osime didn't say anything.

'Can I see her?'

He was going to say no, then shrugged his shoulders. They both went into the house.

Ndudi told them that she had been raped twice on that same morning, first by the departing Biafran soldiers and secondly by the incoming Federal soldiers. And each time, she had been raped by two men. Looking at Sergeant Kesh Kesh and at Ndudi, he told himself that it did not really matter any more. Rape, murder and stealing were not given with human nature but were the products of particular times and relationships. Between people in society. This war was not a game of virtue. Hadn't somebody told him that some time ago? He was experienced enough to realise that now. *The competition in war is not about who is more virtuous. The problem is whether this rape, this murder, this stealing, this cruelty will carry over into peacetime. My guess is that even if they do they will not go unchallenged because the ordinary soldiers and people on both sides will have learnt something from this war, something that Sergeant Kesh Kesh as a new recruit of the third army represents.*

Sergeant Kesh Kesh slapped him on the back and he came out of his reverie.

'I must be going, journalist,' the man said. 'We are going to take Nkesio and then after that, Onitsha. Look after your woman.' He held out his hand, his eyes bright with his hope.

Osime took the man's outstretched hand and shook it and followed him out of the house.

He watched Sergeant Kesh Kesh walk down the road and then get into the jeep. Sergeant Kesh Kesh closed the door of the jeep and waved to him and the jeep began to move away, slowly at first and then quickly down the road. Osime stood there, watching the jeep go down the road and the words of Sergeant Audu came back to him, like the lines of a long forgotten poem . . .

'After this war many generals will write their accounts in which they will attempt to show that they were the heroes of this war, that it was their grand strategies that won the war. They will tell the world that they single-handedly fought and won the war. The names of soldiers like Otun, Emmanuel, Ikeshi and Yemi will never be mentioned. The soldiers take all the dirt and the ambushes and the bullets with their lives. The soliders pay for the unity of this country with their lives and yet, what happens? Always the officers are the heroes. Always the generals take the credit. Always the generals get the praise. Always they are the heroes.'

No, he told himself now. *It will not always be like that even if the generals on both sides conspire to make it appear so. It will not always be like that because a movement is bound to emerge from this war and if not from this war, then after this war. A movement which will write the history of this war and give each man and woman his or her proper due. You, Sergeant Kesh Kesh, and your comrades will never be forgotten. Never.*

Also in Longman African Writers

Loyalties and other stories

Adewale Maja-Pearce

A chilling collection of tales set in a country once ravaged by civil war and now torn apart by sudden wealth.

In this brutal world bars, brothels and small-town hotels are havens for the sad and lonely, escaping from the hustlers on the streets outside. But the short-lived comforts of a cold embrace or the oblivion of drunkenness are no more than brief respites in the larger struggle for survival.

Adewale Maja-Pearce's first collection of short stories breaks new ground in contemporary African fiction. The detached and enigmatic narratives brilliantly evoke the tensions of a society in transition and which threatens to go out of control.

ISBN 0 582 78628.2

Flamingo and other plays

Bode Sowande

Four new one-act plays from one of Nigeria's foremost playwrights.

In this collection Bode Sowande explores major political and social issues of modern Africa using a unique blend of contemporary Western dramatic techniques and traditional Yoruba theatre.

Running through all the plays is the central question of how individuals should respond to the moral decline of the society in which they live. As the author writes in his introduction to *Flamingo*: 'The final choice for me as a writer is to ask, with a degree of anxiety, if violence should be used to deal with the crushing fate of tragic history.'

ISBN 0 582 78630.4

Longman African Classics

The Last Duty

Isidore Okpewho

Winner of the African Arts Prize for Literature

Against the backcloth of the violent and murderous Nigerian Civil War six individuals linked by conflicting ties of honour, greed, lust, fear and love play out a drama of their own that is no less bloody than the war itself. The resolution of the drama has the cathartic force of classical tragedy, as the individuals recognise their final duty to reclaim their self-respect from the quagmire of corruption and betrayal into which they have all been led.

'*The Last Duty* is a highly sophisticated and successfully achieved piece of work . . . an imaginative reconstruction of the experience of the Nigerian Civil War. In its deep moral concern and in its technical accomplishment, *The Last Duty* has earned an honourable place in the development of African literature.'

British Book News

'A strong and original voice in Nigerian literature.'

Books Abroad

'C'est un beau livre.' *Afrique Contemporaine*

ISBN 0 582 64622.7